D0734530

New

Never Lie to a Lady

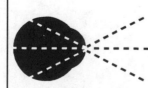

This Large Print Book carries the
Seal of Approval of N.A.V.H.

NEVER LIE TO A LADY

LIZ CARLYLE

THORNDIKE PRESS

An imprint of Thomson Gale, a part of The Thomson Corporation

Mishawaka-Penn-Harris
Public Library
Mishawaka, Indiana

Detroit • New York • San Francisco • New Haven, Conn. • Waterville, Maine • London

THOMSON

GALE

LIBRARY OF CONGRESS CATALOGING-IN-PUBLICATION DATA

Carlyle, Liz.
    Never lie to a lady / by Liz Carlyle.
        p. cm. — (The never series ; #1.)
    "Thorndike Press large print core"—T.p. verso.
    ISBN-13: 978-0-7862-9801-3 (hardcover : alk. paper)
    ISBN-10: 0-7862-9801-4 (hardcover : alk. paper)
    1. Upper class — Fiction. 2. London (England) — Fiction. 3. Large type
books. I. Title.
PS3553.A739N48 2007
813'.54—dc22   2007022069

Published in 2007 by arrangement with Pocket Books,
a division of Simon & Schuster, Inc.

Printed in the United States of America on permanent paper
10 9 8 7 6 5 4 3 2 1

NEVER LIE TO A LADY

PROLOGUE:
AN ASSIGNATION IN CRESCENT MEWS LATE WINTER 1828

The library was hushed in every possible way, its heavy velvet drapes long since drawn against the flickering gaslight beyond. The lush Turkish carpet silenced every footfall, and the room's cavernous depths would have swallowed every whisper, had there been any. Certainly there was no light, save that which was cast in a pool before the hearth.

Lord Nash was many things, but he was not remotely naive. The stage was set, and he knew it. He kept his back to the fire and his eye on the door, which was barely discernible in the shadows.

The door, when it opened, was as soundless as it had been upon his arrival. The Comtesse de Montignac came toward him, her fine, frail hands outstretched as if she were greeting her dearest friend. She wore a red silk peignoir, which was far more suited to the boudoir, and her heavy golden hair swung seductively about her waist.

"*Bonsoir,* my lord," she purred, the red silk shimmering in the firelight as she moved. "At long last, I am to have the pleasure, *oui?*"

He did not take her hands, forcing her to let them drop. "This is not a social call," he said. "Show me what I have come for."

Her smile deepened almost mischievously. "I like a man who knows his business," she purred. Before he knew what she was about, the comtesse's elegant fingers went to her shoulders, and drew the silk peignoir down her arms. It caught on her fingertips just an instant before it slithered to the floor.

Nash cursed the little stab of lust which needled him. But by God, the woman was beautifully made, and she wore a negligee so thin it served but one purpose. Beneath it, her delicate, milk white breasts rose as the breath shuddered expectantly out of her. She touched one hardened nipple through the gossamer fabric.

"Many men have paid well for this," she said throatily. "But for you, Nash — oh, *mon dieu!* A woman almost wishes to give it away."

Nash slid a hand beneath her left breast, and squeezed — not hard enough to hurt her. Not *quite.* A strange mélange of fear and lust sketched across her face. "The papers," he gritted. "Get them. Do not toy with me."

She backed away, cutting him a dark, sidelong glance as she moved into the shadows. He heard a drawer slide open, then slam shut again. She returned with a thick fold of foolscap. Nash took the papers and unfolded them toward the firelight. His eyes swept over the first, then the others, more quickly. "How much?" he asked emotionlessly.

"Ten thousand."

He hesitated.

The comtesse stepped so near he could smell the scent of jasmine in her hair. "This bargain was hard earned, my lord," she said. "My every feminine wile was required in order to obtain what you needed."

"All save one, I daresay," murmured the marquess.

The comtesse did not so much as blush. "And I am sure I need not tell you, my lord, the political ramifications which this could have," she purred, drawing a warm hand down his arm. "Ten thousand, and the pleasure of my body for the evening?"

Nash tried to divert his eyes from the rise and fall of the woman's breasts. "I cannot think your husband would appreciate being cuckolded beneath his own roof, *madame.*"

She smiled, pressed the length of her body to his. "Pierre is very understanding, *mon cher,*" she murmured. "And I have . . . particular needs. Needs which I will gladly demonstrate — if you can be persuaded into my bed?"

"I cannot," he said.

She drew her hand from his arm — in surrender, he thought. Until it settled firmly and warmly in an altogether different location. To his humiliation, his rigid cock twitched insistently against her palm. "Are you quite sure, *mon cher?*" she whispered. "You feel very firmly persuaded — and I cannot but wonder, Nash, if you are all that rumor claims."

He tossed the papers aside. "You play a dangerous game, *madame.*"

"I live a dangerous life," she returned. But with a muted smile, she dropped her hand and stepped away.

He watched her in silence for a time, as one might watch a snake in the grass. She cut an uncertain glance at him. "*Mon dieu,* do not look so sanctimonious, Nash!" she finally snapped. "We are alike, you and I. We are not of this restrained, oppressive English world. We never shall be, you know. Come, why may we not learn to pleasure one another?"

Nash did not answer, but instead bent down and picked up the red silk peignoir. "Just put it on, comtesse," he answered. "There is very little anyone could teach a woman of your experience."

Again, the coquettish smile. *"Oui, my lord, c'est vrai,"* she agreed. She took the red silk robe from his outstretched hand.

They concluded their transaction swiftly enough, the comtesse making no further overtures, save for the occasional torrid, sidelong glance — and not at his face. Nash was relieved to make his way back through the house and out into the damp, silent streets of Belgravia. The mist had grown heavier now, rolling in off the Thames with a cutting January chill. Nash turned up his collar and set off along Upper Belgrave Street. Behind him, the newly minted church bell at St. Peter's tolled twice, the sound oddly sharp in the drizzle.

The broad, elegant thoroughfares were empty at this hour, at this time of year. No one observed Nash as he made his way soundlessly into the rabbit warren of Crescent Mews. This was an old place which the new perfection of Belgravia had swallowed up and risen above. A place not easily found, which made it perfect for his purpose.

In the distance, Nash could see a lamp swinging from its brass bracket, casting a feeble light down the steps of a small and unimportant-looking establishment. As he neared the entrance, a man in a brilliantly hued Guards uniform staggered from the shrubbery, hitching up the fall of his trousers. They nodded politely, and Nash pressed on. From the foot of the steps, Nash could hear raucous laughter ringing out. He stepped beneath a tree just beyond the lantern's glow, lit a cheroot, and settled in for a wait. He had long ago learned patience.

From time to time a military man or a gentleman would burst from the laughter to make his way down the narrow stairs and stagger up the mews. But eventually, a man came out and made his way to the tree. He was slight and quick, and his gait held the sureness of sobriety.

"Good evening, sir."

"Good evening," said Nash. "Is every drunken soldier from the Guards' barracks in there tonight?"

The smaller man smiled faintly. "It would seem so, my lord," he said. "Swann says you wish to engage my services?"

Nash withdrew his purse and jerked his

head toward Wilton Crescent. "Do you know the woman who lives in the third house this side of Chester Street?"

"Who does not?" he answered. "The Comtesse de Montignac."

"Yes," said Nash. "Is that her real name?"

The smaller man smiled faintly. "It is thought unlikely," he said. "But she has well-placed friends, and her husband is an attaché to the French embassy. What is it you wish, my lord?"

"Three men observing the house night and day," said Nash, his voice emotionless. "The names of everyone who comes and goes, from the chimney sweep to the dinner guests. Should she leave the house, I wish to know where she goes, with whom, and for how long. Report to Swann once a week. I shan't seek you out again."

The smaller man bowed. "It shall be arranged." Then he hesitated. "My I speak frankly, my lord?"

Nash's dark, harsh eyebrows went up a notch. "By all means."

"Have a care, sir," he said quietly. "The diplomatic corps is a nest of vipers — and the Comtesse de Montignac writhes at its center. For a price, she would betray her own mother."

The marquess's mouth curved with bitter

satisfaction. "As I am too well aware," he said. "But I thank you for the warning all the same."

CHAPTER ONE:
A GALA IN
HANOVER STREET
SPRING 1828

Miss Xanthia Neville was thinking of having an *affaire.* Thinking of it quite vividly, in fact, as she watched the tide of handsome, elegantly attired gentlemen sweep their partners through the intricacies of the waltz. Cutaway coats and diaphanous skirts swirled and unfurled beneath the glow of a thousand candles. Champagne glasses clinked, and sidelong gazes lingered. Everyone was lighthearted. No one was alone.

Well, that was not quite true, was it? *She* was alone. At the great age of not-quite-thirty — a brittle precipice indeed — Xanthia was a confirmed spinster. Nonetheless, tonight she had worn red; the deepest, most daring shade of claret-colored velvet to be found in the whole of Pall Mall, as if doing so might send some subtle signal within the rarefied confines of Lord Sharpe's ballroom.

Ah, but perhaps she was just deluding herself. Perhaps she'd had too much of

Sharpe's champagne. In this country, unmarried ladies did not have liaisons. They had weddings. Even her cynical-hearted brother would not tolerate a scandal. Moreover, Xanthia, the consummate negotiator, had no notion how one went about parlaying *that* sort of deal. She could finesse the flintiest of customs agents, consign cargo in three languages, and spot a thieving purser with a doctored manifest at fifty paces. But this — her personal life — so often felt beyond her.

So this romance of hers was just another fantasy. Another unattainable thing which, while painfully absent from her life, simply came at too great a price.

Was she lonely? She hardly knew. She knew only that her life had required hard choices — and she made them, for the most part, with her eyes open. Lord Sharpe's ballroom was awash in pretty, virginal debutantes. They were not wearing red. Life's many possibilities were still open to them. Xanthia was envious, and yet she would not have traded places with even the most beautiful amongst them.

She turned away from the ocean of beautiful men and pretty virgins and went out onto the terrace in search of solitude. The heels of her slippers sounded softly on the flagstones, until at last the strains of the orchestra faded, and the murmur of voices quieted. Even the illicit lovers had not ventured so deep into the gloom as this. Perhaps she ought not have, either — the English *ton* did seem to frown on the oddest things — but something in the silence drew her.

At the distant end of the terrace, Xanthia at last paused to lean against the brickwork and let her shoulders relax against the masonry, which still held a hint of heat from an unseasonably sunny day. She had been all of four months in London now, but never once had she been *warm.* She let her head tip back and her eyes close as she savored the faint heat, and swallowed the last of her champagne.

"Ah, if only I were the cause of that expression!" murmured a deep, rueful voice. "Rarely do I see a woman so enraptured — unless she is in bed with me."

Xanthia's eyes flew open on a faint gasp.

A tall, elegantly built man blocked the terrace before her, and even in the dark, she could feel the heat of his gaze drifting over her. She recognized him vaguely, for she had noticed him earlier, reclining languidly in a chair deep inside the cardroom — and she had seen the female heads turning as he left it, too. He was the sort of man who caught a woman's notice; not for his beauty, but for something far more primitive than that.

Xanthia lifted her chin. "Sharpe has a dreadful crush tonight," she said coolly. "I thought my escape had gone unobserved."

"Perhaps it did." His voice was a low rumble. "I could not say. I have been hiding out here all of a quarter hour myself." There was chagrin in his voice, which unexpectedly made her laugh.

He stepped fully into the shaft of moonlight and glanced down at her empty flute. "Sharpe has unimpeachable taste in champagne, does he not?" he murmured. "And your intriguing expression aside, my dear, I wonder if it wouldn't be prudent for you to return to the ballroom?"

Xanthia, however, caught neither his suggestion, nor its subtle implication, for she was absorbed in the study of his face. No, he definitely was not beautiful. Instead, his features held a remarkable ruthlessness, with a hawkish nose, a too-hard jaw, and extraordinary eyes, which were set at just the slightest angle. His hair was dark, and far too long to be fashionable. More disturbing still, there was just the slightest aura of danger about him. Inexplicably, Xanthia did not heed it.

"No," she said quietly. "No, I think I shall stay."

He lifted one of his solid-looking shoulders. "Suit yourself, my dear," he said. "You looked like a cat soaking up warmth just now. Are you cold?"

Fleetingly, Xanthia closed her eyes and thought of the Bajan sun. "I am always cold," she answered. "I haven't been warm in an age."

"What a pity." He leaned nearer and offered his hand. "I believe I have not had the pleasure, ma'am. In fact, I am quite persuaded you are new to Town."

She looked down at his hand, but did not take it. "And do you know everyone?"

"It is my business to do so," he said simply.

"Indeed?" Xanthia set her glass down atop a nearby baluster. "What sort of business are you in?"

"The business of knowing people."

"Ah, a man of mystery," she answered a little drolly. "And from whom, I wonder, are you hiding? An angry husband? A woman scorned? Or that little coterie of matchmaking mammas which keeps eyeing you so greedily?"

He flashed a crooked, rueful smile. "Noticed that, did you?" he asked. "It's devilish awkward, really. They seem to keep expecting me to — ah, but never mind that."

She looked at him intently. *"Expectations,"* she murmured. "Yes, that is the very trouble, isn't it? People are so very reluctant to surrender them, are they not? We are all expected to do certain things, make certain choices — and when we do not, well, *we* are accounted stubborn. Or eccentric. Or that most horrid euphemism of all — *difficult.* Why is that, I wonder?"

"Why indeed?" he murmured. The man's gaze held hers steadily. "I wonder, my dear — are you the sort of woman who does the unexpected? You strike me as being . . . oh, I don't know — a little different, perhaps, from those other people whirling about the ballroom."

Those other people.

With those three simple words, he seemed to draw a dark and certain line between the two of them and — well, everyone else. He was not like them, either. She sensed it. A sudden frisson of some unfathomable emotion slid down her spine. For an instant, it was as if he looked not at her, but at something deeper. His gaze was watchful. Assessing. And yet understanding, all at once.

But what nonsense that was. What was she

doing here in the dark, chatting with a perfect stranger?

His slashing black eyebrows went up a notch. "You have grown very quiet, my dear."

"I fear I have nothing of interest to say." Xanthia relaxed against the brickwork again. "I lead a rather austere life and do not generally go about in society."

"Nor do I," he confessed, dropping his voice. "And yet . . . here we are."

He leaned so near she could smell his cologne, an intriguing combination of smoke and citrus. His gaze caught hers again, more heated now, and Xanthia felt suddenly as if the stone portico beneath her feet had shifted. Even in the dark, his eyes seemed to glitter. "I beg your pardon," she said a little breathlessly. "You . . . you are wearing amber oil, are you not?"

He inclined his head. "Amongst other things."

"And neroli," she said. "But the amber — it is quite a rare scent."

He looked vaguely pleased. "I am surprised you know it."

"I have some knowledge of spices and oils."

"Have you indeed?" he murmured. "My perfumer in St. James imports it for me. Do you like it?"

"I am not quite sure," she said honestly.

"Then I shan't wear it tomorrow."

"Tomorrow?"

"When I call on you," he said. "By the way, my dear, do you mean to tell me your name? Just the name of your husband will do. That way, I can ascertain his club hours and determine when he is most apt to be out."

"I do not know *your* name," she said archly. "But I see that you are quite forward."

"Yes, well, being backward gets one nowhere, does it?" he suggested, smiling.

Xanthia gave a bitter laugh. "Indeed, it does not," she answered. "I learnt that much the hard way."

He watched her warily for a moment. "No, you do not look the shy, retiring type," he said in a musing tone. "Tell me, my dear, are you as bold as that red dress you are wearing might suggest?"

"In some situations, yes," she confessed, holding his gaze. "If there is something one wants badly, one must often be bold."

Suddenly, he slid one hand beneath her elbow, and it was as if something electric passed between them. "You are a most intriguing woman, my dear." His voice was raspy in the gloom. "Indeed, it has been a very long time since I felt . . . well, *intrigued*."

"Perhaps I understand," Xanthia found herself saying. "I wish we could . . . oh, never mind. I am very foolish, I think. Perhaps I ought to go."

But his hand on her arm stilled her. "What?" he murmured. "What do you wish, my dear? If it is within my power to fulfill your desire, it would be my greatest pleasure."

His words left her shivering. "No, it was nothing," she answered. "You are a dangerously charming man, sir. I think I ought not linger here."

"Wait," he said, pulling her to him. "Let us make a bargain, my dear. I shall tell you my name — and my line of business. And in exchange, you will —" He paused, and let his eyes run over her again.

Xanthia was undone by the suspense. "What?"

"You will kiss me," he commanded. "And not some sisterly peck, by God."

Xanthia's eyes widened, but she was inordinately curious. After all, it was she who had started this silly game of cat and mouse. But more foolish, even, than that, she *did* wish to kiss him. To feel that hard, harsh mouth settle over hers, and —

He did not await permission. His hands grasped her shoulders, drawing her abruptly against him as his lips molded firmly over hers. He made no pretext of gentleness, or of polite restraint, opening his mouth over hers, and stroking his tongue hungrily across her lips. Desire surged, and Xanthia opened beneath him, allowing him to explore the depths of her mouth with his slow, sensual strokes.

She felt suddenly alive, yet almost enervated in his embrace, as if she had no will of her own. His wish was hers; his quickening desire echoed her own. It had been so long since she had been kissed by anyone — and never had she been kissed like this. She twined her arms round his neck and allowed his hands to roam restlessly over her, setting her skin to shivering. Their tongues entwined as their breath quickened. He tasted of champagne and raw lust. The smoky scent of his cologne grew to a dizzying intensity as his skin heated. Xanthia was caught up in his madness, pressing her body almost shamelessly against his and allowing his roaming hands and hungry mouth a lover's every intimacy.

"Good God, this is madness," she heard herself say, but it was distant. Disembodied.

"Yes, a glorious madness," he murmured.

His hand was on her hip now, erotically circling the weight of it through the velvet of her gown. Another inch lower, and he was lifting her urgently against him. There was no mistaking the throbbing ridge of his arousal, nor of his intent. Xanthia rose greedily onto her tiptoes, pressing herself to him as she ached for something dangerous.

Somehow, he drew up the fabric of her skirt and slipped his hand beneath, caressing the swell of her hips, stroking suggestively. Over and over he caressed her there. Then, without lifting his mouth away, he urged her firmly against the brick wall and eased the hand between them, delving lower and lower.

Xanthia managed to tear her mouth from his. "Wait, I —"

"We are all alone, my dear," he reassured her between the little kisses he planted along her jaw. "I am sure of it. Just trust me."

His words melted over her. Foolishly, she gave in to him; ached for him with a need she had never known. This really was madness. But on a soft sound of surrender, Xanthia returned her mouth to his, and let the dark stranger have his way. And yet, in this wild, timeless moment, he did not seem a stranger. He knew her; knew just where to touch her. His palm was warm through the thin lawn of her drawers. Without lifting his mouth from hers, he gave a deep, hungry groan and caressed her there, in her most private place. Like a wanton, Xanthia surrendered, her knees going weak. His stroke became more urgent, and then she was panting for him, reveling in each delicate stroke as her need ratcheted up, and her body began to ache.

She was going to explode. She could not bear it. The ache was bone-deep and shuddering now. She felt reality edge away, felt the dark of night swirl about them, and, suddenly, she was frightened. Dear God, had she lost her mind?

He pressed his mouth to her ear and sucked lightly at her lobe. "Give in to it, my dear," he murmured, nipping lightly at her flesh. "Good Lord, have you any idea how beautiful you are just now?"

"I — I think . . ." Xanthia was still shaking. "Oh, please. I think . . . we must stop."

He groaned as if in pain, but his hand stilled.

"Stop," she said again, as much to herself as to him.

Lightly, he let his forehead touch hers. "Must we, my dear?" His words were thick. "Come, slip away with me. Spend the evening in my bed. I promise to pleasure you until morning — and we can do anything your imagination might conjure up."

She shook her head, her hair scrubbing against the brickwork. "I dare not," she said. "I can't think what has come over me. You . . . you must already think me some sort of whore."

He was already smoothing her skirts back down, his touch gentle. "What I think is that you are a sensual woman with a well of unslaked needs," he murmured, lightly kissing her cheek. "And that you should let me rectify that regrettable circumstance."

She gave a short, sharp laugh. "Dear God, I must be mad," she murmured. "I was half-considering it — and I do not even know who you are!"

His eyes still simmering with desire, he stepped back, and sketched her a surprisingly formal bow. "I am called Nash," he said quietly. "Gamester and professional sybarite, at your service, ma'am."

Professional sybarite?

The appalling recklessness of what she had just done was swiftly sinking in. Xanthia still couldn't catch her breath. She opened her mouth to speak, but no sound came out. And suddenly, she did perhaps the most idiotic, most humiliating thing a woman could have done. She turned and ran.

She dashed along the terrace, her mind in a panic. But there was nothing. No footfalls. No shouts. The light spilling from the ballroom was but a few yards away. Just short of the door, she somehow found the presence of mind to stop to tidy her hair and right her clothing. Still no sound. He was not following, thank God.

What had she been thinking? Her breath still rough, Xanthia set her hand flat against the outer window frame and struggled to turn her legs from jelly into something substantial enough to gracefully walk on. Well. She had wanted to do something slightly scandalous. And she certainly had. She had allowed a strange man to kiss her senseless — and had very nearly allowed him a vast deal more than that. And now, absent the warm strength of his body, she felt colder than ever and uncharacteristically shaken.

Furious with herself, Xanthia stiffened her spine and plunged into the crowded ballroom, an artificial smile plastered upon her face. Dear God, what a fool she was. It was one thing to drink a little too much champagne and wallow in mawkish fantasies, and quite another to behave brazenly with a common stranger — or, in Mr. Nash's case, a most *uncommon* one. But however intriguing he was, there was nothing metaphysical between them. He had not looked into her eyes and seen her soul, for pity's sake. How had she conjured up such a notion? Celibacy must be affecting her brain.

Well, there was nothing left to do but pray to God that Nash was a gentleman. Oh, Xanthia was not afraid of gossip for her own sake, but there was her brother Kieran to think about. He might yet turn his life around. And there was her much-loved niece, Martinique. Lord and Lady Sharpe, cousins whom she adored, and their daughter Louisa, whose come-out ball this was. Xanthia's behavior could reflect badly on all of them.

Somehow, she managed to nod to the few people she knew as she passed through the crowd. She wondered if she looked like some just-tumbled wanton, but no one she passed raised so much as an eyebrow. The panic was fading now, but the memory of his touch was not. Dear heaven, she really must find her brother and ask him to see her home, before she did something unutterably foolish — like search out Mr. Nash, and toss him her garter.

With a hand which still shook, Xanthia stopped a passing footman to ask Kieran's whereabouts. The footman bowed, resplendent in his deep blue livery. "Lord Rothewell is in the cardroom, ma'am."

Xanthia smiled politely. "Kindly tell him I should like to go now."

She really did not want to disturb her brother's gaming, but it was either that, or remain here and risk running into Mr. Nash again. Suddenly, amidst all the confusion, it struck her. *Mr. Nash still did not know her name.* She had bolted before giving it to him, and he had not followed her. It was as if he had lost interest.

Perhaps he had. Perhaps she was not as skilled at kissing as she had hoped? The thought was a little lowering. But indeed, it was all for the best. Mr. Nash did not know her name, and she barely knew his. They would almost certainly never lay eyes on one another again, for she did not go about in society — indeed, she scarce had the time — and Mr. Nash had possessed the unqualified arrogance of a man who knew his place in the *haut monde.* And unless Xanthia missed her guess, it was very high up indeed. A sense of mild relief swept over her, restoring her composure.

In the entrance hall, Lady Sharpe was saying good-bye to her sister-in-law. Mrs. Ambrose kissed Xanthia effusively on both cheeks. "Xanthia, my dear, you really must get out more," she said. "You are looking perfectly colorless."

"How charitable of you to concern yourself," said Xanthia politely. "By the way, have you seen Kieran?"

Mrs. Ambrose flashed an acerbic smile. "I left him in the cardroom," she answered. "He is in one of his moods."

Lady Sharpe laughed aloud as soon as her sister-in-law had gone. "What a cat she is, Zee," she whispered as she set her lips to Xanthia's cheek. "And how flattered I am that my reclusive relations have actually deigned to attend my little ball."

"Oh, Pamela, we could not possibly miss Louisa's come-out." Xanthia leaned in to embrace her. But at that very moment, Lady Sharpe went a little limp and slumped almost imperceptibly against her.

Startled, Xanthia slid an arm awkwardly beneath her cousin's elbow. "Pamela?" she said sharply. Then, to the footman, "A chair, if you please! And her maid. Fetch her at once."

A chair was brought in an instant, and Lady Sharpe collapsed into it most gratefully. "The crush and the excitement," she explained as Xanthia snapped open her fan and knelt. "Oh, thank you! That breeze is most restorative. Yes, I've worn myself a little thin, I daresay. Oh, but *please* do not tell Sharpe."

Just then, Xanthia's brother appeared. "Pamela?" he said sharply. "You look most unwell."

Lady Sharpe turned pink. "It is just the heat," she said. "And perhaps my *age*, Kieran. Now pray *do not* ask me any more questions, or I vow I shall answer them and utterly mortify you."

Kieran had the good grace to blush and go at once in search of their carriage. As soon as Lady Sharpe's maid arrived, Xanthia stood. "I do not like your color, Pamela," she said, reluctant to leave her. "But there! I sound like Mrs. Ambrose, do I not?"

Lady Sharpe looked up sheepishly. "Not without reason," she muttered. "I am sorry to have given you such a turn."

"But you have." Xanthia reached down to squeeze her hand. "Which is why you shall see me again tomorrow. Shall we say tea, my dear, at three-ish?"

CHAPTER TWO:
A ROW IN WAPPING
HIGH STREET

By dawn, the unseasonable warmth had given way to a rainstorm, which met the day in slicing gray sheets and continued, unrelenting, into what felt like the following week. Attired in a dressing gown of creamy tussah silk, Nash stood at his bedchamber window in a grim mood, staring across Park Lane and sipping pensively at his morning coffee. But it was not, in point of fact, anywhere near morning.

After leaving Lord and Lady Sharpe with a dozen burning questions still unanswered, Nash had passed the hours after midnight tossing the ivory at White's — not one of his more common vices — and then gone on to his mistress's maisonette in Henrietta Street, coming away vaguely unsatisfied from both. Oh, he'd taken a monkey off Sir Henry Dunnan at hazard, without even paying attention. And Lisette had looked resplendent in a filmy French negligee — a vision hampered only by his recollection of how much it had cost him, and how it had become her habit of late to pout and sulk when he did not dance attendance on her.

Well, she had been pouting and sulking last night. He could hardly blame her; he'd not been at his best. Their interlude had ended in tears, blood, and three shattered wineglasses. He looked down at his empty hand and flexed it experimentally. No, the wound did not gape. He had escaped the surgeon's needle this time. Perhaps it was time to give Lisette her *congé.* His mind was elsewhere now, though he was little pleased to admit it, even to himself.

Absent the fog of lust and champagne, Nash knew he had done an excessively foolish thing last night — and an unnecessary thing, too. How long would it have taken him to discover the name, and more importantly, the circumstances, of the woman in red? Thirty minutes, perhaps, had he troubled himself to do so. But he had not, and now he was deeply angry — with himself, and perhaps with her.

Nonetheless, he had been unable to escape the memory of what they had done together on the terrace last night. And what price, if any, was he going to pay for those few moments of exquisite temptation? What was it about her that had affected him so? He was rarely so willing to let his guard down. But in his embrace, she had been the embodiment of fiery feminine passion, a woman undeniably hungry for all the pleasures his body had offered.

Out of his arms, however, she had panicked like some green schoolgirl — and in the light of day, it was that contrast which so greatly troubled him.

Well, he'd be damned if he would sit back and wait for trouble; he decided as he watched the raindrops race one another down the windowpanes. If there was mischief afoot, he meant to go out and find it, before it found him. The element of surprise was a vastly underestimated advantage.

Just then, his valet breezed efficiently into the room. "Good morning, my lord," said Gibbons, going straight to the dressing room. "I've set your shirt to soak in cold water. I think the bloodstain will come out. Shall I lay out your morning coat? Or will you ride?"

"I shall ride if the rain lets up," said Nash. "I have some urgent business this morning."

"And a grim business, too, it sounds." Gibbons was altogether too forward. "Dare I hope that you mean to turn Miss Lyle off?"

Nash smiled faintly. "One does grow weary of artistic temperament," he murmured. "Have you any notion, Gibbons, what that woman has cost me?"

"A king's ransom, Mr. Swann says."

"Ah, Mr. Swann!" Nash paused to swirl the last of his coffee about in his cup, wondering if one could read one's fortune in coffee dregs. He really did not care for the English habit of tea. "Tell me, Gibbons, do all my servants gossip about me? Or is it just you and Swann?"

"All of us," Gibbons grunted. He was up his rolling ladder now, and poking about on the top shelf of the dressing room. "Alas, we lead small lives, my lord. We must look to you for our excitement."

"Sometimes, Gibbons, I think that I should like a small life," Nash mused. "Or perhaps just a moderately sized life. My stepbrother's life, perhaps? Enough money to live well without being burdened by it, and a career of service to the nation. What would that be like, do you imagine?"

"I'm sure I couldn't say, sir." With one last grunt, Gibbons heaved down a large bandbox. "But if you mean to exchange lives, kindly give a fortnight's notice."

"What? You do not fancy being in service to a prominent member of the Commons?"

"You could not afford me, sir," said Gibbons.

He was quite correct, too. Nash possessed life's every luxury. Indeed, his every whim was anticipated by someone, somewhere, from his boot-boy to his French chef, all the way up to Swann, his man of affairs, and all of them had to be paid a living wage.

Then there was his banker, his butler, his bootmaker, his vintner. His haberdasher and green grocer. Mentally, he added his step-mother and his two sisters to the list. Then all of the servants at all of his estates. His stepbrother Tony. His two great-aunts in Cumbria. The colliers in that Cornish coal mine he'd taken off old Talbot at *vingt-et-un.* It was almost medieval in its simplicity. To every name, he owed a duty, for such was the dominion of the Marquess of Nash. It was a damnable yoke they'd hung round his neck, by God. And he wondered if it was soon to grow heavier.

"I think it must be the carriage today, my lord." Gibbons was at his elbow now, staring at the befogged vista which would perhaps reappear as Hyde Park someday. "I should hate you to take pneumonia."

"Very well," said Nash unhappily. He meant to have a name to go with the miserable unslaked lust his body was suffering, and trotting about London in a crested carriage was far from anonymous. But the carriage it would be, he supposed. It was just another of the many privileges which came to him by way of his title.

It was almost laughable, really. He was certainly not to the manner born. He was just a second son of a second son, and had possessed no prospects at all save for a grueling military career, a cold grave, and, most probably, a Turkish knife in his back.

Still, it was what he had been born and bred to do, his mother had always insisted. And strangely, it was what he had wanted. As a child, he had lived an adventurous life flitting about Europe — at least, he had thought it adventurous. He had not realized they were simply running from one political tinderbox to the next, until the whole of the Continent was consumed in Napoleon's flame and fury.

It was not until his brother Petar, long promised to Czar Alexander I, had been on the verge of leaving for the Russian army and earning his younger sibling's undying envy, that the astonishing news had come all the way to St. Petersburg from faraway Hampshire. Their English relations could not have picked a more opportune time to die, God rest them.

But alas, the Grim Reaper had not finished with what was left. The ensuing years had been hard ones. And when all the bloody battles were done, and all the funeral dirges sung, he was Nash — the very thing he had never expected to be nor ever wished to be.

The door hinge squealed, jerking him into the present. He turned to see his stepbrother peering into the room. "Ah, there you are, Stefan," he said. "Have you another cup? I vow, I am soaked through to my drawers."

"What a charming picture you paint, Tony." Nash motioned for Gibbons, but he was already bringing another cup. "It does look a nasty day out. What brings you?"

The Honorable Anthony Hayden-Worth smiled warmly and took the best chair, which was also the one nearest the coffee service. "May a chap not call upon his brother merely to see how he goes on?" asked Tony, filling the empty cup.

Nash pushed away from the window and joined him by the hearth. "Yes, of course," he said. "But if you need anything, Tony — ?"

An inscrutable look passed over his stepbrother's face. "I'm quite all right," he said. "But thank you just the same."

"Jenny is well?" said Nash.

Tony lifted one shoulder. "She went back

down to Brierwood last week," he remarked. "She seems to have developed quite a fondness for the place. Perhaps she misses Mamma and the girls. I hope you do not mind?"

"Do not be ridiculous, Tony," he replied. "Brierwood is Jenny's home, too. I wish her to be happy there."

"Oh, Jenny is happy enough, so long as her bills are paid." Tony smiled faintly. "She will pop over to France, I daresay, whilst she's in Hampshire, and run up a few more."

"Her father really has cut her off this time?"

Tony shook his head. "Not really," he answered. "She is a pampered princess, our Jenny. Papa threatens, but once in a while, a fat bank draft will still turn up."

"Perhaps it would be better if he did cut her off," Nash suggested.

"Why?" asked Tony pointedly. "So you would be left to pay her bills? And I would be further indebted you? Thank you, no."

Nash sat down and poured himself another cup of coffee, struggling to hold his temper in check. "I have never interfered in your marriage, Tony," he finally said. "And I do not mean to do so now."

Tony smiled, and the sour mood was

broken. "Actually, old man, I only came round to see what went with you last night," he said. "I thought you'd be at White's."

It was an olive branch, and Nash took it. "I finally caught up with Lord Hastley," he said, slowly stirring his coffee. "He has agreed to part with that broodmare after all — for the right price, of course."

Tony's face broke into a grin. "Congratulations, Stefan!" said his stepbrother. "How the devil did you manage it?"

Nash smiled wryly. "An act of sheer desperation, I do assure you," he said. "I ran him to ground at Sharpe's ball last night."

"Good God, you attended a come-out? That *was* desperate."

"It was, rather," Nash agreed.

Tony scowled across the table. "Mind what you do in such places, Stefan," he warned, "or one of those sly, matchmaking mammas will have you in a fix from which your money cannot extract you."

His words sent a chill down Nash's spine though he did not show it. "Wealth can extract a man from nearly everything," he said, hoping he spoke the truth. "And then there is always my vile reputation to fall back on, is there not? In any case, I found Hastley in Sharpe's cardroom. The poor devil's in so deep, he *has* taken to bride-shopping. And he's glad enough now to take my money."

"Yes, aren't we all," said Tony on a laugh.

Nash laid his spoon down carefully. "You are entitled to an allowance from the estate, Tony," he said, measuring his words. "Father arranged it. I could not undo it, even if I wished to — and I do not."

Tony smiled again and changed the subject, turning it instead to his favorite, politics, and the growing strain between Wellington and Lord Eldon. Nash did not much concern himself with English politics, but he knew Tony lived for it, so he murmured polite responses and nodded at all the right places.

"I tell you, Stefan, this damned Catholic question is going to be the death of somebody," Tony finally finished. "At best, it is slow political suicide for the prime minister."

"And trouble in the family is never a good thing," said Nash wryly.

Tony just laughed again. "By the way, old fellow, that reminds me," he said. "Mamma is to celebrate her fiftieth birthday next month."

"Yes," said Nash. "I had not forgotten."

"I believe I shall have a celebration," said

Tony. "Something more than her usual birthday dinner party. Perhaps a ball, and a few guests up to Brierwood for the week, if you do not mind?"

"Of course I do not," said Nash. "Jenny will be pleased to have something to do, won't she? I'm told females enjoy such things."

"I am not sure a house party for Mamma's friends is Jenny's idea of excitement," said Tony. "Still, will you come, Stefan? It *is* your home — and Mamma would be so pleased."

There was an almost imperceptible tightening of Nash's mouth. "We shall see," he finally said. "What are your plans for the day, Tony? Shall I see you at White's this evening?"

"I shouldn't think so," said his stepbrother. "We're to meet after dinner to whinge over the Test and Corporation Acts, but we are just beating a dead horse if you ask me. And then there'll be a by-election strategy meeting."

"Why do you not dine here, then?"

"Certainly, if you will forgive me for rushing away afterwards," said Tony. "These bloody meetings will likely drag into the night as it is."

"But your seat in the Commons is quite

safe. You have been reelected. What more must you do?"

Tony pushed back his chair and rose. "It is the nature of English politics, Stefan," he said. "Elections do not simply cost pots of money, they take effort. One hand washing the other, and all that rot. And rotten boroughs do not come cheap. You are fortunate to be in the Lords, old fellow, where one need not concern oneself with the opinions — or the palms — of the common man."

Nash smiled and languidly took up his coffee. "Indeed, I never give him a thought, Tony," he said, staring over the brim of his cup. "I am too preoccupied with exercising my upper-class prerogatives — and, of course, my upper-class vices."

His stepbrother scowled down at him. "It is just that sort of talk, Stefan, which blackens your reputation," he chided. "I beg you to have a care — and to think of Mamma, at the very least."

"I cannot think anyone imagines my stepmother responsible for my character, Tony," said Nash. "I am fond of Edwina, as she is fond of me. But she did not raise me, more's the pity."

Whatever argument his brother might have countered with was forestalled by Gibbons, who crossed from the dressing room to the window. "It is a miracle, my lord," he announced, staring down at the street below. "The rain has stopped. I think you may safely go out now."

But Nash was not simply going out. He was going on the offensive. "Excellent, Gibbons," he answered. "Send word to bring round my gig, and fetch my charcoal morning coat."

In Wapping, the skies did not clear until midafternoon. Xanthia stood at her office window, staring across the Upper Pool toward St. Savior's Docks and trying to keep her mind on her work. London's weather had done little to still the traffic on the Thames, for this sort of hustle and bustle was driven by hardier men than that.

The whole of London's Docklands was still a constant fascination to her. Even now, some four months after her arrival, she was awed by the industry and commerce of the East End. To Xanthia, England was Wapping. She remembered nothing of her infancy in Lincolnshire. Indeed, she had never in her memory ventured beyond the West Indies until five years past, when she and Kieran had visited London to open a second office for Neville Shipping.

But the moment her trunk hit the dock in this teeming city, she had felt at once as if she belonged. Not in the countryside, nor even in Mayfair, where their home was, but here, amidst all this grime and stench and pulsating activity. If the Thames was London's main artery, then surely Wapping was its heart.

Six days a week, Kieran's barouche brought her from the luxurious confines of Berkeley Square, along the Strand and Fleet Street, and thence into another world. This was the world of the workingman; the mastmakers and the coopers, the lightermen and the watermen. The place where black-garbed customs clerks with ink-stained fingers brushed shoulders with aldermen and bankers. Where the East End merchant princes strode down from their opulent town homes in Wellclose Square to watch their fortunes sail into the Pool of London.

Along this part of the Thames, the languages, the shops, and even the churches were as apt to be foreign as English. The Swedes and the Norwegians were preeminent. The Chinese and the Africans brought strange music and exotic foods. The French and the Italians were as at home in Wapping as in Cherbourg or Genoa. It was a glorious melting pot of humanity.

Just then, the door behind Xanthia opened, sending another chill through the room. She turned from the window to see Gareth Lloyd, their business agent, coming into the office. He went at once to his desk in the corner and slapped down the baize ledger he had carried into the room. "The *Belle Weather* is in," he said matter-of-factly. "She's coming up Limehouse Reach just now."

Xanthia's eyes widened. "What a splendid run!" Inordinately pleased, she left the window and went to her own desk to check the schedules. "All went well? Or has anyone come ashore?"

"The boatswain came in. He says Captain Stretton took on an extra ton of ivory when she rounded the Cape." Lloyd dragged a hand through his thick, golden hair. "Unfortunately, there's been spoilage in the citrus. A black fungus. About a third has been lost, I collect."

That was unfortunate, but not wholly unexpected. Xanthia settled into her chair and began to rub her hands absently up and down her arms.

Lloyd crossed to the fireplace and knelt. "You are freezing again." He spoke without looking at her and began to poke at the coals. "I shall build up the fire."

"Thank you."

She watched him in silence. When the fire was thoroughly rekindled, Lloyd went to the huge map which all but covered the adjacent wall, and began to study the blood-red lines dotted with bright yellow pins, each of which represented one of Neville's ships at sea. The red lines were their preferred trade routes, and Lloyd could likely have traced them in with a fingertip in the dark of night, so well did he know them.

Gareth Lloyd had been with Neville Shipping since before her elder brother's death a dozen years past. Luke had taken him on as an errand boy in the counting house. But Lloyd had quickly shown an uncanny knack for all things financial, and the West Indies was not precisely awash in talent. Those who risked the treacherous journey came to make their own fortunes, not someone else's. A few succeeded, as Kieran had. Sugar was a lucrative business, often more lucrative than shipping.

Gareth Lloyd, however, had continued to toil quietly in the service of another. After Luke's death, Neville Shipping had floundered under a series of business agents, each more dishonest than the last. Kieran had profoundly disliked the company their brother had begun, and he was already worked to the bone by the plantations and mills which provided the bulk of the family's wealth. But Xanthia had grown up at Luke's feet, going regularly with him to the shipping office. It had been the best place to keep a little sister occupied and out of trouble when there were no female relations to depend upon.

Xanthia did not even remember when she had ceased to play at working and had begun to work in earnest. She could not recall the first occasion when one of the men had come to her with a problem to be solved or a decision to be made. Or when she had fired the first worthless business agent and watched disbelief sketch across his face. But at some point, even the bankers and the merchants and the sea captains had ceased patting her on the head and begun to accept that she was a force with which to be reckoned.

By slow default, the management of Neville Shipping had fallen to Xanthia and the operations to Gareth Lloyd. Kieran had not strongly objected. It was Barbados; one did what one must with whatever resources one had. Moreover, they were good — both of them — *bloody good* at what they did. Negotiate and strategize. Invest and hedge. They could send ships and money and commodities flying halfway round the world with the ease of falling off a ladder.

Lloyd moved the pin to show the relocation of the *Belle Weather,* then set one shoulder against the mantelpiece, surveying Xanthia across the room with a gaze which was steady but unreadable. "You went to Lord Sharpe's last night?" he finally said.

"Reluctantly, yes." Xanthia laid aside her pen.

"A Mayfair ball at the height of the season, attended by the height of society," he murmured. "Was it all that a woman might dream of?"

"Some women, perhaps." Xanthia closed the schedule she'd been looking at and stood.

He crossed the room and set one hand beside her on the desk. The tension in the room was suddenly palpable. "You do know that you cannot live two lives, Xanthia, do you not?" he said coolly. "You cannot be both society belle and business owner. This is England. The *ton* will not accept you."

"Then the *ton* be damned," she answered. This was not the first time these past four months this particular issue had arisen. "If my choices did not suit you, Gareth, then you should have stayed in Bridgetown."

"And do what?" he returned.

She lifted her accusing gaze to his. "You had prospects, Gareth," she said quietly. "Fine ones, too. Hancock's offered you a good deal more than Neville's pays you, even with your minority ownership. Did you think me fool enough not to know that? So why are you still here? That's what I wonder."

"Damn it, Xanthia, you know *why.*" His hands seized her shoulders before she could shove him away, and his mouth took hers roughly. Demandingly.

For an instant, she let herself give in, let her weight fall against him, giving in to the strain and the loneliness. He was rock solid and warm. Against her will, the memory of a long-ago passion stirred in her chest. Gareth sensed her surrender and deepened the kiss, claiming her — or so he thought.

But he could never claim her. Whatever there had once been was no more, and she dared not rekindle it. She needed him — needed his friendship, his wisdom — but no, *not* this. Desire was nothing without love. Xanthia, set her hands against his shoulders and forced him back with surprising strength.

He lifted his head, his wild, hot gaze holding hers.

"I ought to slap you senseless." Xanthia's

voice trembled.

The wildfire died. "Have at it, my dear," he said. "If it will make you feel better about being a woman — and having a woman's needs."

Incensed, she drew back her arm, but Gareth's eyes dared her. Chilled her. Somehow, she found the presence of mind to lower her hand and set her palm flat on the back of her chair instead, so that he would not see how it trembled.

"Get out, Gareth," she said, refusing to look at him. "I have grown weary of this. Draw yourself next quarter's pay, and go. You are sacked."

"You cannot sack me, Xanthia," he said as he turned and walked stiffly away. "Not without a two-thirds vote of your directors. And that would be you, me, and Rothewell. Do you want to solicit his vote, my dear? Do you want to tell him why? And do you want to tell him what we've been to one another?"

"I begin to think it might be worth it," she snapped, addressing his back. "Sometimes, Gareth, I despise you."

It was his turn to stare blindly out the window. "No, you don't," he said, setting one hand on his hip. "I almost wish, Xanthia, that you did, for it would be easier.

But good God, sometimes I despise myself enough for the both of us."

She was utterly shaking inside now. Dear heaven, she had played this badly! She really did not want to lose Gareth, either as a friend or as an employee. It was a horrid, horrid balancing act she played.

"I have to go," she said, shoving her chair abruptly to her desk. The argument was over for now, and they both knew that neither had won.

"Go where?" he said, almost as if nothing had happened. "Captain Stretton and the purser will be coming ashore with the manifest and cashbox."

"Lady Sharpe is expecting me," said Xanthia, piling her files together untidily.

"Very well." Lloyd went to the door. "I'll deal with Stretton. Shall I call your carriage?"

"I shall take a skiff from Hermitage Stairs," she said abruptly. "It will be quicker. The rain has let up, and the tide is coming in."

Lloyd turned from the door, frowning. "In London, you are a lady, Xanthia," he said. "Overlooking the fact that ladies do not work, they certainly do not hail watermen unaccompanied."

"And what would you have me do, Gareth?" she snapped. "Loll about in Mayfair tatting sofa cushions and leave you to run Neville Shipping?"

Lloyd drew back as if she had slapped him. "That was beneath you, Xanthia," he said. "And I did not deserve it."

"I am sorry." Xanthia returned to the window, crossing her arms over her chest, as if she were cold again. "You are right, of course. My remark was uncalled for."

He followed her, and turned her roughly by the shoulders. "You do not have to live like this, Xanthia," he said. "Here, in England, you can be what you really are — a lady by birth."

"As opposed to what?" she retorted. "The impoverished ward of Bridgetown's most disgusting wastrel?"

Even Gareth knew better than to bring up the topic of her uncle, the vile man who had reluctantly taken in Xanthia and her brothers. "You are the sister of Baron Rothewell," he gritted. "Cousin by marriage to the Earl of Sharpe. The blood niece of that grand dragon, Lady Bledsoe. Why can't you give this up, Xanthia? Why can't you be what you were destined to be?"

"Because, Gareth, I can never forget what I was." Her voice was low and hard now. "Nothing but my uncle's unwanted refuse.

This company *made me.* By the grace of God, my brother gave me a chance — and now Neville Shipping defines me in a way a man could never understand. I will never, ever give it up, Gareth — not for any reason on God's earth — and if you think otherwise, you'll have a long, miserable wait ahead of you."

His eyes held hers for a long, expectant moment, then, with an awkward jerk, he drew open the door. "I am not waiting for anything," he said. "I was done with the waiting years ago. I shall send Bakely down for your skiff." And then he was gone.

Angry and shaken, Xanthia gathered the papers she would need for the evening, stuffed them into her leather bag, and hastily threw on her cloak. When she went downstairs, into the clerks' domain, Gareth had vanished. She tucked her portfolio under one arm, bid the staff a good evening, and went out into the late-day bustle along Wapping High Street.

The rhythmic *clank! clank! clank!* which rang from the cooperage echoed off the towering walls of the buildings and warehouses lining both sides of the street. The sour scent of fermenting hops from the brewery upriver filled her nostrils. And overlying all of it was the sharp stench of low tide.

A cart rumbled by, laden with wooden slats, destined for the cooperage, no doubt. Xanthia let it pass, then turned down the narrow, cobbled lane which led to Hermitage Stairs. Gareth Lloyd awaited her at the top, and below, the skiff he had summoned bobbed against the slapping current. It looked to be new and sturdy, and the waterman bore his brass license badge proudly on his coat sleeve.

Clearly, Gareth meant to accompany her. "It is late," he said, his voice emotionless. "I've sent Bakely down to the dock. He'll send a lighter out when the *Belle Weather* drops anchor and tell Stretton to report tomorrow."

For an instant, she considered refusing his company. But Xanthia was nothing if not practical. It would look far better to arrive in Westminster in the company of a gentleman — or a man who certainly looked the part — rather than to arrive alone, and she did have Pamela to think about. So she placed her hand in Gareth's, as she had done perhaps a thousand times before. "You really needn't do this, you know."

"I know," he said, and took her carefully down the stairs.

They settled themselves into the boat, and

the waterman pushed away from the stairs, stroking his oars deeply and powerfully into the roiling murk.

Xanthia tried to focus on the riverbank and not on the man who sat beside her. She loved this view of London. This was not the stiff, elegant world of Mayfair and Belgravia, but the living, breathing world of commerce, dominated by the vast East India warehouses, and the tall construction cranes of the new St. Katharine's Docks. In the pool, massive merchantmen and sleek clippers rocked on the turning tide, their towering masts now stripped bare. Lighters hastened to and fro to off-load precious cargo from the larger vessels, then see it safely ashore. And if man were dwarfed by this great, teeming world, a woman was . . . well, blatantly out of place. Gareth was not wrong on that score.

Oh, Xanthia felt as if she belonged — but the occasional sidelong stare told her that she still did not blend in. Of course there were women in the docklands. But they were shopkeepers, seamstresses, and merchants' wives, or the ubiquitous prostitutes who frequented every inch of every port on God's green earth. They were a part of life from which the ladies of Mayfair would undoubtedly have recoiled. Xanthia was well accustomed to them. Gareth was wrong. She was not a lady, she thought, craning her neck in search of the *Belle Weather.* Not really. And that did not trouble her as much as it perhaps should have done.

She was very troubled, however, when she arrived in Hanover Street to be told that Lady Sharpe was still abed. Instructions had been left to show Xanthia to her ladyship's chamber, and a footman took her up at once.

Xanthia went in to see that Pamela was not precisely in bed, but on a long, velvet divan and wrapped in a woolen shawl. Her daughter Louisa sat rigidly in a chair beside her. Lady Louisa's dainty blond ringlets seemed to have lost a bit of their bounce, and the girl's eyes and nose were swollen to a pathetic shade of pink.

"Heavens, Pamela!" said Xanthia, stripping off her gloves as she came into the room. "And Louisa — ? What on earth has happened?"

At that, Louisa burst into tears, sprang from her chair, and rushed toward the still-open door.

"Oh, my," said Xanthia, watching the girl's flounced skirts vanish.

Pamela looked up with a wry smile, and patted the empty chair. "Pay her no mind,

Zee," said her cousin. "The child is seventeen. Everything is a melodrama when one is that age."

Xanthia tossed her gloves aside and sank into the chair. "Pamela, what is going on?" she demanded, taking her cousin's hand. "This house seems perfectly topsy-turvy today. The servants are jumpy as cats — and you, in your dressing gown at teatime! You are unwell. I can see it in your eyes."

The wry smile returned. "I am just a little weak, my dear," said Pamela, squeezing her fingers. "But it shan't last. Now, listen, Zee. I am going to tell you the most *amazing* thing! Sharpe is quite simply beside himself."

Xanthia's eyes widened. "What? Tell me, for I'm worried sick."

Pamela set a hand on her somewhat ample belly. "Xanthia, I am with child."

Xanthia gasped. "Dear heaven! Are you . . . are you quite sure?"

With a weak smile, Pamela nodded. "Oh, Xanthia, *can* you believe it? I am so excited — and so very frightened, too."

Xanthia was a little frightened herself. Pamela was but a few years shy of forty, and after two decades of marriage and at least half a dozen pregnancies, she had carried but two children to term. Daughters.

Lovely girls, but daughters all the same.

"Oh, Zee, do say you are happy for me!" exclaimed Pamela. "Oh, do not think what you are thinking, my dear, and think only of this wonderful chance which I have been given. A chance to give Sharpe his heir. Oh, my life would be quite perfectly complete!"

Xanthia smiled deeply and leaned over the divan to kiss her cousin's cheek. "I am ecstatic," she said. "I could not be more pleased. I cannot wait to tell Kieran. He will be so happy for you, Pamela. But my dear, you must be so very careful. You know that, do you not?"

"I do know," she said grimly. "The midwives and doctors have already been here this morning to poke and prod me, and to confirm what I was afraid even to hope. And now, I'm not to be allowed to do anything — scarcely even go downstairs! — for the next six months. I shall go quite mad, of course. But it will be worth it if I can but give Sharpe a son."

Suddenly, the vision of Louisa's red nose and eyes returned to Xanthia. "Oh, dear!" she said. "Poor Louisa!"

Pamela's eyes began to flood. "Frightful timing, is it not?" she said. "This is her come-out, Zee! This is *her* season! We've spent a small fortune dressing her, and she has taken quite nicely. And now I'm to be stuck abed until Michaelmas!"

"What is she to do, Pamela?" asked Xanthia. "There is her father, of course . . . but that is not quite the thing, is it?"

"She must have a chaperone," Pamela insisted. "Of course, there is always Christine. She is Sharpe's sister, after all. But she is thought to be — well, a little *outré,* is she not? I cannot think her a proper companion for a girl of Louisa's tender years."

"No, I think not," muttered Xanthia.

The truth was, Christine Ambrose was an amoral cat — one who from time to time had sunk her claws into Kieran. But Kieran knew the woman for what she was, and used her about as well as she used him. Sometimes Xanthia thought that perhaps they deserved one another. But Christine chaperoning Louisa? No, it would not do. Slowly, it dawned on her that Pamela's hand was holding hers in a near death grip. She looked down to see an unmistakable pleading in her cousin's eyes.

"Oh, Xanthia, my dear, *may* I count on you?"

Xanthia barely suppressed a gasp. "Count on *me?*" she echoed. "To . . . to do what, pray?"

"To see Louisa through the rest of her

season."

"To . . . to take her about to balls and assemblies and such, do you mean?" said Xanthia hollowly. "Oh, Pamela. I do not think . . . no, I am not versed in such . . . I could not possibly . . ." But the desperation in Pamela's eyes was perfectly heartwrenching.

Pamela sat up a little on the divan. "I shall arrange invitations to all the best houses in town," she wheedled. "And Almack's every Wednesday, of course."

Xanthia made a slight sound of exasperation. "Do not be silly, Pamela," she said. "We haven't a subscription and likely cannot get one."

Pamela laughed. "Oh, Rothewell will be admitted *instantly,* dear child," she said. "His title ensures it. And I shall put it about that you are to be Louisa's chaperone and made as welcome as I would be. After all, I am not without influence in Town, my dear. And — and why, perhaps you will have fun, too! Oh, my dear, *do* say you will do it."

Xanthia hesitated. Dear heaven! Her hope of never seeing Mr. Nash again was on the verge of collapse. "But I am an unmarried woman," she protested. "That really is not ideal. *Is* it?"

"But you are a mature woman," said Pamela firmly. "It must be you or Christine. It *must* be family, and Mamma cannot do it. Besides, she and Louisa always quarrel. All you will need is Kieran's escort, or Sharpe's. There will almost always be a cardroom to pacify them."

Xanthia let out her breath on a sigh. Kieran would not like this any better than she, but he had an uncharacteristic fondness for Cousin Pamela. "Of course we shall be happy to help, Pamela," she answered. "But there are a few things, my dear, which you ought to consider."

Pamela's pale eyebrows lifted. "Yes? Of what sort?"

Xanthia dared not tell her about the intriguing Mr. Nash. "Well, you know that I am greatly involved with Neville Shipping," she said instead.

"Oh, yes, dear," she said. "You so often speak of it."

"But what you may not realize is that I — well, I spend a good deal of time there. Literally. At the business."

Pamela seemed to consider it. "Well, you do own a third of it," she mused. "One must look after one's interests, I daresay."

"Actually, I own twenty-five percent," she said. "Kieran has twenty-five, and Martinique the twenty-five she inherited when

Luke died. Gareth Lloyd, our business agent, now owns the remaining twenty-five percent."

"Does he indeed?" said Pamela. "I was not aware."

"Well, that is neither here nor there," Xanthia continued. "The truth is, I more or less manage Neville Shipping."

Pamela nodded cheerfully. "Yes, you once suggested something of that sort."

Xanthia took her cousin's hand again and vowed to make her listen. "Pamela, I go into the East End in a carriage to work every day," she said, her voice firm. "I sit in an office surrounded by men, in a grimy little house in an especially grimy street in Wapping — which is filled with some of the most disreputable people imaginable — and I dearly love it. People stare at me, Pamela. One day a man near the London docks *spat* at me. Most of them do not think I belong — and no one amongst the *ton* is apt to disagree with that assessment."

"Oh. Oh, I see." Pamela was blinking owlishly. "Is it . . . is it rather like having a shop, would you say? Mrs. Reynolds once had a shop, you know. But now she is Lady Warding."

"Yes, but I never shall be Lady Warding, or anything like it," Xanthia gently pressed.

"I shall always be Miss Neville who has the utter lack of breeding to keep a job — and to do men's work. For that is what they shall say, Pam, if the word gets out. And it will sound worse, I fear, than being a mere shopkeeper."

Pamela pursed her lips, and shook her head. "You have a right, Xanthia, to look after yourself," she insisted. "If Kieran supports your doing that, then it is no one else's business."

"No, it is not," Xanthia agreed with asperity. "But if it gets out — which it will — then the gossips shall make it their business."

Pamela relaxed against the chaise and patted Xanthia's hand. "Oh, if it gets out, you will merely be thought an eccentric," she answered. "Indeed, my dear, with your charm and your dash, you might make it quite the rage. Perhaps it will become fashionable to have one's own company? I should choose hats, myself. How does one make them, do you suppose? In any case, I am not worried on Louisa's behalf."

Xanthia smiled faintly. Employment really was a foreign concept to her cousin, who had been raised every inch a lady. "Very well, then," she murmured. "You have been warned."

"So I have, and now that that is all settled, I want you to put your hand here," said Pamela, placing Xanthia's palm atop her belly. "Say hello to your new cousin, the future Earl of Sharpe."

Xanthia's smile deepened. "Am I to feel anything?" she asked, curious. "Will he . . . will he move? Or kick my hand?"

Pamela laughed. "Oh, Xanthia, you can be shockingly innocent," she said. "No, he shan't do a thing for weeks and weeks. But he is in there, all the same. Shall I tell you when he starts to move about? Would you like to feel him kick?"

Xanthia felt suddenly shy, and, to her shock, more than a little envious. "I would, yes," she admitted. "It is such a wonderful, unfathomable thing to me."

Pamela's face took on a serious expression. "You must have children of your own soon, Xanthia," she said quietly. "Time marches on. You are what? Seven-and-twenty now?"

Xanthia gave an embarrassed laugh. "Oh, Pamela, I shall be thirty in a few months' time," she said. "And there is one serious flaw in your plan, my dear. One ought not have children without a husband."

Pamela's expression brightened. "Well, you are about to enter the marriage mart!"

she answered. "Louisa is determined to look about quite carefully for just the right sort of gentleman. I would suggest, my dear girl, that you do the same."

Xanthia shook her head. "I do not mean to marry, Pamela."

"Well, why on earth not?" demanded her cousin. "It is the most natural thing in the world."

Xanthia looked away and chose her words carefully. "Gentlemen wish their brides to be . . . well, younger and more naive," she answered. "Besides, there is Neville Shipping to worry about. If I marry, it becomes my husband's. Even if it did not, no husband would permit me to work as I do."

"Oh, heavens, let Kieran take care of Neville Shipping!" said Pamela impatiently. "What else has he to do? He has sold his plantations, and he has leased out all of his estates. Honestly, Xanthia, if he cannot find something to occupy his time, Sharpe says he is going to drink and whore himself into an early grave."

Xanthia stiffened. "Kieran knows nothing of shipping, nor does he wish to," she replied. "He will simply sell the company to the highest bidder."

"Yes, as he did the Barbados properties," Pamela remarked. "I vow, that made no sense to me."

"He did not sell to the highest bidder, Pamela," Xanthia gently chided. "He leased the land in allotments to the men who had worked it year after year. And if you had lived all your life in Barbados as I have done, you would understand why he wanted to do that. The days of slavery, Pamela, are over. It is time we all accepted that. It is a vile and corrupting institution, no matter how gentle one's hand."

"Yes, it is very dreadful, to be sure, but could he not just —"

A sound at the door cut her off. Pamela's maid came into the room. "The girl from Madame Claudette's has come with Lady Louisa's new gowns, ma'am," she said after curtsying. "Shall you wish her to try them on before the girl goes?"

Pamela and Xanthia exchanged vaguely apologetic glances. Clearly, there would be no more talk of slavery's evils on this particular afternoon. It was time to get back to that evil which was far more troubling to the ladies of Mayfair — the unspeakable horror of a badly fitted ball gown.

CHAPTER THREE:
A GRAVE
MISUNDERSTANDING
IN MAYFAIR

Baron Rothewell was savoring a brandy and a black, nasty humor when he heard the knocker drop upon his elegant front door in Berkeley Square. He had been savoring his brandy since teatime, actually, and was not now disposed to break what had thus far been a solitary interlude.

Rothewell was the sort of man who believed very firmly the old adage that silence was the true friend that never betrayed. He made few acquaintances and kept far fewer. Nor was he a man with any fondness for idle conversation — and it was all idle, so far as Rothewell could see.

But he likely needn't be concerned, the baron consoled himself, going to the small sideboard in his study to pour himself another tot. He knew almost no one in London, and certainly had invited no one to call upon him. He was surprised, therefore, when one of his newly employed footmen came in bearing the card of a gentle-man whose name he had never before heard.

"I am not at home," he growled.

But the servant looked ill at ease. "I think he means to wait, my lord," said the foot-man. "After all, it *is* Lord Nash."

Rothewell scowled. "Who the devil is Lord Nash?" grumbled the baron. "And why should I give a damn?"

"Well, he is the sort of fellow who gener-ally gets what he wants," said the footman.

This was enough to pique Rothewell's curiosity. "Oh, very well," he said. "Show the fellow in."

Naturalists say that when certain carni-vores meet in the wild, they circle and scent one another, each assessing the other's willingness to back away. Rothewell never backed away from anyone, and his hackles went up the moment the man crossed his threshold.

The man called Nash was whipcord-lean and moved with a controlled strength which was rather more formidable than outright brawn might have been. His hair was black as a raven's wing, with perhaps a suggestion of silver at the temples. He carried an expensive-looking driving cape over one arm, and his gloves in one hand, as if his stay was to be brief.

"Good evening, Lord Rothewell." The man had eyes like obsidian ice. "How kind of you to receive me."

Glittering eyes. Expensive clothes. A voice too soft — and not quite English, either, he thought. *This, at least, should be interesting.*

Rothewell waved a hand toward a chair. "Do sit down," he said. "How may I assist you?"

As if to make a point, Nash repositioned the chair nearer the desk. "I am here on a matter which is of a personal nature."

"I can't think what the devil that might be," said Rothewell, "since I never before laid eyes on you."

The man smiled faintly, as if he did not believe him. "No, I have not the pleasure of a formal acquaintance," he answered coolly. "But I believe I had the honor of meeting your sister last night at Lord Sharpe's ball. Miss Xanthia Neville — she *is* your sister, is she not?"

The man, Rothewell decided, looked like a wolf; a wolf with a lean and hungry look about him. "I do not remember you from Sharpe's ball," he said, holding the man's gaze. "But yes, Miss Neville is my sister. What of it?"

"I collect you are her guardian," said Lord Nash in his too-quiet voice. "I should like your permission to pay court to her."

"You should *what* — ?"

"I should like to court Miss Neville." If anything, his voice was even quieter, and more ominous. "I somehow feel certain that my suit will be acceptable to you."

Rothewell was not remotely intimidated. "It certainly is not," he barked. "Why should it be? My sister is an exceptional woman. And she is not in need of — nor, so far as I know, even in *want of* — a husband. Moreover, it is Xanthia's permission you'll need — and if you knew a bloody thing about her, you would already know *that*."

"Ah, an independent-minded young lady," remarked Nash. "How very charming."

"She is not independent-minded," said Rothewell. "She is *independent*. And stubborn. And imperious, when she's in the right — which she is, more often than one wishes to admit. Good God, Nash, she's nearly thirty years old. Moreover, she . . . she is not *like* other women. Have you any notion what you are asking?"

"I am asking if I may court your sister."

"Why?"

"I beg your pardon?"

"Why Xanthia?" he demanded. "If you want a wife, why not chose some young, biddable miss, Nash? Life will go a damned sight easier for you, trust me."

Lord Nash was looking faintly uncomfortable now. "Miss Neville is the managing sort, is she?"

"Yes, and quite good at it," said Rothewell. "Indeed, I believe I would back her ten to one against any man I know — but press your attentions where they are not wanted, Lord Nash, and you will answer to *me*."

Nash looked truly puzzled. This meeting obviously was not going as he had planned. But what the devil had he expected? Suddenly, an unpleasant thought struck Rothewell. He let his eyes drift over Lord Nash's expensive attire, and pondered it. "Frankly, Nash," he finally said, "now that I think on it, I know of but one reason why you might have an interest in my sister — and it is not flattering."

Nash's eyes glittered. "Pray speak plainly, Rothewell."

"I am referring to her fortune," Rothewell answered. "As you doubtless know, my sister is quite a wealthy woman. But she will not give it up, Nash — and a marriage would require her to do just that."

The marquess drew back an inch, his confusion replaced by outright hauteur. "You dare to suggest I am a fortune hunter?" he snapped. "Good God. Certainly not."

Rothewell steepled his fingers together thoughtfully. "Then I beg your pardon, of course," he said curtly. "I suppose Xanthia is not precisely what one would consider parson's bait, however lovely she may be. And her strong personality . . . well, I daresay I have made my point in that regard."

Nash's posture was so rigid now, he looked as if he'd swallowed a poker. "Perhaps there has been some mistake," he finally acknowledged. "I begin to collect that your Miss Neville would not make an ideal wife after all."

Rothewell flashed a faint smile. "For the right man, Xanthia would make an admirable wife indeed," he said. "But I am relatively confident that you are not that man. I will not see such an intelligent and lovely woman wasted on someone who neither loves her nor deserves her."

Nash lifted a piercing, steady gaze to meet his host's. "You make it sound as if you had someone else in mind."

It was Rothewell's turn to shift uncomfortably in his chair. "My sister has an offer, yes," he admitted. "A proposal of long standing from a family friend. I daresay they will get round to tying the knot one of these days."

"I see." Abruptly, Nash rose, his eyes suddenly flat and inscrutable. "My apologies, Lord Rothewell. I have inconvenienced you quite unnecess—"

Suddenly, the study door burst open, and a whirlwind carrying a stuffed leather folio swept in. "Kieran, I have the most *shocking* news ever!" said his sister as both men rose. "And the *Belle Weather* is in six weeks early, so I thought that we might —" Her eyes had shied wild in the direction of Rothewell's guest. "Oh. Good Lord. I . . . I do beg your pardon."

She was halfway out the door when Rothewell caught her. "Not so fast, old thing," he said. "I take it you know our new friend Lord Nash?"

"*Lord* Nash?" Xanthia had flushed three shades of pink. "I — no, I do not. That is to say . . . that is to say I did not perfectly understand who . . . or why . . ."

Rothewell could not recall ever having seen his sister at a loss for words. He let his eyes drift over her face, to reassure himself that she did not fear this man.

No, there was nothing but grave embarrassment etched on her face. "Obviously, this unfortunate business does not concern me," he said, releasing his sister's arm. "I shall leave you to it."

"Leave us to what, pray?" Xanthia was looking at Nash with a sidelong suspicion now.

"I'm damned if I know." Rothewell shrugged, and took up his brandy glass. Then, thinking better of it, he snared the bottle, too. It might be a long night.

"Good evening, Miss Neville," said Nash, when the door was closed. "We meet again."

Nash watched Miss Neville's suspicion shift to outrage. "Oh, *Lord* Nash, is it?"

"Please do not claim you did not know," he said.

"I did not know." Each word was crisply enunciated. "What are you doing here? How did you find me?"

"You have been much on my mind, my dear, since abandoning me last night," he said. "So I asked a few discreetly placed questions and was a little disturbed by what I discovered."

Anger sketched across her face. "As I am a little disturbed to have been run to ground as if I were some sort of prey," she returned. "I apologize, sir, as I hope you do, for what happened last night. However, when a lady abruptly leaves a gentleman under such circumstances, there are but a few conclusions one can draw."

"Are there indeed?" he murmured. "I could think of only one."

"And yet you followed me here?" she challenged, entirely missing his point. "Followed me into the privacy of my home? That, sir, is unacceptable."

Nash watched her warily for a moment. Even amidst his confusion, he could not help but be aware of her proximity and of her almost palpable allure. She was an unconventional beauty to be sure, with her dark chestnut hair, thin nose, and eyes too widely set — eyes which were focused on him unblinkingly, demanding an answer to her challenge.

"You must pardon me, Miss Neville," he finally said. "I have misjudged the situation."

"It would seem so," she returned. "What on earth possessed you to call upon my brother?"

"I was entering the lion's den, I thought," he answered. "I am not the sort of man who waits for trouble to find me, and I wished to see which way the wind blew."

"Oh, how ridiculous!" she answered. "What did you say?"

"Very little that made sense," Nash confessed.

"I wish you to stay away from him," she commanded. "Rothewell eats dandies like you for breakfast, Lord Nash. Trust me, you do not want to irritate him."

Nash drew in his breath sharply. "I beg your pardon. Did you say *dandy* — ?"

Miss Neville colored. "Well, a fashion plate, then. Or a tulip. Or an exquisite, perhaps?" She stopped and pursed her lips. "I beg your pardon. I meant no insult, and I obviously don't know the proper words. But whatever you are, just stop antagonizing my brother."

Nash stepped closer, and grasped her arm. "And talking about what we were doing on Sharpe's terrace might antagonize him?"

"Good God!" Her eyes sparked with blue fire. "Surely you did not?"

He set his head to one side and studied her, still gripping her arm quite firmly. "No, I did not," he answered musingly. "Tell me, Miss Neville, what do you think his reaction would have been?"

She jerked her arm away, and stepped back. "I cannot say," she confessed. "Nothing, perhaps. Or perhaps he would have shot you dead where you stood. That is the very trouble with Rothewell, don't you see? One never knows. Kindly go away, Lord Nash. And stay away. I think you will be saving all of us from a vast amount of grief."

He stepped closer, strangely unwilling to let her escape. "Tell me, Miss Neville, why did you kiss me last night?" he asked quietly. "Indeed, what in God's name were you doing alone on that terrace in the first place?"

"England is a free country," she responded. "I went out for air."

"Miss Neville, you are an unmarried woman," he protested. "Society generally expects —"

"Kindly save your breath," she interjected. "I neither need nor want another lecture about what English society expects. I am unwed, sir, not witless. If I wish a breath of fresh air, I shall have it, and your *beau monde* will simply have to wrestle with their ridiculous notion of propriety."

Against his will, Nash's mouth began to tug into a grin. "Well, it would appear our discussion here is finished," he said, taking up his cape and gloves. "You are, if I may say so, Miss Neville, a most fascinating woman. I wish to God you were a willing widow — or even some poor devil's willing wife — but you aren't, are you? And now I'm to suffer for it."

"Oh, for pity's sake, Lord Nash." She looked at him uncertainly. "No one need suffer."

"Alas, there is but one way to avoid that," he murmured. "And it is quite out of the question. Thank you, my dear, for a remarkable evening — two of them, actually."

He heard a sound of relief escape her lips as she turned toward the door. But at the last instant, she caught him by the arm. "Wait, Lord Nash." Her eyes were still wary. "I should like to know — what was your conclusion?"

"I beg your pardon?"

"On the terrace," she reminded him. "You said you could think of but one conclusion to draw. Obviously, it was the wrong one."

"Ah, that!" He smiled faintly. "When I learnt you were unmarried, I supposed that I had been followed onto the terrace and entrapped."

"Entrapped?" It took her a moment to comprehend, then understanding dawned. "*Entrapped?* Good Lord, what an insult."

He lifted one shoulder. "It is a constant threat to a man in my position."

She glowered at him. "You flatter yourself, Lord Nash. Were I a man, I might just call you out for such an affront and put a period to both you and your self-absorbed concerns."

"I begin to wonder you don't do it anyway," he said honestly. "Are you a very good shot?"

"Yes, but a tad out of practice," she said. "I'd likely miss your heart and hit your bowels, so it would be a long, painful, and putrefying death."

He winced. "Then I have been saved from a terrible fate indeed," he said, bowing to her. "You are a rare beauty, my dear, but not worth dying for — slowly or otherwise. I give you good evening, Miss Neville. And I wish you joy of your unwed state. Long may it continue."

Xanthia watched Lord Nash suspiciously, but his regret did indeed seem sincere. She gave the slightest nod of acknowledgment, then escorted her unexpected visitor to the door. Nash set his hand on the brass doorknob, but on impulse, Xanthia covered it with her own. "Will you answer one last question for me?"

He looked down his hawkish, arrogant nose, and lifted one eyebrow. "I cannot say," he answered. "Will it result in further threats to my life or my manhood?"

She ignored that, for she could see that he was struggling mightily to suppress a grin. "Could I ask you — or what I meant was —" She paused to lick her lips uncertainly. "Is it possible that you might be able to forget that . . . that last night ever happened?"

The crook in his eyebrow went up another notch. "Oh, not in a million years," he murmured, leaning just a little nearer. "I shall take the memory of that lush, sensuous mouth of yours to the grave, my dear. And then there is the perfect turn of your fine, firm derrière beneath my hand, and the almost searing heat of your —"

"I did not mean it quite literally," she interjected.

"Ah," he said, his eyes drifting down her length. "But you will not mind if I occasionally fantasize, Miss Neville, about what might have been? Here in London, the nights can be cold and lonely."

"Lord Nash, please." Xanthia felt the heat rise to her face. "I exhibited an unfathomable lack of judgment, and I wish you would not remind me of it."

"But if I cannot forget it, why should you?" His voice flowed over her like warm velvet. "Indeed, Miss Neville, you have cut me to the quick. I had hoped that there was some small remnant of that little interlude which you, too, might wish to cling to."

Xanthia tried to look grave. "Never mind that," she said. "All I am saying, sir, is that . . . well, I am going to be out in society a little more than I had expected. I beg you to never, ever mention what happened to anyone else."

He drew back a pace. "Good Lord, Miss Neville!" he answered. "What manner of man do you think me?"

She bit her lip, and glanced up at him. "A gentleman, I hope?"

"A gentleman, indeed," he murmured. "I should sooner have my fingernails ripped out by a French inquisitionist than share such an intimate and treasured memory."

Xanthia looked away. "Thank you," she said. "I do not ask this lightly — and not even for myself."

He shocked her then by touching her gently under the chin and drawing her face back to his. "If not for yourself," he asked quietly, "then for whom do you ask it?"

She lowered her gaze, and he dropped his hand. "For Lord and Lady Sharpe," she managed to say. "I must chaperone Lady Louisa through the remainder of her season. I shall even have to appear at Almack's. I fear my cousin's health has taken a fragile turn, and she cannot attend to it."

"Good Lord! Almack's?" His black eyes danced with laughter. "And you shall *go?*"

Her gaze snapped back to his. "You doubtless find that humorous," she returned. "But

I have little choice in the matter. And you may believe me when I say there are a thousand things I should rather be doing than rubbing elbows with the *ton*."

He held her eyes for a long moment, some nameless emotion sketching over his features. "Well, then," he finally said. "Perhaps we are destined to meet again after all, Miss Neville."

"Oh, I doubt it." She managed a teasing smile. "You do not look the Almack's type to me. I should lay odds they won't even let you in the front door."

Again, he lifted one elegant shoulder. "One never knows," he murmured. "What sort of odds are you offering?"

Xanthia laughed. "Oh, just a straight wager," she said. "I must have a spare twenty-pound note lying about the house somewhere."

Nash smiled tightly. "Tempting, Miss Neville, but I think the take would have to be a good deal richer to get me into *that* sort of gaming hell," he said. "Too many men have lost their most valuable asset inside Almack's lofty portals."

Xanthia lifted her eyebrows. "What sort of asset?"

Lord Nash flashed his wolfish grin. "Their priceless bachelorhood," he answered.

"Now I bid you good evening, my dear, until we meet again. I believe I can find my own way out."

Amidst a tempest of emotions, Xanthia bathed and dressed for dinner. What a shock it had been to find Nash — *Lord* Nash — casually reclined in her brother's best chair and looking very much at home. Today he had seemed so very dark and tall — and altogether more *man* than she had remembered. In all the rush of Xanthia's workday, and in all the consternation over Pamela's health, she had somehow forced away the memory of last night's foolhardy escapade.

Well, that was not wholly true, she admitted, studying herself in the dressing mirror as she fastened her second earbob. The memory of Lord Nash's touch had lingered, hovering in the back of her mind, and engendering vague feelings of embarrassment — interspersed with more than a few stabs of regret. And upon seeing him again, once the initial shock was past, the regret had cut like a keen blade. In the light of day, it was obvious just how striking a gentleman he was.

He was not handsome, no. Not in the English way. But he was elegance personified; lean and dark, like a cat prowling through a moonlit wood. There was an air of intrigue about the man which made one yearn to know him better in every sense of the word. Today Lord Nash had worn his heavy, too-long hair swept off his high forehead like a mane of sable. His cloak, an almost old-fashioned bit of elegance, had looked to be made of the most supple, finely draped wool imaginable, and his dark gray coat had molded beautifully to the width of his shoulders.

His face, too, was remarkable. Those hard planes and angles held a severity and a certain majesty which she had not noticed the previous evening. And his eyes — oh, God, those obsidian eyes! They were almost exotic in appearance, and set at just a hint of an angle, as if the blood of a Mongol horde coursed through his veins.

All of it left Xanthia wondering. What if she had not left him standing on the balcony last night? What if she had been daring enough to act on her fantasies? What if she had simply given him her name and accepted his bold invitation into his bed?

He would have refused her, that was what would have happened. Once Lord Nash had learned she was unwed, he would have backed away as surely as if she had just burst into flames. He had the air of a man who had been singed before.

On a sigh, Xanthia straightened up from the mirror and looked herself straight in the eye. *Forget him,* she told herself. *It will never happen. Not with Nash, and not with any other man.* Well, not unless she wanted Gareth — and Gareth wanted far more than Xanthia was prepared to give.

With Gareth there had once been passion, yes. And a sincere friendship, too. But Xanthia understood too well that a woman, once she married, became nothing but her husband's property. It was not that she *believed* Gareth would have wrested control of Neville Shipping from her, but merely that he would have had the legal right to do so. And it would have been *her* choice to give him that power over her and all that she had worked for. She loved him. But she did not love him enough for that.

In the dining room, she and Kieran passed the first two courses of dinner catching up on the day's post. Kieran was not a man given to casual conversation, but there was a little news from home in the form of a letter from a neighboring plantation, and one of Kieran's tenants in Barbados had written to ask a rather convoluted question about water rights. Mundane business, to be sure, but it was the essence of their life together.

Kieran and Luke, and eventually Martinique, whom Luke had adopted, were all the real family Xanthia had ever known. And they were all she needed. Suddenly, however, in the midst of passing a platter of buttered parsnips down the table, Xanthia was struck with a vision of her hand on Pamela's gently rounding belly. She must have faltered, for Kieran grabbed the dish and drew it from her grasp. "All right, Zee?" he murmured, casting her a curious glance.

Xanthia forced a smile. "The dish was a little heavy."

Kieran motioned for more wine, then sent the footmen from the room. Xanthia knew the pointed questions were about to begin, but she rarely feared her brother's wrath. Indeed, she understood him better than anyone — which was to say not very well, and yet well enough to grasp the one truth which eluded almost everyone. Each blunt and heavy-handed thing the great Baron Rothewell did was motivated by a bone-deep sense of duty; a duty he had been neither born to nor trained for. A duty which he had brought upon himself — or so he believed.

Their elder brother's untimely death had scared them both deeply, for in one horrifying instant, the brave trio of orphans had become but two. And neither she nor Kieran had been prepared for it. So she forgave Kieran his meddling and his barking, and bore it with as much fortitude as she could muster.

Kieran was circling the wine around the bowl of his glass and staring into it almost blindly. "I wish to hear all about this Nash fellow, my dear," he said. "I gather you met him at Pamela's?"

Xanthia lowered her eyes. "In passing."

"Well, you must have made quite an impression, Zee," he went on. "You realize, of course, that Gareth Lloyd's heart will be broken if you marry your Lord Dark-and-Dangerous?"

Xanthia stopped nudging her peas from one side of the plate to the other. "I beg your pardon?" she said. "If I *what?*"

Kieran eyed her from across the table. "If you marry Nash."

Xanthia's eyes felt as round as her dinner plate. "What in heaven's name gave you such a notion?"

"Perhaps it was the fact that the man asked permission to court you," Kieran returned. "What, did he not come to the point?"

Xanthia was aghast. "He certainly did not."

"Good." Kieran took up his knife and deftly sliced the leg off his roast chicken. "I hoped he had cast aside the notion."

"Surely —" Xanthia's voice hit an oddly sharp note. "Surely, Kieran, you cannot be serious about this?"

"He asked permission to court you," said Kieran more firmly. "And I put him off. I suggested he find someone younger, and more biddable. Besides, he clearly knows next to nothing *about* you, Zee, so —" Suddenly, he halted. "I hope, my dear, that I have not misinterpreted your feelings for the fellow?"

Xanthia shook her head. "No."

No. The answer was definitely *no*. And now the only feeling Xanthia was suffering was the slightest sense of light-headedness. Lord Nash must be perfectly mad. Had he really believed he had somehow tainted Xanthia's precious virtue? With just a *kiss*?

But it had not been just a kiss, had it? At the mere memory, a faint tug of desire went twisting through her, ratcheting up her breath. Xanthia closed her eyes. Good Lord, if she allowed herself to think of it, even for an instant, she could still feel that sweet, languorous yearning which his mouth and his touch had aroused. It made one think of candlelight, and of soft linen sheets, and of . . .

No. It was not just a kiss. And Nash was right. Had it been Lady Louisa whom he had so flagrantly caressed on the terrace last night, Sharpe would have had him leg-shackled before noon. And he would have deserved it, for Louisa was obviously an innocent. But Xanthia was not — and therein lay all the difference. She marveled that Nash had not noticed it. Perhaps he had. Perhaps that was why he had begun to fear the snap of a parson's mousetrap.

Kieran was looking at her strangely.

Xanthia took up her fork and forced a bemused expression. "Lord Dark-and-Dangerous," she murmured. "Why do you call him that?"

Kieran forked up another bite of chicken. "I find a malevolent sort of air about the man," he said after thoughtfully chewing it. "He isn't English, either. Or perhaps I should say English is not his first language. Did you notice?"

Xanthia's eyes widened. "You may be right," she answered. "I have rubbed elbows with sailors so long, I pay scant heed to a faint accent."

Kieran looked introspective. "Well, wher-ever he is from, I am not sure I care for his

91

effrontery," he remarked. "I believe I shall ask Sharpe about the man's character."

"Oh, pray do not." Xanthia frowned at her brother. "Indeed, I forbid it."

"You forbid it?" Kieran shot a dark look across the table, then relented. "Well, suit yourself, Zee. It's your wedding, not mine."

"It isn't anyone's wedding," she insisted.

"And you did not answer my question about Gareth, my dear," he went on. "I hope I need not remind you that Gareth is still our dear friend. Indeed, he is all but family to us both."

"What are you trying to say, Kieran?" she demanded.

"Just do not hurt him, Zee, any more than is absolutely necessary," said her brother quietly. "If you do not mean to have him, then tell him plainly."

Xanthia dropped her fork. "I have told him plainly," she said. "I have been telling him for about half a decade now, Kieran. Kindly hush about Gareth. I have something far more important to discuss."

"Have at it, my dear," said her brother, his tone instantly lightening. "But for God's sake, do not speak to me of Neville Shipping, or of what you and Gareth have been about all day. I should rather hear an alphabetical recitation of the Westminster tax rolls."

Xanthia shot him a chiding look. "I wish to speak to you of Pamela," she said. "And do listen, Kieran, if you please. It is important."

Now that she was over the shock of seeing Nash again, all of Xanthia's fear and excitement over Pamela's situation sprang forth anew. But it took her all of half an hour to explain Pamela's predicament, and enlist her brother's cooperation. It came grudgingly, for Kieran had not the least interest in English society. Indeed, since letting his mills and plantations go, and moving back to England, he had shown little interest in anything.

They finished the meal in silence. From time to time, Xanthia eyed him across the table. She was worried. Kieran spent most of his days reading and drinking, and his nights prowling about in the stews and hells of Covent Garden. He feigned no interest in life's higher purposes or finer virtues, and had thus far refused to join even the most humble of clubs or societies. Kieran kept low company, odd hours, and bad women. His occasional trysts with Mrs. Ambrose were almost a relief to her.

Xanthia loved her brother desperately. For so long, it had been just the three of them

— she, Kieran, and Luke — fighting against the world. They had lived for one another. Sacrificed for one another. She could not count on all her fingers and toes the times when her elder brothers had literally taken the brunt of their uncle's wrath for something she had done, or later, the times they had hidden her away from his dangerously drunken friends. Kieran, of course, had always taken the worst of it, for even as a young man, he'd been rash, and far too bold. Luke had possessed a degree of diplomacy. Kieran had possessed a soul filled with passion and anger.

Xanthia was not perfectly sure what was to become of her brother. *He is going to drink and whore himself into an early grave,* Cousin Pamela had said. Pray God she was wrong. Still, hearing the words spoken aloud had troubled Xanthia. She had been thoroughly unsuccessful in drawing Kieran into the shipping business, for he had claimed — and not wrongly — that she and Gareth did not need him. Xanthia then tried to convince him not to renew the lease on his vast estate in Cheshire. He would not listen, saying he had no wish to live in the country watching the sheep and grass grow.

And that was that. Xanthia had her hands

full with the business, which occupied most of her waking moments in one way or another. Indeed, with dinner all but done, it was time to attend to it. Mentally, she began to recount the papers she had brought home for review. There was a suspiciously high invoice from the victualling yard for six of Neville's ships which had gone out in January and were not due back in port for another fortnight at best. She was disinclined to pay the bill until she had compared it to the inventory of provisions they had taken on. There was a stack of insurance forms from Lloyd's, and a proposal from an insolvent competitor to sell them three dilapidated merchantmen — but at a price Xanthia found hard to resist. She needed to do a little arithmetic to make sure the time in dry dock for refurbishment would not eat significantly into Neville's profit, for the cost of —

"Ah," said a quiet voice. "I see I have lost you again."

Xanthia looked up to see that Kieran was already pouring his port, which one of the footmen had carried in on a tray.

"My apologies," she said mechanically. "My thoughts were elsewhere."

Kieran's mouth turned up at one corner. "Yes, in Wapping, I suspect."

Xanthia moved to slide back her chair. "I fear so," she said, rising as the footman leapt forth to assist her. "Which reminds me, I have a raft of papers I must see to by evening's end. You will be going out, I collect?"

He smiled faintly and tossed off a portion of his port. "I daresay I shall."

"Then I will bid you good night."

"Yes. Good night, Zee."

At his elbow, however, Xanthia hesitated, then impulsively, she bent and brushed her lips over his cheek. "Do be careful, Kieran," she murmured. "Promise that you shall?"

He tossed a dark, sidelong look up at her as if he might snap at her with one of his ugly retorts, but at the last instant, the expression faltered. "All right, old thing," he said quietly. "I shall be careful."

In Park Lane, the evening was drawing to a close. Working London had long since gone home to dinner, and traffic up and down the hill had waned to little more than the occasional brisk rattle of a fine carriage passing by. Agnes, the first-floor parlor maid, was working her way through the house, methodically sweeping the hearths and drawing the draperies as she went.

In Lord Nash's vast library, she hesitated.

96

Coals yet glowed in the grate, casting an eerie red light along the mantelpiece. She began instead with the floor-to-ceiling curtains, drawing snug the weighty velvet panels using a long brass rod. When the last was drawn against the evening's chill, she put down the rod and turned to the hearth.

"Thank you, Agnes," said a deep voice in the shadows.

Agnes shrieked, nearly leaping from her skin.

"Thank you, Agnes," Lord Nash repeated. "You may go now."

Agnes bobbed unsteadily. "Beg pardon, m'lord," she squeaked. "I d-did not see you. D-Do you not wish a lamp lit?"

"Thank you, no." There was the sharp *chink* of a vodka decanter as he refilled his glass. "The dark can cover a multitude of sins, can it not?"

Agnes bobbed again, as if for good measure. "I — I daresay, sir," she whispered. "Am I to do the hearth now?"

"See to it tomorrow." The marquess's voice rumbled in the gloom. "You are excused. No — wait."

"Yes, m'lord?"

"Is Mr. Swann still in, by chance?"

"I — I don't know, sir," admitted the parlor maid. "Shall I send a footman to fetch him, sir?"

"Please do."

The girl darted out, leaving Nash alone again with his thoughts. He slid deeper into his armchair, cradling his snifter of *okhotnichya* against his shirtfront. He had been sitting thus more or less since his return from Rothewell's mansion in Berkeley Square, his solitude broken only by dinner. Perhaps he would not have thought to eat at all, but Tony had come to dine, blowing in and out like an August thunderstorm.

Nash wished he had not invited him. Not tonight.

Though they had always been close, they were like chalk and cheese, he and his stepbrother. Tony lived in the present, Nash in the past — or somewhere in between. They shared little by way of personality, and nothing at all in appearance. Tony was fair and handsome to Nash's dark glower. Tony was slender, elegant, blue-eyed, and Oxford-educated. Yes, Tony was the one thing Savile Row's finest tailoring would never make Nash — the perfect English gentleman. But like most of them, Tony held a provincial view of the world, and England's place within it. To him, there was nothing which mattered beyond Albion's white shores.

So whilst Tony was left to fight and finesse

and scrap his way up the government ladder, here was Nash, being . . . well, *Nash* — a title almost as old and as grand as fair Albion herself. It seemed contrary to the laws of nature. It seemed . . . a little unjust, really. Tony was the grandson of a duke — which in England counted for quite a lot, even if two dozen cousins would have to perish to put him within sniffing distance of the title.

It was a pity, Nash often thought, that Tony could not simply have had the marquessate — and he could not escape the feeling that Nash's late father had probably thought so, too. The perfect English gentleman for the perfect English title. And by now, left to his own devices, Nash might have been a major in the czar's Imperial Guard. Or left in peace to stroll the hills of home with his favorite wolfhound.

Ah, but his life was in England now. Nash had been fourteen when his father had married Edwina, his very distant, very English cousin in a match arranged within the family. It was a far cry from his first marriage, for Edwina was a pale, pretty girl, newly widowed by a blue-blooded, black sheep of a husband. She had a small child in tow and scarcely two shillings to rub together.

Nash's mother had descended from the noble houses of Russia and Eastern Europe.

The blood of czars, *vladikas,* and the great khans had coursed hot and fierce through her veins — and told in her temper, too. She had been a dark, vibrant beauty. But she had also been spoilt, given to terrible tantrums, and entirely too certain of her own worth. And never, ever had she been satisfied with her lot in life.

She had been particularly dissatisfied with her short life in England, and had made no secret of her disdain. Perhaps that was why society so often cut Nash a sidelong glance. Perhaps they were wondering just how alike he and his volatile mother were.

Nash was stirred from his reverie by the sound of someone softly clearing his throat. He looked up to see Swann hovering in the gloom, already wearing his overcoat and clutching his tall beaver hat. "You wished to see me, sir?"

"Working late again, eh?" Not that he left the poor devil much choice, Nash reminded himself. "Pour yourself a dram, Swann, and sit down."

His man of affairs did as he was bid. "What may I do for you, my lord?" he asked when he was settled.

Nash gently swirled his vodka in his glass. "What do you hear, Swann, from our friend in Belgravia?" he asked. "Has the Comtesse

100

de Montignac returned to England?"

"Not yet, my lord," said Swann. "She remains in Cherbourg, so far as it is known."

"And what of her husband?"

"He remains with her," said his man of affairs. "De Montignac has quarreled again with the French foreign minister — a lover's spat, or so 'tis whispered — and it is believed he has been sent away in disgrace."

Nash relaxed into his chair. "Excellent news," he murmured. "Perhaps they will both stay in Cherbourg."

Swann smiled ruefully. "I doubt it, my lord," he said. "They love too well the diplomatic limelight and the privilege it grants them."

"Not to mention the opportunities it gives them," said Nash sourly. He put it from his mind, however, and turned the topic to the one which he found inexplicably more pressing. "The woman I was enquiring about this morning, Swann," he began. "I wish to learn one thing more — something which you may more discreetly discover than I."

"You are speaking of Miss Neville?"

"Indeed," said Nash. "I paid the lady's brother a call this afternoon."

"Did you?" said Swann in mild surprise. "May I ask, sir, what manner of man you found him to be?"

"A man who lives hard, by the look of him," said Nash grimly. "A hulking, rather rough-edged fellow, with the hands of a farm laborer — and yet he possessed no artifice which I could see. What is it the English call such a man? Ah, yes, *a colonial*."

"One ought not be surprised, I daresay," said Swann. "He was not above five or six years when sent out to the West Indies."

"Yes, but do you not find it odd the girl was sent as well?" mused Nash. "She must have been an infant. One wonders a more genteel situation could not have been found for her."

"I'm told their aunt is Lady Bledsoe," said Swann. "Hardly the most charitable of women."

"Yes, she's an old battle-axe, as I recall," Nash murmured. "But her daughter, Lady Sharpe, is thought quite kind, is she not?"

"So it is said," Swann agreed. "In any case, the children were sent out to Lady Bledsoe's elder brother, who had been exiled to the West Indies by the family when quite a young man."

"Exiled, eh?"

"He shot a man dead, sir," said Swann. "Not in a duel, but in a drunken rage. The family had to cover it up, and now, no one seems to remember much about him."

"Rothewell and his sister have been back in England but four months," said Nash, almost to himself. "I wonder what brought them?"

"Was that what you wished to learn, my lord?"

"Actually, no." Nash set his glass aside with an awkward clatter. "No, the young lady is said to be betrothed — or something just short of it. I should like to know to whom."

"To whom she is *betrothed?*" Swann was staring at him.

"Yes, if it can be learnt discreetly," Nash snapped. "What of it?"

Despite the gloom, Swann looked to be blushing. "I — I beg your pardon, sir," he said swiftly. "I shall make enquiries. *Discreet* enquiries."

"Yes, damned discreet," gritted Nash. "I shall meet you here tomorrow at — say, half past four?"

"Tomorrow, sir?" Swann shifted uneasily in his chair.

Nash lifted one eyebrow. "Have you a problem with that?"

"My . . . my mother, sir?" he gently prompted.

Nash cursed beneath his breath. Just this

morning, a message had arrived to say that Swann's mother had been taken ill. That, no doubt, was the reason the man had worked so late tonight. "Bloody hell," he said. "Swann, my apologies. Never mind this foolishness. What time do you go?"

Swann swallowed hard. "Tomorrow morning at five, my lord. On the Brighton coach."

Nash rose, forcing Swann to do likewise. "I shall bid you a safe journey, then," he said, offering his hand. "And your mother a swift recovery. Go and snatch a few hours' sleep while you may."

"Thank you, my lord." Swann already had his hat in hand. His vodka sat untouched.

Nash watched him depart, feeling altogether too self-centered, and more than a little sheepish. *To whom she was betrothed indeed!* What difference did it make? The woman was plainly no threat to him.

Or was she?

There were many kinds of threats, Nash considered, going to the nearest window and drawing back one of the drapes. He wondered at the twist of fate which had left it to him to guard himself and his family from all of them — some nebulous, and some frightfully well defined. There was Edwina's regrettable habit of taking too much wine, then playing too deep at the card table. His elderly aunts' predilection to believe every rotter and scoundrel with a tale of misfortune to tell and a pair of pockets to let. And then there was Tony's unfortunate tendency to —

Oh, how ridiculous! This threat fell into none of those categories, did it? This could not taint his stepmother's good name, or ruin his brother's political career. No, the only thing threatened by Miss Neville seemed to be Nash's peace of mind. But peace of mind could be bought with enough vodka and enough sex.

Nash took one last look at the flickering lamps along Park Lane, then let the heavy drape fall and returned to his shadows and his decanter. The coals were half-dead now, their fierce glow reduced to a mere tracery of crimson, blood-bright against the heap of dark cinders. Ashes to ashes. And thus went the world and everything in it, eventually. Nash took up his vodka again and resolved to think no more of Miss Neville's breathless sighs. His lust, too, would eventually burn down to nothing.

Just then, there was a faint sound at the library door. He looked up to see Vernon in the shadows. "Your pardon, my lord, but Mrs. Hayden-Worth has called."

Jenny? How very odd. "Show her in, Vernon."

A moment later, Tony's wife swept in. She wore a carriage dress of deep blue, and her fiery hair was swept up beneath a small but elaborate hat. "Nash!" she said, leaning forward to kiss his cheek. "I was trying to catch up with Tony, but Vernon tells me I have missed him."

"Yes, gone back to Whitehall, I'm afraid." Nash gestured toward the fire. "Will you join me, my dear? I shall send for a little sherry."

"Oh, no, I can stay but a moment." Jenny smiled and seated herself on the very edge of the chair. "How do you go on, Nash?"

"Quite well, I thank you," he said. "What of you? I thought you were in Hampshire."

"I've just this instant got back from Brierwood," she said brightly. "Nash, you really must see Phaedra. She is looking quite the grown-up lady nowadays."

"I saw her at Christmastime," Nash reminded her. "Yes, Phae is a beauty — but a clever beauty, thank God."

Jenny shot him a chiding look. "That's all very well, Nash," said his sister-in-law. "But she must be clever enough to hide it. Men do not wish to marry intelligent girls, but merely young and pretty girls."

"I do not think you speak for all men, Jenny," Nash countered.

Jenny was undeterred. "And the spectacles must go," she continued. "They are not in the least becoming. You must speak to her, Nash. Edwina is perfectly cowed by the chit."

"Edwina leans on Phae," said Nash. "There is nothing wrong with that."

Jenny made a pout with her lips. "Well, I am going to haul the child off to Paris one day," she warned, "and have some decent gowns made up. She looks depressingly drab."

"Thank you, Jenny," said Nash. "You may send the bills to me, of course."

Jenny's warm smile returned. "I shall, then," she said. "What fun. Thank you, Nash."

Nash tapped thoughtfully on his chair arm. "That reminds me, Jenny," he said. "The bills for Edwina's house party next month — you must send them to me as well. I was thinking that since this is her fiftieth, there should be a nice gift. A tiara, perhaps? Or a diamond necklace? Tony will wish you to choose it, of course. Your taste in finery is impeccable."

Jenny tossed her hand dismissively. "Yes, but that's eons away," she said. "I shall think of something." She had already begun to shift restlessly in her chair.

"Well," said Nash, setting his hands on his thighs as if to rise. "I mustn't keep you. I am sure you must be road-weary."

Jenny was out of her chair in an instant. "A little, yes," she admitted. "So sorry to trouble you."

"It is no trouble whatsoever," said Nash, showing her to the door. "If I should run into Tony at White's later, may I give him a message?"

Jenny smiled again. "Just tell him that I am back in London for a few days, that is all."

"Yes, of course," he said, as they strolled down the passageway. "I am sure he will wish to come straight home."

"No, he needn't," said Jenny, as Vernon came forward with her cloak. "I am just going home to dress. I've a little soiree in Bloomsbury to drop in on." She stood on her toes, and kissed his cheek again. "Good night, Nash."

"Good night, Jenny."

Nash watched her go down the steps with a little sadness in his heart. Jenny, he feared, was not particularly satisfied with her marriage — not that she had put forth much effort in that regard. But Nash did not especially blame her. It was Tony who had begun this debacle. Their marriage had been a mistake from the outset. But then, most marriages were, weren't they?

Perhaps there was a lesson there somewhere, Nash thought, as Jenny's carriage began to roll down Park Lane. But did he need a lesson? Certainly not. The notion was almost laughable.

"Shut the door, Vernon," he said dully. "And ring for Gibbons. I believe I shall go out for the evening after all."

CHAPTER FOUR:
AN INTRIGUE IN
BERKELEY SQUARE

Less than a se'night after her promise to
Cousin Pamela, Xanthia found herself in
Kieran's study, wading through a fresh tide
of invitations. Thus far they had attended
only small, rather intimate events, save for
one dreadful foray into Almack's, but the
season was nearing full swing. The reclusive
Baron Rothewell and his spinster sister were
suddenly the most popular couple in town
— or so it felt — and Kieran was none too
pleased about it.

Today Xanthia had left Wapping a few
minutes early, stealing away with a bolt of
pale pink shantung which had arrived on
the *Maiden Fair* just in from Shanghai. She'd
glimpsed it being off-loaded, and found it
irresistible. The shade was the perfect foil
for Pamela's eyes and hair, and would make
up admirably into a dressing gown for her
later months of confinement. When she
delivered it to Hanover Street, Pamela cried

most affectedly and thanked her again for helping Louisa.

But in Berkeley Square, things were not so amiable. Her brother was in one of his cold moods and drinking as heavily as usual. With a flick of her wrist, Xanthia tossed the latest envelope onto the "unavoidable" pile as a heavy cart went rumbling past the open window. "Another musicale," she said. "I know you despise them, but it's Mrs. Fitzhugh, so there's little to be done for it."

Her brother cursed beneath his breath. "Another evening of overweening prigs sawing back and forth on fiddles like a pair of cats mating?" he snarled. "Good God, I think I should rather be shot."

Do not tempt me, thought Xanthia. "I do not have time for this, either, Kieran," she said warningly. "I feel as if am leaving everything to Gareth, merely to go gadding about London in satin and silk. Indeed, I can scarce sleep for thinking of what's been left undone. And tomorrow is Lady Henslow's picnic, which will consume the whole of my day."

Her brother's dark glower did not abate. He sat in stony silence as a newsboy cried the day's headlines, the rapid patter borne on the spring breeze from the depths of

Berkeley Square. A sleek black gig whirled past the window, a pair of matched grays stepping high and sharp on the cobbles.

When at last Kieran spoke, his tone had gentled. "Perhaps I should just remove to Cheshire after all, Zee," he said. "You can hardly go about in society without my escort. Were I to leave Town, you would have an excuse."

For an instant, Xanthia was tempted. "But what of your tenant?" she asked. "And where would poor Louisa be? No, it is our family duty, Kieran."

He grunted, and tossed off the last of his brandy. "Family duty, my arse," he said. "Who gave a damn for family duty when we were children? I should think losing one's parents is a bloody sight more tragic than missing one's come-out season."

Xanthia was silent for a long moment. "You are quite right," she finally said. "But that was not Pamela's doing. She was but a child, too."

"Yes, and what of Aunt Olivia?" he snapped. "She could fly down here on her broomstick tomorrow and see to the chit herself. But Aunt Olivia has never been much given to inconveniencing herself."

"She is Louisa's grandmother," Xanthia admitted. "And yes, you are right. She *should* do it. But she will not, Kieran, and we both know it. Besides, she is old. And so it falls to us. We must do our duty, even if others have at times failed us. Besides, it is not as though we were left to starve. Uncle put food on the table. He put a roof over our heads."

Kieran looked at her with an old, long-remembered hurt in his eyes. "I cannot believe you just said that, Zee," he said quietly. "You, of all people."

There was no more to be said on the topic. The long years in Barbados were in the past, and best left there, too. Xanthia turned her attention back to the teetering pile of invitations.

"Here is a ball for next Tuesday," she said placatingly. "There will be a cardroom for you there, I am confident. And surely Louisa would rather dance than sit? I shall send our regrets to Mrs. Fitzhugh."

Her brother said nothing, but instead got up and went to the sideboard to refill his brandy. The decanter thudded lightly on the silver gallery tray just as the door opened to admit Trammel, their butler. "I beg your pardon, my lord," he said. "Two gentlemen have called."

Kieran turned, glass in hand. "At this hour?"

"Indeed, sir. From the Home Office." Trammel extended an oval salver, which held two calling cards and a letter sealed with red wax.

"What, to see *me*?"

"How very odd!" said Xanthia, laying aside the ball invitations. "What sort of missive have you there, Trammel?"

"A letter of introduction from Lord Sharpe, I collect," said Trammel on something of a sigh. "The callers are a Lord Vendenheim de — something-or-other. I cannot pronounce it. And a Mr. Kemble, who looks like a French fop — begging your lordship's pardon, sir."

"They sound a merry pair," said Kieran.

Trammel relaxed. "I've put them in the upstairs parlor."

One eyebrow raised, Kieran opened the letter. "Sharpe begs me to give these gentlemen a moment of my time on a matter pertaining to . . . yes, to *urgent government business,*" he murmured. "What the devil, Zee?"

Xanthia leaned forward in her chair. "I cannot think what these men might want of you."

Kieran shook his head. "I'm damned if I can make heads or tails of it," he answered as his sister rose to take her leave. "Sharpe's clearly in a state. He says it's something to do with shipping. Or . . . or with transporting something to . . . to *Greece?* Bloody hell! What do I know of such things?" He motioned her back to her chair. "No, no, you'd best stay put, Zee."

Slowly, she sat back down.

"Show them in here, Trammel," said Kieran, flinging himself back into his desk chair. "I am disinclined to go far from my brandy. I'll lay you a monkey this will be dull as ditchwater."

But Lord Rothewell was soon to be proven wrong. The men came into the room with a clear sense of purpose. The taller of the two, a lean, rather sinister-looking man, led the way, and introduced himself as the Vicomte de Vendenheim-Sélestat. More surprising than his foreign name and exotic appearance was his position.

"I should tell you that I am attached — in the vaguest sense of the word — to Mr. Peel's staff in the Home Office," he said after Xanthia had been introduced and refreshment offered. "This is my associate, Mr. Kemble."

Kieran turned to the second, more foppish gentleman. "And you work for the Home Office, as well?" he asked, laying aside the man's thick ivory calling card.

"I work for whoever is willing to pay my price," said Mr. Kemble, who had settled himself with exquisite grace into the chair next to Xanthia's. "In this case, it happens to be Mr. Peel."

Lord de Vendenheim shifted uncomfortably in the chair adjacent. "Mr. Kemble is — er, something of an expert in a field which has lately become of great interest to the Home Secretary and the Prime Minister," he explained.

Kieran looked bored. "And what, pray, would that be?"

De Vendenheim looked grim. "The transportation and illegal importation of misappropriated, untaxed, and — er, usually illicit goods."

"Good heavens!" said Xanthia. *"Smuggling?"*

Kieran's face went tight. "Now see here, de Vendenheim — Neville's is an honest business," he snapped, shoving his brandy glass so roughly it scratched the wood. "And my sister is of unimpeachable charac—"

Mr. Kemble threw up one hand. "Lord Rothewell, please!" he cried, his face a mask of horror. "Good brandy bruises! And your desk! That finely grained mahogany! I must beg you to think of it."

Kieran's mouth fell open.

"And I must beg your pardon," Xanthia interjected firmly. "What, pray, are we talking about? Surely not the furniture?"

De Vendenheim glowered at Mr. Kemble again. There was a decided tension between the two men. "Miss Neville, Lord Sharpe has suggested that your family's firm might be in a unique position to help the Home Office with an enquiry," he said. "You are doubtless aware that Sharpe chairs Peel's Select Committee on —"

Xanthia held up a forestalling hand. "I fear we know very little of English politics," she answered. "We understand Sharpe is active in the House of Lords, but we have lived here only a short while."

"Which makes you all the more desirable, for Peel's purpose." De Vendenheim folded his long, elegant hands neatly one across the other, an ornate signet ring glinting from one finger. "May I ask both of you to hold this discussion in highest confidence, whatever your decision?"

"I was not aware there was a decision to be made," said Kieran. "But we are patriots, for pity's sake, if that is what you are asking."

"In a manner of speaking," said de Vendenheim, "it is."

"Then pray continue," said Kieran, with

an impatient gesture of his hand. "We'll hear you out, at the very least."

De Vendenheim and his associate exchanged glances. "Might we close the window?" asked the vicomte.

Kieran did so at once.

"You are aware, are you not, of the ongoing difficulties between Greece and Turkey?" asked the vicomte when Kieran returned to his chair.

"Barbados is not quite the back side of the moon," said Kieran wryly. "I am aware the Greeks revolted against their Turkish rulers some years past, and that things are not much improved. But Neville's goes to neither of those places — do we, Xanthia?"

"Yes, to Constantinople," she murmured. "And to Athens on occasion, when the political climate permits. But what can this possibly have to do with Neville Shipping?"

De Vendenheim leaned intently forward. "The peace forced upon Turkey last year by Canning has proven nearly worthless," he said. "Once again, the Greek revolutionaries are said to be regrouping. They mean to seize Athens and Thebes in one bold strike, and we think Russia is back to her old tricks, supplying covert assistance."

"There will be open rebellion again?" asked Xanthia.

"Wellington fears so," said de Vendenheim. "And to add fuel to a smoldering fire, plans were recently uncovered to smuggle American-made rifles into Greece — one thousand Carlow carbines, one of the most accurate and lethal weapons on earth."

Kieran propped one elbow casually on his desk. "And we should care?"

"You, more so than most," warned de Vendenheim. "The balance of power in the Near East grows more precarious by the day, and now there is a traitor in our midst — a traitor whose acts will do nothing but encourage the Greeks to fight on, and perhaps persuade the Russians to jump fully into the fray on their behalf."

"But why is that a problem?" Xanthia was tapping one finger thoughtfully on her chair arm. "Isn't England in sympathy with the Greeks?"

De Vendenheim frowned. "There is popular sentiment, Miss Neville," he said grimly. "And then there is the economic and political reality. England can ill afford an expanding Russia, and what Russia really wants is not to help Greece but to gain control of the Turkish Straits and threaten our Mediterranean trade routes."

Kieran frowned. "But aren't the Russians our allies?"

De Vendenheim shrugged. "Ostensibly, perhaps," he said. "But the reality is that the fall of Constantinople would lay open a clear path for Russian expansion in the East. Eventually, perhaps even India could be jeopardized. Given the nature of your family's business, Lord Rothewell, surely you can comprehend the significance of such trade disruptions?"

Perhaps Kieran did not, but Xanthia comprehended the significance with disturbing clarity. A war in the Mediterranean? That could prove to be a devastating economic blow to Neville Shipping.

"In time, the whole of Europe might explode into conflict again," added Mr. Kemble. "The Continent cannot sustain such strife again so soon — not politically, and not economically."

"That I know firsthand," said de Vendenheim vehemently. "And that is precisely why it is in England's best interest to support the Turks, even though popular British sympathy still lies with the Greeks."

"Well, you may thank Lord Byron for that nonsense," said Mr. Kemble with a simpering smile. "Just add together one hideous headdress and some frightful poetry, stir in a measure of political intrigue with a dash of premature death — and *voilà! A cause célèbre!*"

"He was not helpful," admitted de Vendenheim. "But let us not speak ill of the dead."

Kiernan was toying with the wax jack which sat upon his desk. "I do not understand," he said as if to himself. "Why is the Home Office concerned about a war in a foreign nation?"

De Vendenheim straightened in his chair. "An excellent question," he said. "It has to do with those rifles. And a plot which was recently uncovered on British soil, which suggests many more such shipments are planned. The money is being laundered through diplomatic channels in London — by the French, we think, though it makes no sense. But we are certain that a vast deal of ordnance is being moved out of Boston, perhaps directly into Athens, or more likely via an obscure Eastern European port."

"An interesting theory," Xanthia mused. "There are several ports which could be used for unlading contraband. What was the tonnage on the vessel which was seized, my lord? I am wondering, of course, about its draft. That might tell us which ports could be used most inconspicuously."

De Vendenheim looked embarrassed.

"Ma'am, you catch me short on technicalities."

"It might be important," said Xanthia, keenly interested now.

De Vendenheim cleared his throat. "No doubt," he conceded. "I shall endeavor to discover those details for you, Miss Neville. In any case, Peel has reason to believe the perpetrator is a British citizen who is gunrunning for profit — and perhaps for personal reasons. But it little matters. He is still a traitor under British law."

"And what will happen to him when caught?" asked Xanthia.

"He will be hanged," said de Vendenheim.

"And very slowly," added Kemble rather too cheerfully.

"Dear me!" said Kieran drolly. "A nasty business."

De Vendenheim looked at Kieran from beneath carefully hooded eyes. "Which is why we would understand, Lord Rothewell, if you want no part of it," he said. "It is nasty, and it is dangerous. But after speaking with Sharpe, and learning of your unique situation — well, the temptation to come straight here was simply too great."

"Why such urgency?" asked Xanthia. "What has happened?"

Again, de Vendenheim and Mr. Kemble

exchanged glances. "Two nights ago, at a village inn south of Basingstoke, a man was found with his throat slit," said de Vendenheim.

"From ear to ear," chimed Mr. Kemble, drawing an illustrative finger across his neck.

"Dear God!" Xanthia shuddered.

"The killer was looking for something," Kemble continued. "Something he did not find. Sewn inside the lining of his portmanteau, agents of the Home Office found papers detailing — or allowing Peel to extrapolate — much of what we have just told you."

"But most of it was in code," de Vendenheim added. "Government cryptographers are working on it even as we speak. In any case, the dead courier was very near the country house of a somewhat notorious nobleman; a gentleman who is not without power and influence, and who has many contacts in Eastern Europe and Russia. It is not the first time such coincidences have occurred, yet Peel dares not investigate him openly."

"Why?" said Kieran bluntly. "What is another bloody nobleman in this country? England seems awash in them."

De Vendenheim's eyes flashed with frustration. "This one has a family member who is well placed in the Commons, and becoming increasingly influential within the party," he answered. "The family is very close. Peel can hardly suggest this man is a traitor by word or deed — certainly not without irrefutable evidence. If Peel is wrong — *if* — then great damage might be done on any number of fronts."

Kieran appeared unsympathetic. "In Barbados, we would just hang him."

Xanthia shot Kieran a chiding look, then turned to de Vendenheim. "The man is wealthy, too, I collect?"

"His marquessate is a rich one," the vicomte admitted. "And he has multiplied the family fortune many times over, ostensibly by means of high-stakes gaming. It is said he has nerves of steel at the table, and can anticipate his opponent's every move. But he could just as easily be feathering his nest by smuggling and gunrunning. Who would be the wiser?"

Mr. Kemble gave an impatient toss of his hand. "You are going to have to give them a name, Max," he warned. "We can go no further with this until you do."

De Vendenheim hesitated. He looked at Kieran very directly. "May I have your word as a gentleman that neither you nor your sister will divulge this name?"

"To whom would we divulge it?" asked Kieran. "We scarcely know anyone. But my cousin Sharpe sent you here, so of course you have our word."

De Vendenheim paused to consider it. "The man's name is Stefan Mihailo Northampton," he said quietly. "But he is called Nash. The Marquess of Nash."

Xanthia suppressed a gasp. Kieran set the wax jack down awkwardly, and cut his eyes toward her. "Lord Dark-and-Dangerous," he murmured.

"I beg your pardon?" said de Vendenheim.

"A little jest between us," said Kieran, shifting his eyes away. "We do know him vaguely. He . . . he was at Sharpe's ball."

"Yes, Sharpe invited him for a reason," admitted the vicomte. "He is keeping an eye on the fellow."

Kieran studied their visitors. "Nash is an imposing sort of man," he went on. "However, I found him a tad presumptuous. What do you know of him?"

"His background is unusual," said the vicomte. "He was born in Montenegro, to an old and very noble family with a good bit of Russian blood on one side."

"Montenegro?" Kieran echoed.

"The *black mountain*," murmured Xanthia. "It is a rugged place between the Adriatic and the southern Carpathians."

"Do you know it, Miss Neville?" asked Mr. Kemble.

"Not well," said Xanthia. "But I know that the Bay of Kotor is the largest on the Adriatic — a sort of fjord, and very deep — yet it is extremely well hidden."

"Yes, a point which has not escaped us," said Mr. Kemble.

"The country was once known as the ancient principality of Zeta," the vicomte went on. "His family's estate was in Danilovgrad — and still is, I daresay. Nash's maternal grandfather was a renowned military leader who fought with Vladika Petar I, and helped crush the Turks at Martinici. Amongst the region's nobility, the family is both powerful and wealthy — and more than a little dangerous."

"Dangerous?" said Kieran. "In what way?"

"The region has a violent history, and deep clan loyalties which are often incomprehensible to us," the vicomte said. "The family has close ties to Russia and no love lost for the Turks."

"But is Lord Nash close to that side of his family?" asked Xanthia pointedly.

De Vendenheim lifted one shoulder. "It was once assumed not," he admitted. "But with Eastern Europe perched on the edge of this nasty little war, we can ill afford assumptions."

"At present, Wellington hopes merely to keep the lid on an already-boiling pot," said Mr. Kemble. "So, as you might deduce, the last thing England needs in the region is a gunrunner with uncertain loyalties."

"It all sounds so very complicated," said Xanthia. "But we did wonder at Lord Nash's faint accent."

Mr. Kemble looked at her oddly. "What do you know of him?"

"As my brother said, I met him at Sharpe's ball," she returned. "He is quite dramatic in appearance. And his dark eyes . . . yes, very exotic."

"Yet his father was as English as yours or mine," said Mr. Kemble. "He was a second son — a strikingly handsome man, by all accounts — who met his wife in Prague whilst making the Grand Tour. They drifted about Europe and Russia until Nash was perhaps twelve, then his father came into the title most unexpectedly."

Kieran propped an elbow on his chair arm, and waved his hand vaguely. "And you wish us to do . . . what, precisely? Knock on his front door and offer to transport his munitions to Kotor? Bloody obvious, I should say."

"Good Lord, no," said de Vendenheim. "Just make his acquaintance, Lord Rothewell. And suggest, ever so vaguely, that your morals can be compromised."

"That would be nothing new," Kieran murmured.

"And you have been in England but four months," said Mr. Kemble. "Play upon your colonial past. Complain about the King and his taxation policies. Suggest that Barbados should go the way of America. He will not think it odd if you feel little obligation to the Crown."

Kieran was staring pensively into the distance, and tapping one finger on his desk. "It will not do," he said, almost to himself. "He can too easily discover that I've nothing to do with Neville Shipping. I daresay I could not plot the ports of Europe on a map with a sledgehammer."

De Vendenheim and Kemble looked at him in bewilderment.

Xanthia sat up stiffly in her chair. "I shall do it," she said abruptly.

Their gazes turned to her in unison. "I beg your pardon?" said the vicomte. "You shall do what?"

She managed a look of cool competence. "I shall befriend Lord Nash," she said. "I know rather more of this business than does my brother."

Kieran nodded. "Regrettably true," he acknowledged. "I am not at all sure poor Sharpe believes it, but I am just the family farmer. It is Xanthia here who tends our little world of wood and water — and she will do anything to keep her business interests from being threatened."

Their initial confusion past, the two gentlemen did not look particularly disbelieving. "I see," said de Vendenheim. "This rather complicates matters."

"Or perhaps not," murmured Mr. Kemble. "Indeed, perhaps it simplifies them."

Kieran was frowning. "I think Xanthia's getting involved with this Nash character might be unwise," he said. "Gentlemen, you'd best find another bit of bait for your hook."

"Oh, come now, Kieran!" Xanthia interjected. "Lord Nash can scarce be more unsavory than the sea dogs and scoundrels I am accustomed to. And I have Mr. Lloyd, our business agent, to help me." She turned to Mr. Kemble and the vicomte. "Besides, I have already made the gentleman's acquaintance."

Kieran lifted one of his dark, haughty eyebrows quite high at that. "Yes, and quite thoroughly, I begin to think," he murmured. "And you now propose to strike up a deeper acquaintance?"

Xanthia smiled coolly. "He was not altogether indifferent to my charms, Kieran," she said. "And while Nash hardly strikes me as a traitor, any risk to England's trade routes — indeed, to *our* trade routes — cannot be tolerated. Someone must get at the truth of this business, and quickly."

De Vendenheim was looking both appalled and hopeful. "With all respect, Miss Neville, Lord Nash is not the sort — well, he is not a gentleman with whom one —"

"He is not thought quite *nice,* Miss Neville," Mr. Kemble interjected. "And unmarried ladies dare not risk his acquaintance."

Xanthia looked at him skeptically. "I must have seen a dozen mammas shove their daughters in his direction at Lord Sharpe's," she chided. "And I do not think his exchanging a word or two with a confirmed spinster will much discourage them, either. Gentlemen, I suggest you put this matter in my hands. I shan't risk my neck, my good name, or my business, of that you may be certain."

"Yes, especially the latter," said Kieran dryly.

"But Miss Neville," protested de Vendenheim. "Your reputation —"

"No, my *trade routes*," she interjected.

"He may learn more about you, Zee, than you wish him to know," warned her brother.

"Lord Nash is hardly the sort of man who gossips," said Xanthia.

"Yes, and what if Nash turns up at Neville Shipping one day?" grumbled de Vendenheim. "What then? Is your Mr. Lloyd always in?"

"No, he is often in the warehouses, or on the docks," Xanthia admitted. "It is his job to oversee and account for the movement of freight. But we've a counting house full of clerks below."

Lord de Vendenheim looked at Kieran, who smiled faintly. "She is bullheaded," he said matter-of-factly. "But far from stupid."

Mr. Kemble gave a slow, wicked smile. "I say let her have at it, old chap," he said to de Vendenheim. "You know that old saw about women being the weaker vessel? Well, it's a damned lie."

"Then I shall leave you to explain that to the Prime Minister," the vicomte snapped.

"Just remember, old chap, that there are but two things Nash cannot resist," warned Kemble. "A well-staked card game and a beautiful woman."

"I've yet to hear him accused of seducing

unmarried ladies," countered de Vendenheim.

Xanthia realized de Vendenheim had a
point. She wished she'd had the forethought
to invent a conveniently dead husband
before clambering off the *Merry Widow* on
All Saints' Day. Her new life in London
would have been far simpler — in any
number of ways.

Just then, Kieran pushed back his chair.
"Gentlemen, we will help you so far as we
can, but I shan't permit my sister to risk
her safety. Is that understood?"

It was. After a few more moments of
debate, the three gentlemen could not quite
reach an agreement as to how best to
proceed. De Vendenheim was clearly uneasy,
and declared his intention of discussing the
plan with Mr. Peel, whilst Mr. Kemble was
already contemplating the best way to
ensure Xanthia's safety. They parted company agreeing that the vicomte would call
upon them in two days' time to tell them of
any new developments.

Mr. Kemble bowed low over Xanthia's
hand as he went. "Cobalt, my dear, is your
color," he mused, his careful, assessing gaze
running down her length. "Yes, accented
with ice blue to match your eyes. Moreover,
I have it on the best authority that blue is

Nash's favorite color."

Xanthia smiled. "Well, we would not wish to see Lord Nash disappointed, would we?"

"No, we certainly would not." And with that, Mr. Kemble bowed again and disappeared into the shadowy depths of the corridor.

"Kem," said de Vendenheim as soon as the door was shut. "How would you fancy being a shipping clerk?"

"Why, I shouldn't fancy it in the least!" Nose in the air, Kemble went down Lord Rothewell's steps. "It must be sheer drudgery. Why do you ask?"

De Vendenheim set a brisk pace in the direction of Whitehall, more or less dragging Kem after him. "Well, it is like this, old chap," he said. "You are the brilliant mind who encouraged this notion of Miss Neville's helping us. But I can tell you right now that Peel will not let us troll through London using *her* as bait — not unless she is carefully guarded."

Kemble came to an abrupt halt, causing a grumbling pedestrian to step off the pavement and into the street to avoid them. "Oh, no, Max," he said. "No, no, no. I am a businessman — and a bloody busy one. Do not even think of it. I agreed to help you out with a few discreet enquiries and to do a little poking about, but no more."

"Well," said the vicomte equivocally, "we shall see how it all sorts out."

"Oh, I can tell you, *mon ami,* how it will all sort out — with me going back to my shop in the Strand for a glass of Quinta do Noval '18 and a very expensive cheroot, and you going home to your put-upon wife and those drooling twins."

"Oh, for pity's sake, Kem." The vicomte had set off again. "Children drool when they cut teeth. The stuff is hardly toxic."

"Tell that to my best blue superfine morning coat!" said Kemble with a sniff. "Maurice was beside himself, Max, when he saw it! Simply *beside* himself!"

"Another of your Cheltenham tragedies," muttered de Vendenheim, setting off again. "But on another topic, tell me, Kem, was that not a van Ruisdael landscape I saw being cleaned in your back office yesterday? Such a lovely piece. Those fluffy white clouds above the windmill. Those almost Turneresque trees. Yes, a van Ruisdael, surely?"

Kemble cut a chary, sidelong look at his companion. "You have a good eye, Max."

"I do, don't I?" De Vendenheim smiled and clasped his hands behind his back as he walked. "And I also have a list of stolen property from an art theft which occurred in Bruges some six months past. The gentleman was quite a collector of van Ruisdael. Alas, not one piece has been recovered."

"How perfectly dreadful for him," said Kemble.

Suddenly, the vicomte jerked to a halt on the pavement again. "Kem, old fellow, I've a splendid notion!" he said. "Why do we not write to the poor chap and tell him about *yours?* He would doubtless be interested. Indeed, he might come over on the next Oostende packet, just to have a look."

Kemble's eyes flashed with ire. "Damn you, Max."

De Vendenheim pressed his fingertips to his chest. "*Me?* What for, pray?"

Kemble was silent for a moment. "I cannot close my shop, Max," he finally said. "And Miss Neville probably works in Wapping. Right on the river, I do not doubt. *Quelles horreurs!* The sounds. The stench. I could not bear it."

"But on the river is precisely where one finds smugglers," said the vicomte calmly. "Moreover, your clerk John-Claude is perfectly capable of managing the shop. Maurice can keep an eye on him."

Kemble gave one last little quake of rage, then surrendered. "Her interior decorator, then," he said. "*Not* a clerk."

"*Interior decorator?*" Max stopped again, and set his hands on his hips. "I don't even know what that is, Kem, but I am relatively certain a counting house in Wapping does not require one."

"It probably requires one quite desperately," Kemble countered. "But very well then, I shall be . . . her personal secretary! Yes, her man of affairs, so to speak. That way it will seem perfectly logical for me to be seen in both her home and her business."

Now this was the kind of logic with which the vicomte could not argue. "That really is quite a capital notion," he said musingly. "Unusual, yes. But then, she is an unusual woman."

"I can give you no more than a fortnight, Max," warned Kemble. "And you must bear all the expenses."

"Fine, but I want you with her every possible moment," said the vicomte warningly. "And Kem?"

"*What?*"

De Vendenheim paused but a heartbeat. "If Nash gives her any trouble — if she ends up in any immediate danger whatsoever — kill him."

"How?" asked Kemble matter-of-factly.

"Snap his neck," suggested the vicomte.

"Then shove him down the stairs and say he fell."

"Well, trips and falls are a leading cause of injury," murmured Kemble solicitously.

But de Vendenheim's attention was focused farther down the street. "Kem, do you see that hackney coach turning the corner into the Haymarket?" he asked. "If we hurry, we can catch it."

"Why?" asked Kemble. "I am just going down to the Strand."

"No, you are going to Wapping," said the vicomte. "I believe we shall just pay a call to the River Police. Let's see what they might know about munitions smuggling. And then, why, I think we will search out the offices of Neville Shipping. No time like the present, Kem, for you to get the lay of the land — and the river, whilst we're at it."

Upon the departure of their unexpected guests, Xanthia went at once to her room and remained there alone, thinking. So lost was she in her contemplations, she failed to so much as light a lamp, despite the falling dusk. Vaguely, she was aware that dinnertime approached and that Kieran would doubtless wish to discuss de Vendenheim's request — perhaps even to scold her just a bit for her audacity. But Xanthia wished first to replay the conversation in her own head, to come to terms with her reasons for making such a bold and ill-considered offer.

Help de Vendenheim indeed. In hindsight, she was shocked he had not refused her offer outright. Perhaps it was a measure of his desperation. It was a very serious charge which had been leveled against Lord Nash — and a horrific charge, too, when one considered that a man had been murdered. She remembered Mr. Kemble, ghoulishly slicing his finger across his throat. It made it impossible to put de Vendenheim's allegations from her mind.

Could Nash be a traitor? He certainly exuded wealth and power, and possessed the aura of a man who usually got what he wanted. There was an unmistakable dichotomy to his character; a strange mix of darkness and light which was just a bit unnerving. Xanthia was quite certain the man could be ruthless when it was warranted. But gunrunning? Was he capable of it?

Xanthia gazed blindly into the falling gloom and realized the answer was yes. But *had* he done it? Ah, now that was another question altogether. Would Nash be a traitor to the Crown in order to protect his interests elsewhere? Or would he do it simply for money? It was a complicated question.

Xanthia knew what she wished to believe. She wished to believe the best of him — which was silly when one considered she scarcely knew the man. At first, de Vendenheim's allegations had made her feel inexplicably wronged by Lord Nash. How could he be . . . what? *Not* her knight in shining armor.

That was laughable. If Nash possessed armor, it would be gunmetal black and chain mail. Xanthia looked down to see that she had begun to twist her handkerchief in knots. *Damn it, she wanted to know!* She needed to know the truth about Lord Nash's character — which was frightening when one considered the implication of such a need. Her promise to de Vendenheim had little to do with patriotism or duty, and everything to do with plain old feminine curiosity. And therein lay the danger. But already Xanthia knew that she would not be dissuaded. One way or another, she meant to have the truth about Lord Nash.

Suddenly, a faint sound drew her back to the present. She looked up to see one of the housemaids silhouetted in the door. "Shall I light your lamp, miss?" said the girl. "It is almost time for dinner."

Xanthia laid aside her well-wrenched

handkerchief and stood. "Thank you, Amy," she said. "A little light of any sort would be most welcome just now."

CHAPTER FIVE:
A SHOCKING PROPOSAL IN RICHMOND

Lord and Lady Henslow were a prominent couple amongst the upper echelons of the *ton,* and much admired for the gala picnic which they held at their Richmond estate each season. Today looked to be another great success, for the guests who surrounded the buffet tent were already agog. Her ladyship's French chef had somehow managed to roast a pig the size of a beer barrel, and was presently engaged in carving the beast *al fresco* with swift, showy flashes of his kitchen knives.

Suddenly, one of the knives slipped on a bone, glinting dangerously in the sun. A collective gasp arose. Lord Nash passed on by the tent and the unlucky pig. It would not do to meet his Maker by means of an exhibitionistic Frenchman — not when one had been expected by one's family to die a hero's death at the hands of a bloodthirsty sultan.

He strolled toward to the top of the stairs, which led down the lush lawns of Henslow House. They rolled out like carpets of emerald beneath the sun, each a littler lower than the last. One of the lower terraces held a bowling green to one side, whilst the opposite flank was set with tables and chairs trimmed in white-and-yellow bunting. Below it all lay the Thames, which here appeared to be a glistening, pristine waterway, rather than the almost fetid, roiling surge which it became but a few miles downstream.

Amidst a gaggle of ladies below him, Nash could see his hostess, floating like a pink balloon in a sea of pastel muslin. Lady Henslow's ample girth made her unmistakable in the crowd. Nash set off in her direction. He rather liked Lady Henslow. His stepmother's elder sister, Lady Henslow had always fawned over his young sisters, Phaedra and Phoebe. She had enlisted the influence of her husband, an ardent Tory, in assuring Tony's swift rise to power. And to Edwina, she provided a sisterly shoulder to cry on. For all those things, Nash was grateful to Lady Henslow. But none of them, he inwardly admitted, was the reason he had come to her picnic.

But Lady Henslow had espied him and

was wading from the pastel froth of her guests, her face aglow with delight. "Nash, do my eyes deceive?" she said, reaching up — very far up — to set her palms against his cheeks. "I never thought to see you here."

Nash took one of her hands and carried it to his lips. "My dear, it is a pleasure," he said, bowing low. "I see you mean to outshine the season's debutantes. That shade of pink greatly becomes you."

Lady Henslow's eyes twinkled. "And I see you keep to your racy Continental habits, my boy," she returned. "No proper Englishman would let his lips actually *touch* my hand."

Nash raised both eyebrows. "Alas, madam, it is gloved," he said. "You have cheated me of a long-anticipated pleasure."

At this her ladyship guffawed most indelicately. "Be honest with me, my boy," she said. "What brings you slinking around before nightfall? Surely not my little affair?"

Nash gave a muted smile. "May I not call upon my stepaunt when the mood strikes me?"

"Certainly, you may do," said her ladyship. "But the mood has not struck you these last twenty years or better. You are up to some sort of intrigue, Stefan. I know it.

Just remember — there will be no pigeon-plucking at my picnic. Some of these lads are just down from school and green as grass."

Nash gave a muted smile. "I only pluck pigeons who are old enough to know what they are about, ma'am, and fool enough to deserve it."

Lady Henslow laughed again. But just then, she was called away to some crisis in the buffet tent — a severed finger, most probably. Nash snared a drink from a passing footman and continued his amble down the terraces, all the while aware of the not infrequent stares and whispers which came his way. He ignored them and paused to speak to those few gentlemen whom he knew. But the truth was, London society, even the very best of it, was cleanly cut into two halves. There were those in the *ton's* inner circle, and there were those who moved along the darker fringe. Nash was clinging to the ends of the fringe.

Nash looked about at the crowd, seeing no one under the age of twenty whom he knew. No, the gentlemen — and the women — with whom he associated were older and harder, and they recognized one another by their cynical eyes and jaded expressions. They were not apt to be seen at afternoon picnics. Indeed, they were not apt to be seen much before midnight.

Nash felt a little foolish, but he shook it off and moved on. On the last terrace, the crowd thickened considerably. Here, the ladies in pastel ruffles twirled their matching parasols as they clung to the arms of the dashing young beaus who took them down to promenade along the riverbank whilst doting mothers looked on. Suddenly, Nash wished to escape. He half turned on the step, but unexpectedly, someone touched his elbow.

"Stefan? You? At a picnic?"

He turned to see that Tony stood nearby.

"Remarkable is it not?" Nash murmured.

"I should say so," agreed Tony. "Aunt must be in alt. This will provide the *ton* with a week's worth of gossip."

Nash lifted his hat to the two gentlemen with his brother. "Mr. Sofford, Lord Ogle," he said with a bow. "I trust I find you well?"

Tony's political cronies were quite well, and apparently engaged in a rather animated debate about the Civil Rights of Convicts Act. After exchanging pleasantries, they went on to argue about banking, poaching, and something to do with the Catholics, though what, if anything, one had to do with the other, Nash could not have said. He was struggling mightily not to yawn when Mr. Safford pointed up the steps.

"Ah, look!" he said. "Here comes Sharpe. He will know how the Whigs are expected to split."

"No doubt he shall," said Lord Ogle. "But on a more pressing point, gentlemen, who are the visions of beauty clinging to the fellow's arms?"

Tony set a hand above his eyes to shield the sun. "That sugarplum with the ringlets is his daughter, Lady Louisa," he answered. "And the slender lady with the dark hair is a cousin, a Mrs. — Mrs. — damn, but I forget her name."

"*Miss* Neville," Nash supplied. "She is unwed and newly arrived from the West Indies."

Tony dropped his hand, and looked at Nash oddly. "Is she indeed?" he murmured. "And unwed? At her age?"

"Come, Hayden-Worth!" said Mr. Safford. "She is hardly in her dotage. Besides, I hear she is possessed of a huge fortune."

"Heavens!" murmured Lord Ogle. "I wonder if there is any hope of *dis*possessing her of it?"

"I should have a care, if I were you," said Safford quietly. "Her brother is Baron Rothewell. Have you met him?"

146

Ogle shook his head. "No."

"Well, you don't wish to," said Sofford. He looked as if he might say more, but the new arrivals were drifting down the terraced lawn now. When they reached the stairs above, Lord Ogle called out for Sharpe to join them.

Nash knew it the instant Miss Neville laid eyes on him. But to the lady's credit, she neither faltered nor blushed. In fact, he realized as the introductions were being made, she seemed almost glad to see him. Or perhaps *mildly amused* was the better term, for a strange little smile lurked at one corner of her wide, good-humored mouth, and there was a glint of something intriguing in her eyes.

And what eyes they were. How odd he had not noticed them before. They were an unusual color, a deep shade of blue, which was rimmed with silver-gray. Odder still, the look which was fixed upon him was steady — like a man's. Rather than casting her gaze downward or sideways in some silly effort to appear demure, she looked directly at him; not boldly, but simply eye to eye, as if she knew precisely what she was about.

"And how shall you vote, Lord Nash?" asked Miss Neville, drawing him back to the present.

Nash tried to pretend he'd been listening. "I rather doubt I shall vote at all, ma'am."

"But you should do, Nash!" grumbled Lord Sharpe. "We could use you on our side now and again, you know." The earl looked as if he was about to launch some tirade on *noblesse oblige,* but Nash was saved by Lady Louisa, who tugged gently on her father's arm.

"Papa, the bowling!" she whined. "You promised we might watch. Mr. Sofford, are you not to play?"

"Gad!" said Sofford, tugging out his watch. "Is it time already?"

Lord Ogle bowed. "Good luck to you, old chap," he said. "Hayden-Worth and I are promised to Lady Henslow for archery on the east lawn."

"Miss Neville, are you a fan of bowls?" asked Nash.

"I fear I know little about it," she replied. "But I am sure I shall enjoy it."

Lord Sharpe laughed. "I daresay Xanthia would rather go shoot at something," he said. "Feel free, my dear, if archery is more to your liking?"

"Perhaps Miss Neville would instead favor me with a walk along the river?" Nash suggested.

Lord Sharpe looked hesitant.

"I should love a good walk," declared Miss Neville before Sharpe could refuse. "But a real walk, if you please, not a promenade. Louisa, shall we meet at the tent after the game?"

"Yes, of course," said Lady Louisa, obviously pleased to have her way.

Her father, however, looked less pleased. "Very well, then," he said. "You will stay near, Xanthia, will you not? In case — well, in case you are needed?"

Nash suspected his true meaning was something altogether less charitable. Miss Neville finally succumbed to a faint blush. Nash watched the group disperse to their various entertainments, and wondered what the devil he'd been thinking to suggest such a quixotic thing as a walk along the river. Good Lord, the woman was temptation personified — and she had no business being seen on his arm, even at such a benign affair as a picnic. But she had agreed, and she was not exactly green from the schoolroom. He might as well enjoy himself.

Nash let his eyes run appreciatively down Miss Neville. She had worn not pastel, thank God, but a dress striped in rich shades of blue and gray. Not a woman in a thousand could have pulled it off, but the gown beautifully emphasized her slenderness and height. "I do not think your cousin approves of me, my dear," he said. "Perhaps you ought to take in that bowling match after all?"

"Thank you, no," said Miss Neville, starting down the steps without him. "I mean to have that walk. Are you coming? Or shall I go alone?"

"Taking the air again, my dear?"

"I beg your pardon?"

"I believe you once said that if you wished for a breath of fresh air, you would have it, and damn the consequences."

She looked up at him, her deep blue eyes narrowing against the sun. "I cannot imagine the consequence of taking a turn up and down an open path in the middle of the afternoon will amount to much, my lord," she returned. "Even if one is hanging off the arm of an unrepentant rake."

"Ah, that is good news." Nash smiled down at her.

"I beg your pardon?" she said again.

"It seems I have been elevated from *dandy* to *rake*," he said. "My masculinity is much reassured."

Her wide mouth twitched with humor. She extended her hand up to him. "Come along, Lord Nash," she said. "And kindly do not poke fun at my limited vocabulary."

True to her word, she set off downstream at a brisk pace as soon as they reached the path. Nash's usual gravitas was somewhat undercut by her long stride. "Miss Neville, I thought you meant to hang off my arm," he said when the crowd thinned. "You are moving as if all of London is afire, and you wish to watch it burn."

She slowed at once. "I do beg your pardon," she said, settling her hand just above his elbow. "But there are so many people here, and that makes the empty path beyond so very tempting."

"The social whirl holds no attraction for you?" he asked, matching his steps to hers.

"Not especially," she said. "At home in Barbados . . . well, society was not so rarefied as this. I feel a little out of place here."

"You do not look out of place," he said. "You look every inch a lady born to this life."

Her gaze moved over his face, quickly assessing him. "You mean that as a compliment, I am sure," she said. "But . . ."

"But what?" he encouraged.

"Frankly, I take little satisfaction from it," she said. "This sort of life has so little purpose."

"I see," he said quietly. "You would rather . . . what? Work for the betterment of the underclasses? Run a charity school? Knit stockings for the poor?"

She laughed lightly. "Lord, no," she said. "Not I!" But she offered no further explanation.

They walked in silence for a time, her hand lying light and warm on his arm. Nash found it surprisingly pleasant. On the river to their left, a pair of broad-shouldered scullers glided past, their oars glinting in perfect rhythm, the far boat ahead by half a length.

"What, then, would you rather do with your life, Miss Neville?" he finally prodded. "Retire to the country and raise a brood of children, perhaps?"

"No," she answered. "No, Lord Nash, I am already doing what I please with my life."

She stopped abruptly along the path, her gaze fixed on the scullers, but he sensed she was not really watching them. Nash glanced up and down the path. Though still well in sight of the house, they were the only guests this far downriver.

Finally, she cleared her throat, and resumed walking. "Lord Nash, did my brother tell you that we are quite wealthy?"

"I was made aware of that fact, yes."

She smiled faintly. "The barony, of course, brings my brother a good income. But we have other interests as well."

"Yes, you have plantations in Barbados, do you not?"

"But they are let now," she said. "And my brother is at present without an occupation. We own a business — Neville Shipping Company. Have you heard of it?"

"I do not believe so."

"No, I cannot think shipping is the sort of thing an English gentleman would much concern himself with," she mused. "But we Nevilles, you see, have no such compunction. In fact, one might say we are more or less in trade."

"Many gentlemen invest in such businesses, Miss Neville," he said. "I own several mines; Lord Ogle, a railroad — or a part of one. You need not speak as if you and Rothewell are running a haberdashery. Where is your charming brother, by the way?"

She smiled faintly. "Sharpe stepped in for him at the last moment," she answered. "Rothewell was much relieved."

"Yes, he seems a private, almost secretive sort of man."

"Indeed, very much so." Her strong blue

gaze turned to him again. "And I have a secret, too, my lord," she said quietly. "May I depend upon you once again to keep my confidence?"

He laughed, though he wondered vaguely what she was getting at. "Pray tell me all your secrets, my dear," he answered. "I should love to have you in my power."

"Nash, do be serious," she chided.

Nash inclined his head. "Of course you have my word, Miss Neville," he said more seriously. "Pray what is this secret?"

Slowly, she leaned closer. "Neville Shipping is mine," she whispered. "Oh, it is family-owned — but my brother leaves the running of it to me. And it is a very profitable concern, if one knows the tricks of the trade."

"I see," he said quietly. "And you . . . know all the tricks, do you?"

A slow, mischievous smile curved her wide mouth. "I am very good, Lord Nash, at everything I do," she said. "Would it not shock these proper English ladies to know that tomorrow, whilst they are lying languidly in their beds at noon, awaiting their ladies' maids and their hot chocolate, I will already be at my grimy little office in Wapping, rubbing shoulders with sea dogs and stevedores?"

She sounded entirely serious. "Surely you jest?"

Miss Neville lifted one of her dark, finely arched brows, and spoke with surprising passion. "Not in the least," she answered. "Indeed, were it left to me, everyone would be gainfully employed."

"Dear God!" he said. "Perish the thought, Miss Neville."

"I am quite serious," she insisted. "This insidious rot of living only to be served by others, this . . . this utter lack of drive or ambition — well, is it any wonder half the *ton* suffer from chronic *ennui?* Their lives have no challenge. No purpose."

"And your life does?" he asked. "I mean, I do not doubt you, my dear. But what is that purpose?"

Despite the bright sun, her eyes glinted with excitement. *"Commerce,"* she said. *"Enterprise.* The thrill and the challenge of competition — financial competition. These are the things that move the world, Lord Nash, not the foolish intrigues of the *ton,* no matter how blindly they might think otherwise."

He chuckled quietly. "They will be crushed, my dear, to hear it."

Miss Neville lifted her slender shoulders beneath the rich fabric of her gown. "Oh, they will realize soon enough that the reign of upper-class elitists is coming to an end," she said. "We are entering a new age, Nash. An age of progress and industrialization. And England will change — much as America has done — into a nation of self-made men and women."

They stood opposite one another now, his eyes intently studying her. "Good Lord," he finally said. "You are not just another pretty face, are you?"

"No, I am a businesswoman," she said with icy certainty. "And my allegiance is to the bottom line on Neville's financial statement, not some silly ideal of blue-blooded Crown and country."

He took her arm then and drew her near. "Careful, my dear," he murmured, his eyes drifting over her face. "Those words sound faintly treasonous."

Her chin came up, and her eyes sparkled. "My God, Nash. Are you a high-stickler after all?"

Nash shook his head. "No, but nor am I a rash fool."

Miss Neville seemed to relax a little. "You are quite right to be careful," she answered. "But sometimes I despair of not having moved this business to America. England's taxation policies have become onerous, and the political restrictions placed on our business are . . . ah, but enough of this. I shall bore you unforgivably."

"I rather doubt you could ever do that, Miss Neville," he said. "You might shock me, perhaps, with your *laissez-faire* notions. And you understand, do you not, that it is considered most unseemly for a woman of your class to espouse such ideas, let alone engage in business?"

She cast a curious, sidelong glance in his direction. "But do *you* find it unseemly, Lord Nash?" she asked. "Or are you intrigued by it? Are you put off by a woman who rejects the traditional role of wife in favor of personal and economic freedom?"

Nash was taken aback by the clarity her words. Was that what she was? *And was he put off?* It was a valid, if strange question. "I am not sure," he answered honestly. "I did not realize your views went so far as to cast aside that more traditional role."

"Come, Nash, you must never lie to a lady," she said sardonically. "Of course you realized it. Otherwise, you would not be walking arm in arm with me. You are hardly in the market for a wife."

"Indeed not. But what has that to do with anything?"

"You invited an unattached, ostensibly

eligible female to stroll with you in front of half the *ton*," she answered. "Surely you comprehend the implication of your act?" She paused to turn around on the path. "Look, we are now out of sight of the others. But you do not care, because you already know, Nash, that your 'most prized asset' — your beloved bachelorhood — is safe with me."

Nash stared down the length of the river behind them and realized that she was right. He was not concerned. Moreover, Miss Neville was perhaps the one woman here with whom he could be himself. And, distracted by the heat of their debate, he had forgotten to keep his guard up. They had long ago left the grounds of Henslow House. He reluctantly acknowledged that it was time to turn around.

"There was a little bench beneath the trees some distance back," he said. "Why do we not return to it?"

"A return to the bounds of propriety?" she teased.

"I am trying to show concern for your virtue, Miss Neville, much as it surprises me," he said dryly. "I suppose that the ruin of your good name is a guilt I should rather not live with."

"How very patronizing of you, Nash," she

complained. "I believe you did not listen to a word I said."

"I listened," he returned. "But you are very young, my dear. And there is always Lady Louisa to consider."

Miss Neville's expressive face fell just a little. "I will own, Nash, that you are right about my young cousin," she confessed. "I wish to do nothing which might wrongly influence her, or hinder her chance at a good marriage. But I am almost thirty. I am not *very young.*"

"My goodness, all of that, are you?" he said, smiling down at her. "You are a well-preserved specimen for such a great age. Have you all your teeth still?"

"You are teasing me, sir," she chided. "You think I will still end up at the altar when all is said and done. But consider this, Nash: Why should I subjugate myself to a man when I am perfectly capable of managing on my own?"

"You have your brother," he challenged. "Legally, it is he who is responsible for you."

"Come now, Nash," she said with a muted smile. "For all his harsh ways and blunt tongue, it would never occur to Kieran that it was his duty to govern me. You must understand how we grew up. And that in Barbados, women often own businesses.

They travel unaccompanied, and even quietly take lovers if they wish."

"Do they indeed?" he murmured. *What was Miss Neville suggesting?*

Nash's mind turned back to his meeting in Lord Rothewell's study. The views Rothewell had expressed then were very much in keeping with Miss Neville's now. But he had suggested something else, too. "Actually, my dear, it was your brother who implied that you might soon marry."

She jerked at once to a halt. "Did he? Good Lord. I thought he'd given up that notion."

"Apparently not," said Nash. "Is there a gentleman pining for your hand?"

Miss Neville shifted her gaze back to the river. "There once was, perhaps," she answered. "But we have agreed we do not suit. My brother is naive if he thinks that will ever change."

"Nonetheless, the man still wishes to marry you."

She flicked an uncertain gaze in his direction. "How would you know?"

"I think, Miss Neville, that once a man had fallen in love with you, he would be hard-pressed to fall out of it again," said Nash in a lightly teasing voice. "I believe I shall keep my distance from you, my dear. I suffer my frustrations with little enough grace as it is."

"Heavens!" she said. "Have you a great many?"

"Frustrations?" He looked down at her, and took in her intelligent face and the expanse of ivory skin which revealed just a hint of what he already knew was a lush, enticing bosom. Hell yes, he was frustrated. But what the devil was he to do about it now? If he were going to seduce Miss Neville, he could at least do her the courtesy of seducing her in private. Against his will, Nash felt his mouth quirk with humor. "Yes, I have one or two frustrations, Miss Neville. And your hip brushing against mine from time to time is not helping them any."

Xanthia did not miss the innuendo. Her steps faltered just an instant, and at once, Nash's warm, steady hand slipped beneath her elbow. She flicked a quick glance up at him. The heat in his gaze was unmistakable, and once again she was struck with the strangest notion that she was staring into the eyes of a kindred spirit. Another soul who was drifting, perhaps, and living a life which was somehow incomplete.

But what romantic drivel that was! She was wasting her chance. This was the perfect opportunity to learn more about Nash. To assess his character and attempt to find out if he was the man de Vendenheim believed him. To give him just a little rope and see if he was inclined to hang himself. She looked up to see the stone bench just beyond. It faced the water and was flanked by willows. It was private, yes — but not quite hidden, either. It was, in fact, quite perfect. The terraced lawns were just coming into view around the bend, and above, she could already hear the laughter from Lady Henslow's makeshift archery range.

She said nothing until they were comfortably situated on the bench. "There!" she said, carefully neatening the folds of her skirt. "This is quite nicely secluded, is it not? We may be seen, perhaps, from the lawns — but only our backs."

"Your words suggest we've something to hide," he teased.

"Have we?" Xanthia dropped her eyes to the faint bulge in his trousers and, tossing caution aside, leaned into Lord Nash and very deliberately set her hand on his knee.

His eyes lit with an inscrutable emotion. "Miss Neville, I beg you to be careful."

She let her lashes fall nearly shut. "We cannot be seen from this angle," she whispered. "Besides, it was you, Nash, who first spoke of your frustrations, was it not?"

He sat as stoically as was humanly possible under the circumstance, his eyes fixed intently on her slender, tempting fingers. To his extreme torment, she eased them higher. "Christ Jesus," he gritted. "I am trying to be a gentleman, Miss Neville. But someone is going to see you."

"Oh dear, you might be right," she murmured. But instead of moving her hand, she merely scooted a little nearer. "There, I think they cannot see now."

He looked at her a little grimly. "That was not quite what I meant."

"Nonetheless, it solves the problem," she said. The ridge of his erection was straining against the fine wool of his trousers.

Shamelessly tempted, Xanthia wondered how it would feel to stroke the hot, hard length of Lord Nash's obviously stiffening manhood. Somehow, she stilled her hand and squeezed her eyes shut. Fleetingly, she forgot her purpose — forgot completely what de Vendenheim had asked of her — and thought only of what it would be like to lie pinned beneath Lord Nash's weight. To have that warm, spicy scent of his settle over her like a sensuous cloud. To take the heat and strength of him deep inside, and —

"My dear Miss Neville," he murmured. "I think now is not the time and place."

Her eyes flew open, and she realized her hand was inching toward a most dangerous position. "When?" The word came out low and husky. "When, Nash, would be the time and place?"

"In another lifetime, I fear," he responded. "It would be unwise of you to tempt me in this one."

Xanthia smiled lightly. "But there is something undeniable between us, Nash," she murmured. "A simmering heat which keeps flaring to life when we are near. Tell me you do not feel it."

He gave a bark of sharp laughter. "I think that what I am feeling is bloody obvious." Then he covered her hand with his, gave it a hard squeeze, and deliberately returned it to her own lap.

Xanthia ignored the hint. "Are you . . . *interested*, Lord Nash?" she asked.

Something flared hotly in his eyes. "Do you understand what you are asking for, Miss Neville?"

She lifted her head and pinned him with her gaze. "I am asking if you will be my lover," she said. "For as long as it pleases us. Have you any commitment to another?"

Nash smiled sardonically. "Miss Neville, do I look the faithful type?" he returned. "I enjoy variety in my bedmates and tire of them quickly. And I must tell you frankly, my dear, that the very last thing I want or need is an innocent — particularly a well-bred innocent — in my bed."

"I am not precisely innocent, Nash," she murmured, allowing her bottom lip to lightly catch between her teeth. "I would, I daresay, be considered tainted merchandise — so none of your aristocratic friends would have me in their marriage bed anyway."

He drew away, something which looked like anger glittering in his eyes. "That is a little harsh."

"It is also true," she said. "Does it not ease your guilt?"

"As of yet, I've done nothing for which to feel guilty," he answered. "Not unless one counts that foolish kiss on Sharpe's portico. I knew, even then, that you were going to be trouble."

Xanthia gave him a slow, teasing smile. "Nash, if I no longer interest you, then you have only to say so," she murmured. "I am lonely but hardly desperate. London is filled with handsome gentlemen, and whilst I am not a beauty, I have been told I possess a certain charm."

For a long moment, he was silent, his expression darkening, his jaw tightly clenched. "I hope, Miss Neville, that you will not have a discussion of this nature with any other gentleman of your acquaintance," he finally said. Then abruptly, he rose. "I shall think on — indeed, I shall probably be obsessed by — your mad proposal, my dear. And I pray for your sake I'll do no more than that. Now, please allow me to see you safely back to your cousin."

Xanthia caught his hand. He bent over her, his dark, heavy-lidded eyes seemingly focused on her mouth, and for an instant, she thought he might kiss her again. Her heart fluttered wildly in her chest. But he did not bend lower. Instead, his eyes searched her face, as if looking for something.

Xanthia held his gaze. "Nash?"

Fleetingly, he hesitated. "No," he finally said. "No, this simply is not possible."

Again, she smiled. "Of course it is possible," she said. "Nothing is impossible if one dares to make it so."

His seemingly black eyes flashed again. He did not answer, but instead straightened up, and, taking her arm, he drew her up and set off in the direction of the picnic. "Nash, you are going to dislocate my shoulder," she complained.

He said no more until they had almost reached the first cluster of guests upriver.

Then he stopped abruptly and turned to face her. "Miss Neville, you are playing with fire," he said tightly. "Please remember that whilst I am not a rake, I am certainly not a saint, nor anything remotely near it."

"No, I believe you once said you were a sybarite."

"Yes, selfishly and impenitently so," he said. "And a sybarite takes what he wants, then casts it aside when he has extracted from it all the pleasure he may. You would do well to remember that."

Then Lord Nash turned on his heel and went swiftly up the path.

Xanthia made the journey home that afternoon in a state of dreadful confusion. She was not perfectly sure just what she had managed to accomplish at Lady Henslow's. Utter humiliation, perhaps? She had tried to seduce Lord Nash — and she had almost accomplished it. As he said, he was no saint. He certainly did not look a saint. Indeed, he looked perfectly capable of all that de Vendenheim had accused him. So why had her brain been unable to keep hold of the fact that there was a purpose — a purpose far greater than physical pleasure — in what she was doing?

Xanthia was a person who carefully assessed her adversary, but something in Nash circumvented her usual caution. She kept thinking — imagining, really — that he knew her; that he understood her on some level which escaped most people. There was this terrible temptation simply to let herself go when she was in his company — to be . . . well, *herself,* really. But she was just deluding herself, or perhaps making silly, romantic excuses for the almost overwhelming desire she felt for him.

The man was quite likely a traitor. A smuggler. And someone had been killed, either at his word, or by his hand. Absent the heat of desire, Xanthia could remember de Vendenheim's warnings. There was a great deal at stake, politically and economically. *Power and money.* The two things people were so often willing to kill for. All that aside, de Vendenheim would have been appalled to know she had tried to sleep with the man. Xanthia herself was a little appalled; she wasn't even sure just what had taken hold of her. She had meant merely to flirt with Nash just enough to put him off his guard.

Blindly, she stared through the window at the thinning crowds along Piccadilly, and reminded herself that this was not about *her.* This was about greater things. It was a serious business, not some impassioned *af-*

faire of the heart. And yet, sitting with him this afternoon — touching him almost intimately, and yearning for his touch in return — Xanthia had trouble accepting that de Vendenheim's allegations could be true.

Was she really such a fool? Nash was as cold and controlled a man as ever she had met. Indeed, she understood perfectly well that, with this man, she was in over her head. He was not a scorned and prideful man like Gareth Lloyd, whom she could manage. He was unmanageable in every sense, and she knew it. And yet, she was not dissuaded. Oh, yes. *Fool* was indeed the right word.

She felt the carriage rock to a halt in Berkeley Square and heard Sharpe's footman leap down to drop the steps. Her mind forced back to the present, Xanthia kissed Louisa on the cheek and thanked Sharpe for the lovely afternoon. Then she went in, craving only a hot bath, a glass of sherry, and the solitude of her bedchamber, to receive instead the news that a caller had been awaiting her return for the last hour or better.

Apparently, her frustration showed.

"It is that foppish gentleman again, miss," whispered Trammel. "And he's brought a bandbox. His lordship is out, but the cheeky fellow asked for you, anyway. So I put him in the yellow salon with a glass of his lordship's best brandy, but he won't drink it. Sniffed it and put it down again. Have you ever heard of such a thing, miss?"

Miss had not. Perhaps she would just go into the yellow salon and drink it for him. God knows she needed something restorative. She went upstairs, mildly annoyed.

"Good afternoon, Mr. Kemble," she said, sailing as breezily as she could into the room. "What a delightful surprise."

"My dear Miss Neville." The dapper gentleman made her a deep, elegant bow. "I see you took my advice — or very nearly."

She looked at him blankly for a moment, then realized he was looking at her dress. "Oh, this?" she said, lightly touching the fabric. "Yes, but it is just blue and gray."

"Yet very flattering nonetheless," replied Mr. Kemble. But it was said clinically, almost as if they discussed a business matter. Perhaps they did. Indeed, Xanthia would do well to think of it in just that perspective. A business matter.

"I have brought you a gift," said Mr. Kemble, producing the small bandbox.

"A gift?" Xanthia took it, and sat down. "You really should not have."

170

Mr. Kemble, too, sat. "You must open it, my dear. We must see if it fits."

Xanthia felt her eyes widen with surprise, but she did as he asked. It was quite inappropriate for a gentleman to give any sort of gift to an unmarried lady, and yet she sensed that this gift was somehow different.

Her eyes widened when she lifted the lid. Oh, yes. Definitely different. Nestled in a pile of wood shavings was a sort of little leather harness with a pocket — and tucked into the pocket was a small silver pistol. Gingerly, she lifted it out.

"Have you any idea how to use it?" asked Mr. Kemble hopefully.

Xanthia laid it across her knees. "Yes, actually. But I am out of practice."

"It is for close range only," said Mr. Kemble with a dismissive gesture. "Now I shall turn around, Miss Neville. I wish you to hike up your skirts, and make perfectly sure it fits."

She looked at him blankly. "If it . . . fits *where*, precisely?"

"Around your thigh," he answered, turning to face the wall. "And pull it tight, if you please. That pistol is deceptively heavy."

Feeling more than a little silly, Xanthia set her slipper on a footstool, drew up her petticoats, and did as he asked. The leather strap buckled snugly, as though it had been made for her. She put her foot down. "Yes, it fits," she said. "But do you really think —"

"Absolutely," interjected Kemble, spinning around on one heel. The man was quick as a cat, she noticed. "We cannot know what predicament might befall you, my dear, or how far away I might be."

Xanthia looked at him blankly. "How far away from what?"

"Dear me." There was a flash of black humor in his eyes. "Max did not tell you?"

"Lord de Vendenheim?" Xanthia shook her head. "No, he has told me nothing."

Mr. Kemble opened his arms expansively. "My dear, it seems we are to become inseparable," he declared. "I am your new man of affairs."

"I can't think what you mean," she said.

Mr. Kemble smiled tightly. "Your personal secretary," he clarified. "Your aide-de-camp. Your chaperone, one might almost say."

"But I do not require one," she said. "I have Mr. Lloyd and a counting house full of clerks. Besides, *a chaperone?* The notion is absurd."

"Cela va sans dire!" said Mr. Kemble, his brown eyes rueful. "But Maximilian would insist. So I am to accompany you

172

to your place of business and give you whatever assistance I may whilst you are at home."

Xanthia pursed her lips. "You may inform Lord de Vendenheim that I have never had a governess and do not mean to have one now," she finally said. "I am quite accustomed to the Docklands, and I rather doubt I'll come across anything more dangerous than that here in Mayfair."

Mr. Kemble looked at her chidingly. "That is all very well, Miss Neville, but what of me?"

Xanthia lifted one eyebrow. "What about you?"

Mr. Kemble gave a theatrical sigh. "Well, it is like this, my dear. Max has caught me in something of" — here, he paused to lay a finger aside his cheek — "well, let us call it a little indiscretion. A sort of *affaire d'amour,* as it were. An unnatural attachment that is just — well, a tad illicit. And it is the very sort of thing a man in my position should not wish to have made public."

Xanthia lifted both eyebrows, then suddenly, his intimation struck her. "Oh. Oh, dear." She cleared her throat decorously. "I cannot think *that* is anyone's business but yours, sir. And, of course, the — the — well, the *person* with whom — oh, good Lord!

Never mind. What has any of this to do with me?"

"Max is blackmailing me."

It took a moment for his words to sink in. "But that is quite outrageous!"

"So it is, Miss Neville," he replied. "But I beg you to think of me. If you turn me off, why, Max will think it my doing. He will say I did not make an earnest attempt. That I failed to impress you with my dedication and my diligence."

Xanthia looked at him suspiciously. "I somehow imagined the two of you were friends."

"My dear, nothing could be further from the truth!" said Mr. Kemble, with a little toss of his hand. "Sadly, Max has no friends. He is a singularly grim, humorless, and un-affectionate man who thinks only of himself and his precious Home Office."

"Oh, I do not for one moment believe *that*."

Kemble smiled, and folded his hands together on one knee. "Well, it was worth a try, was it not?" he said lightly. "Come now, Miss Neville — what harm will it do if I dog your footsteps for a fortnight or so? Perhaps you will even find me of some use. I am, if I do say so myself, a man of many talents."

Xanthia did not doubt that. And he was entertaining, in a flamboyant and faintly dangerous sort of way. Indeed, there was an unmistakably dark edge to his personality, but at least he was not dull.

"Very well," she finally said. "You may accompany me to Wapping each day, and we shall make a little place for you in the office. Are you a very organized person?"

"Frightfully so."

"Excellent," said Xanthia. "I've a vast storage room filled with logs and manifests from Bridgetown which need indexing and filing. But I shan't need you otherwise, Mr. Kemble, particularly here, where I have my brother to . . . to *safeguard* me — which is an utterly silly notion anyway. And I certainly shan't be wearing this clumsy pistol strapped to my leg."

"But my dear, you should," he averred. "A lady ought never go past Temple Bar unarmed. Particularly a lady in your line of work and given the assignment you have undertaken. Lord Nash is believed to be a very dangerous man."

"Oh, of that I am quite certain," Xanthia murmured. "But I am not at all sure he is a traitor."

"The Home Office is quite sure he is,"

said Kemble. "And they mean to see him in prison."

"Without first having the truth?" said Xanthia archly. "Why do I begin to believe you people have already tried and sentenced Lord Nash? I am happy to help, Mr. Kemble, when it is in my company's best interests to do so, but I won't be a part of a mockery of justice — not at any cost. Do I make myself plain?"

"Quite plain." Kemble looked vaguely contrite. "And perhaps you are right."

"I think I am," she said. "But if I am wrong — if Nash is behind this — we will know it soon enough."

Mr. Kemble smiled and folded his hands neatly together. "And until then, wear the pistol anyway, my dear," he pressed. "After all, a lady can never have too many silver accessories."

She deliberately lifted one eyebrow. "Yes, and what if Lord Nash should happen across it?" she murmured. "Accidents do happen."

Mr. Kemble gave a slow, wicked grin. "In your reticule, then?" he suggested. "But you'll need quite a large one."

"That is a more practical notion." Xanthia pursed her lips again. "Very well. I shall do it."

Mr. Kemble unfolded his hands, and smiled triumphantly.

Following the debacle at Lady Henslow's picnic, Lord Nash went home with every intention of dining in, and *staying* in — to privately lick his wounds or his claw marks or whatever it was Miss Xanthia Neville had sunk into him. Her very presence left a damnable itch, one which he couldn't seem to scratch, a bone-deep frustration as vexing as it was foreign.

He was expecting Tony for dinner, but his brother did not appear. So he ate alone, silently chewing on his own frustration, and washing it down with a bottle of Hungarian *bikavér* — bull's blood, a wine stiff enough to peel the paint off the dining room walls.

It was not enough. He roamed the house like a wraith. Poked through the library shelves. Practiced *vingt-et-un* until his eyes crossed. Soon his restlessness drove him into the dark streets again, and he found himself halfway to Berkeley Square before he realized what he was about. He stopped abruptly on the pavement, his greatcoat swirling around his ankles in the evening's leaden mist.

What good would it do him to go there? What did he mean to do when he arrived?

Stand in the street and gaze up at the woman's windows like some besotted lunatic?

No. No, the price for that was too high. He would take instead what he had already paid for. And he was not besotted; he was just . . . maddeningly intrigued. Yes, that was the word. With that decided, he strode off in the direction of Covent Garden. He would find physical satisfaction in Lisette's bed, as he had done a hundred times before. And if that did not work, he would go to Mother Lucy's, and ask for a willowy brunette with bottomless blue eyes. He would ask her for — well, not for anything especially unusual, though some of Lucy's girls could satisfy the most depraved of appetites. Nash was not interested in depravity. All he wanted was a few hours' peace in someone's arms.

But it was not to be Lisette's. Not if he wished for peace. He was well into his second glass of vodka by the time she arrived home from the theater, her eyes alight with barely veiled indignation. "Why, fancy seeing you here!" she said, tossing her cloak at the cowering butler.

Nash looked up from his glass. "You are late, Lisette."

The actress shrugged and went to the

mahogany bureau. Lisette might be indignant, but she knew on which side her bread was really buttered — and it was not at Drury Lane. "I did not expect you, darling," she said, pulling the pins from her hat. "Your habits have changed of late."

"But I pay you to be here."

"No, my dear, you pay me to fuck you." She shook out her ice blond hair, eyeing his reflection in the mirror. "But there was a little après-theater soiree at Millie Dow's. Had I seen you at all, perhaps I would have invited you."

He snatched his drink and stood. "Come upstairs when you have finished primping."

"Yes, I wish always to look my best for you, Nash." Her eyes followed him in the mirror. "Why do you not take up the madeira as you go?"

"I don't care for any," he said.

"Well, I *do*," she said. "So take a glass as well, if you please."

There was just one glass left on the tray. Nash snatched it and the decanter, then stomped up the steps alone. Once upstairs, he set them on Lisette's night table and slowly began to undress.

When at last she slid naked beneath the covers, he took her fiercely, thrusting deep on the first stroke, and driving himself almost madly into her, in some futile effort to push away his demons. Lisette responded — she was, after all, an actress. But in truth, she had always liked it this way. It was, perhaps, what had first drawn them together. The need to spend their frustrations and their bodies. The hunger for sexual satisfaction — but without intimacy.

There had been a time, he admitted, when this had been all he had wanted. Surely it still was? He had simply tired of Lisette, that was all. And at the moment, he had tired of this performance, too. Lisette looked up at him through somnolent eyes, her red mouth half open and gasping. It felt so . . . *insufficient*. It was as if he watched them thrusting and panting and reaching for one another from a distance, and through someone else's eyes. Someone detached. Passionless.

Nash watched Lisette stiffen and tremble beneath him, then he finished mechanically, pulling himself from her body at the last possible instant, allowing his seed to spill across her milk white thighs. It was perhaps the blandest, most mundane performance of his lifetime. Lisette smiled lazily up at him, but he could sense her discontent. Perhaps she had simply feigned satisfaction. Indeed, perhaps she had been doing so for a long time now. What a harrowing thought that was. By remaining in this farce of an *affaire,* had he simply been making both of them miserable?

There came a time, he knew, in every sexual liaison, when things either shifted to something deeper, or they did not. And once that point was reached, the days and months which followed would bring nothing but resentment and recrimination. Nash did not want anything deeper, and the resentment — well, its taste was already old and bitter. Yes, with Lisette — as with every other lover he had ever taken — the time had come.

After catching his breath, he rolled to one side and dragged an arm over his eyes to shut out the feeble lamplight. Lisette did not turn down the wick as was her habit, but instead sat up a little in bed, her weight shifting on the mattress. For a long, expectant moment, there was nothing but the sound of his breathing in the room.

"Did you play tonight?" she finally asked. "Was it . . . grim?"

"No," he said. "I stayed home."

The truth was, he had not sat down at a card table in days. He had not been to White's, nor to any of the more nefarious hells he frequented — places crawling with

181

sharks and blacklegs of every ilk. Places which ordinarily would not have given him pause. But of late he'd had no taste for the sport — and he knew better than to gamble when his edge was off. Sharpers were naught but carnivores; they cut the weak from the crowd, and gutted them. None knew this better than he.

"I used to know, Nash, when you came to bed whether you had won or lost." Her voice held a hard edge. "Tonight you fucked me as if you had lost."

"Lisette, for God's sake," he grunted. "Not tonight."

"Am I wrong, Nash," she finally said, "in thinking you have tired of my favors?"

He could hear her picking at the coverlet with her fingernail, almost as a child might pick at a scab. She meant to make them both bleed. He could feel it. And peace meant to elude him yet again. Well, perhaps he deserved no better.

Resigned to his fate, Nash rolled from the bed and went to the window, which overlooked Henrietta Street. He braced his hands wide on the window frame, and stared out into the night. The bells of St. Paul's were tolling the hour, sounding as if they were swathed in cottonwool. The fog had rolled in so cold and so dense, one could probably swim through Covent Garden, and the streetlamps seemed no more than oily yellow smears.

"Nash, I have been thinking," said Lisette from behind him. "We . . . we could have another girl again, could we not? Just for a while. Helen Manders has enormous breasts — and not a scruple to her name, so far as bed sport goes."

Nash had thrown up the window, and was drawing the cool, acrid air into his lungs in some hope that it would clear his mind. "I do not think so, Lisette."

"But she is playing Titania this run," Lisette cajoled. "Perhaps she would even wear her costume. She looks very fetching as a fairy, I do assure you."

"No, not Helen," he said. "She is not the answer."

"Then another man, Nash, if you wish," she suggested, her voice low and seductive. "Would you like that? Would you? I could be a very bad girl, and afterwards — why, you could punish me. What of Tony? He is very handsome. I should fancy a go at him, I think."

He whirled about at the window, disgusted by her suggestions. "Good Lord, don't bring Tony into this," he snapped. "The man has trouble enough as it is — and a wife, too, I would remind you."

Lisette rolled her eyes. "Oh, God, Nash!" she said. "Must you be so frightfully conventional? I do not care if he has a wife — and I can assure you that *he* does not care. Not if all I hear is true."

"Well, he bloody well ought to care," said Nash. "Why? What have you heard?"

Lisette smiled up at him from the bed. "Come back to bed, Nash," she purred. "Come back and let me have you again, *hmm?* This time, the way *I* like it. And then perhaps I'll answer your question."

Nash turned back again, and dragged a hand through his hair. "No, I . . . I have to go, Lisette."

"Nash!" she chided. "It is three in the morning."

"I have to go," he muttered, snatching up his shirt.

Lisette crushed her fists into the bedcovers. "Damn it, Nash!" she said. "I grow weary of this . . . this lackluster, halfhearted *affaire.*"

"My apologies," he managed, shaking the wrinkles from his coat. "You are perfectly right."

"Nash, it is like this," she began, her voice now edged with anger. "I have had enough. And, I suspect, you have, too. I am leaving you for Lord Cuthert. Do you hear me? I am perfectly serious."

Nash was nodding as he drew on his trousers. "Cuthert, yes," he muttered. "By all means."

"And I shall be out by tomorrow, Nash," she screeched, "if you don't say *something* which will make me wish to stay!"

Nash shoved his arms through his waistcoat and looked at her blankly. "He's a nice chap, Cuthert — isn't he?" he answered. "I shouldn't wish you unhappy, Lisette. I just — well, I just wish you out of my life. And I out of yours, of course."

Honesty, it seemed, was not the best policy. Lisette's expression stiffened to one of utter rage. "Oh, God, how I hate you!" she shrieked, snatching up the decanter of red wine. "I hate you utterly! Completely!"

Her aim was true, but at that very instant, Nash had knelt to find his stockings. The spray of shattering glass just above his head brought him up again. He looked over his shoulder to see the madeira running blood-red down the ivory silk walls.

He stared at the mess in stupefaction for a moment. "Didn't that decanter match the goblets you broke last week?" he finally asked.

"Yes," she hissed, sending the last glass

crashing into the mirror. "And look! Now you've a matched set!"

CHAPTER SIX:
A SULTRY
AFTERNOON
IN WAPPING

It was just a short visit to the new St. Katharine's Docks, Xanthia had decided. A little stroll upriver, not even half a mile. Modern times were coming to Wapping, by way of improved cranes, deeper basins, and expansive, well-lit warehousing. And Neville Shipping, Xanthia had vowed, was to be at the vanguard. With that logic, three months earlier she had plunked down a king's ransom in a preconstruction leasing arrangement for twelve thousand square feet of warehouse space. The negotiations had been long and hard, but the deal had at last been struck. Today had been her first opportunity to inspect the progress of the construction.

Mr. Kemble, of course, had protested her going. But there was nothing as yet which Xanthia required protection *from,* and she told him so. So she left him in the upstairs office with a crate of old manifests, which had been dumped beside the extra desk Mr. Bakely had found for him, then she went downstairs to find Gareth Lloyd. They could not have been away more than two hours, she would have sworn, but the moment they stepped from Wapping High Street back into Neville's dim, dingy counting house, everything had gone topsy-turvy. The first hint was the sour, chalky smell which assailed her nostrils.

"Good God," said Lloyd. His feet were frozen to the threshold as his eyes roamed the room.

Beside him, Xanthia could only stare. Their six clerks were cowering in one corner. Mr. Bakely rushed forward, wringing his hands, his glasses hanging off the tip of his nose. "I tried to stop him, Miss Neville," he said in a low, wretched voice. "I told him it just *would not do!* But he wouldn't hear of it!"

Xanthia stepped farther into the room. "Mr. George," she began, using the name they had agreed upon. "What, pray, is the meaning of this . . . this *disorder* in my counting house?"

In the distant corner, Kemble's head whipped around, and his face lit with pleasure. He swished his way around the clump of desks and cabinets. "I call it *pale*

188

melon," he said almost gleefully. "The Duchess of Devonshire painted her drawing room in it last spring — she is thought all the rage, you know — and now it is all the rage in Mayfair."

Gareth Lloyd was still staring at the two workmen on ladders who were slathering the wall with a pinkish orange paint. Three of the tall desks had been covered in paint-spattered Holland-cloth, and the others shoved to one side, leaving the clerks looking like sheep cornered in a pen. At the back windows, another pair of men dressed in stiff black suits were unrolling bolts of vivid fabric and holding them up to the windows in animated discussion about color and contrast.

"That's Phillipe and his assistant," said Kemble. "From the mercer's over in Fenchurch. After all, why pay Bond Street prices? I mean, it *is* just a counting house."

"Indeed, Mr. George, this is *just a counting house,*" Xanthia echoed angrily. "And one which lives and dies by its profit and loss statement each month. We cannot possibly justify such an expense."

Mr. Kemble seemed to draw himself up three inches. "Madam, everyone must decorate!" he pronounced. "Ugliness is so depressing. So tiring. How can these people be expected to work under such conditions?"

Just then, a loud fist sounded on the open door behind Xanthia. "Oy, Georgie!" cried the caller from the doorstep. "We're 'ere wiv 'is green carpet. Wot yer want done wiv it?"

"It is called *summer celery,* Mr. Hamm!" Kemble called through the door.

Xanthia turned to see two burly men outside, and a dray cart in the street beyond. "A — a *carpet?*" she managed.

Mr. Kemble gave her a doting smile, and lightly patted her arm. "Do not fret, dear girl," he whispered. "My friend Max will pay for this. And then the place will look *so* much brighter, will it not? So much more inviting, and — dare I say it? — yes, *cheerful.* And cheer is so important in one's daily surroundings, do you not think?"

"I . . ." Xanthia swallowed hard. "I am sure I do not know."

Gareth Lloyd was surveying the situation with obvious disgust. "Well, I can tell you what *I* should like to know," he grumbled. "I should like to know what kind of — of *personal secretary* calls his employer 'dear girl.' And I would venture to say further, Mr. George, that you are about to find yourself unemployed — though why you were ever hired to begin with is quite beyond me."

Lloyd vanished up the stairs, his feet thundering on the steps. He had been opposed to Kemble's presence from the outset and clearly thought Xanthia had lost her mind.

Kemble just smiled and patted Xanthia again. "My dear, is your Mr. Lloyd always this testy? Oh, never mind! I am sure he'll come round — especially when he sees the lavender silk moiré I'm going to hang upstairs."

Just then, another knock sounded.

"Good Lord, what now?" Xanthia spun around again.

To her shock, the Marquess of Nash stood on the doorstep. Behind him, Mr. Hamm and his minion were wrestling the rolled carpet from their cart. Kemble vanished into the depths of the room. Xanthia felt faintly unsteady. "Lord Nash," she managed to say. "What on earth?"

Nash had his hat in his hand. "I was just in the neighborhood," he said. "I thought I should like to see precisely what a 'grimy little office' in Wapping looks like. May I come in?"

Xanthia stood aside. "You may as well," she said. "Everyone else has."

Kemble, however, had leapt to attention, albeit at a distance. He was rearranging the Holland-covers for the painters, but Xanthia could sense that the man was watching Nash from one eye, quivering like a bird dog on point. Even the cowed clerks were peeking up from their ledgers.

Nash let his gaze drift round the large room. "You are redecorating, I see."

"There is no *re-* to it." In the back of the room, Kemble snapped out the next cover like a freshly starched bedsheet. "This place has always been a nightmare. Mustard-colored walls, fly-specked windows, oily, unfinished floors — utterly depressing."

Xanthia flashed a muted smile in Nash's direction. "Some of our servants are opinionated," she murmured.

"Miss Neville, shall I bring up tea now?" Kemble was on his knees, carefully tucking the cloth around the edges of a desk. "And kindly tell Mr. Lloyd I need his opinion on this cabbage-rose pattern for the curtains, if he would be so good as to come back down."

Xanthia blinked uncertainly. "Mr. George, I do not think Lloyd will much care wh—"

"Nonetheless," Kemble interjected. "I wish him to come *down.*"

Suddenly Xanthia understood. Kemble

wanted her to take Lord Nash upstairs. Alone. Which was perfectly logical, really. There could be but two reasons for Nash's visit — and neither could be discussed in front of the staff. As to Nash, he had drifted off to examine a set of Hogarth prints, which had been cheaply framed and badly hung on the wall by the door.

Kemble snatched a ledger from Mr. Bakely's desk. "And Miss Neville, pray take this with you as you go."

Bakely opened his mouth to protest, and Kemble stepped discreetly on his toe. But when Kemble made no move to bring her the ledger, Xanthia crossed the room a little impatiently and snatched it from his hand. "My goodness, aren't you a fast worker!" he murmured. "I stand in awe."

"Thank you," she murmured, stepping away. "Tea would be delightful."

"Right away, ma'am,"

"Oh, and Mr. George?" she said quietly.

"Yes, Miss Neville?"

"The *pale melon* must go," she said. "I am sorry, but I cannot bear it. And no rug. About that, I am adamant. We have too many muddy boots in and out of here. It would soon be ruined."

Kemble's eyes sparked with temper. "And the draperies?"

"You and Lloyd must decide," she answered. "But no ruffles. No fluff. No frill. Do we understand one another?"

"Indeed not," he said huffily. "But the choices are yours to make."

Exasperated, Xanthia returned to the door, and to her unexpected guest. "Will you come up to my luxuriously appointed office, Lord Nash?" she asked dryly. "I have a view of St. Savior's Docks which will simply take your breath away."

"And God knows I love nothing so much as the sight of a picturesque dockyard," said Nash. "Lead on, Macduff."

"*Lay* on," Xanthia corrected, starting up the stairs.

"I beg your pardon?"

"It is *'Lay on, Macduff,'*" she said. "Macbeth is inviting Macduff to fight him. To come forward and attack. Really, Lord Nash, did you not learn your Shakespeare properly at Eton?"

"I'm afraid I have never learnt it at all," said Nash quietly.

She glanced over her shoulder. "I beg your pardon?"

"I was struggling to learn English when the boys my age were at Eton," he said. "I do not think I would have quite fit in."

Something in his tone made Xanthia

falter. And again, there was that sudden flash of understanding; of kinship. Yes, she knew too well what he felt. "Forgive me," she said. "I — I meant only to tease you, not to insult you."

"No insult is taken," said Nash. "I make every effort to look the part of a proper British nobleman, Miss Neville, but it is all a bit of a ruse, you see. Deep down, I am just rough-elbowed, Continental riffraff."

Xanthia managed a grin. "Continental riffraff?" she said. "That sounds exciting."

He laughed and leaned past her to open the door.

"Oh, no, the next one, please," she said. "That door leads to our rather untidy storage room. I should die of embarrassment were you to see it."

Lord Nash smiled and opened the next door. Behind his desk, Gareth Lloyd jerked to his feet. Quickly, Xanthia made the introductions, then instructed Lloyd to go downstairs and attend to the draperies. A few heated words ensued; but in the end, Lloyd stomped back down the stairs.

Suddenly, Xanthia found herself alone with Nash. It was dashed unnerving, too, when she recalled her rather risqué behavior by the river. What must the man think of her?

Nash was prowling about the untidy work space, which now held three desks, the broken crate, a long worktable, and the map which covered one wall. There were also two armchairs and a small tea table by the cold, clean-swept hearth.

"Won't you sit down?" she asked politely.

"Not until I have seen your glorious view." Nash was still holding his hat.

"Do forgive the staff, my lord." Xanthia took the hat and laid it on her desk. "They are not especially skilled in the art of office etiquette." Then she led him to the deep casement window. "There," she said, pointing to the opposite shore. "That is Rotherhithe Wall, and the entrance to St. Savior's. And you see Mill Stairs, just there? And the stave yard, and the timber yard? Oh, and that building, I believe, was the cooperage — before the roof fell and the rats moved in."

"Good Lord."

"And, of course, beneath it all, is the Thames, churning with mud and God only knows what else," she finished. "Scenic, is it not?"

Nash leaned close; so close, she could feel the heat of him against her shoulder. She felt her discomfiture — and her pulse — ratchet up. "Utterly idyllic," he answered. "I wonder you get any work done."

She laughed and tried to turn from the window. But Nash did not give way. "And I also wonder," he murmured, his eyes roaming her face, "— yes, I wonder what the devil possessed me to come down here."

For an instant, Xanthia couldn't catch her breath. When she finally did, it was tinged with his warm, deeply masculine scent. "Perhaps you've something you wish shipped?" she said with specious cheer. "You may, of course, trust all your transportation needs to Neville's. We are the very best in the business."

The strange intimacy was broken. Nash chuckled, and let her pass. "I shall remember that, my dear, when next I need something sent to — oh, where *do* you go, anyway?"

"To hell and back, Lord Nash, if there's money to be made." She motioned him to the chairs by the hearth. "But whatever it is you've come for, you may as well have tea first."

Her timing was excellent. One of the clerks rapped softly on the door, then shouldered his way through with the battered old pewter tea service. "That Mr. George fellow is upset we haven't any cakes, ma'am," he said. "I'm to go up to the bakery and fetch some."

Xanthia refused the cakes and sent him out again. She poured tea, and she and Nash exchanged opinions about the weather. Nash thought it might rain. She did not.

It felt so strange to discuss such mundane things after all that had passed between them. Xanthia knew she should concentrate on what de Vendenheim had asked of her, but she could not get past the fact that Nash was *here* — in her office, prowling around like a caged panther and interjecting himself into her ordinary world in a way which sent her senses reeling.

The man was the stuff of female fantasies; a man who made one think of breathless sighs and tangled sheets, not the sort of man who turned up for tea in the middle of one's workday afternoon. But he was here, and he was behaving with restrained civility — though his dark, too-long hair and obsidian eyes made him look just a little untamed. She let her eyes drift over his snug breeches and tall, black Hessians, which emphasized his height and lean musculature. His riding coat was close-fitted across a pair of fine, broad shoulders, and tailored with a decidedly Continental cut.

Good manners took over and kept Xanthia

from staring at him as pointedly and as intently as she might have wished. "You rode, I collect?"

"Yes, I wished to take the air," he said.

She laughed. "In Wapping?" she asked. "Oh, never mind! Tell me, my lord, of your background. Was English not your mother tongue?"

He smiled self-deprecatingly. "No, not *my* mother's," he agreed. "She despised England and everything in it, I think."

"Ah," said Xanthia. "Where was she from? The Continent, I daresay, with that sort of attitude."

He laughed again. "Yes, you are quite right," he admitted. "She was from Montenegro. Do you know it?"

Xanthia nodded. "Oh, indeed," she answered, setting down her cup and saucer. "It is a breathtakingly beautiful country, or so I'm told. I can imagine one might miss it a great deal."

"You cannot imagine how truly lovely it is, Miss Neville, until you have seen it," he answered. "The vivid blue of the Adriatic set against a backdrop of dark, richly forested mountains. As a child, I thought it an almost magical place."

"You grew up there?"

The marquess shrugged. "Mother was a

bit of a vagabond," he said. "She was of Russian descent on one side, and she moved in only the best circles. We traveled incessantly. Vienna. Prague. St. Petersburg. But if we had a home — yes, it was Montenegro."

"And Montenegro is to the north of" — Deliberately, she furrowed her brow — "yes, Albania, correct? And Greece?"

Nash smiled. "I suppose that in your line of work, one must have a good sense of geography."

"Indeed," she agreed. "And of politics, too. For example, we are not always able to refit in Athens when we might otherwise prefer to do so. Revolution can be a dreadful inconvenience to commerce."

"I can assure you, my dear, that no one is more inconvenienced by the revolution than the Greeks themselves," he said quietly. "But in the end, they will prevail."

"Is that your wish?" she asked lightly.

Nash visibly stiffened. "I am no friend to the Turks," he admitted. "My family has been fighting them for centuries. For what little it is worth, yes, by God, I hope the Greeks run the Aegean red with Turkish blood."

Xanthia had struck a nerve, it seemed. It would be unwise to press this line of conversation. "Do you miss your homeland greatly?"

Nash nodded when she lifted the teapot. "I did miss it quite desperately, at first," he answered, as she refreshed his cup. "But the war was raging, and my father had inherited an English title. He had responsibilities here."

"Your line had not been expected to inherit?" she asked.

Nash shook his head. "By no means," he said. "My brother and I were promised from childhood to Czar Peter — for his Imperial Guard — when we came of age. That was to have been our destiny, you see. But then Father's brother and nephew died in a yachting accident" — here, he lifted his hands in a remarkably Continental gesture — "and destiny changed her mind, I suppose, and sent us to Brierwood, the family seat in Hampshire."

Xanthia tried to relax in her chair. *Hampshire.* The man who had been murdered had been traveling through Hampshire. "How exciting it must have been for you," she managed. "What was it like to first see your family estate and know that one day it would all be yours?"

"At the time, I was not the heir." He paused to sip politely from his tea. "My brother Petar was the elder. Regrettably, he died young."

This, Xanthia had not heard. "I am so sorry," she said. "I gather your mother disliked England on sight?"

Nash smiled sardonically. "My mother remained in Hampshire but a short while, then chose to return to her old life. My father . . . well, things had been turbulent. I think by then he was not sorry to see her go."

"How sad that sounds," said Xanthia.

Nash shrugged as if it scarcely mattered. "My father had a new life; a life of wealth and English privilege," he said. "And English duty. But those things meant nothing to her; she was cut off from her world. She said she could not breathe here. So she left — and died shortly thereafter."

Xanthia did not miss the remorse in his voice. "How tragic," she murmured. "But it was no one's fault, was it?"

Nash lifted one eyebrow. "No, no one's fault," he answered, setting down his teacup. "Tell me, Miss Neville how does your business go on?"

Xanthia glanced at him across the table. Clearly the discussion of his family was at an end, too. "Quite well, I thank you," she said. "We have increased our sailings by thirty-five percent, and our profits by almost ten since relocating."

"Good Lord." He shot her a look of surprise. "You must be minting money in the cellars and buying ships at a prodigious rate."

Xanthia inclined her head in agreement. "Yet another reason for being here," she said. "One can buy — or lease — almost anything easily and quickly."

"And yet with all this expenditure of capital, you are still turning a huge profit?" he said. "I wonder you did not relocate sooner."

Xanthia cut her gaze toward the window and the thronging river beyond. She tried to focus not on the deep, seductive rumble of Lord Nash's voice, but on the task de Vendenheim had laid before her. She *had* to know if he was guilty. She could not delay — for any number of reasons.

"Unfortunately, London has its disadvantages, too," she finally said. "Where there is opportunity, Lord Nash, there is always danger. Is that not an old Chinese proverb?"

"Danger? Of what sort?"

She smiled tightly. "Customs men are everywhere, for example," she said. "And they are sticklers for the letter of the law."

He looked at her darkly. "Miss Neville, you shock me."

"Oh, come now, Nash," she said. "Have you never drunk untaxed brandy?"

"God, no," he said with a faint shudder. "I do not drink the stuff at all."

She looked at him in mild surprise. "What, pray, do you drink?"

He hesitated. "The occasional glass of red wine," he said. "And *okhotnichya*."

Xanthia furrowed her brow. "What is that?"

He smiled faintly. "A spirit made of rye."

"Rye?" Xanthia wrinkled her nose. "Like a . . . what do the Russians call it? Like a vodka?"

He set his head to one side and studied at her. "Yes, a strong vodka," he said. "You know it?"

Xanthia laughed. "Lord Nash, if it can be bottled or barreled, I have likely heard of it — and probably transported it," she said. "I also know it is not a libation for the faint of heart."

He laughed, a rich but faintly sardonic sound. "Deceivingly, Miss Neville, the word *vodka* means 'little water,' " he said. "Russians are masters of the understatement."

"And how is *okhotnichya* different from vodka?"

"*Okhotnichya* means the spirits were distilled with strong herbs," he explained.

"Like cloves and citrus peel — or even anise."

"Anise?" said Xanthia sharply. "Like absinthe?"

Lord Nash shot her a strange look. "Ah, the French vice," he said. "Surely, Miss Neville, you do not partake? It is a dangerous business."

She shook her head. "I've never seen it," she admitted. "But I daresay you have."

He smiled faintly. "Yes, a time or two, in my misspent youth," he confessed. Then his voice seemed to drop another octave. "But taken to excess, my dear, absinthe is a poison and a convulsant. I am the sort of man who prefers always to indulge my vices to excess — and if someone is having convulsions, I prefer it to be of the more pleasurable sort."

Swiftly, she looked away. There was no mistaking the heat in his words, and if his intent was to make her heart flutter and her stomach bottom out, he had succeeded. Dear heaven! It was all too easy to imagine the sort of vices Lord Nash would enjoy to excess — and with a connoisseur's skill, too, she did not doubt. Somehow, Xanthia found the grace to return her gaze to his, and to feign a mischievous smile.

"Your overly indulged vices aside, my lord,

might I assume that your vodka always bears a customs stamp?" she teased. "And what of your cheroots? Your tobacconist imports his goods from where? Virginia? North Carolina? And he dutifully pays his taxes, does he not?"

Nash looked faintly chagrined. "Actually, I get my vodka through a rather disreputable fellow in Whitechapel, and my cheroots by courier from Seville," he said. "I am very particular as to the taste."

"Ah!" said Xanthia. "Indeed you must be. Spanish tobacco comes mostly from Cuba, or Venezuela. *Tut tut,* Nash! I do not think the King would approve."

"Painting me a sinner and a tax cheat, are you, my dear?" he asked. "Really, what is a little untaxed tobacco? And vodka — it can scarce be had here, taxed or otherwise. But you, Miss Neville, are talking of doing something a good deal more dangerous."

"I did not say I did such things, but merely that I know how they are done." Driven by restless anxiety, Xanthia had left her chair to roam about the room. "It is not difficult, Nash, to circumvent a customs agent, or even to take on contraband cargo in a foreign port. A little grease to the right palm is usually sufficient — but one must choose that palm with great care. It is no business for amateurs."

He coughed discreetly. "My dear, you frighten me," he said.

But Xanthia could see she that she did not. Not really. There was a pensive light in Nash's eyes, but whether from ordinary curiosity or something more speculative, she could not say.

In any case, she had pushed this business far enough. Were Nash the man de Vendenheim thought him, another word might kindle suspicion. She whirled about and laughed lightly. "But why are we speaking of this nonsense?" she said. "It must bore you. Tell me, Nash, why did you really come here this afternoon? Not, I think, to discuss customs agents?"

As etiquette required, he, too, had risen. "I just wished to see this for myself," he said, making an expansive gesture about the room.

Xanthia opened her hands. "See what?" she demanded. "A woman doing an honest day's work? Have you no servants to watch, my lord?"

He stepped closer and studied her from beneath his hawkish black brows. "I think you have the makings of a shrew, Miss Neville."

"Thank you." She smiled. "I thought

perhaps you were here to take me up on my offer."

He hesitated, as if surprised she had mentioned it again. "I am afraid not, my dear."

"Well," she said briskly, going to the map on the wall, "then I shan't humiliate myself by repeating it."

"Oh, but I wish you would," he returned in his deep, resonating voice. "Nothing feeds a man's psyche like a beautiful woman pleading for his sexual favors."

Xanthia pulled out one of the yellow pins — the *Mae Rose* — and stabbed it a half inch nearer the Straits of Gibraltar. "I am not pleading, Nash," she said coolly. "Nor am I particularly beautiful —"

"No, not in any conventional way," he interjected.

Bloody hell. She liked him all the better for his honesty. "— and if you want me, Nash," she managed to continue, "then *you* will be the next to make an offer. I have no wish to continue flinging myself at a man who will let conventional notions about breeding and conduct and — and *virginity* get in the way of what ought to be perfectly healthy appetites."

Xanthia was still moving pins, sometimes just for the satisfaction of stabbing them into the wall again. She did not realize how close Nash was until she felt the heat of his body behind her. "Do you know," he said, his breath stirring the hair near her ear, "I believe I am done with conversing."

Caught in midstab, Xanthia's arm froze. At once, she felt the heat of his breath on her neck. Felt his warm hands slide around her waist. "Miss Neville," he murmured, "how you do intrigue me." Then his lips settled against the turn of her neck, searing and sure.

"Umm." It was an exhalation of pure pleasure.

Nash never lifted his mouth from her flesh, though it was only her throat, her ear, then her jaw he kissed. But when his mouth brushed over the pulse point beneath her ear, Xanthia melted. She let the pin in her hand go skittering across the floor and let her body sag backward against the hard wall of Nash's chest. Her head fell back onto his shoulder, giving him every opportunity to touch her.

His hands moved restlessly over her, stroking her waist, her ribs, then moving higher. He palmed the weight of her breasts, then lightly thumbed her nipples, which were already peaked with desire. In the slanting afternoon light, neither spoke — fearing, perhaps, to destroy the strange spell. Instead, he still nuzzled her throat, planting feverish kisses down the length, all the way to her shoulder whilst her breath ratcheted ever higher.

At last, when he touched her earlobe with the warm tip of his tongue, a sigh escaped her lips. In response, Nash drew a hitching breath and set one wide palm over her belly as the other slid lower. And lower — until Xanthia wished desperately to tear away her clothes, to give him free rein. To feel the heat and passion of his mouth in other, more secret, places.

Apparently, they were of a mind. Xanthia shivered when cool air breezed over her calves. Inch by inch, Nash was fisting up one side of her skirts, sending them slithering over her knee and up her thigh. A tremble of raw desire ran through her then, bone-deep and eviscerating.

Xanthia set her hands flat against the map, steadying herself. And then his mouth was on the nape of her neck, biting just hard enough to heighten her awareness. And his hand — *oh, God, his hand.* The froth of her petticoat and the fine lawn of her drawers was no barrier. Already Nash was sliding one finger back and forth in her wet, silken heat. The man was a master, wicked and tormenting as he twisted the fine thread of her desire to the breaking point.

Xanthia's breath began to hitch with little gasps of pleasure. Nash sensed her need, easing his finger higher, stroking and teasing, ever so lightly brushing the swollen nub of her desire. As the intensity heightened, she collapsed fully against the wall, setting her feverish cheek against the chill of the map, her hands planted wide. She was trapped against the wall by his weight, the hard ridge of his cock pressing firmly and insistently into the cleft of her backside.

"God," he rasped against her neck. "Good God, what I would not give to rip off those drawers and lift you onto —"

But it was too late. Xanthia's hitching breath had become a soft, rhythmic sob. She could not wait. He was drawing her, making her throb and ache and pulse with need. Her entire being convulsed. She raked her hand wide, sending more pins scattering across the floor. Then, flat against the wall, with his hand working her into madness, Xanthia felt the world spin away. Felt the grime and grit and mustard yellow paint of her tawdry office whirl about her, then explode into shards of white light. The trembling rocked her, and washed over her, leaving everything pure and perfect in its wake.

When she came back to herself, still trembling, Nash had turned her in his arms, and was swallowing her gasping breath with his kisses. "Shush, shush," he crooned, his mouth stroking over her brow bone. "Careful, love."

Then it struck her. *The office. The staff. Good God, Gareth.*

Xanthia tried to nod, but Nash chose that moment to ignore his own advice and take her mouth on a tormented groan. Still greedy, she opened to him at once, and felt his tongue slide deep, plumbing the secrets of her mouth. He twisted his fist in her skirts again, and held her to him as if he were a drowning man and she his only hope. Over and over he kissed her, his nostrils wide, his breath rough, and one hand firmly grasping her derrière. Lifting her body firmly to his, he tore his mouth away, his eyes filled with something which looked like a mix of chagrin and regret.

Unable to look at him, Xanthia fell against him, and set her forehead to his shoulder. "I thought you were a sybarite, my lord," she whispered. "I understood you thought only of your own pleasure."

"It was enough of a pleasure, my dear, simply to watch you," he murmured into her hair.

"Liar," she said on a spurt of laughter. And somehow, the embarrassment was over. She lifted her head, and held his gaze. "I think I should quite like to make love with a sybarite. To . . . be caressed by the hands of a man bent only on his pleasure — and mine."

"Are you inviting?" He whispered the words into her ear.

Xanthia swallowed again, and squeezed her eyes shut. "No," she rasped. "I — I shan't ask again, Nash. You know what I want."

He smiled. "I obviously know what you need," he admitted, tucking a wayward lock of hair behind her ear. "Though whether or not it is what you ought to *have* remains un—"

There was a sharp knock at the door.

They burst apart like the conspirators they were. Gareth Lloyd entered and dropped a stack of green baize account books onto his desk. He said nothing to Nash, who had returned to the window to stare at the river below. With a stiff nod to Xanthia, Gareth went to the map and frowned at it. "I have sent for your carriage, Zee," he said without looking at her. "Otherwise, you will be late."

Xanthia went to her desk, and ran a finger

down her calendar. "Oh, Lord!" she said. "My fitting for Lady Cartselle's masque! What is the time?"

"Half past three."

Nash turned from the window. "You mean to attend Lady Cartselle's masque next week?"

Xanthia was shoving papers into her bulging leather satchel. "Yes, Lady Louisa fancies herself desperately in love with Cartselle's heir." She jerked her head up. "Why? Shall you go?"

Nash gave a muted smile. "I never attend such larks," he admitted. "But forgive me, Miss Neville. I am now detaining you from your work." He turned and bowed stiffly in Gareth's direction. "Mr. Lloyd, it was a pleasure."

Gareth grunted at him dismissively. He was picking the yellow pins from the floor where Xanthia had dropped them. Almost ruthlessly, he began jamming them into the Arabian Sea, as if Neville's had a whole fleet positioned strategically off the coast of India.

Nash took his hat from Xanthia's desk. "Good afternoon, my dear," he said quietly. "And thank you again for the lovely . . . view."

The door closed quietly behind him, leaving a terrible emptiness in the room.

Gareth's posture was rigid, a sure sign of his temper. At last he turned from the map and returned to his desk.

"Are we declaring war on Bombay?" she asked, her voice light.

Something inside him seemed to snap. "God damn it, Xanthia!" He picked up one of the ledgers and slammed it so hard pages flew. A shock of heavy gold hair had fallen forward, shadowing his face. "Just what do you think you are doing? *What?*"

"I beg your pardon," she said, stalking toward the desk. "To what are you referring?"

"To your acting like a common gutter slut," he snapped. "For God's sake, do you know who that man is?"

Before she knew what she was doing, Xanthia had drawn back her arm and slapped him full through the face. "Yes, I know who he is." Her voice was low and tremulous. "How *dare* you, Gareth? How dare you speak to me that way?"

"You know why I dare." His words were laced with pain. "Because you should be *mine*, Xanthia. And you know it."

Xanthia leaned over his desk. "So let me understand this — if I allow you certain liberties, I am 'yours,' " she said. "But if I allow them to another man, then I am a slut? Have I fully grasped your meaning, Gareth?"

He tore his gaze from hers and looked away. She was horrified to see the mark her hand had left. "I did not call you a slut, Zee," he whispered. "I said that — or what I meant was —"

"Never mind what you meant."

Xanthia returned to her desk and hefted the stuffed satchel from her chair. "And by the way, Gareth, I had reason to believe that Lord Nash might require our services. This was business — at least it began that way. And if it ends as something else, then . . . then it really is none of your business, is it?"

He looked at her with hurt in his eyes. "No," he said quietly. "No, apparently it is not."

"Then I will wish you good day, Gareth," she said. "I am sorry I struck you. It was no more excusable than your words, and I am ashamed, as I hope you are."

With that, Xanthia pushed through the door and went down the stairs. Her entire body seemed to tremble with repressed emotion. Below, the painters were still at work — a pale yellow this time. The clerks had their heads down, pens *skritch-skritching* diligently across their desks, and Mr. Kemble was nowhere to be seen. She burst out into the last golden light of afternoon, and climbed into the waiting carriage, strangely blinking back tears.

Dear God, she was so angry and confused! She did not want trouble with Gareth, nor did she wish to hurt him. So often she wished that she *did* love him, that she loved him enough to be what he wanted her to be — a benevolent wife and mother, not just a businesswoman with a bad temper. But she did not love him enough, and it was a shame. He was a good man. A shrewd business partner. And perhaps, seen through his eyes, what she had just done was quite beyond the pale. She pondered her alternatives as the driver cracked his whip, jerking the carriage into motion.

No, she still did not mean to tell Gareth of Lord de Vendenheim's suspicions. There was no reason to blacken Lord Nash's name when he mightn't be guilty of anything worse than leading a hedonistic life. And he was not guilty of worse. She was suddenly, overwhelmingly, certain.

Yes, Nash possessed a fondness for his homeland. He was filled with nationalistic pride. But were those not honorable things? He wished fervently that the Greeks would prevail in their struggle — as did the overwhelming majority of the English people. He was an unrepentant gambler and libertine — and though he apparently raised decadence to an art form, it was a behavior not unusual in London.

But was he a traitor to his adopted country? No. He had shown no interest whatsoever in rising to her bait — and she had offered it most generously. Oh, she had piqued his interest, yes, but it had been interest in *her,* she could have sworn. Xanthia had watched his mind mulling through it. He had been studying her face. Weighing her nature. Wondering if he dared take her up on her offer.

If anything more nefarious than that had crossed Lord Nash's mind, then Xanthia was not the judge of character she believed herself — and she had staked half her family's fortune on her ability to do just that. But would *de Vendenheim* believe her?

No. He would not. Indeed, he could scarce afford to. The Home Office had too much at stake. And that left but one possibility: Xanthia could find proof of Nash's innocence. If she had imagined it possible to find evidence of his guilt, why was not the opposite possible? Or was she just a fool? Had she simply allowed his lips and his touch and his whispered words to addle her brain?

Lord, surely not? Xanthia collapsed against the plush banquette of Kieran's carriage. Suddenly, it all seemed too much. She was utterly exhausted. She had a business to run; she did not have time for a *life.* Certainly she had no time for de Vendenheim's intrigues. And now she had not just her costume fitting to survive, for this was the dreaded Wednesday — which meant she and Kieran must take Lady Louisa to Almack's tonight.

Cursing men in general, Nash in particular, and praying Almack's would soon be struck by lightning, Xanthia let her eyes drop shut and her fatigue and her worry and the rhythm of the rocking carriage lull her into a fretful sleep.

CHAPTER SEVEN:
A FLAP
IN PARK LANE

"There's been a letter from Swann, my lord." Gibbons was brushing — well, thrashing, actually — the previous evening's frock coat at Nash's bedchamber window. "I am afraid the news is not good."

Still in his dressing gown and slippers, Nash looked up from his newspaper. "Lord, what now?"

"It is his mother," said Gibbons, energetically flapping the coat out the open window.

"I know about his mother," Nash snapped. "Good God, man — what are you doing to my coat?"

Gibbons straightened up, bumping his head on the window frame. "Making a futile attempt to dispel the stench of tobacco smoke and cheap *eau de toilette*," he said over his shoulder. "It utterly *reeks,* my lord. Where in God's name did you go last night?"

Nash gave a disgusted grunt. "Played

macao with Struthers at some Soho hell-hole," he answered, returning his gaze to the paper. "Now stop waving my coat at Hyde Park before you spook a horse."

"My lord, it *stinks*."

"Take it down to the butler's pantry."

Gibbons shot him a testy look. "I cannot," he said. "Agnes has asthma. If I take it below-stairs, she'll wheeze for a week."

Nash put the paper down with a crush. "Just how long, Gibbons, have you been brushing soiled clothes in my bedchamber?" he complained. "And precisely when did my servants become masters and I their slave?"

Gibbons snatched the coat back inside. "Very well, my lord," he responded. "If you cannot spare a thought for poor Agnes, then I shall take it down at once."

"Oh, for God's sake!" Nash waved his hand in obviation. "I don't mean it. You know I do not. I'm just . . . out of sorts."

Gibbons looked inordinately self-satisfied. "I know, my lord," he said more solicitously. "We've all noticed it."

"Aye, and gossiped about it no end, too, I daresay," muttered Nash, snapping his paper back into form. "Now what were you saying about a letter?"

"She died," said Gibbons.

Nash felt another burst of impatience. "*Who* died?"

"Swann's *mother*." Gibbons frowned censoriously. "He's to be away at least another se'night, arranging the funeral and letting the cottage. He sends his profuse apologies and hopes you have no urgent need for his services."

Nash scowled down at his coffee. The truth was, he could do without Swann for another week though he did not like it. He very much wished to know what the Comtesse de Montignac was up to nowadays, but he had not thought to ask Swann to set up a meeting before leaving town. Then there was the paperwork on his desk, which was fast becoming a dangerously teetering pile.

Still, a mother's death was a hard thing at any age, and presumably Swann cared for his mother as much as Nash had cared for his — which was to say, quite a lot. Like many women too beautiful for their own good, his mother had been at times cruel, and always selfish, but he had loved her. Her death had marked the end of his innocence and the beginning of his new life. Life as the English heir. Life without Petar. Until she had abandoned him in England, Nash had thought himself a mere visitor to this place.

He cleared his throat and laid the paper aside. "Have you Swann's direction to hand, Gibbons?" he asked, going to the mahogany escritoire. "I shall send my deepest condolences and reassure him there is nothing pressing."

There was, however, one small thing which Swann had left undone, Nash thought, as Gibbons went haring off in search of the letter. But during Nash's visit to Miss Neville's offices last Wednesday, he had answered the question for himself. Her former fiancé — if he had ever been quite that — was Mr. Gareth Lloyd. Nash was quite sure of it.

A proposal of long standing from a family friend, Lord Rothewell had said. How many people in London had known Miss Neville in the West Indies? Very few, Nash guessed. But it little mattered. Lloyd had given himself away with his cold, hard gaze and abrupt manners. He had disliked Nash on sight, and his every gesture toward Xanthia had spoken of patronization and, less perceptibly, of possession.

He marveled Xanthia put up with it. Perhaps she still had a *tendré* for the fellow? The thought sent an uncomfortable chill down Nash's spine. At once he jerked himself back from that emotional precipice.

The woman's past was none of his concern
— nor was her future. If they were to have
anything together, which he doubted, it
would be in the here and now.

Nash had kept his distance from the
woman these last few days and cleared his
head enough to play a hand or two of cards.
He had also begun looking about for Lisette's replacement. But to his eye, none
could compare with the intriguing Miss
Neville. Where she was concerned, however,
he was unsure of what next he ought to do
— or even what he wanted to do. The
woman was still dangerously unwed, and he
was having a devil of a time making out her
. . . well, her *character*. And what a strange
thing with which to concern himself! He
wanted only to bed Xanthia Neville —
wanted it quite desperately, in fact — and
character had heretofore been of no impor-
tance in choosing a woman to fuck.

Damn. He did not even like that choice of
word. Not when it was used in the same
sentence as her name. Where had these finer
feelings come from? They were bloody an-
noying. And he could not escape the suspicion that such things probably mattered
more to him than they did to Xanthia, for if
one believed all that the lady said, her morals were decidedly ambiguous.

It was not just her obvious willingness to have sex without benefit of clergy — a notion which was shocking in itself — but in her business dealings, she seemed more than a little ruthless, which made her seem to him like . . . well, like your average businessman, he supposed.

Nash threw down his pen in disgust. What right had he to question someone else's moral fiber? He had made a career of bankrupting fools for sport. He was not above bedding other men's wives and, indirectly, impoverishing their children. He had always had his choice of highly skilled courtesans with whom to slake his baser needs. In years past, he had favored the most lecherous entertainments imaginable — with females both high and low, and sometimes all at once. Was his horse any higher than Miss Neville's? What was the difference between them?

Ah, from society's standpoint, that question was easy to answer. She was a gently bred, unwed female. She should be demure, kind, and not just virtuous, but naive, too. Her innocence was to be preserved at all cost, for it was the vehicle by which blue-blooded privilege would be borne forth into the next generation. Once she had married and performed that noble duty, however,

Miss Neville could whore herself pretty much as she pleased. That was the dirty little secret of British aristocracy. And the thought of *her* being — *good God* . . .

He prayed Rothewell meant what he said. He hoped no one would push that vibrant creature into a marriage of convenience. For so sensual a woman, it would be like trapping an exotic bird and throwing a dark cloth over the cage. It would be hell. But she was almost thirty. She really was quite on the shelf, and of her own doing, too.

All this left him with too many unanswered questions. Who was Xanthia Neville? Was she the cunning, perhaps faintly duplicitous business owner? Or was she the sensual, breathless almost-innocent he had found in his arms? The duality of her nature troubled him. There was something . . . something lurking there, just beyond his mental grasp. Something which did not ring true — but it would come to him in good time.

Just then, Gibbons came back into the room, a folded piece of foolscap in hand. "Here we are, my lord," he said, placing it on the escritoire.

Nash thanked him and picked it up. "Gibbons, you have been handling my invitations in Swann's absence," he murmured.

"Tell me — what became of that card for Lady Cartselle's masque?"

"It is still on your desk downstairs." The valet had commenced thrashing the frock coat again. "I am to send your regrets, I collect?"

Nash was tapping the edge of Swann's letter pensively on the desktop. "Actually, Gibbons, I think I shall go."

"My lord, it *is* Lady Cartselle," Gibbons cautioned. "I fear the affair will be a little tame for your — er, your *tastes.*"

Nash flashed a wry smile. "Ah, but perhaps my tastes are changing?" he suggested. "Or perhaps it is just old age setting in. In any case, I shall need a costume — something which does not involve the total annihilation of my dignity."

"Indeed, sir." There was a hint of excitement in the valet's voice. "Something in keeping with your character?"

"Precisely," said Nash. "Have you an idea?"

Gibbons had tossed the coat down on the bed, and was already rummaging about in the dressing room. "You have only to put yourself in my hands, sir," he said through the door. "I shall prepare just the perfect thing."

■ ■ ■ ■

"Well, Xanthia, you are nothing if not creative." Lord Sharpe stood in the center of his wife's sitting room, turning this way and that before her gilt cheval glass.

Xanthia and Lady Louisa circled him assessingly. From the divan, Pamela clapped her hands. "Oh, Sharpe, pink flannel really does become you," she said. "And your bald head — well, it does look perfectly porcine once the little ears are attached."

Louisa knelt behind her father. "Hold still, Papa," she said. "I am going to pin your tail on now."

"A tail?" Sharpe craned his head to see. "Oh, good Lord, must you?"

"I think it's very fetching," said his wife.

"There!" said his daughter, standing.

"Mind your tail feathers, Louisa," said Xanthia, stooping to untangle Louisa's costume. "They are getting caught in my purple train."

Pamela laughed. "My dears, I hope you make it to Lady Cartselle's with all your bits and pieces intact," she said. "Circe and the Sirens! And Circe's pig! What a mythological trio you make. Now, Louisa, which siren are you again?"

"Pisinoe," said Lady Louisa. "The one with the lute, I think? It seemed best, since my singing would not lure anyone to do anything — except flee."

Xanthia looked on admiringly. "Nonetheless, you make a beautiful half human half bird, my dear," she said. "Your wings and your tail feathers — well, Lord Cartselle's son cannot but notice you tonight, I am sure."

"Let us pray he is quick about his business, then," said Sharpe a little peevishly. "I shall never hear the end of this in the House."

"But it takes a bold, confident man to wear a pig costume, my love," said his wife solemnly. "Besides, you will be masked. Oh, I wish quite desperately that I was going."

Lady Louisa's smile fell. She bent low to kiss her mother's cheek. Just then, one of Sharpe's footmen appeared. "Your carriage has come round, my lord."

"Oh, wait! Wait!" Pamela was shaking something jingly. "Pray do not forget Circe's bowl of magic herbs. And here is Sharpe's leash!"

Xanthia took the long, gold chain, and the elegant footed bowl, which Pamela's cook had filled with what was probably just bay leaves and thyme. Sharpe bent to kiss

Pamela's cheek, too. "Thank you, my dear," he said gruffly. "But I think I may go safely across to Belgravia without being leashed."

Amidst much laughter, they made their way downstairs and into Sharpe's barouche. They arrived to find Belgrave Square choked with elegant carriages. Along the pavement, all manner of fictional and historical characters were being disgorged onto the red carpet which ran up Lord Cartselle's marble steps.

Lady Louisa's nose was pressed to the window. "Look, a Marie Antoinette!" she cried. "And a Robespierre! And who is that man giving out apples?"

"Sir Isaac Newton, perhaps?" said Xanthia. "Come now, Louisa, sit up straight and let me fluff your wings. It will soon be our turn."

Nash arrived among the last of Lady Cartselle's guests, stepping into her entrance hall amidst much curtsying and tittering from the good lady's daughters. Lady Cartselle herself looked both stunned and gratified by his presence. As Gibbons had pointed out, this one was to be a relatively genteel entertainment, and save for his forays into White's, Nash was rarely seen in genteel society. He was quite confident his reputation had preceded him here tonight, but apparently, it little mattered. A wealthy, unattached marquess was a much-sought-after guest.

Inside the grand ballroom, Lady Cartselle's orchestra had struck up a waltz. Nash positioned his mask carefully and waded into the crowd, his eyes searching for a good vantage point. A handful of guests had trickled up the steps and onto the narrow gallery which encircled the room. An excellent place to see but not be seen. Save for his greeting to Lady Cartselle, Nash had no intention of making himself known, and no intention of seeking anyone out — not whilst wearing the damnable rig which Gibbons had forced upon him. In keeping with his character, indeed! He felt so bloody silly he was not sure he could approach Miss Neville even if he recognized her.

Alas, he barely noticed Marie Antoinette, who had followed him up the red carpet and into the house. Indeed, she was following him still. Nash finally realized it, for the scent of her perfume was strong and unpleasantly familiar. She caught his arm at the foot of the gallery steps.

"*Alors*, speak of the devil!" said the woman in a French accent. "*Bonsoir*, Monsieur Satan. You look splendid in your black silk cloak. And those horns! *Oui,* I always thought you would have a very fine pair."

Despite her powder and patch, the Comtesse de Montignac was easily recognized. *"Bonsoir, madame,"* said Nash stiffly.

She had not released his arm, but her hand felt faintly tremulous. "Come, my lord, and finish this waltz with me, *s'il vous plait?"*

"Thank you, no." His voice was cold.

The comtesse smiled up at him, a dangerous, devious look. "Ah, monsieur, I think you must," she said, still holding his arm. "I have something you should see. Something better discussed, I think, on the dance floor, *oui?"*

Nash's very last wish was to make a scene. "Very well," he said coolly, drawing the comtesse's slender frame into his arms. "How much is this to cost me?"

"Perhaps we can negotiate something to our mutual benefit," she answered, as they entered the first turn. "I wish only to be of help to you, Nash. Tell me, shall we see your beautiful stepbrother tonight?"

"I have no notion," he said, drawing her deeper into the crowd. "My brother's comings and goings are none of my concern."

At that, she laughed. "Come now, Nash," she said. "We both know that is not so."

He swept her into the next turn, their gazes locked. He realized in some shock that she was not wearing powder after all. Her skin tonight was parchment pale, her throat more swanlike than ever. Yes, the comtesse's frail beauty was becoming more frail than beautiful.

She realized he was still staring and licked her lips almost lasciviously. "I wish to see you, Nash." Her voice was suddenly low and sultry. "For more than just . . . a business arrangement."

"I am afraid that is not possible."

The comtesse drew him nearer and set her mouth very near his ear. "I have invited a group of friends, *mon cher* — very close friends — to join me later tonight," she whispered. "And Pierre has brought me a very fine absinthe from Paris — his little way of atoning for his sins. My friends have certain . . . predilections. So bring your mask, Monsieur Satan. I think you know what I mean?"

The comtesse had pressed herself inappropriately close. He regarded her with thinly veiled disgust. "And in exchange for my . . . *performance,* you will what? Reward me with more of your treasures?"

"*Oui,* I could doubtless be persuaded." He drew her into the next turn, and the comtesse brushed her pelvis quite deliberately across his. "Is it true, Nash, that you have tired of the lovely Lisette?"

"Certainly not," he answered. "Miss Lyle has tired of me."

The comtesse laughed so hard she drew stares. "Oh, there is not a man in a hundred here who would admit such a thing," she said. "Even were it true — and of you, it cannot be."

But Nash had grown weary of her cloying scent and gaunt, pressing body. He wished he had never fallen victim to her scheming. *"Madame,"* he said quietly, "you could not recognize the truth if it bit you in that lovely arse of yours, so little acquaintance with it do you have."

Her expression froze. "I beg your pardon?"

He took the unpardonable step of stopping and dropping her hand. "No, it is I who beg yours," he said stiffly. "I have decided that I no longer wish to dance to your tune, Comtesse de Montignac. Whatever the price." With that, he nodded curtly and stepped away. "I give you good evening, *madame.*"

"Nash," she hissed beneath her breath. "Nash, you will regret this. I swear it to God."

He probably would, he thought, turning

away. But in his anger and disgust, he did not care. The dancers nearest them were already staring. The one thing he had wished for — to remain unnoticed — had slipped from his grasp. Good God, he had wanted to choke the breath of life from that bitch.

He started up the gallery steps, intent on putting as much space between them as was possible. It was then that he noticed her. Not Xanthia Neville. No, the first person who caught his eye — a little slip of a girl — looked suspiciously like Sharpe's chit. Then again, he'd seen the girl but once. Whoever she was, she was dressed in solid white, and wore white paint instead of a mask. She carried a golden lute, and was adorned with a vast deal of feathery plumage.

But the woman beside her — ah, there he was less certain. She was very tall and reed-slender, a look which was further emphasized by the close-fitting Grecian gown she wore. The white bodice was cut almost to her nipples, and over it she wore a sheer purple robe, the train of which she caught over one wrist. The gown and robe were encircled by a golden girdle which rose to a peak between her full breasts, lifting them most tantalizingly. The woman's dark hair hung to her waist in thick waves, which were entwined with gold ribbons. Before her, she carried a golden bowl, and in her opposite hand she held a long, gold chain which was leashed to . . . *a pink pig.*

Yes, it was a very large, very bald man dressed, unmistakably, as a pig.

Just then, someone brushed by him on the stairs. "An impressive show, is it not?" said a Napoleon Bonaparte. "That chap in the pig suit must have ballocks the size of Brazil."

"Yes, but the woman —" Until that moment, Nash had not realized he had stopped on the stairs. "Who the devil is she? Or *what* the devil is she?"

"Circe the Sorceress, someone said," answered Napoleon casually. "And by Jove, she can cast a spell over me if she pleases. That's a Siren on her left, and one of Odysseus's sailors. Circe changed them into pigs and led them around by their snouts, did she not?"

"So the legend says," murmured Nash.

He turned and followed Napoleon down the stairs, then plunged into the crowd. But by the time he had crossed to the ballroom's entrance, the pig, the bird, and the woman in purple were gone. Perhaps it was just as well, he thought. Still, it had been Xanthia.

236

He was unaccountably certain of it. Nash decided to return to the gallery and keep watch. The evening was growing late. If she had not appeared within the hour, he would strip off his dramatic black costume and its silly accoutrements, then go up to White's in search of Tony.

The orchestra had struck up a lively country dance, the merry strains of the violins carrying up the steps. On the dance floor below, the dancers whirled, clapped, and circled one another with high steps and flashes of color. Nash strolled along the balustrade, taking in the crowd's jovial chatter. He watched from a distance — in more ways than one. Sometimes he thought that that was the one thing he had in common with Xanthia Neville; the thing which perhaps drew him so inexorably to her. In their own ways, they were outsiders. They would never truly fit in.

He wished, damn it, that she were here. If she were, he might simply ask her what manner of spell she had cast over him. Perhaps she was Circe in the flesh. God knew she tormented him. And yes, for her he was beginning to fear that even he might wear the golden leash.

Oh, the feeling would pass. But while he waited for the inevitable, Miss Xanthia Neville haunted him, those deep blue eyes beseeching him, taunting him — and yes, even comforting him, in his dreams, and sometimes in his waking moments, too. He wished the woman did not seem so . . . so *sane*. So steady and dependable. She was a woman, he thought, that a man could trust — and Nash had had little enough of that in his life.

Just then, a pair of Barbary pirates brushed past, loudly laughing and drawing him from his reverie. He scanned the dance floor again and saw no sign of the woman in purple. But from the corner of his eye, he spied a Queen Elizabeth in deep green satin. Her bright, burning hair was unmistakable, as were the heavy circles of pearls which she wore.

Lord, it was Jenny. The pearls had been his wedding gift to her. He wondered, fleetingly, if Tony were here, but dismissed the notion. The couple lived rather independent lives, an arrangement which apparently suited both. Nash did not approve, though he could not have said why. It could scarcely be argued that he held the sanctity of marriage especially high — he had helped too many women violate it.

Tony married, Nash supposed, for political reasons. Jenny had been a great heiress whose money had helped launch her husband's career. But to Nash it seemed a bit like a deal with the devil. And he feared there was an equally fiendish deal being struck below at this moment, for the Comtesse de Montignac was whispering in Jenny's ear. Seen beside Jenny's vivid coloring, the comtesse looked more pale and more wraithlike than ever. She looked . . . *otherworldly.* And dangerous.

Jenny and the comtesse had once been fast friends — a double entendre if ever there was one — but until a few weeks past, Nash had believed the friendship had faded. Had it resumed? And if so, when? Nash's hands tightened on the balustrade, as if they might crush it to splinters. Bloody hell, this was an inconvenient time for Swann to be away. The women linked arms most companionably and set off across the ballroom toward a group of young bucks who were idling about near the champagne fountain. Alarm bells began to ring in Nash's head.

Good God. This would not do. He would have to speak to Tony.

As midnight neared, Xanthia found herself left to her own devices. Lady Louisa had fallen in with a gaggle of young people who were being closely chaperoned by Lady

Cartselle's sister. Sharpe, after being unleashed, had trotted off to Lord Cartselle's billiards' room to smoke cheroots and talk of politics.

Xanthia wandered the fringe of the ballroom, feeling rather pathetically alone. She knew almost no one, and could bestir little interest in making new acquaintances. After her third circle, Xanthia decided to slip onto the veranda. Picking up her train, she sneaked out the nearest door, acutely aware of what had happened the last time she had done such a thing.

It seemed a lifetime ago, she thought, as the breeze caught her hair. Her rash behavior with Lord Nash that night had been inordinately foolish, she knew. But in hindsight, she was not at all sure she regretted it. She had met a man she might otherwise never have known, a man who stirred her in a way nothing else ever had, not even her work. And she had learned some things about herself, and about desire.

Outside, the air was chilly, but Xanthia did not mind. She leaned back against one of the massive columns and thought of Nash's kiss that night — and of his touch several days past. At the memory of what they had done together, she could feel a faint heat radiate up her throat to her cheeks, and a shiver of sensual awareness run down her spine. She was *not* ashamed. Indeed, she yearned to be with him again. If only he were —

A sound from the rear startled her. "It is Circe, I believe?" said a low, steady voice.

Xanthia whirled about, fingertips pressed to her lips. For an instant, her heart stopped. Could it possibly be — ? *No.* It was not he. This voice was unmistakable.

"There are not many women with your height, Miss Neville," said the Vicomte de Vendenheim from the depths of a monk's hood. "Nor with your elegance of bearing."

"Good evening, my lord," she murmured. "You have joined the Franciscan brotherhood, I see."

"Nay, madam, the Jesuits," he insisted. "Their philosophy is rather more to my liking."

Xanthia smiled knowingly. "Yes, I can believe that," she answered. "How may I be of service, sir?"

De Vendenheim leaned so close their shoulders brushed. "By keeping yourself safe at all times," he said, his words almost inaudible. "From what Mr. Kemble reports, I fear you have been overzealous in your task."

She shook her head. "No, in fact, I assure you —"

"Nonetheless," the vicomte interjected, "do you see the gentleman there? In the court jester's costume just beyond the French window?"

Xanthia nodded. One could not miss his sprouting, jingling hat and green tights. No one had seemed to know his identity, but he had been drawing laughter all evening with his faintly ribald jokes and silly parlor tricks.

"That is Mr. Kemble," said the vicomte. "Lord Sharpe is in the billiards' room. Do not stray far from one of us, Miss Neville, I implore you."

"Then you have seen Lord Nash?" she asked a little breathlessly.

De Vendenheim shook his head. "No, and I think it unlikely he would put in an appearance at such an affair," he answered. "But his brother, Mr. Hayden-Worth, is here — and that makes me unaccountably ill at ease."

"His brother?" Xanthia looked at him blankly. "Oh, yes! I had almost forgotten. The M.P. whom you do not wish to antagonize."

Despite the shadows of his hood, de Vendenheim looked morose. "The likelihood of that is growing more slender every day," he answered. "There have been developments. Our cryptographers have broken a part of the code. But I cannot speak openly here." Swiftly, he bowed and kissed the air above her bare hand. "Good evening, Miss Neville. I will call in Berkeley Square as soon as I may."

Xanthia watched him go with a measure of concern. His suspicions, it seemed, had been renewed, and the vicomte was a man of remarkable determination. It would not be easy to convince him that his assumptions had been wrong. Xanthia must take him proof. But to do that, she must first *find* the proof — which would require gaining access to Nash's home. And thus far, gaining access to Nash — in any way at all — had proven a challenge. But matters were growing increasingly more urgent. De Vendenheim now seethed with frustration, and he would not wait long to strike. She would simply have to think of a way to get close — very close — to the Marquess of Nash.

In the end, it was the gentlemen's retiring room which proved to be Tony's undoing. Seeing a fellow in Elizabethan dress who looked vaguely familiar, Nash followed him and slipped in unnoticed to find Tony relieving himself in a vigorous torrent. At the sight of Nash, however, Tony almost pissed on his shoe.

"Good God!" Tony's eyes ran down Nash's costume. "What the devil?"

Nash flashed a wry smile. "Yes, it is I. The Dark Prince himself."

His stepbrother shook his head. "You are turning up in the damnedest places, old man," he said, restoring his costume to order. "And hard to miss, too, in that red damask waistcoat and sweeping black cloak."

"Yes," said Nash solemnly. "I am making a statement."

"And that would be?"

"That my valet is a sadistic idiot." Nash glanced at Tony's attire. "White tights, old chap? At least you've got the knees for it. Who the hell are you?"

"The Earl of Leicester," said Tony. "He was Queen Elizabeth's lover."

"Yes, I am aware," said Nash. "I have learnt a little of your English history, you know."

"Right, sorry." Tony flashed an embarrassed smile, then opened the door for his stepbrother. "Anyway, Jenny insisted. She's Elizabeth — the red hair and all that."

"Yes," said Nash quietly. "I saw her."

Tony did not catch the concern in Nash's tone. "By the way, Nash, you have not forgot, I hope, Mamma's birthday party?" he said, as they strode toward the ballroom.

In the passageway, Nash hesitated.

"Nash!" Tony chided. "At least put in an appearance. Phaedra and Phoebe will be thrilled."

Nash's conscience stirred. He was his half sisters' guardian. He really should look in on them more often. "Thrilled, eh?" he murmured. "What day do you go down?"

"Thursday next, I should think," he said. "The guests will come on Saturday for the grand dinner party, and a few will stay a day or two. We'll have a little dancing one evening, some cricket, perhaps a picnic at the old ruins."

Inwardly, Nash groaned. It was definitely not his usual sort of entertainment. But it was Edwina's birthday — and though she was often silly, and occasionally imprudent, he was fond of her. He was loath to see her hurt. "I shall try to meet you there," Nash hedged, looking about the ballroom. "Tell me, Tony, where is Jenny now?"

Tony's expression soured almost imperceptibly. "Lord, how the devil should I know?"

Nash leaned very near. "You should know

because you are her husband," he said firmly. "Think how it looks to your political career if you cannot think of your wife."

Tony's expression softened. "You are right," he admitted.

"What is wrong, Tony?"

Fleetingly, he hesitated. "It is just that fast crowd she runs with," he finally said. "I saw them last in the cardroom, and God only knows how much she will lose before the night is out. What does she expect me to do, Nash? Cut a vein and bleed gold sovereigns?"

It was one of his stepbrother's more unguarded moments, and Nash was not without sympathy. "I saw her laughing with the Comtesse de Montignac earlier," he remarked. "I am quite sure it was Jenny — I have not seen another Queen Elizabeth."

His stepbrother smiled weakly. "Nor have I."

"I do not like this friendship, Tony," Nash warned. "You, of all people, know how dangerous that woman is."

"You overstate the matter, Nash," said Tony lightly. "They are acquaintances, no more."

Nash felt his temper spike. "Good God, Tony, do not lie to me, of all people," he snapped. "I am your brother. I am on *your* side. You must order Jenny not to see her."

"Not to see her?" echoed Tony. "Easier said than done, Nash. We see them socially. Besides, I must remain on good terms with her husband."

"De Montignac?" spit Nash. "The hell you do! Tony, don't be a fool. Everyone knows they are conniving, dangerous people."

"My job requires it," said Tony coldly. "And I would have a devil of a time explaining to my wife why she must then give up a friendship with the man's wife."

Nash felt his temper spike. "I once said I would never meddle in your marriage, Tony," he snapped. "But in this case I am about to make an exception. Either *you* tell her — or I shall. Both of you must stay as far from the comtesse and her husband as possible — indeed, so far as you can, stay away from the entire French diplomatic corps."

Despite his black domino, Tony had lost a noticeable amount of color. "Very well, Nash, if you demand it," he said stiffly. "I owe you that, I daresay, at the very least."

"Yes, Tony," said the marquess, turning to leave him, "I daresay you do."

Struggling to contain his temper, Nash

returned from the terrace just as the supper dance was ending. The girl who he'd thought was Lady Louisa was stepping reluctantly away from a slender blond lad wearing a wreath and toga. Lady Cartselle urged the pair toward a group of equally callow-looking young people and shooed them in the direction of the buffet.

Well. If Xanthia were here, it seemed she was free from her duties for the nonce. Inexplicably, he wished to see her now more than ever. He wanted to escape his own anger and his stepbrother's stupidity. He wished simply to forget it all — his obligations, his frustrations — and lose himself in something beautiful and bewitching.

He pressed through the crowd, moving against the stream, his eyes searching. Halfway across the ballroom, he spotted her — the woman sheathed in purple and white, making her way through the thinning crowd toward one of the rear doors. Absent the crush of the dance floor, his every instinct told him it was her. The way she moved — her elegant, queenly grace — was somehow unmistakable. And she was alone.

On impulse, Nash set a path for the second entrance. The rear doors of the ballroom opened onto a dimly lit corridor, a more private part of the house. He wondered where she was going.

They entered the passageway within an instant of one another. She turned in his direction, and he stepped from the shadows to block her path. "Looking for your Odysseus, Madame Circe?"

The woman in purple looked him up and down boldly. "Ah, but Odysseus was immune to Circe's spell, was he not?" she said, her voice sultry. "I should prefer a man who can be entranced by my magic."

"Very wise, Madame Circe," said Nash. "Have you someone in mind?"

"Alas, I did have," she murmured, lowering her gaze. "But the man I seek does not attend such foolish entertainments."

"Then he is unworthy of you, fair sorceress," Nash replied. "Might another man tempt you in his absence?"

"I daresay the devil could tempt a woman to be quite wicked indeed." Madame Circe's eyes swept over his costume again, and a faint half smile curved her lips. "I am impressed by your fine horns, Lord Lucifer, and your flowing black robes. But tell me — have you brought your staff? I should need to see it, of course, as proof of your powers of temptation."

It was she. No one else could be so witty, and yet so bold.

"Come with me, my sorceress," he growled, grabbing her by the arm, "and I will show you my staff, so that you may judge its worth for yourself."

By God, he was tired of being teased. Tired of being honorable when he was nothing of the sort. And tired of seeing to everyone else's troubles. Perhaps it was time he caused a little trouble for himself.

Xanthia spoke not a word but followed him, her golden bowl in hand. He moved in haste, heated curiosity and thwarted lust churning in his gut. At the end of the corridor lay a plain, narrow staircase. Without hesitation, they descended, her diaphanous robes billowing out like a vapor.

Cool air rose up to meet them as they descended, but it was not enough to cool his strange emotions. At the bottom step, a single sconce burned in a long, flagstone passageway. The servants' quarters. It would have to do. Nash seized the first door he came to and flung it open.

A narrow sitting room — the housekeeper's, most likely. Another flickering sconce revealed its tidy chairs covered in chintz, a worn spinning wheel, and a small brick hearth, now cold. On the worktable sat a sewing basket, its wicker lid set to one side. Nash slammed the door and, releasing

Madame Circe, snatched a ladder-back chair and wedged it under the doorknob.

"There, by God," he said. "Let the enchantment begin."

Circe set down her bowl of herbs and floated toward him. He really could believe her a sorceress. Nash's eyes swept over the snug sheath of white silk which nearly bared her bosom, and the golden girdle which circled beneath, pushing her breasts up into plump, delectable swells — breasts which were rising a little rapidly from her exertions. Her mask was purple satin dusted with gold. Bangles of gold encircled her wrists, and at her neck she wore a heavy gold chain from which an amethyst drop fell almost to her cleavage. If the ensemble was meant to draw the eye, it was succeeding admirably.

Nash caught her hand and drew her toward him. She came easily against his length, enfolding her body to his and lifting her mouth to be taken. He obliged her, kissing her deeply and languidly for long moments, until at last she drew back a fraction, her breath already rough and fast. "What if the servants should return?"

His mouth had found her throat, and was lingering there. "They are otherwise engaged," he said, his tongue playing lightly along her pulse point. "And what if they do? The door is blocked, and we are masked. We are . . . *anonymous,* Madame Circe. Our identities are a secret — even to one another."

In his arms, she shivered.

He pressed his lips to her ear. "Do you know who I am?"

For an instant, she hesitated. "Yes," she rasped.

He drew back and smiled wickedly. "Ah, but what if you are wrong?" he whispered. "Are you still willing?"

Rising onto her tiptoes, Xanthia set one hand to his chest and her lips to the turn of his neck. "Entice me to willingness," she softly challenged. "Are you not the devil himself?"

He tightened his embrace and returned his mouth to hers. He found her mask wildly erotic, her words more so. And yet he had kissed many women, and done far more, without ever having seen their faces, or even knowing their names, for women of the *ton* preferred to enjoy their saturnalia incognito, and the anonymity served only to heighten the sexual pleasure.

Circe had let her head fall back, exposing her long, slender throat, a pair of delightful collarbones, and a plunging expanse of white flesh below. He circled his hands around the golden girdle and lifted her breasts in his hands. As he suspected, she wore nothing beneath. The creamy swells burst from the white silk like ripe fruit to his greedy mouth, the delicate pink-brown nipples already taut beneath the sheer purple fabric.

He lowered his head and drew one between his teeth, nibbling gently through the purple gauze. With a soft cry, Xanthia speared her fingers through his hair, almost dislodging his horns. On impulse, he pushed the purple tunic off her shoulders, then slid his hands beneath her derrière, moving as if to lift her onto the table.

To his shock, she slipped from his grasp. "Impatient demon," she chided. "First, you have something to prove, Lord Lucifer. Are you worthy?"

For a moment, her meaning escaped him. She stepped close again, so close he could smell the scent of her skin, then she eased a hand between the folds of his cloak. *"Umm,"* she said, setting her warm palm fully against his erection. "Very tempting — *so far.*" At that, her nimble fingers went to the close of his black trousers and deftly slipped one button free.

Good Lord but she was bold! Nash moved

as if to help, but she pushed his hand away, and finished the job herself, shoving impatiently at the black wool and white linen until his cock sprang free from the folds of fabric.

She made a low, appreciative sound in the back of her throat, then took him almost reverently into her hands, stroking firmly up his length. "Now that is a staff to incite true wickedness," she murmured. "I think we may proceed with the enchantment." And then she shocked him by going down onto one knee and cupping him fully in one palm.

Nash was having a little trouble catching his breath. Circe — *Xanthia* — turned her face, and set the softness of her cheek against the hot, hardness of his flesh, and he almost came undone. He had been fondled avariciously a thousand times, but this was — this was — *intimate.* Something shot through him, hot and fierce. Not lust, but something far more disturbing.

She must have sensed it and misunderstood, for she lifted her face to his. "May I . . ." She faltered. "Would you enjoy it if . . ."

"I would enjoy anything you chose to do, my sorceress," he rasped, scarcely daring to hope. "So long as you do only what you *wish* to do." But when she took the base of his cock in one hand, and closed her mouth around the tip, Nash's breath seized. Shuddering like a schoolboy, he lashed out for something to hold on to. In the gloom, his fingertips found some sort of chest.

Her lashes fluttered up at him uncertainly. "Am I . . . I am doing it right, Lord Lucifer?" she asked. "I fear I am something of a novice at this particular . . . *enchantment.*"

"You're bloody well enchanting me," he choked, holding tight to the edge of the chest.

She returned to her erotic ministrations, the silken warmth of her mouth devoured him, inch by throbbing inch. With one hand holding fast to the base of his shaft, and the other gently cradling him beneath, Circe worked his length until his breath came hard, and his every muscle was rigid. Until he knew her for a sorceress indeed. And knew himself to be hopelessly lost.

She drew at him, her wide, full mouth suckling him with motions both erotic and tender. He threw back his head, savoring the indescribable pleasure, and praying it would never stop, until his flesh was slick and his ballocks spasmed. *Close. Oh, so close.*

Gently, he twined his free hand into her

hair and drew her up. He kissed her, hot and openmouthed, plunging over and over into the sweetness of her mouth, entwining his tongue with hers. He burned to rip the mask from her face — yet he dared not break the spell.

"I want you," he said, lifting his mouth but a fraction.

"Yes," she whispered. The word was hungry. Urgent.

This time she allowed him to lift her onto the edge of the worktable. Her long, dark hair had swung over one shoulder to tease at her areola. He pushed it back and set his mouth to her nipple again. God, but she was beautifully shaped, with high, full breasts which were made for a man's mouth. He suckled her there on the edge of the table, first one breast, then the other, until time spun away, and there was only the two of them, their breath hot and fast in the dimly lit room.

When he could bear it no more, he drew up the white silk skirts of her gown and slithered her drawers down her long, milky thighs. Good Lord, she had legs which went on forever. Legs which might wrap around a man, enticing him to madness and self-destruction. A sorceress indeed.

He urged her back onto the table, her long

hair fanning out across the wooden surface like a mantle of dark silk. Then he set his hands to the inside of her thighs and pushed them wide. She cried out when he took her with his mouth, a tremulous, uncertain sound. Her hand fluttered to her thigh almost apprehensively. He sensed that this was new to her.

"Shush, love," he whispered, catching her hand, and setting it flat to the tabletop. "Let me enchant *you,* sweet Circe."

He delved into her sweet, secret places, tormenting and teasing with a skill honed by years of practice. She cried out again, her whole body trembling. Sensing the risk, he drew his tongue away, and slid one finger into her tight, creamy sheath. She rode down greedily onto his hand, and he slipped another finger inside. She was more than ready.

Unable to wait, he dragged his weight onto the table, crawling over her like some predatory cat. Beneath the mask, her eyes looked wild and uncertain. He kissed her again, stared into her eyes, and told her just what he meant to do next.

"All right." She choked out the words, and swallowed hard. Then, more certainly, *"Yes."*

Nash took himself in hand, and eased his cock into the slick heat of her desire. She gasped at the intrusion but set one purple slipper on the table edge and lifted her hips a little awkwardly, as if to meet his next thrust. He meant, he supposed, to go slowly. But the sweet artlessness of her gesture caught him unaware. And caught his heart in his throat. He could not wait. Could not think. Instinct seized him. He slid deep inside on a triumphant grunt.

Damn. If she was not a virgin, she was close enough to scare the hell out of a man. Beneath him, she had frozen at the intrusion.

"Are you — is it — all right?" he croaked.

She nodded, her hair scrubbing softly on the table. "Yes. Good."

He held himself perfectly still, biting his lip to still the urge to thrust again. Slowly, he felt her go limp, felt the walls of her womanly sheath begin to relax. And to tempt. He answered, moving gingerly back and forth.

"Ah," she said, exhaling. "Lord Lucifer, that . . . ah, *that* is exquisite."

He moved again, lifting himself high, and entering her in what he hoped was a perfectly positioned stroke. She met him thrust for thrust, rising eagerly to take him. To take him deep, and to take him into a world of unspeakable bliss. He knew it already.

Her flesh pulled at him, coaxed him, seduced him in every possible way. Her small, capable hands settled on his shoulders, then slid down to his waist. There was an unmistakable urgency to her motions, a hunger he knew and answered. She lifted one leg, and wrapped it around his waist. The sewing basket tumbled from the table onto the floor. The sounds of their lovemaking — the soft sighs and silken wetness — were glorious in the gloom. Then he felt her quiver against him, and knew.

He lost himself then, driving into her with a physical furor he had never known. She cried out, a soft, keening sound, and he held her to him as she trembled and shuddered beneath him. The last thing he felt was like a lightning strike, except the jolt was one of pure joy. A dangerous, almost certainly addictive, emotion.

Speechless and gasping, Xanthia lay in her lover's arms for what seemed to her an eternity and yet an infinitesimal moment all the same. Slowly, their breathing returned to normal, and when at last she had returned fully to the here and now — and to the shocking realization that she had just made love to the man of her dreams on a housekeeper's worktable — she was compelled to stifle a groan of mortification.

Just then, a clattering of heels arose in the stone stairwell beyond. Servants' voices echoed down the passageway, shouting out orders about prawns and champagne and pâté; things which were apparently wanted in the dining room above.

He had rolled off the table and drawn her to his feet before the echoes died. "Good God, this was madness," he muttered, swiftly neatening her clothing. "It is but a matter of time before one of the servants tries to come in, looking for clean table-cloths or some damned thing."

"Don't fret," she whispered, with a neatening tug on his red waistcoat. "As you say, we are still masked."

His gaze caught hers, fierce and hard. "God, I am such a fool," he whispered — just before he kissed her again. His mouth hungrily upon hers, he set her back against the doorjamb and kissed her deeply and passionately, as if his need had been in no way slaked by the lovemaking.

They came apart breathless and gasping. For an instant, he hesitated, then, "Go," he rasped, setting her firmly away. "You must go out without me." He jerked the chair from beneath the brass knob, gingerly opened the door, and peered out.

"Anyone?" she whispered.

"They must have all gone down to the kitchens," he said. "Hurry back up to the ballroom. Should anyone see you, you must say you are lost."

Xanthia looked at him solemnly. "Oh, I rather fear that I might be," she murmured. "Thank you, Lord Lucifer, for a most wicked evening."

As if he were embarrassed, he looked away and jerked open the door. "Go," he rasped. "I shall follow you after a time."

But he would not, and she knew it.

Xanthia stepped into the passageway, knowing full well she had seen the last of her dark prince this night. The man in black silk would vanish into the gloom as swiftly as he had come — and nothing between them had really changed.

She heard the heavy wooden door close softly behind her, shutting her away from him. The magic and the seductive anonymity of the evening were at an end. Beyond, the stone steps loomed in the flickering lamplight.

Xanthia went up them alone.

CHAPTER EIGHT:
A TRYST AT
HORSEFERRY WHARF

May came to Berkeley Square, and with it, a period of quiet. Lady Louisa and her father were invited to spend a few days in Brighton with friends, granting Xanthia a respite from the social whirl, if not from the demands of daily living. Nothing was heard from Lord Nash, and Xanthia mentally flogged herself about a dozen times each day for hoping — and perhaps expecting — otherwise.

Rather than permit herself to slip into low spirits, Xanthia worked long hours in an attempt to catch up on the tasks she had been shirking. Gareth grew more silent and more volatile with every passing day. And Rothewell simply grew more dissipated. One could no longer miss the deeply etched wrinkles about his eyes and the perpetual frown lines which gave his face character but little else.

None of this went unnoticed by Mr.

Kemble, who seemed to make it his business to meddle in everyone else's. One day when Xanthia was late coming down for dinner, Rothewell found himself faced with the full force of Kemble's officiousness. He came upon the gentleman in question in the study, where he was attempting to reorganize the contents of Xanthia's leather satchel.

"A hopeless task, Mr. Kemble," he warned, going to the sideboard to pour himself a brandy. "She'll only stuff it full again as soon as you are gone — when *will* you be gone, by the way?"

"As soon as Max releases me," he said fretfully. Having got all the papers out, he was having a devil of a time getting them back in again.

Rothewell tossed back a generous sip of his brandy. "Surely if Nash were going to make his move, he would have given some sign by now," he remarked, staring into the depths of the amber fluid. "Xanthia has given him ample opportunity, has she not?"

"Oh, she has given him ample opportunity," said Kemble. "But to do what? That, I think, is the question."

Rothewell set his brandy down with a thud. "I beg your pardon?"

"Oh, never mind!" Kemble turned the

satchel around on the desktop, and with a graceful hop, hefted himself up, and simply sat on it. "Ah, victory!" he said, as the thing compressed another inch.

"You are a clever fellow, Mr. Kemble," said Rothewell over the rim of his glass. "I will give you that. Your tact, however —"

"Sadly lacking, is it not?" Kemble interjected. "Alas, it is the bane of my existence. I often cannot help but say what I mean. It is my life's mission, I sometimes think, to help others see truth and folly for what it is."

"I beg your pardon?" said Rothewell again.

"Well, take yourself, for example, my lord." Kemble had slid off the leather bag and was neatly lashing both buckles. "I hear you have been spending a vast deal of time at the Satyr's Club."

Rothewell stared at him blankly. "*That* is none of your damned business."

Kemble shrugged his elegant shoulders. "Perhaps not," he agreed. "But the Satyr's Club is a perniciously wicked place, Lord Rothewell. You would do well to find another establishment in which to seek your — er, your sort of entertainments. I can suggest a couple of rather innovative brothels, if you'd care to try them?"

Rothewell felt both temples begin to

throb. "Who the hell are you, to give me advice?"

"A man with vast experience in this city," said Kemble calmly, "of both the high and the low sort. There is not a bawd, a black-leg, a cracksman, or even the most base-born cutpurse in London whom I do not know by sight. I can pinpoint on a map every whorehouse, every rookery, and every fence, from Stepney to Chelsea."

"Good God, man. Make your point!"

"I practically cut my teeth in the stews and hells of London, my lord," he said quietly. "You, by contrast, have been here but what? Four or five months? Forgive me, Rothewell, but in *this* town, you are just a babe in the woods."

Rothewell set down his brandy and stalked toward him. "Why, you pompous little prick," he growled. "How dare you —"

Kemble held up an admonishing finger, and, inexplicably, Rothewell stopped in his tracks. "I am also the man appointed to keep your sister safe from all harm," he said. "And a dead brother would, in my consid-ered opinion, constitute harm, since the lady seems inexplicably attached to you. Ordinarily, her taste is more discerning."

To give the devil his due, the fellow had a sense of humor. And for all his foppish appearance, he was not easily intimidated, either. Rothewell relaxed and gave a disgusted grunt. "A bit of a dramatist, aren't you?" he said, strolling aimlessly back to his own desk. "I think I can take care of myself, wherever it is I choose to seek my entertainments. I do not think the Grim Reaper is as yet on my heels."

"Have you any idea, my lord," said Kemble, "how many men died in London last month of eating opium?"

"I haven't a bloody clue."

"There were six, my lord," said Kemble. "Six *that were found.* Three pulled out of Limehouse Reach, and another three farther downriver. And of those six, four had been lately seen at the Satyr's Club. Moreover, those French girls they keep will tip you the token without so much as a word of warning, for the place is riddled with the pox and they daren't speak of it — and I mean syphilis, Rothewell, not the common clap. It robs a man of all sense, you know. But slowly, so that you have time to truly appreciate the horror of it all."

Rothewell tossed off the last of his brandy in one swallow. "Aren't you the crapehanger from hell," he grumbled. "Life is fraught with risk, Kemble. And death comes to us all."

"To some sooner than others," muttered Kemble. "And *you* are begging for it."

"What did you say?"

Kemble set the satchel on the floor, and whirled around. "I said, my lord, that you are losing your looks," he answered. "You have all the charm and beauty of a violent death warmed over. Honestly, have you seen yourself lately? Your skin tone is gone, your eyes are shot bloodred, and it appears that a drunken stonemason carved those lines into your face with a hammer and chisel."

"Lines?" Absently, Rothewell slid a hand over his faint stubble. "Skin tone?"

Kemble leaned across the table, and took a full pinch of Rothewell's cheek, then let it go again. "Do you see that? Do you?"

"No. It's my skin — and I'm wearing it."

"Yes, and it has no resiliency!" said Kemble. "No vigor! And that shade! Why, if you hadn't a bit of your island bronze left, I daresay you'd have no color at all. What, pray, will you do in another six months?"

"Hang myself?" Rothewell suggested. "I mean, once a chap's looks are gone, what else has he to live for? Good tailoring and a tight corset can only go so far."

"Precisely!" said Kemble, missing the sarcasm.

A faint motion at the door caught

267

Rothewell's attention. He turned to see Xanthia entering. "Heavens, Mr. Kemble, are you still here?"

Kemble bowed stiffly. "If you are in for the evening, Miss Neville, I shall take myself off."

"I am in," she assured him. "But will you stay to dinner?"

"Thank you, no," he said. "Good evening to you both. I shall find my way out."

"And good riddance," grumbled Rothewell, going to refill his glass.

Xanthia caught him lightly by the arm. "Must you, Kieran?" Her eyes darted toward the decanter. "I think we ought to dine now."

She watched as her brother smiled stiffly. "By all means," he said. "I would not keep a lady waiting."

Xanthia forced a light laugh. "Not even when the lady has kept *you* waiting?" she asked. "And by her absence, subjected you to the advice and ministrations of Mr. Kemble?"

"Oh, you'll pay for it, old thing," he warned, offering his arm.

Xanthia shot him a look of sympathy. "Was it dreadful?"

"Yes, apparently, I am an aging old roué," said Kieran, steering her toward the dining room. "A drunkard who has lost his looks and now subsists on Turkish opium and the purchased affections of pox-riddled prostitutes."

"Dear me," said Xanthia quietly. "I am very glad to have missed *that* conversation."

They dined in companionable silence. Xanthia wondered what Mr. Kemble had really said to Kieran. Whatever it was, her brother appeared to be mulling it over. Or perhaps he was just suffering the blue devils again. She sighed inwardly, and motioned for the footman to refill her wineglass. Kieran would have to deal with his devils alone tonight. Xanthia hadn't the strength.

It had been a long, hard slog in Wapping today. In between the rush of real work, she had written not just one, but *two* notes to Nash — and promptly torn them up, of course. Then she and Gareth had quarreled about the scheduling again, and it had ended in her overriding several of his decisions, something she tried to avoid. But the demands he made of the ships and their captains had become intolerable. It really was inhumane to turn crews around on so little notice and to behave as if everyone else ought to be the sort of emotionless automaton *he* had apparently become.

Oh, Xanthia was fond of Gareth. In her

own way, she even loved him. And in loving him, she had come to know him for what he was: an intelligent, somewhat arrogant man who was honest to a fault and too handsome for his own good. Kieran believed her a fool for not marrying Gareth, but Xanthia knew something was missing. She wished to love with her whole heart — and perhaps when she did, the sacrifices marriage would require of her would not seem too great a price to pay.

She had often considered saying yes to Gareth's proposals. But she had realized she could not when she found herself obsessed by how their marriage might affect Neville Shipping. Would he insist on taking over once they were wed? Probably. Gareth had once hinted that he believed Xanthia would be happier if she had a home and children to care for. Indeed, he might have tried to insist on it. But if they continued working cheek by jowl for years on end, might they simply come to find one another dull?

The risk was too great, Xanthia had soon realized. The continued success of the business had to come first. And if she were able to so easily put it first — to think of it as the thing around which their marriage must revolve — then Gareth was not the man for her. And Gareth deserved something better than a wife who did not love him enough to make him her utmost priority.

Lord Nash, on the other hand, had become a terrible distraction. But that aside, Xanthia rather doubted that he would ever trouble himself to consciously interfere in her work. And it sometimes felt as if her thoughts already revolved around him. Certainly she was unable to think clearly when he was in the same room — a bad sign, she feared. When Nash kissed her, the world swirled from beneath her feet, and her every thought was of his touch. Neville's could go hang when she was in his arms. And that was a risk of an altogether different sort.

Suddenly Kieran's voice cut into her consciousness. "So what of this business with Nash?" he asked out of the blue. "Just what is going on, Zee?"

"Going on?" Xanthia swallowed hard. Her brother looked in an ill mood. "With . . . Lord Nash?"

"Yes, Nash," said Kieran. "Look here, Zee — did anything . . . *happen* at that masque last week?"

Xanthia feigned surprise. "Well, I *saw* Lord Nash," she answered. "We spoke. He was very . . . amiable, I daresay, is the word I am looking for. But he did not press a wad

271

of banknotes into my hand and beg me to run a load of rifles to Kotor. And he isn't going to, if you ask me."

"Humph," said Kieran. "He's got no dog in this fight?"

"Oh, I would not say that," Xanthia admitted. "I almost think he *would* do it, were he asked. But he hasn't been. I'm quite sure of it."

"Are you?"

"Utterly," Xanthia confirmed. "I think Nash's idea of aiding the motherland would be to run away and join the Russian Imperial Guard. And somehow, I must make de Vendenheim and Peel believe that."

"If you say Nash is innocent, I believe you," said her brother. "So bugger Peel and de Vendenheim. What are they to us? Or Nash either, come to that?"

Xanthia set her wineglass aside and frowned. "Do mind your language, Kieran," she said. "This is our home, not a cane field."

"I beg your pardon," said her brother stiffly. "You must do as you please, I suppose. But as for that coxcomb Kemble, I should like to get rid of *him,* too. Indeed, I may well do it."

"You have had too much to drink," Xanthia remarked.

Kieran pushed away from the table. "No, my dear," said her brother, jerking to his feet. "I have not had nearly enough. That is my problem."

Xanthia crushed her napkin with both fists. "Kieran, stop," she whispered.

"Stop what?" he demanded.

She lifted her gaze to catch his. "Kieran, can you not see?" she pleaded. "You are all I have. But you . . . you are becoming more like our uncle every day."

Abruptly, his fists crashed down on the tabletop. "By God, Zee, I don't need this!" he roared, as the glass and cutlery jumped. "Not from that upstart Kemble, and especially not from *you*. Like Uncle, indeed! I have not yet taken my riding crop to your hide, have I? Nor locked you in the cellar with the rats and the damp? Nor let my dissolute friends chase you round the dinner table?" His face was black with rage.

"That is not what I meant," said Xanthia, unwilling to back down. "And I think you know it."

Kieran braced both hands on the table's edge and bowed his head. She could feel him grappling for control. "I know I do not need your advice, damn it," he finally rasped, falling back into his chair. "I am not something for you to manage or to fix, Zee.

I am not Neville Shipping. I am just a man, and I am living my life as I see fit. I will thank you to stay out of it."

Xanthia forced her hands to relax. "You leave me little choice," she answered, as her napkin slithered into the floor.

He had turned his face away. "No choice at all," he said, as one of the footmen entered with a decanter of port. "I am well enough, Zee. Leave me be."

Xanthia declined to stay for Kieran's port and excused herself from the table. Pausing only long enough to snatch her satchel from the study, she went upstairs. But once alone in her suite, she was seized with a restless frustration and paced the floors for the better part of an hour. Eventually, she decided to skim some correspondence she'd brought home from work. Soon she had read four letters — without comprehending a word.

In frustration, she snapped the file shut and tossed it onto the bed. Would Kieran try to insist she put an end to this intrigue with Nash? For all his slipshod ways and *laissez-faire* attitude, her brother always put her happiness — and her safety — first. He had clearly decided she was wasting her time with Nash. Xanthia wished to God she felt the same. But slowly, by agonizing little increments, she had come to believe that no moment spent in Nash's company was wasted.

The man was, however, dangerous. A hardened gamester and a well-practiced libertine. Possibly worse. But he was no traitor to his country. Again Xanthia wondered how close de Vendenheim was to making an arrest. Surely he would have to have proof? Or perhaps not. Perhaps de Vendenheim had decided that the mere allegation of treason would throw enough light on the smuggling operation to end it? Even more chilling was the fact that at Lady Cartselle's masque, he had implied that he was no longer as concerned about Mr. Hayden-Worth's influence in Parliament.

Unfortunately, the longer de Vendenheim's hounds chased the wrong fox, the greater the risk to Nash — and the greater the chance that the real smuggler would continue unchecked. The precarious balance of power in the Mediterranean might easily be tilted toward chaos. On her fingers, Xanthia counted the number of Neville's ships which could be passing through the Strait of Gibraltar within the next fortnight. She ran out of fingers.

Impulsively, but with a surprisingly clear head, Xanthia went to her writing desk, scratched out yet a third, nearly illegible note, and sealed it with red wax. Then before she could think better of it, she threw on her woolen walking cloak and rummaged through her wardrobe for a hat which would shadow her face.

Downstairs, the house was quiet. Kieran had obviously gone out, for the lamp in his study was unlit. She was not above slipping out the back door, but it was unnecessary. The servants had apparently gone below-stairs for dinner. Xanthia let herself out and locked the door behind. She tried not to consider the rashness of her actions, and instead set a brisk pace along Upper Brook Street, thankful for what little light leached through the evening's brume.

Number Six Park Lane was the address of the Marquess of Nash. Xanthia had learnt that much from Mr. Kemble, and it was but a few minutes' walk from Berkeley Square. How odd to think that the object of her obsession lived scarcely a stone's throw away. But Xanthia had learned that every-one who was anyone lived in Mayfair, and all of them right atop one another.

The spring fog clung to her face like damp cotton wool, the metallic scent of coal smoke acrid in her nostrils. Shivering, Xanthia pulled her cloak tighter and turned into Park Lane. The street below was quiet.

She paced down a few yards, then back up again. Some five minutes into her vigil, a boy in a scruffy brown coat rounded the corner, whistling a merry tune.

She called him to her, and extracted her purse. "I wish you to run an errand for me," she said solemnly. "Are you willing?"

"Are yer payin'?" He eyed her purse almost lasciviously.

Xanthia extracted a sixpence and pressed both it and the sealed note into the boy's hand. "Take this down to Number Six," she instructed. "The front door, mind, not the rear. Come back when you've done it, and I'll have a shilling for your trouble."

"Gor, mum!" Eyes wide, he tugged his forelock and went scurrying down the street.

In the gloom, she could barely make him out. His hunched form stood on the doorstep for what seemed an eternity. At last, the door must have opened, for she heard it shut again with a heavy thud. The lad leapt off the steps and hastened back up the hill.

"To whom did you give it?" she asked.

The lad shrugged. "Some stiff-arsed footman."

"Mind your language," Xanthia gently admonished. "Now, go home to your mother, young man. It is very late at night."

The boy just grinned, snatched the shilling, and darted away into the fog.

Xanthia turned and retraced her steps to Park Lane, where she wound her way down some lesser-traveled lanes, across Piccadilly, and through the parks. On the opposite side of St. James's Park, Westminster was quiet but far from empty. Fine carriages still rattled in and out, conveying important members of Parliament in splendid Tory isolation, no doubt. Xanthia preferred to walk — and in the opposite direction from Mayfair. Here, she was unknown. Anonymous. She could smell the river nearing now as she wound her way through the narrow streets unaccosted.

At the foot of Queen Anne's Gate, she could see the sconces which flanked the entrance to the Two Chairmen. They flickered unsteadily, casting the corner in eerie light. As she approached, the pub's taproom door swung wide, staccato laughter cutting through the fog. A pair of staggering nightingales came out and turned toward the park. Xanthia pulled her hat a fraction lower, stepped into the shadows, then headed toward the river.

It took but a few moments to make her way to the Westminster wharves. Here, vast quantities of stone and timber were offloaded and carted into greater London to build the new homes and shops which the wealthy required. Pallets of brick and carts laden with coal lined the narrow lane which edged the water. The river was quiet tonight, the tide high and turning. A lighter came skimming past, taking advantage of the tide to sail back down to await tomorrow's cargo.

She turned and paced again. He was not coming. Xanthia bit her lip. No, he probably had not even been at home. She drew in a deep, steadying breath. The stench of mud and rot was strong along the wharf, but inured to it, Xanthia drew her cloak tighter and paced down to the water's edge. Below, a faint wake sloshed incessantly at the stone steps, which descended into the murky current. In the distance, she could see the lights of Lambeth glowing like gauzy yellow cotton balls in the murk.

It must be nearing midnight now. No self-respecting sybarite would be alone at such an hour. He was likely throwing the dice in Covent Garden — or wallowing in the arms of some dasher. At that thought, Xanthia squeezed her eyes shut. What a pathetic gudgeon she was! Of course the man had lovers. Many lovers — and he tired of them easily. He had told her so, in plain language. He certainly need not bestir himself in the middle of the night to stroll the riverbank in search of a clandestine romance — or whatever it was Xanthia meant to offer him.

No, he was not coming. And it was just as well. She was only fooling herself if she believed that this late-night escapade had been about nothing but the security of Neville's shipping routes. It was about Nash — about her fascination with him. But she, too, had her pride. Besides, she was freezing to death in the damp.

Along Abingdon Street above, she could hear a watchman calling the hour, his voice strangely disembodied in the fog. Almost an hour had passed since she had set off on this ill-thought escapade. It felt like an eternity.

Xanthia was securing her cloak in preparation to go when she heard the footsteps on the cobblestones, as disembodied as the watchman's cry. She was not perfectly sure from which direction they came until a dark form materialized from the fog, and stepped briskly past her. His height and lean grace were unmistakable. Xanthia reached out and touched the Marquess of Nash on the arm.

He froze, and turned around as she pushed back the brim of her hat. "My dear Miss Neville." Despite the chill, he swept off his hat. "Once again, you shock me."

In her agitation, Xanthia did not quite catch the worried edge to his tone. She drew him between a towering pile of stone and a cart laden with coal. "You received my note?"

"No, I came down to queue up early for the next coal barge," he said. "We're fresh out in Park Lane."

Her shoulders fell. "I have disturbed you," she said coolly. "My apologies."

"No." He set one hand on her arm, and gentled his voice. "No, my dear, never that. But it is not safe for a lady to be out so late at night. I would drag you home this minute, could I do so without risk to your reputation."

"Let me worry about my reputation," she answered. "I wished to see you — and I knew you would not come to me."

"Oh, my dear girl," he said softly. "Whatever for?"

Xanthia shook her head, uncertain of her answer. "After last week —" she began, then faltered. "After what we did together . . . I, well, I have been unable to think clearly."

"Last week." His voice had grown quiet.

The tension inside Xanthia snapped. "Don't you dare," she said. "We are not going to pretend, Nash, it did not happen."

He fell silent for a long moment, then

exhaled sharply in the gloom. "No, that would not do at all, would it?" he said almost to himself. "It did happen. And given our nature, I very much fear it is apt to happen again."

"You sound as if you regret it," Xanthia whispered, shaking her head. "Don't do that to us, Nash. That is worse than pretending it never happened. It is like . . . like wishing we did not know one another at all. But it is too late for that."

His grip on her arm tightened. "My dear, that is the very point." His voice was raw now, and tinged with some powerful emotion. "You do not know me. And I — well, I should never have come to your office that day. Certainly I should not have followed you to Lady Cartselle's masque. My intentions were far from honorable. And by God, they aren't honorable now."

On some wild, insane impulse, she rose onto her tiptoes and kissed him hard on the lips. His body stiffened, but his mouth softened. His fingers curled into the wool of her cloak. And then the fire burst hot and fierce between them.

On a raw moan, Nash drew his tongue across the seam of her lips. Xanthia opened her mouth at once, thrilling to the taste of him. Her hands found his waist, worked their way into his coat, and slid round to the small of his back. His fine beaver hat fell to the cobblestones. One of his arms banded her to him, strong and resolute, while the other hand cradled the back of her head in a kiss which was infinite in its sweetness. Unmistakable in its desperation.

They came apart with small, lingering kisses, lovers parting with an enduring reluctance. "My dear, you are dangerously tempting," he whispered.

"I wish to see you again, Nash," she said fervently. "*Alone.* Let me come to you. Who will know?"

He drew back to look at her. "I am too much the cad to refuse you, my dear," he murmured. "But I will at least remind you that you deserve better. Or at the very least, you deserve *more.*"

She looked up at him unflinchingly. "More than you can give?" she whispered. "That is what you mean, I know. But would it not be fairer to let *me* decide what enough is? Would it not be more equitable to let me determine how daring I wish to be?"

He leaned toward her and set his forehead to hers. "I begin to think, my dear, that you are very daring indeed," he murmured. "Very well then. Suit yourself. I think you know the address. Number Six Park Lane."

She brushed her lips along his jawline. He pulled her more tightly against him. "My poor girl, come here. You are shivering."

"It is this dreadful English damp," she said on half a laugh. "I never imagined one could be so homesick for a place one did not like all that well."

He set his lips to her forehead. "In Barbados, I daresay, the tropical flowers would be bursting with blooms, the days would be long, and the sun would be hot," he murmured. "Yes, I know what it is to be homesick for something far different from this, my dear. You have my sympathy."

She pulled away, and grinned. "Ah, but in Barbados, the men are not nearly so handsome," she said. "Or so skilled. I believe I will put up with this vile weather for a while."

"I hope, Xanthia, that you will." He kissed her again, feverishly and a little desperately. "Now for God's sake, *go home.*"

"Tomorrow evening, then?" she whispered. "I shall claim a headache and go to bed early — and I will wear a veil, I swear it. No one will recognize me."

"You will wear a veil, yes," he firmly repeated. "And I shall send my servants away."

"You would do that for me?"

"I will do whatever I must to live with the guilt," he said.

"Where shall I meet you?" she asked breathlessly. "What time?"

"Come up through King Street Mews, if good sense does not overtake you first," he said. "There is a gate into the yard, and the rear door which is always lit. I will await you there. If you have not come by eight o'clock, I will assume you have come to see reason — and I will try to be glad of it."

"Oh, I fear that reason and I parted ways in Lady Cartselle's livery room," said Xanthia honestly. "I will be there."

His eyes softened and lingered on her face. "I will be waiting for you," he said. "Now kindly appease the less daring amongst us by going home. I promise to make it worth your while tomorrow night."

Xanthia shivered, half from the chill and half from anticipation. "Good night, then," she whispered. On impulse, she rose onto her toes and kissed him swiftly. "Until tomorrow."

"Good night . . . *Zee*." Nash turned, snatched up his hat and, with one last look of regret, melted into the gloom.

He wished, she knew, to escort her home. But it would not do for her to be seen alone after midnight on the arm of any man, and certainly not Nash's. A pity she had not thought of a veil sooner. Pulling her cloak snugly about her, she left the wharf and set a quick pace back up toward St. James's. Her mind was awhirl with plans and possibilities. *She had done it.* She had convinced him.

She wanted, of course, to prove his innocence. To herself. And to de Vendenheim. Surely, once inside his home, she would see something — at the very least, some sort of sign — which would cast doubt upon the Government's theory? Her shoulders fell. What if she had no opportunity? Or what if she did — and found nothing? Would it matter to her? No, very little, she admitted. De Vendenheim had by far the easier task. Guilt was so much easier to prove than innocence.

At the corner of Great George Street, she turned left, but here the fog seemed to have thickened, if such a thing were possible. Even the gaslights were useless. Keeping a careful eye on the pavement, Xanthia quickened her pace. But something behind caught her ear. *Footsteps.* They echoed hollowly off the towering town houses which lined the street.

Foolishly, she slowed. Was it Nash? Perhaps he had decided to follow her? Or perhaps her imagination had just run wild.

No. The steps were closer now. Xanthia picked up her pace, her heels sharp and quick on the pavement. She could sense St. James's Park just ahead. In a few more minutes, she would be back in Berkeley Square. There would be a good fire in her bedchamber. A decanter of sherry on the night table. Warmth. Security. Comfort.

Suddenly, something — *someone* — snared her arm, spinning her roughly around. "Yer money or yer life," rasped an almost inhuman voice. "Scream, and I'll slit yer from ear ter ear."

"Unhand me," ordered Xanthia, giving a hard try. "Let go!"

The man merely jerked her closer. His breath was sour and reeked of onions. "Let's 'ave it, now," he ordered, laying something cold and menacing against her throat. "That little leather purse full of coins? Toss it onto the pavement, milady, afore yer gets a nasty bloodstain on that fine cloak."

Her blood was running cold now. The blade against her throat was like ice. Like death. "Release me," she whispered. "And I shall reach insi—"

Suddenly, the man's arm jerked high, as if God himself had seized it. He cried out, grabbing his elbow as the knife clattered to the pavement. "What the bloody — ?"

The question was never finished. Something black — a boot? — flashed in the gloom, catching the man square across the throat. His head snapped back like a broken doll's, then he slithered to the pavement.

"Good God," said a dark, deeply irritated voice. "Where *is* your pistol, Miss Neville?"

Xanthia sagged with relief as Mr. Kemble materialized from the gloom. "Oh, thank heaven!" she said. "My pistol — oh. Oh, dear. I left it."

"And did you leave your common sense behind to keep it company?" he snapped. The urbane coxcomb was gone, and Kemble was all business. "Do not ever flash a purse in the street again, Miss Neville. Especially not in the middle of the night. Indeed, you should know better."

Xanthia had grabbed hold of a lamppost to steady herself. "But — but I didn't flash it."

The man on the pavement began to moan. Without missing a beat, Kemble set his boot firmly against the man's throat. "The boy you hired," he said irritably. "He was not out for a midnight stroll, Miss Neville. He was making marks."

"Making . . . marks?"

"Looking for victims to rob," Kemble

clarified. "He works for a ring. Pickpockets, cracksmen, common ruffians. They all come out at night, Miss Neville — and the daylight, too. How in God's name have you survived down in Wapping?"

She blushed. "My mind . . . it was elsewhere tonight."

"Yes," said Kemble dryly. "I noticed."

"You — you were following me?" Xanthia had finally stopped shaking, her fear succumbing to her indignation. "You were *spying* on me?"

"I am watching out for you," Kemble corrected. "With good reason, as it happens."

"But — but how dare you?" Xanthia sputtered.

"Go home, Miss Neville," said Kemble almost wearily. "Go home, find your pistol, and put it in your reticule. Never flash your purse in the street again. Burn that hideous excuse of a hat as soon as you arrive home. And for God's sake, do not ever turn your back on the Marquess of Nash. Peel wishes you merely to serve your country — not to die for it."

"Are you following me everywhere?" she demanded.

"Someone is," he said. "Max has seen to it."

For an instant, Xanthia shook with fury.

"Then *someone* may prepare to follow me back to Park Lane tomorrow night," she hissed. "For I am going back — and I am going to prove once and for all that Nash had *nothing* to do with this gunrunning business."

"Miss Neville, I urge you to be cautious."

"Yes, as de Vendenheim is being cautious?" Xanthia retorted. "He has all but convicted Nash."

Across the street, a shade had flown up, and a lamp now hovered at the window. The man on the pavement moaned again, his eyes fluttering open. He looked up, saw Kemble, and raw fear sketched across his face.

"Good evening, Mr. Tomkins," said Kemble, hauling the man to his feet. "Working nights again, are we?"

"Georgie Kemble!" he gritted. "God rot yer, yer sneaky peachin' bastard!"

Kemble smiled. "Yes, I have missed you, too, Tommy," he said, deftly twisting the man's arm up behind his back. "Let's have a little stroll up to the Queen's Square Magistrate's Office, shall we? The weather is so lovely tonight."

The man writhed. "Sod off, yer son of a bitch."

"What a moving offer," said Kemble, "but

you are not quite my type. Now *move.*"

The man moved, his eyes shying over one shoulder like a nervous horse's. He clearly feared his captor. But Mr. Kemble seemed quite thoroughly at ease. Chattering amiably about the weather, he frog-marched Xanthia's assailant into the gloom.

Xanthia stared after them in amazement and clutched her reticule to her chest. "Mr. Kemble," she said into the swirling haze, "*you* are a very strange man."

CHAPTER NINE:
A CUP OF COFFEE
IN PARK LANE

Across Westminster, the day dawned fair, the morning sun quickly burning off the last of the evening's fog and bathing the verdant slopes of Hyde Park in shafts of light which shifted gently as the clouds drifted overhead. Today, Lord Nash was up at dawn, much to his staff's surprise, for he had a few errands to run. By the late afternoon, however, he had returned to Park Lane to dress for the evening and await his fate.

A fine, strong breeze periodically ballooned the draperies about his shoulders, bathing him in cool air as he braced his palms on the window frame. The shafts of late sunlight across the park reminded him, he decided, of a scene from a Constable exhibit which he'd admired at the Royal Academy. Fleetingly, he was struck with the strangest impulse to take Miss Neville to see it.

Good Lord. What a notion!

"There," said Gibbons, giving one last tug upon the back of Nash's collar. "It looks splendid, sir, if I do say so myself. Now, are you quite sure you can extract yourself from this finery without my help?"

"I shall manage." Nash turned to give himself one last going-over in the pier glass, then picked up his cup of coffee. It was his third; he kept pouring them, then forgetting to drink them.

Gibbons was looking at him slyly. "It will be no trouble at all, my lord, for me to return in time to help you undress."

Nash glowered at him over the cold coffee. "I said you were to have the evening off," he replied. "Let me rephrase that. *Go away* — and do not come back until noon tomorrow."

Gibbons trembled with feigned indignation. "Well!" answered the valet. "Such ingratitude!"

Nash handed him the coffee. "But whilst you're still here, be so good as to pour this out," he said. "It's gone cold."

With a tight smile, Gibbons went to the window and summarily dumped it.

Below, someone shrieked.

Nash glowered at the valet. "Bloody hell!" he said, hastening toward the window. "Sorry! Very sorry!" he called out.

"Yes, gardy-loo!" shouted Gibbons, with a waggle of his fingers. "Have a lovely day!"

Nash withdrew from the window. "You needn't take your snit out on innocent passersby," he said. "If you must ruin someone's wardrobe, let it be the usual one — *mine*."

Gibbons threw his arms over his chest. "Oh, this is all about your scorched cravat, isn't it?" he said. "Well, you can thank Mr. Vernon for that one! It was he who over-heated the irons, then set them on the worktable, innocent as a little lamb!"

"Vernon has the evening off, too," Nash reminded him. "And he's damned grateful for it." He had returned to the pier glass to stare at the lapels of his frock coat. "What do you think? Ought I have chosen the bottle green?"

"It depends," said Gibbons, "on whether or not she'll be sober enough to notice what color you are wearing."

Nash drew away from the mirror, and this time his glower made Gibbons blanch. "She is *not* that sort of woman," he said coldly.

The valet clasped his hands together. "Oh, I knew it," he said. "I just knew it! You have planned some sort of tryst!"

"Of course I have," Nash snapped. "Why else would I suffer the inconvenience of waiting on myself?"

Gibbons's elation faded to curiosity. "Have you got rid of the Henrietta Street house?"

"No." Nash felt a faint heat rise to his face. "She is not *that* sort of woman, either."

Gibbons's expression faltered. "Dear God!" he said. "Oh, heavens!"

"What now?"

"Monsieur René will not approve."

"I had not planned to ask his permission," said Nash, turning his head to brush his knuckles assessingly over his fresh shave.

"It doesn't matter," said Gibbons. "He does not approve of females."

"He's the bloody chef," said Nash. "What business is it of his?"

"He will give you the sack," warned Gibbons.

"I am the employer," Nash reminded him. "I do the sacking. And remind me again, Gibbons — why is it I don't sack *you?*"

"Because your last three valets quit," he answered. "You are difficult to work for. You have *moods,* sir. And you keep odd hours. You come home with your person and your clothes in a shambles. And you definitely don't do the sacking where René is concerned."

"He won't know a thing about this, Gibbons, unless you open your big mouth."

The valet laughed. "Oh, sir, you are deluding yourself if you think it will stop at this."

Nash looked at him incredulously. "If *what* will stop at *what?*"

"A female in the house." Gibbons was holding a finger in the air now. "Once you've let *that* sort in, my lord, they never go out again. Not really."

"What *sort?*" he demanded. "I told you, she is extremely respectable."

"And that, sir, is the very trouble," said Gibbons. "You are having a tryst with a respectable lady. Next you know, you'll be caught in the parson's mousetrap — and perfectly pleased about it, I daresay. But René shan't be pleased. He'll be on the first mail packet out of Dover."

Nash grunted. "René shall have nothing to worry about," he replied, returning to his mirror. "There will be no mousetrap — of anyone's making."

Gibbons drew in his breath sharply. "My lord! I am shocked. Simply shocked."

"You've never been shocked a day in your life," muttered Nash, wondering if perhaps breeches and boots would look more — well, more *dashing* than ordinary trousers. "What the devil are you squawking about, anyway?"

"I am shocked that you would invite *a lady* into your home with dishonorable intentions."

"You know nothing of my intentions, Gibbons," he snapped. "We'll be playing piquet for all you know."

"Now, that I truly doubt," said the valet. "Has she a husband?"

"Well . . . no," he admitted. "Those are the sort I *do* take to Henrietta Street."

"Then this is an outrage!" said the valet. "Sir, I must insist you make an honest woman of this well-bred young lady."

"You do not know if she is young or well-bred or has two heads, Gibbons, so mind your own business."

But his valet was making Nash dashed uneasy. Was this not the very argument he'd already had with himself a dozen times over the last week? And neither side had won. Instead, he had let Miss Neville sink her claws back into his hide — his weak-willed, quixotic hide — whilst he surrendered to desire.

Well, weak-willed he might be, but this argument was over. He went to the chair by the dressing room door, and picked up Gibbons's portmanteau. Just then, Vernon, the footman, entered. "Begging your pardon, my lord, but there's a van round back."

"A van?"

"Yes, my lord. He said he came round to the front as he was told, but someone threw cold coffee on his head."

Nash scowled at Gibbons.

"In any case, he's round back now, unloading boxes," said Vernon. "He says they are for you."

"Boxes?" said Gibbons as the footman vanished. "What sort of boxes?"

"Bloody greenhouses!" said Nash under his breath.

Gibbons looked at him incredulously. "I beg your pardon? Did you say greenhouses?"

Nash turned to look at him. "I might have done," he said. "What of it?"

"A greenhouse with *boxes?*"

Nash shrugged sheepishly. "I got rather carried away," he answered. "And the fellow's turned up an hour early."

"I think," said Gibbons, "that you have lost your mind."

Nash was afraid to answer that. He rather thought perhaps he *had* lost his mind. Nowadays, his every deed — and his every thought — seemed most out of character. This entire plan reeked of scandal and danger — not to mention absurdity. And now the flowers were starting to arrive.

What in God's name had possessed him to order them? Perhaps Gibbons was right. Perhaps he was simply poking one toe over a dangerous, slippery slope.

Ah, well! Too late to worry about it now.

"Here," he said, thrusting the portmanteau at Gibbons. "Give my regards to your sister."

Xanthia arrived home that evening and went straight upstairs to her bedchamber. "Tell my brother that I have a headache and shan't be dining with him tonight," she instructed the housemaid who answered her bell. "And be so good as to send up hot water for my bath — lots of it, please."

The maid nodded sympathetically. "A hot bath'll do you good, miss, to be sure."

Once the old brass slipper-tub was pulled from the dressing room and filled, Xanthia dismissed the servants, saying she was going straight to bed and did not wish to be disturbed again. Then she slipped into the deep, hot water and tried to steady her nerves — or perhaps her *anticipation* was a better word.

Tonight she would make love with Nash. Not some impulsive, illicit act performed in haste and desperation, but a slow and deliberate savoring of one another. And

Nash was a man well worth savoring. With a deep exhalation, Xanthia let her head fall back against the high rim, and slid deeper into the bath.

Perhaps she should have been more apprehensive. Nash was a connoisseur of female flesh. He had doubtless made love to many women; women skilled in the arts of arousal and satisfaction. Xanthia, by contrast, knew little about either. But strangely, she felt she *knew* Nash. He was intrigued with her, of that Xanthia had little doubt. Whether or not simple intrigue would become anything more remained to be seen. Xanthia accepted that life was fraught with uncertainties, and she had learned to take her pleasure — and her comfort — where and when she could. She would take all that Lord Nash could offer her, and be glad of it. She would not look beyond tonight.

So resolved, Xanthia took up the soap and her brush, and scrubbed herself head to toe, all the while thinking of Nash. In the warm, sudsy water, she lifted her breasts in her hands. She was no beauty, it was true, but she was made generously enough, she thought. She had the sort of trim, vigorous body which some men appreciated — Nash apparently amongst them. Last night, despite his obvious anger and frustration, the simmering heat in his gaze had been unmistakable.

And tonight . . . would he look at her again in just that way? Would his black eyes melt with ardor as he stripped the clothes from her body? At the mere thought, something in Xanthia's stomach seemed to twist; it was a sweet, yearning sensation which melted through her body, leaving her longing for something ill defined. But Nash would know just what she needed. Xanthia understood that instinctively. She touched herself there — where his mouth had been but a few days past — and shivered with anticipation.

Good Lord, it was time to get dressed.

She dried, and drew on one of her few extravagances — hideously expensive silk undergarments. Soon, a dozen dresses had been drawn from her wardrobe, and rejected again. Xanthia, who scarce gave a thought to her wardrobe, was suddenly beset by doubt. She held up two gowns, studying each in the mirror. What did the well-dressed woman wear to an assignation? Red? She wrinkled her nose and tossed it aside. Deep blue silk? Xanthia lifted it higher and remembered Mr. Kemble's advice. That shade of blue did indeed do wonders for her eyes.

When she was dressed in her dark cloak and veil, Xanthia slipped down the back stairs and out the rear door. She made her way through Mayfair, once again shrouded in fog, but not quite the all-enveloping pea soup of the previous evening. She wondered vaguely if Mr. Kemble was following her. Someone likely was — and for all his protestations, she rather doubted Kemble had entrusted the job to another.

But she would not think of that, nor of what de Vendenheim had asked of her. The intrigues of men no longer interested Xanthia; she wished only to prove Nash's innocence and move on with her life. The identity of de Vendenheim's mysterious villain was best left to the devices of those more clever — and more concerned — than she.

It was an easy enough task to go through the mews and identify Nash's house. His was the only door lit. She made her way through the gloom, and went up the three steps to the stoop. But when she lifted her hand to knock, the door opened. Nash stood on the threshold, his wide, solid shoulders blocking the dimly lit passageway beyond.

"You came," he said.

"Yes." She stepped inside and lifted off

the veiled hat, cutting a sidelong glance at him. Tonight he was dressed for the comfort of his own home, wearing no coat, but only a waistcoat of muted black brocade. His shirtsleeves billowed faintly around his arms, and he wore his hair caught back in a black silk cord, a look which was unfashionable yet, on him, quite striking.

He lifted her cloak from her shoulders. For an instant, they stood there awkwardly. Then Xanthia cupped his face in her hands and rose onto her tiptoes to set her cheek to his. "I came."

A hard, strong arm banded about her waist, whilst his opposite hand settled almost comfortingly between her shoulder blades. He buried his face in her loosely arranged hair. "Is it wrong of me to wish to see you so desperately?" he whispered.

Xanthia laughed a little nervously. "What choice did you have?" she answered. "I have thrust myself upon you."

Nash heard the edge in Xanthia's voice. He set her away and slid his wide, warm palms around her face. "You mustn't think that," he whispered, his eyes roaming over her face. "I want you madly, Zee." Nonetheless, at that moment, Nash was questioning his own sanity and wondering if there was any way he could summon the fortitude to kiss her quickly then send her back out the door.

No. He knew it the instant he felt her lush breasts against his chest. Their lips had not met, and yet the hot rush of desire already pooled heavily in his loins. She must have sensed it, for she lifted her chin, and parted her lips enticingly. Her rich blue eyes were soft and welcoming in the dim light of the corridor. He took her lips in a kiss which became endless in its sweetness. Over and over Nash kissed her, slanting his mouth over hers in caresses which left them both weak-kneed and a little shaken.

"Zee, come upstairs." He whispered the words against her lips. "I should be patient, love, but it is beyond me."

Xanthia's dark lashes lowered, feathering across her ivory cheeks. "I wish you to make love to me, Nash," she rasped. "Slowly — as if we had all the time in the world. Not just a few stolen moments. Not just this one night."

This one night. Was that all she meant it to be?

It would be wise of her, but Nash could not bear to think of it. And although it was a romantic, almost silly gesture, he swept her off her feet and into his arms. She pressed her cheek against the softness of his coat, and, suddenly, it did not feel silly at all. She said nothing as he carried her up the two flights of steps to his suite.

"I have a surprise for you," he murmured.

He laid her down in the middle of his bed and set his knee to the mattress. Half of her long, heavy hair had already slipped from its loose arrangement, and was cascading across the brocade of his coverlet like a waterfall of dark silk. Her hands lay to either side of her head, her fingers gently curled to her palms, in an almost submissive gesture, and Nash was struck with the almost primitive urge to take her — to take her fiercely, to bind her to him then and there, without another word.

But it was then that she noticed the flowers. She sat up a little and looked about in obvious amazement. "Good heavens!" she murmured. "Hibiscus blossoms? Nash, what on earth?"

He braced one hand on the headboard, leaned over her. "I thought they might remind you of home."

Vases of tropical hibiscus blossoms were everywhere — pink, peach, and even crimson — and the bed on which she lay had been scattered with petals. Nash plucked a pink one from a vase by the bed — a huge, double-blossomed beauty, and passed it to her.

Xanthia held it to her nose to inhale the familiar scent. "Oh, they *do,* remind me of home," she murmured. "Do you know, we had an entire hedge of these round our house. Goodness, Nash, where did you find so many?"

"I robbed every hothouse in the south of England," he confessed.

Her eyes widened farther still, and she laughed. "You didn't?"

"Well, my messengers probably harangued them until they likely wished I had." He took her empty hand in his. "But you struck me as the sort of woman who ought to be made love to on a bed of flower petals — and what better than these?"

She drew the blossom down the turn of his jaw. "Ah, it seems I have you in my power," she said. "You must want desperately to please me."

Nash gave a sharp laugh. "My dear, I think I should hate you to know just how desperate."

Xanthia stroked the flower beneath his chin. "Then undress for me," she whispered. "I wish to see something beautiful."

"That's what the hibiscus blossoms were for," he teased. "Have my poor florists suffered for naught?"

"Oh, Nash, you wretch!" She choked out the word on a sound which was half a laugh, but perhaps half a sob, too. "Damn you for being such a — a *romantic!* They *are* beautiful — too beautiful. What kind of libertine are you, sprinkling hibiscus petals over your bed?"

He carried her knuckles to his lips. "I am wooing you, you practical-minded shrew," he said, kissing the back of her hand. "Be still, and let me properly seduce you."

"*Properly seduce* was not the phrase I had in mind," she assured him, sitting up amidst the flower petals, and kicking off her slippers. "Undress for me, Nash. Please. I want to feast my eyes on something that is both beautiful and wicked."

Nash felt suddenly taken aback. Oh, he had undressed for women a thousand times — but what she asked for — it was somehow more than he had given before. But her hands were already at his cravat, and in seconds, she was unfurling it from his neck like an expert.

He looked down at her, and lifted one eyebrow.

"Two brothers," she answered dryly. "Brothers who often came home cup-shot, only to promptly pass out. Valets were in short supply — but I am, if I do say so myself, not a bad one."

Her clever fingers were already slipping free the buttons of his waistcoat. She pushed it from his shoulders, taking his braces with it. Nash drew his shirt hems from his trousers and dragged it off over his head. He was gratified by a sharp inhalation of breath — the unmistakable sound of feminine appreciation.

Xanthia leaned into him, lifting her mouth to his. As their already-swollen lips met, she began to deftly unfasten his trousers. But Nash kissed her lingeringly, refusing to be hurried despite the increasingly urgent sound of her breathing.

By God, the woman was not going to rush him into scratching an itch that could not wait. It very well *would* wait — and by the time he had done with her, Nash vowed, she'd be on her knees and shedding the tears of a grateful woman. He pushed her back down into the softness of the bed, braced his hands beside her shoulders, and told her so, in no uncertain words.

Xanthia's eyes widened, and her chest rose with a deep, anticipatory breath. Nash got up, ruthlessly toed off his slippers, then shucked off trousers, stockings, and drawers in one practiced move.

On the bed, Xanthia swallowed. Hard. "Oh, my!" she whispered, her eyes trailing lower. And lower. "You really are . . . quite magnificent."

Nash was no longer sure that was so — he had long ago ceased to be a beautiful boy, but was instead a man — in his prime, yes, but with all the attendant battle scars. He accepted her compliment, however, and drew her up from the bed.

"Now, wench, it is your turn," he answered. Quickly, he unbuttoned her gown down the back. It sagged open to reveal an elegant chemise of fine white silk and a pair of slender shoulder blades that made his mouth go strangely dry.

They were just shoulder blades. Good God. He drew the pins from her hair, then sat down and pulled her a little roughly between his thighs. Xanthia watched almost passively as he divested her of most of her garments, until at last he was rolling her stockings down her legs. But when she was then left in nothing but her drawers, she crossed her arms a little shyly over her bare breasts, and looked away.

"Oh, no," he murmured, slithering them down her hips.

Dear God, he thought. *Her thighs really did go on forever.* Her hips curved gently, her belly was a soft, beautiful swell, and her navel turned inward in a way which made a man want rather desperately to tease it with his tongue. But the thatch of dark hair at the joining of her thighs — oh, it was almost enough to drive a man mad. He inhaled her scent, then, on a wild, irrepressible impulse, slid his hands around to cradle her derrière. She gasped faintly. But he drew her body to his mouth without preamble, thrusting his tongue deep.

Xanthia cried out, a faint, quavering sound. A jolt of pleasure. Her hands settled lightly on his shoulders, as if for balance. Nash drove his tongue in again, stroking it as deep as the position permitted. The scent of her was maddening. Over and over he flicked his tongue through the warmth, feeling her buttocks tremble in his hand and her fingernails dig into his shoulders.

It was not enough. He set his lips to her belly, and closed his eyes. Dear God, when *would* he have enough? He could make love to her like this all night, he feared — and never ease this aching hunger.

"Lie down," he said, a little roughly.

Xanthia did as she was told. He dragged his body over her nakedness and pushed her legs wide with one knee. For long moments he kissed her, his fingers buried in

310

her hair, his cock throbbing hot and urgent against the warm velvet of her thigh. Kissing her so deeply, so intimately, Nash began to lose touch with the present, began to lose himself in the raw need as he slid, hopelessly and inexorably, into that blinding sensual abyss he knew so well.

Xanthia's breathing was ragged when his lips left hers. He sat back and let his eyes sweep over her — *feast* on her, just as she had said. Her breasts rose rapidly, their large areolas dark pink against the ivory of her skin, skin so pale he could trace the blue veins just beneath the creamy surface. Her nipples were hard nubs now, and her skin prickled with sensual awareness.

Nash set his mouth to her breast and drew her nipple between his teeth, biting just enough to make her gasp. Her hips bucked beneath him instinctively, a clear signal of what her body wanted. For long minutes, Nash suckled her, tasting and nipping, until her trembling and her breathing had risen to a fevered pitch.

When he sat up, her mouth was slightly parted, her face turned half-away. Her breasts were still rising and falling as she gasped. He gently turned her face back to his, and held her wide-eyed gaze.

"Do I frighten you?" His voice was abrupt

and husky.

"Yes," came her whispered response. "We both frighten me."

And she frightened him just a little. Though he would never have admitted it, Nash was on unsteady ground, and he knew it. But best not to think of that too deeply. Instead, he pushed her thighs wider with the flats of his hands, then trailed one thumb through her glistening wetness. She gasped twice, like a woman on the verge of release — and yes, just a little afraid of herself.

On impulse, Nash picked up the pink hibiscus blossom and stroked it down her breastbone. The stiff green leaves were almost black against her fairness, and he found the contrast deeply erotic. Slowly, he brushed the flower over her left nipple, hardening it even further, as if such a thing were possible. Over and over, he stroked her with the heavy pink flower, fixated on the way her flesh shivered as the rough leaves lightly prickled at her skin. Then the wide, milk-soft petals would follow, almost soothing it. He stroked her throat, her breasts, the crooks of her arms, slowly working his way toward the sweet swell of her belly.

He toyed with that perfect little navel. With the slight curve of her pelvic bones.

Then down the quivering flesh that guarded her womb. Her breath was rough now, almost as if she were crying. She was looking not at him, and not at the flower, but at his hand. With the opposite fingers, he gently parted her, then drew the blossom through her slick, creamy flesh. She cried out, a tremulous, uncertain sound.

Again, he stroked. And again, until she was shivering. Until the shivering became something more. "Come for me, Xanthia," he crooned after a time. "Let yourself go."

"I — I — can't," she gasped. "I want — I want — you inside."

He wasn't sure why he urged her on. "Just feel it, Zee," he whispered. "Feel the soft touch of the flower on your sweet, hard — there, do you feel it?"

"Yes —" she gasped. "Oh! But I want . . . oh, Nash!"

"You want *this,* Zee," he whispered, lightly tormenting her with the hibiscus. "Come for me, my tropical flower. Let it go. Tremble, and let me watch. Here — take your own hand and —"

She jerked her hand away. "I need . . . more," she said. "I want *you.*"

"This *is* me," he rasped. "And you don't need more, Zee. You are such a wild, sensual creature at heart. Think of the silk drawers

313

you wear — so slick, so erotic. You wear them, Zee, because you like that silky softness against your skin."

"Yes," she gasped. "I . . . like it."

He drew the hibiscus just a fraction deeper. "The next time you draw them over your thighs, Zee," he whispered, "I want you to think of this flower. To think of *me* — making love to you with this flower. Making you cry out like the beautiful, sensual woman you —"

And then she was crying — and trembling to her very core, her hands curling deep into the loose petals and the softness of the coverlet. When her cries subsided, he dropped the hibiscus and crawled up the length of the bed to cover her shuddering body with his own. He felt . . . *deeply* gratified. Amazed. Inspired. Xanthia was beautiful — beautiful in her passion — both in bed and out. He held her close, planting light, reassuring kisses down the swanlike length of her neck.

When Xanthia came back to the present, she found herself inextricably entwined with Nash — literally and figuratively, she feared. Her arms were around his waist, and one of his rock-hard thighs was between her legs. But her heart — oh, that he held in the palm of his hand. In that perfect moment, however, time held suspended, and her life beyond this — this room, this night, this *man* — seemed fleetingly to hold no meaning.

Making love with Nash, she feared, would ever be like that. It would shut out the world, leaving only the two of them.

She felt Nash's weight shift smoothly upward, the rough, dark hair of his chest prickling at her breasts as he moved. Xanthia, still trembling, reached instinctively down to grasp his swollen manhood. Nash made a sound, an almost raw, urgent groan, then he mounted her. In the candlelight, his hard thighs bulged, and his shoulders seemed impossibly wide. Still fascinated, she slipping one palm down to cradle his heavy sac, then slowly she guided the firm, hot length of him between her legs.

"Now, Nash," she whispered. "Make me . . . make me yours again."

He entered her almost reverently, inching slowly deeper as the sound of his breath roughened. At the last, Xanthia lifted her hips to take him. Nash slid inside on a triumphant grunt. He set his hands to either side of her head, closed his eyes, drew out, and thrust again. "Good God, Zee," he rasped. "You . . . you madden me. *Bewitch* me."

She lifted her hips again, and slid her hands down the hard muscles which layered his ribs, then his thighs. "Make love to me, Nash," she pleaded.

Apparently, he did not need a second invitation. Soon his thrusts were deep and strong. His powerful hands were everywhere — on her shoulders, clutching her hips, stilling her buttocks as he thrust in a wild, carnal rhythm. His hands caught hers, pushing her arms high above her head. Xanthia rose to meet him, curling one leg about his waist. His too-long hair had long since fallen forward to shadow his face, and the glistening sheen of exertion lit his skin. Their bodies slid over one another, his dark, glittering gaze like that of something wild and untamable.

For long moments, they thrust and exhaled and melted to one another, the rhythm rising to an almost dizzying pitch until Xanthia's heart was like a drumbeat in her ears. She felt her whole body begin to throb with it; felt her passion draw tight as a bowstring — and then his fingers dug deeper into the flesh of her hips, and he cried out, a guttural, almost agonizing sound. Xanthia went over the black precipice with him, her hands entangled with his, her leg still wrapped around his lean, taut waist.

She came back to the sounds of their roughened breath. After long, wordless moments had passed, Nash lifted his body from hers and shifted his weight to one side. She rolled over, and he curled himself almost protectively about her. Xanthia's last thought, before she slipped into a deep and dreamless sleep, was of Nash's hand, curling possessively beneath her right breast.

CHAPTER TEN:
A LONG WAY
FROM YORKSHIRE

To sleep. Oh, to sleep the sleep that knits up the ravell'd sleeve of care! Nash had not had such a night of rest in a score of years or better. And now, he was vaguely aware that someone — something — was set upon dragging him from it. He buried his face in Xanthia's neck, forced the racket away, and drifted off again. But the clamor began anew.

It was Gibbons, devil take him. No one else could knock so hard. Or so relentlessly. Nash tried to bestir himself from Morpheus's depths. In his arms, Xanthia murmured something inaudible and rolled over. He felt her warm fingers touch his face and slide round the turn of his jaw.

"Nash?"

His eyes fluttered open.

"Nash, is there . . . someone downstairs?"

The relentless pounding came again, echoing through the empty house like a drum tattoo.

Alarm shot through him. It was not Gibbons. "Bloody hell!" He jerked upright, and scrubbed his hands down his face. Someone at the front door. And not a servant in the house.

"They . . . they will go away, won't they?" said Xanthia hopefully.

But Nash was already drawing on his trousers. "It would appear not," he said grimly. "It could be Rothewell, my dear. He may have discovered you are here. And if he has, ignoring him will not help matters."

Xanthia sat up, her eyes wide. "Oh!" she said, clutching the sheet to her chest. "Oh, no, Nash, I think it cannot be. He would be gone from home at this hour. What is the time?"

The knocking came again, more rapid. More urgent.

"Almost eleven." Nash was stabbing his shirttails in. He was sorely tempted to ignore the din, but a thousand troubling thoughts were running through his mind. *An accident. An illness. Tony. Edwina. The girls.*

"Good God, the girls," he said aloud.

"What girls?" she echoed from the bed.

"My sisters." Nash was throwing on his

319

waistcoat. "Something might have happened."

Xanthia looked worried. "Perhaps it is just a late caller? A — A friend? Or your brother?"

"I think not," said Nash. "Someone has been pounding on the door a while now. Tony wouldn't dare — not unless someone was bleeding to death." He leaned over the bed and swiftly kissed her. "But if it is Rothewell, love, and he shoots me dead on my doorstep — *you were absolutely worth it.*"

Xanthia could do nothing but stare after him. He had been perfectly serious.

Feeling more than a little anxious, she leapt from the bed the moment the door shut. Absent the warmth of Nash's body, she felt cold to her bones. She looked down at the bed, and at the fringe of hibiscus blossoms which now lay haphazardly around it. How romantic and unreal it all seemed now. And how dreadfully cold it had suddenly become.

For a moment, she debated throwing back the bedcovers, but that seemed . . . oddly presumptuous. She gave a sharp, slightly hysterical laugh, then went into his dressing room. There was a cream silk dressing gown hanging from a brass hook. She put it on and wrapped it around her in voluminous, awkward folds. She crept to the door and heard nothing. She was sorely tempted to tiptoe partway down the stairs. But no, that would not do. Her eyes flew across the room to the mahogany escritoire.

Well. There could scarcely be a better opportunity to do what she had vowed to do. Feeling dreadfully guilty, Xanthia turned up the wick of Nash's lamp and carried it across the room. One by one, she began to pull out the little drawers.

Nash approached the front hall uneasily, dragging his hands through his hair as he went, in some vague hope of neatening it. Now fully awake, his ire was quickly rising. By God, there had better be blood in the streets to justify this sort of intrusion. And damn it, if this was Tony —

He jerked open the door. It was not Tony.

It was a small, frail creature, damp from walking in the fog. She wore a limp gray cloak and carried a huge umbrella which had clearly seen better years — probably better decades. But when she lifted her gaze to the lamplight, he could not miss the righteous indignation which burned there.

Bloody hell. Another moralizer of some ilk?

And a damned determined one, it would seem.

"No reformers," he said, pushing shut the door.

The frail creature rammed her umbrella into the crack, splintering its delicate stretchers. "My name is Mrs. Wescot," she said over the awful crunching sound. "I've come to see the Marquess of Nash."

Wescot? Did he know any Wescots?

Mrs. Wescot shoved her umbrella in another inch. "Please, sir," she begged. "If you've an ounce of Christian charity in your heart, let me in."

Christian charity? Foolish girl. The Marquess of Nash had none. And yet, as he looked down at the ten inches of black oilcloth and shattered bamboo which now protruded into the sanctity of his home, he knew he was going to regret what he was about to do. Why tonight, of all nights, must he actually *feel* that one ounce — for surely there was no more than that in his heart?

But she was damp, and the night was chill. He threw open the door and stepped back.

The girl dipped her head shyly, and set her dripping umbrella carefully to one side. She was terribly young, perhaps eighteen, and seemed to take no notice that she had been greeted by a man in his shirtsleeves and waistcoat. "I must see the Marquess of Nash," she said again. "I'm afraid I haven't a card. Will you be so good as let him know I am here?"

"It is a dashed odd hour to pay a social call," said Nash, gently lifting the sodden cloak from her shoulders. "What is the nature of your business?"

"It is a most personal matter," she said, turning slightly. "He will doubtless recognize the name."

Nash froze, holding the cloak aloft like something contaminated. He stared down at the young woman's belly, and for an instant, the earth seemed to drop from beneath his feet. *Good God, surely not?*

But absent the heavy garment, there was no mistaking the high, round swell for what it was. And yet, he did *not* recognize her. He would . . . *wouldn't* he? Or had it come to this? Had he begun to forget the faces as well as the names?

No. It was not possible. He was almost absurdly careful of such things. And she was no more a whore than she was a lady. She was . . . something in between. Something which looked delicate and ephemeral and almost frighteningly alone. Then it struck Nash that *she* did not recognize *him*. Relief swept over him, washing away some of his ire with it.

Gently, he laid her cloak across his arm, and took up the lamp by the door. "Come into the parlor, child," he said. "I am the Marquess of Nash."

He heard her sharp intake of breath, but he did not look back.

Nash had no idea what one did with a guest's damp cloak, so he laid it across a chair. "Do sit down," he said. Then he turned up the lamp's wick and lit a branch of candles. He could see her better now, and there was no mistaking the lines of worry etched on what might otherwise have been a remarkably pretty face.

"Now," he said, standing before her, "how may I be of service, Mrs. . . . . Wescot, was it? Your business must indeed be urgent if it calls me from my bed so late at night."

"Your b-bed?" The girl had lost what little remained of her color. "I do beg your pardon. I-I was told . . ."

"What?"

She looked embarrassed. "Th-that you did not sleep, really," she confessed. "That you kept late hours and — and b-bad habits."

Nash looked at her very pointedly. "Perhaps I was not sleeping, Mrs. Wescot," he suggested. "Perhaps I was indulging in one of my bad habits. Did you ever think of that?"

She blushed profusely, making Nash feel instantly like the cad he was.

He clasped his hands behind his back and studied her. "I beg your pardon," he said. "That was tactless. Why do you not state your business, ma'am? It really is quite late for a lady to be out alone — which, now that I think on it, begs the question: where is *Mr.* Wescot?"

At that, she burst into tears. No, not tears — *torrents.* Great, heaving sobs which made him wish to spring into some sort of heroic action — but what? Nash dug rather desperately through his pockets until he found a handkerchief.

"You . . . you are a widow?" he tentatively suggested.

"N-n-no," she snuffled into the fine white lawn. "M-Matthew is in — is in — *oh, God!* — a sponging house!"

"Good heavens." Hands still clasped, Nash began to pace before the settee. "Ma'am, I must ask you — do I *know* Mr. Wescot?"

At that, the girl's eyes widened incredulously. "Do you *know* him?" she cried. "Yes, of course you know him, Lord Nash. You have driven him into near bankruptcy. How can you stand there, sir, and ask me such a thing?"

How could he indeed? Wescot. *Wescot.*

Something began to stir in the dark depths of his mind. A few days past, there had been a game of pharaoh at a very low hell in Fetter Lane — quite near most of the sponging houses, much to the convenience of many. Nash had been in a foul mood, angry with himself for lusting after Xanthia and none too eager to play. But Mr. Mainsell had brought an acquaintance — a chap of some five-and-twenty years, with a bold tongue and a cocksure manner. His arrogance had struck Nash very ill, and braggadocio had proven an expensive vice. The fellow had lost something rather large — Nash searched his mind — yes, a *mill.*

"Some sort of mill?" he said, scarcely aware he spoke aloud. "In — good God, *Yorkshire?* Is that it?"

The girl gave a sharp cry. "A finishing mill!" she said. "It was his grandfather's."

Nash scarcely knew where Yorkshire was — and he certainly did not know what a finishing mill was. He had come home, stripped off his gloves, poured himself a healthy measure of *okhotnichya,* and tossed Wescot's note of hand onto the teetering heap of detritus which awaited Swann's return. And there, so far as he knew, it lay to this moment. Swann would finalize the conveyance, then sell it, or trade it — or do whatever it was he did with such things.

But that night — ah, yes, that night! Perhaps, had he not been angry with himself over his own behavior, he would have cared very little about Mr. Wescot's. Perhaps he would have refused to play with him altogether, for it had come clear early on that the chap was but a rustic and in well over his head.

Nash became vaguely aware that the girl was still yammering on about Yorkshire.

"— and so, you see, his grandfather really felt that Matthew *should* have the mill," she was explaining. "And he did die shortly thereafter. But then Matthew found out about the babe" — here, she paused to set a hand on her swollen belly — "and I am persuaded that he wants only the best for the child."

"Are you indeed?" said Nash dryly.

The girl blinked back fresh tears and nodded. "That, you see, is why we *came* to London," she said. "Matthew wants us to live here — to take our place in society, you see — for the child's sake. He swears he shan't squander a dime, no matter what his papa fears — and that with the income from the mill, he really *can* pay off his debts, and buy us a fine town house . . . b-but then *he lost the mill!"*

Good God, what a nightmare! An early widowhood, he feared, was the girl's best hope — and if Wescot's insolent mouth were any indication, that day might not be too far distant. But in the meantime, what was to be done about her? And the child?

Damn it, why was this *his* problem? By God, he had played an honest game — as he always did. And if Wescot's family starved in the street, why must he now be troubled with it? Nash gritted his teeth. "And you are hoping, are you not, that I shall simply give you the mill back?" he said. "Is that it?"

Somehow, the girl managed to nod. She was softly crying now, not the heaving sobs of a few moments past, but the quiet snivels of hopeless resignation. At last, Nash sat down. He felt as worn as she looked — which was a damned shame when, not a moment earlier, he had been wallowing in the greatest pleasure of his life. He stared across the tea table at the girl, and braced his elbows on his knees. "Look, Mrs. Wescot, I am going to do you the favor of being honest," he began.

She looked up at him accusingly. "But you are not an honest man, are you?" she said. "Indeed, they say you are perfectly wicked."

"I am far more honest than most," he returned. "And whilst you may hear many things of me — most of them true — you will hear no one name me a cheat or a sharper or a liar. So here, my dear, is the awful truth — you have a babe in your belly and an arrogant young fool for a husband."

"I beg your pardon!"

But in his anger and frustration, Nash had no intention of stopping. "What your husband lost, Mrs. Wescot, he lost through conceit. What I took was a damned sight less than I might have done. The man played cards as if he had a dozen mills to spare and no family to feed. You must get him out of London — tomorrow would not be too soon — and keep him out. Mill owners from Yorkshire, Mrs. Wescot, rarely find any 'place' in society — and if you did, it would be the last thing you would wish for your child."

She crumpled his handkerchief, and her face crumpled with it. "Oh, I knew it!" she wailed. "I tried to tell him so. We do not belong here."

"When is the child due?" he asked bluntly.

She blinked a little uncertainly. "Why, the end of next month."

"Have you any relations at all nearby?"

She nodded. "My cousin Harold is a

greengrocer in Spitalfields," she said almost sheepishly. "I did marry *up,* you see."

Nash was not at all sure of that. "Is he a decent man, this cousin?"

The girl nodded. "He is plainspoken," she said. "But kind — and honest."

"Then you must send Harold to me, Mrs. Wescot, when the babe is born," he ordered. "He will give to me the full legal name of the child — be it male or female — and I shall give you back your mill."

"You . . . you *will?*"

"To your child," he said bluntly. "*Not* your husband. With Harold the greengrocer as trustee. Do you understand me, Mrs. Wescot?"

"Oh," she said. "Oh, dear."

Nash lifted his hands. "You may take it or leave it," he said. "It is the best offer I can make you, and a bloody generous one."

"Oh, it is generous indeed!" she said. "And very kind, too. But Matthew . . . he mightn't like it."

"Then you may send Matthew to me, ma'am," said Nash. "And I shall put it to him in terms even a fool can understand."

"Yes. Yes, of course. Thank you, Lord Nash."

Nash returned to the chair, and picked up her sodden cloak. "Come with me, Mrs.

Wescot," he said, "and I shall endeavor to hail you a cab."

"No, I thank you," she protested, rising. "I haven't the money."

"I shall pay the fare," he said quietly. "You will catch your death, child, haring about London in a wet cloak — and I greatly fear that your rather imposing umbrella has breathed its last."

She dropped her gaze. "Thank you, my lord."

Nash looked at her very steadily. "Have you a place to stay, ma'am? The spring weather can be vile."

"Our bags are still at the George," she said. "But . . . but they have thrown us out."

"Will your cousin Harold take you in?"

She nodded.

"Then I shall pay the driver to take you to the George to collect your things, and from there on to Spitalfields."

"Oh, dear. That . . . that is a very long way, is it not?"

"Not so very far," he reassured her. "And Mrs. Wescot — a word of advice, if I may?"

She looked back up and nodded.

He set one hand on her shoulder. "You are soon to have a child, my dear," he said. "So I suggest you get yourself a backbone and get the whip hand on that husband of yours. However awful it may seem, the welfare of your child will depend upon your ability to do this."

Her finely arched brows drew together. "But . . . but how?"

Nash set his head to one side. "You are a dashed good-looking girl, Mrs. Wescot," he said. "Must I really explain this further? Use the gifts God gave you and bring him to heel. Never forget that — for the right woman — a man will do very nearly anything."

"Yes." Mrs. Wescot stiffened her spine. "Yes, my lord. I shall endeavor to remember that."

Xanthia was bent over a chair, tidying her clothing, when Nash returned to his bedchamber. She jerked up at once, looking vaguely ill at ease. She dropped the last garment and crossed the room, her arms outstretched. "Nash?" she said. "All is well?"

He sat down on the edge of his bed and told her what had happened. By the time the story was finished, he had shucked back down to his shirtsleeves, and they were lying on the bed again, his head upon her shoulder and his arm about her waist. It was almost disconcertingly comfortable — and comforting.

"I do not know why it bothers me so, Zee," he murmured. "I mean — I am not without feeling, but this is the nature of high-stakes gaming. If we all begin returning that which was fairly won — well, what would be the purpose in it? Pretty soon we'll all be playing penny-loo with our grand-mothers."

Xanthia stroked a hand through his hair. "Part of the fault lies with Mr. Mainsell," she pointed out. "He brought a man to the table who had no business being there."

Nash said nothing for a long moment. "She was with child," he said quietly. "Quite far along. Did I mention that?"

"No." She stroked his hair again. "No, you did not."

Nash curled a little closer. "That, I think, is what unmanned me," he admitted. "The thought of that child, being brought up by a man who likely hasn't the sense to come in out of the rain — or worse, an infant being born into instant poverty, with a father in debtor's prison . . ." His words fell away.

"You felt it would be your fault?"

"And on one level, it would have been." Nash was quiet for a time. "I made a dread-ful mistake tonight, Zee," he finally said. "When we . . . when we made love."

In his embrace, she stiffened. "It did not

feel like a mistake to me," she murmured. "Indeed, I was rather hoping we might do it again."

Nash hugged her hard. "No, I mean that I left my seed inside you," he murmured. "That is a risk I do not normally take — and twice now, I have taken it with you. It was exceedingly careless of me, and I think . . . yes, I think that is a part of what troubled me tonight. Mrs. Wescot is to have a child — and what say, if any, did she have in the matter?"

"Most women want children," Xanthia remarked.

"Well, *she* should not," he said sharply. "Her husband is an idiot."

"Nash!" she chided. "You are in a very strange mood."

"Yes, I daresay," he murmured.

Nash spread his hand wide across her womb, as if doing so might guard her from the worst. He considered the risk he had run tonight and knew he should have been appalled. Terrified. Or at the very least, deeply concerned. But for himself, he was none of those things. To him, the odds of a pregnancy were only a little more calculable than the odds of Rothewell turning up on his doorstep with a brace of dueling pistols. It required a gamester's risk, one which he was prepared to take. For the alternative — not being able to make love to Xanthia — simply was not an option now. But was *she* prepared to take that risk?

Most women want children.

Xanthia was right, of course. But did she want children? At Lady Henslow's she had suggested that she had rejected marriage and motherhood. And now that he knew her better, he was beginning to believe it might be true. Certainly she had refused at least one proposal outright. She lived an unconventional life, and was quite obviously loath to give it up. Moreover, Neville's was the thing around which her world revolved. How could a woman own a business *and* raise a family?

But many women did. Perhaps not women of his class, but it was commonly done. And even amongst England's upper class, some women managed large estates. Others did an almost overwhelming amount of charitable work. If Xanthia conceived, what would they do?

They would do what most everyone in such a predicament did — marry. He would insist upon it — and if he did not, her brother bloody well would. For all his liberal notions about his sister, Rothewell was quite obviously a man of hard resolve.

Xanthia was right about his mood, too. It was very strange tonight. She might well decide she did not wish to see him again. She had come here to enjoy his company and his body, not to jog him from one of his melancholy moods. He forced it away and lifted his head to kiss her. But this time, it was tinged with an altogether different sort of desperation — and one which was wholly foreign to him. It would not do to examine that emotion too closely.

"I like you in that dressing gown," he said, when their lips parted. "It does not look half so fetching on me."

She picked at it a little nervously. "I thought I ought to put something on," she murmured. Then she hesitated, as if there was more she wished to say.

Nash decided that there had been enough serious conversation for one romantic evening. Besides, he was half-afraid of what Xanthia might say were she to give their odd liaison much thought. He rolled up onto his elbow. "Have you dined?" he said, his fingers toying with a strand of her hair. "There is a cold supper laid out in the dining room. Will you join me?"

"Yes, I am famished," she said, smiling widely. "My dinnertime headache seems miraculously to have vanished, and I could eat half a horse now."

"I believe it is just cold roast beef," he said. "Will that do? And will you dine in your dressing gown, madam?"

They laughed together at the absurdity of it all as they dashed down the stairs hand in hand. He felt oddly young and more than a little foolish. And suddenly, he did not give a damn.

On impulse, he decided to stop on every floor and give Xanthia a brief tour of the house's public rooms. Northampton House was one of London's most stately private homes, and it had been purpose-built for the seventh Marquess of Nash when Mayfair was little more than a cow pasture. Nash knew it was much admired. But for the first time, he felt himself actually *looking* at — and admiring — his own home. It was an inexplicable pleasure to see it through Xanthia's eyes.

She *oohed* and *ahhed* appreciatively at the sumptuous furnishings and gilt woodwork of the withdrawing room. She remarked upon every painted ceiling, every pilaster, and every cornice, then gushed at length over the mahogany furnishings and dramatic velvet draperies of the library. They reached the dining room still holding hands. Xanthia gasped when she saw the long, lustrous dining table laid with Northampton's massive silver epergne and its grand flotilla of matching service pieces.

But at the far end of the table, Nash's face fell. For all the splendor set upon the tabletop, there was, of course, but one place laid. He picked up the lone wineglass. "We could share?"

"Have you another fork?" she asked.

"A hundred of them, I daresay," he admitted. "But I couldn't say where."

She laughed again. "You really do live a life of pampered privilege, do you not?" she said. "Pour the wine whilst I poke about in your cupboards."

"That sounds exciting."

Her eyes reluctant to leave his face, Xanthia slowly released his hand. Nash lit the candles, and she carried one into the shadowy passageway which linked the dining room to the opulent gilt withdrawing room. As she had suspected, it was a narrow butler's pantry — and as was proper, everything was locked up tightly. She tugged on the drawers to no avail, then lifted the light to look all around. The pantry was neat as a pin, the marble floors and counters glistened, and behind the glass doors, the plate shone.

"You shall have to share," she said, returning to the table. "No, wait — the sideboard." She went to it, and began opening doors and drawers. There were plates in the left door and a minimal amount of spare cutlery in the top drawer. "By the way," she said, returning to the table, "you have exemplary servants."

Nash was staring at her, some fervent but nameless emotion in his eyes.

"What?" she asked, letting her gaze run the dressing gown. "Have I a smudge?"

"No, it is just —" He jerked out a chair to seat her. "It is just that I am not accustomed to having a woman puttering about the house."

"I am sorry," she said quietly. "It must feel intrusive."

He shook his head, and returned to his chair. "No, it feels — different. Pleasant."

Xanthia leaned back against her chair and surveyed him. "Did you grow up alone, with only your father after your mother's death?"

"What?" Nash's expression cleared, and he lifted the lid of a nearby platter. "Oh, no. Father remarried immediately. My step-mother still lives at Brierwood."

"Yes, of course," she said, taking a slice of the beef from the dish he offered. "You mentioned sisters. And I met your step-brother at Lady Henslow's, did I not?"

"Yes, Anthony Hayden-Worth," he said. "Lady Henslow is his aunt."

"I thought him very charming," Xanthia remarked. "Are the two of you close?"

Nash cleared his throat. "Well, we are vastly different people," he said, passing a dish of cold potatoes. "But I am very fond of him. Tony was seven when our parents wed, and I was a grown-up thirteen. It was good for me, I suppose, to have someone besides myself and my own misery to think about."

"You were a real brother to him?"

Nash smiled, but it was faint. "I wanted to be," he admitted. "I had had an excellent example in my brother Petar. But Tony . . ."

"Yes?" she encouraged. "Go on."

Again, he seemed to hesitate. "I always felt Tony resented me," Nash explained. "Though he certainly never said as much. I was so dark and so foreign and so frightfully ignorant of all things English. Tony used to laugh at me, and say, 'Well, if you are going to be an English lord, you must learn so-and-so —' And of course, I did not know it, whatever it was, so I had to struggle to catch up."

"But you did learn," said Xanthia. "Indeed, you likely know more than I do."

Nash cut her a chary glance. "Oh, I doubt

it, my dear," he said. "That first year, Tony and I shared the same books and tutors, for I was still struggling to learn the language, and I knew almost nothing of English history. It was . . . a little humiliating. Have you any notion, my dear, how long it takes to get rid of an Eastern European accent? I am lucky, I daresay, that my father did not beat it out of me with his razor strop."

How very sad his life had been. Perhaps she should not have dredged up such old and painful memories. Xanthia set down her fork and propped her chin in her hand. "I have a question," she said, studying him. "What does Tony call you?"

"Nash," he said, as if it were obvious.

She shook her head. "No, *before* you were Nash," she said. "What is your Christian name?"

"Oh," he said quietly. "Stefan."

"Stefan," she repeated. "You never said."

"You never asked."

Yes, and there was a reason for that, she inwardly admitted. De Vendenheim had told her his full name early on. But inexplicably, Xanthia wished to hear it from Nash's lips. He pronounced it with an elegant, almost haunting softness over the vowels. "It is a lovely name," she said.

He lifted one shoulder, as if it were of no

consequence. "It is spelled with an *'f,'*" he said. "Father wished me to change it, so that it would look more English. But I refused. It was not my name."

"It was an unreasonable request," she said. "Was he disappointed?"

Nash broke off a bit of bread. "I often disappointed him," he answered. "Deliberately, sometimes, I suppose. I felt that he wanted to strip away that part of me which was not English. Suddenly, after years of ignoring it, England was all that mattered to him. I found it dashed confusing."

"You were young," said Xanthia. "You had been dropped into the midst of a strange land with a strange language and customs which are vastly different from those in the distant reaches of Europe. You wished merely to cling to the familiar."

"How wise you sound."

"Because it was the same for my brothers," she answered. "When our parents died, no one here was willing to take us in, so we were sent out to Barbados to live with my father's elder brother."

"That is a long journey to a strange place — especially for three small children."

She smiled faintly. "Indeed," she said. "And I realize now how terribly traumatic it must have been for them. They remembered

England and the happy life we had as a family. I did not."

"I wonder which is worse," he mused.

It was a question Xanthia had often pondered, but there seemed to be no good answer. Certainly she saw no point in pondering it any further tonight. She picked up a crystal dish of pickled vegetables. "Tell me about your mother," she said casually. "Was she remarkably beautiful?"

He looked up from his plate in some surprise. "Extraordinarily so," he answered. "Why?"

Xanthia lifted one brow. "Well, you are very beautiful," she said, spearing a sliver of cucumber and passing it to him on her fork. "And not in the English way." She watched Nash draw the morsel from her fork, and thought again of how sinfully delicious his mouth was.

"No," he said thoughtfully. "There was nothing remotely English about my mother. I think that is why she was so miserable here. And whilst I believe that her abandoning us was selfish, I do understand how she felt."

"She was homesick?"

"It was more than that." He leaned close to offer her the wineglass, and the warm, erotic scent of neroli teased at her nostrils.

"I have always felt astride two cultures," he went on. "For almost half of my life, it was made plain to me that only two things mattered — our Montenegrin nationality, and our alliance with Mother Russia — this from my father as well as my mother."

"And then . . . ?"

"And then everything was turned upside down," he answered. "In the time it took for my uncle and cousin to drown, my father's ambitions completely altered, and my life entirely changed."

"Yes, my older brothers' lives changed similarly."

"How so?"

"When our parents died, it left my elder brother Luke as my uncle's heir," she said. "The holdings were worth very little then — just a run-down plantation on the island and a neglected estate in England — so it was more of a burden than a stroke of good fortune."

He looked at her with sympathy in his eyes. "Yes, I would gladly give up this life and this wealth — give it all to Petar — were it in any way possible," he said. "A title brings with it much obligation — as you seem to comprehend."

"And as my brother Kieran has learnt," Xanthia agreed. "He, too, was a second son.

He never expected or wanted to inherit. But tragedy often intervenes, does it not? My elder brother died in a fire — a slave rebellion, actually. It was . . . horrific. For all of us."

Nash winced. "A rebellion," he said. "How gruesome."

It was Xanthia's turn to shrug. "I do not think Luke was meant to be killed," she said. "But he was caught in the cross fire, quite literally, in a burning cane field. These things happen. We were not the only family touched by tragedy that day."

"And so the younger brother was left to deal with the aftermath," said Nash. "Good Lord. I suddenly find myself in charity with Rothewell — but do not worry. I rather doubt it shall last."

"No, it rarely does," said Xanthia on a laugh. "He is not one who inspires charity. But I love him. We are . . . close in a way which is difficult to explain."

They ate in silence for a time. Xanthia found it exceedingly pleasant and felt no need to fill the void with unnecessary words. From time to time, Nash glanced at her and smiled. His dark, unusual eyes looked especially mysterious this evening, as if the talk of his homeland and family had heightened something of the exotic in him.

"You have changed your scent," she finally said, glancing over at him. "When we met, you were wearing a hint of amber oil."

His slashing black brows lifted. "Ah, but a beautiful woman told me she did not like it," he explained, sliding another slice of beef onto her plate. "A beautiful woman whom I wished desperately to pursue. So I asked my perfumer to stop blending it in."

Xanthia was touched by his words. He rose from the table and went to the sideboard to decant more wine. She loved the way he moved, with such a languid, fluid grace — and he made love that way, too. A frisson of sensual awareness ran down her spine as she watched him. Yes, tonight one could well believe that the blood of Byzantium ran through his veins, or that his proud stance signified his descent from the Mongol horde.

"You must have your mother's eyes." She blurted out the words unthinkingly.

He flashed a wry smile, and returned to his chair. "Ah, yes," he murmured. "Yet another part of me which will never be mistaken for English."

Xanthia reached out and set her hand over his. "They make my heart stop," she whispered.

His expression softened. "I wish only to

make it skip a beat or two, my dear."

Xanthia settled back against her chair and laid down her fork. She watched his long, elegant hand tip the crystal decanter over the glass which they shared.

"If I am not being too forward," she said quietly, "how did your mother die?"

The exotic eyes grew distant. "We were never entirely sure," he said, setting the decanter down sharply. "When she made ready to leave England, she asked me to escort her to Danilovgrad — I was a big, strapping youth for my age, and well accustomed to travel — but Father said I was too young. So Petar insisted on going, against father's orders. But within a few days, they, too, were caught in — what did you call it? The cross fire?"

Xanthia nodded.

"Well, this was Napoleon's cross fire." The pain in his eyes was unmistakable. "They meant, I suppose, to go round Spain, and perhaps cross over Italy, but they did not make it. We never knew for certain. They died in Barcelona when the French seized the city."

"What a tragedy," murmured Xanthia. "In Barbados, the war did not greatly affect us."

"Then you were fortunate in one way, at least."

Xanthia watched him carefully. "Were you angry with her?" she asked. "Your mother, I mean?"

His head jerked up. "I don't understand how a mother could just leave her children," he said quietly. "Yes, Petar was a young man. To some extent, he could make his own choices. But we were no happier here than she. And yet, she made no effort to take us home."

To take us home . . .

Perhaps he still considered the Continent his home. She hoped de Vendenheim never guessed as much. On impulse, she leaned across the table and set her hand over his.

"Nash, you cannot know what your mother may have tried to do," she said. "Who can say what may have gone on between your parents?"

He looked at her oddly. "What do you mean?"

"The laws in England are very strict," said Xanthia. "A mother has no say as to where her children live, or even with whom they live. It is quite possible she tried to take you. Perhaps her request that you accompany her was but a ruse. Perhaps her real objective was to get you off English soil? How old was your brother?"

"Eighteen," said Nash hollowly. "He had

already purchased his army uniform."

"So you were much younger," Xanthia mused. "That is probably why she asked you first. To get you away."

Nash had obviously never looked at it that way. "My mother always seemed like a force of nature," he said. "She was so prideful. So willful. I cannot imagine her beholden to the laws of England — or any country, really."

"Her pride and her will would have mattered little here," said Xanthia grimly. "To take away an English marquess's son against his express wishes? She could not. It is probably a hanging offense."

Nash considered it, then shrugged. "Well, it makes little difference now," he said. "I am here. I am the Marquess of Nash, and I am carrying out the duties of the title — at least minimally."

She released his hand and said no more. As if to dismiss the topic, Nash began picking over an assortment of fruit. He selected an especially succulent apple, sliced it, and offered her a sliver.

"What was he like, Zee, this uncle of yours?" he asked lightly. "Was he like your brother — a sort of hard-bitten colonial?"

Xanthia laughed. "Is that what you think of Kieran?" she asked, after swallowing a bite of apple. "No, my uncle was what one politely calls a wastrel. A habitual drunkard — and a violent one, too."

Nash winced. "How dreadful for you, my dear."

Xanthia stared into the darkened depths of the room. "I have tried to look upon him with more charity as I've grown older," she said a little wistfully. "He was a bachelor of almost forty when we were thrust upon him. Even with his egregious neglect, the plantation threw off enough money to keep him in rum, dice, and women. He liked his life as it was."

"He could have sent you back," said Nash. "Better that than to hint that you were unwanted."

"Hint?" said Xanthia. "There was no hinting. A litter of sniveling, stinking whelps, he used to call us. He was quick with his riding crop, too, when we annoyed him. But he did not send us back. I think Aunt Olivia threatened him with something."

"Threatened him?"

Xanthia shrugged. "He'd had some sort of legal trouble in England. In any case, we survived. But Uncle did not; he lived less than ten years after that. Kieran used to laugh and say that the horror of inheriting us killed him — but he was so pickled in rum, it took him a decade to keel over."

"That is a grim sort of humor."

"It is the only sort of humor Kieran has," Xanthia returned. "Anyway, Luke inherited the title and the estate in Cheshire."

"Cheshire?"

"It is a county below Merseyside."

Nash grinned. "Yes, I still have the map Tony's tutor gave me," he teased. "But I was unaware that Cheshire was Rothewell's seat."

"Well, he behaves as if he is unaware," said Xanthia. "In any case, it wasn't worth much then, for Uncle had let it go to rack and ruin. The plantation was unentailed. It went to the three of us equally."

"I see," said Nash. "And how did you begin your business?"

"The shipping?" said Xanthia. "Oh, Luke did that. A few years after Uncle's death, he married a woman who owned a couple of dilapidated trading vessels — and Neville's was begun."

Nash lifted the wineglass in a toast. "And did he make you all immediately rich?"

"More or less," Xanthia admitted. "With Luke running the shipping concerns and Kieran buying up new mills and new acreage as fast as he could, it did not take us long to pay off Uncle's debts and begin to prosper."

"No, your brother does not look to be a lazy man," murmured Nash. "What does he do with himself nowadays?"

Xanthia shrugged and looked away. "He drinks and lives in the past," she said. "His life — well, it has never been happy. And now he misses the mills and the sugar plantations. But that way of life in Barbados is gone — or should be. Kieran is wise enough to know this, and to accept it. Many in the West Indies do not."

"Is there no woman in his life?" asked Nash. "He has never been married?"

Xanthia shook her head. "He was in love once, but he handled it very badly," she admitted. "And now there is only Christine, I suppose. That is Lord Sharpe's half sister. They are having an *affaire* — if one can actually call it that."

Nash's harsh eyebrows lifted. "Ah, yes," he murmured. "The lovely Mrs. Ambrose."

"Do you know her?"

He cut a strange glance in her direction. "There are few rich men in London who do not."

"Do you know her *well?*" Xanthia clarified.

"Well enough," Nash hedged.

"Have you slept with her?"

Nash looked at her chidingly. "Zee, have I asked you such questions?" he asked. "Do you wish me to make out a list of names? You will be a long time reading it, I do assure you. And no — I have never *slept* with her."

With a mischievous smile, Xanthia settled back into her chair and crossed her arms over her chest. "Yes, you *do* know her well," she murmured. "I vow, I should not be surprised. I think she is a very wicked woman."

Nash was methodically slicing up the apples and putting them back in the bowl. "It depends, I daresay, on your definition of *wicked.*"

Xanthia leaned conspiratorially nearer. "Mrs. Ambrose and Kieran go to clubs together," she whispered. "Vulgar places in Covent Garden. I overheard the servants giggling about it."

Nash's voice, when he spoke, was measured. "Mrs. Ambrose sometimes provides — well, a service, one might say," he agreed. "A service for men of . . . unusual appetites."

Xanthia felt her eyes widen. "Unusual appetites?"

Nash hesitated. "Mrs. Ambrose knows people and can gain entrance to certain types of houses around town," he said. "Houses of erotic pleasure. And she is, shall we say, a woman of open and liberal habits herself."

"Ah," said Xanthia, taking another fortifying sip of wine. "That explains it."

Nash looked up from the apple he was slicing. "Explains what?"

Xanthia cut her gaze away. "One evening Mrs. Ambrose came to dinner," she said. "And when she took off her gloves — well, there were . . . red marks. Around her wrists, I mean. She wore bracelets, but one could still see if one looked closely."

Nash's expression faltered. "If Mrs. Ambrose had rope burns, my dear, then someone got out of hand," he said. "Restraint is one thing, but —"

"Is it?"

He ignored her. "But wounds — well, let us say that even Mrs. Ambrose is not that debauched — not so far as I know."

Xanthia plucked a sliver of apple from the bowl. "You are mutilating this fruit, Nash," she remarked. "One almost gets the feeling that this discussion makes you uncomfortable."

He was still calmly slicing. "I am not entirely sure this discussion is appropriate for your ears," he acknowledged.

Xanthia nibbled off half the apple sliver. "Do you know, Nash, how many prostitutes live in a port like Bridgetown? Or Wapping, come to that? Have you any notion the things I've seen and heard in my lifetime?"

"I shudder to think, my dear," he answered. "But what we are discussing is . . . a rarefied form of sexual experimentation, not a quick tumble that costs two quid. A talent which is not easily acquired — and the women and men who are highly skilled at it can command quite a price — if they wish to."

"Does Mrs. Ambrose wish to?"

Nash half shrugged. "Mrs. Ambrose likes it both ways," he said.

"Both ways?"

"Never mind, Zee," he said. "Here, have another slice."

Xanthia took one. "Do you think Kieran ties her up before he has his way with her?" she suggested, biting into it. "Or perhaps she does something naughty to him? Perhaps — yes, perhaps she *canes* him. I daresay she dresses up like some slutty governess and just wallops his —"

"Good Lord, Zee!" He looked at her in pure exasperation. "I am sure I do not know. Besides, it is more likely to be the other way round."

355

"The other way round?"

"Mrs. Ambrose likes her men . . . dominant."

Xanthia eyed him carefully across the communal wineglass. "Then Mrs. Ambrose chose the right partner," she replied. "Besides, what woman wants a conventional, unimaginative man in her bed?"

This time, the look he shot her was dark, and assessing.

Xanthia smiled. "In any case, I do hear her say things to him sometimes. Oddly suggestive things — when she thinks no one is listening."

"Mrs. Ambrose and your brother make a dangerous pair," said Nash.

Xanthia had risen from her chair, and circled behind Nash. "Do you think we make a dangerous pair?" she asked him, bending low over his shoulder.

He looked up at her, his gaze suspicious. "At the moment, my dear, you strike me as the most dangerous woman I know."

Xanthia ran her hands over his shoulder, and down his chest. The fine lawn of his shirt was soft, but the muscles beneath were warm and firm. "I must go soon," she said. Lightly, she trailed her tongue around the shell of his ear. "But I should hate us to waste that fruit. Why do we not take it upstairs?"

Wordlessly, he rose, and snatched the bowl from the table.

Xanthia awoke in Nash's embrace some hours later, sated and sore from his languorous lovemaking. The fruit was gone, and most of the hibiscus petals had wilted. Only the brimming vases remained to remind her of Nash's romantic gesture.

Nash lay on his back, breathing deeply. She wondered at the time. Late — very late, she was sure, but the lamp was turned so low, she could not see the mantel clock. With great care, she eased herself from his arms, and sat up on the edge of the bed. She dragged the hair from her face and looked at the untidy pile of clothing she had left on his chair. It was imperative she be home before the servants stirred.

With one eye on the bed, she dressed, then carefully tucked two letters inside her pocket. She had found them in his escritoire. They were not franked, and the darkened folds suggested that perhaps they had traveled far. She hoped they would not be missed — and that she would soon have an opportunity to replace them.

She had seen another, larger desk in the library. On her way out, she meant to have a careful look at it. If it yielded nothing to prove Nash's innocence, then that was it. She was done — and she meant to tell Mr. Kemble so at her first opportunity — tonight, if she caught him skulking home behind her.

Xanthia was beginning to rue the vow of secrecy she had given de Vendenheim. At this point, her word of honor was the only thing which kept her from simply telling Nash the truth — that the Government suspected him of being a traitor. Dear God, how awful that sounded! How could she bring herself to say the words? And what would he say in return?

From the outset, she had been intrigued by Nash, and Lord de Vendenheim's cloak-and-dagger business had served only to inflame that intrigue. The chaos which de Vendenheim had described — the disruption to England's trade routes and the economic ruin which might follow — had deeply concerned her, yes. But perhaps, in the dark reaches of her mind, she had simply been searching for an excuse to seek Nash out.

In any case, her suspicion about his guilt had slowly turned to a certainty of his innocence. And somehow, Xanthia had come to believe his innocence would be easily proven — naive of her, she now realized, given the complexities of this case. Had she foolishly imagined that she would simply hand de Vendenheim some tidbit of exoneration, and he would go haring off in search of other quarry? Certainly she had not imagined that she would fall desperately in love with Lord Nash.

Dear heaven! *Had she?* Had she fallen in love with him?

Xanthia closed her eyes. Lord, what a fool she was. And what a reckless intrigue she had got herself mixed up in.

She could not resist one last look over her shoulder before slipping out the door. Nash had the bedsheet thrown over one leg, but the rest of him could be seen in all his masculine glory by the flickering lamplight. She could still make out the solid rise and fall of his chest, the dark tangle of curls about his half-erect manhood, and the stubble of beard, which had already begun to shadow his lean cheeks. He was a beautiful, virile male — and Xanthia was suddenly grateful that he had chosen to take her to his bed.

Softly, she closed the door and felt her way down the stairs. The sconces had long ago burnt out, and in the library, all was darkness. With hands which shook, she managed to light a lamp on one of the reading tables, and carry it to the desk without incident. Gingerly, she drew open the top drawer. Nothing was locked. The ridiculousness of it struck her yet again. Would a gunrunner and a traitor leave his desk unlocked?

Of course not. But Xanthia poked hastily through it, swallowing down her anxiety, and finding little of interest save for a teetering pile of business correspondence, which included eight notes of hand — gaming debts, she supposed. And none of it was hidden, but rather, heaped in a wooden box on the desktop.

She was bending down to pull out the last drawer when a beam of light cut silently across the desk. Her heart in her throat, Xanthia jerked up, blinking against the brightness, which hovered in the doorway. "Xanthia?"

"Yes?" She closed the cracked drawer with her toe. "Nash? Is that you?"

He approached the desk wearing the ivory silk dressing gown, his lamp held high. "Xanthia, what are you doing?"

"Doing?" she echoed. "I — well — I am writing you a note. Or that is to say, I *was* going to write you a note — to — to say that I had to go. Home. But there seems to be no letter paper."

His eyes never leaving hers, Nash bent down, then slowly drew open the top drawer. A stack of white foolscap glowed pallidly in the lamplight.

"Oh!" she said. "Oh, how foolish of me. There it is."

Nash set down the lamp a little roughly. The flame cast eerie shadows up his face, hardening his jaw, and emphasizing the hollows of his face. "Xanthia," he said quietly. "Xanthia, how could you?"

Nausea welled in her throat. "Well, I th-thought that there would be letter paper," she lied. "Honestly, Nash."

"After the evening we shared . . ." he began. Then his words fell away.

"Nash," she said sharply. "Oh, Nash, I am sorry. I — I can explain. Truly."

"Well, I think the very least you could do," he said bitterly, "would be to wake me and kiss me good-bye."

"To — to *kiss* you?"

"What would you think, my dear, if you woke to find *me* missing from *your* bed after a night of incomparable passion?" he asked. "Would you say — 'Oh, I daresay he left a note in the library! That shall do very nicely!' — And then just roll over and go back to sleep?"

"N-No." She clasped her hands, and bit her lip.

He set his hands on her upper arms. "Xanthia, this . . . this is just an *affaire,*" he said. "I know that. But it is more than that, too, isn't it? Do we not have . . . a friendship? At the very least?"

She dived into his arms. "Yes, of course we do," she said, setting her temple to his strong shoulder. *But I needed to ransack your private papers first.*

Dear God, how dreadful that sounded! What was she thinking? What kind of person was she?

She drew back and let her eyes drift over his harsh, handsome face. "Nash, my dear," she said. "It was thoughtless of me. I — I adore you. Haven't I made a fool of myself proving it? But you have a score of women to choose from. Surely . . . surely you would not lose sleep over me?"

He took hold of her shoulders a little harshly. "I have *one* woman," he said roughly. Then there was a hitch — a hesitation in his tone — as if he was just now thinking it through. "One woman, at present, and that would be you, Zee. And whilst this . . . this very delightful *affaire* continues, there will be no one else. For either of us. Is that clear?"

"Yes, my lord," she said softly.

He tilted his head, one eye narrowing. "And if you *ever* disappear like that on me again, Zee, so help me —"

She covered his mouth with hers, cutting off his words.

"I won't," she said, when their lips parted several moments later. "I promise. I won't do it ever again."

He stepped back, lifted her hand, and kissed it in an elegant, old-fashioned gesture. "Zee, I wish you to do something else for me," he said. "Will you?"

"Yes, I would do anything, I think," she said.

He smiled. "This is an easy thing."

"Then I shall certainly do it."

Nash hesitated for a moment. "I just wish you to call me by my name," he finally said. "Just . . . Stefan. No one does anymore — well, almost no one. But, once in a while, I like to hear it. It reminds me, I think, that I am something more than just this English title."

She smiled, and wrapped her arms around his neck. "Then Stefan it is," she murmured. "Now you must do something for me."

"Anything."

"Kiss me good night again . . . Stefan."

CHAPTER ELEVEN:
GOUT & GUNPOWDER
IN THE DOCKLANDS

"Well, well!" sang Kemble upon entering Xanthia's office the following morning. "It seems someone had a late night."

Xanthia was not in a tolerant mood. Gareth had already remarked upon her bleary-eyed appearance *ad nauseam.* "Be still, my head hurts," she muttered. "Did you see Mr. Lloyd downstairs?"

"Off to the West India Docks already," he said, placing the morning's post on his desk. "You've another letter from that victualler. My, but he is getting testy! Do you wish me to take care of him?"

Xanthia cut a suspicious glance at him. "Take care of him how?"

Kemble shrugged innocently. "Why, just a civil chat," he responded. "What did you think I meant?"

"A civil chat!" Xanthia pushed away her tea in disgust. "What that scoundrel needs is to be drawn and quartered."

"Frankly, I've found that tends to draw a crowd." Kemble was sorting Gareth's post from the pile. "But I know a couple of blokes down in Stepney who'll tie his wrists to his ankles and toss him in Greenwich Reach."

Xanthia scowled. "No one is going hang over this victualling bill."

"Then they can tie his wrists to his ankles and toss him naked into Mother Pendershott's bathhouse," he suggested, waggling his eyebrows. "He won't walk straight for a week once those chaps get done with him."

Xanthia looked up from her desk. "Now *that* is frightfully tempting."

Kemble finished with the mail and returned to her desk. "Well, let's get down to business," he said crisply. "What has Nash said? Have you got the goods on him yet?"

"There are no goods, Mr. Kemble." Xanthia leaned over and extracted the purloined letters from her satchel. "There was nothing to be found save these, and I cannot make them out."

He flipped the first letter open. "Oh, he's a sharp one," Kemble muttered. "When it comes to what he leaves lying about, he's likely very careful."

"Or very innocent," said Xanthia, coming restlessly to her feet.

Kemble looked up. "I beg your pardon?"

Xanthia went to the window and stared out across the Pool of London. "Mr. Kemble, I wish I had never become involved in any of this," she said. "I should never have given you my word of honor to keep this confidential. Lord Nash deserves to know what he stands accused of."

"Miss Neville, what are you saying?"

She turned from the window in frustration. "That it is time we accept that the man is innocent," she snapped. "Nash knows nothing of this smuggling business. Will you kindly explain that to Lord de Vendenheim? He must move on and blight someone else's name with his innuendos and suspicions."

"Dear me!" Kemble began to fan himself with the letters. "Someone's a little short of sleep."

"No, someone's a little short of patience." Xanthia was pacing now, hands on her hips. "I have done everything short of offering to load up Nash's Carlow carbines and captain the ship to Kotor myself. I tell you he *simply is not guilty.*"

"Perhaps he just doesn't trust you?" Kemble had opened the second letter and was skimming it.

"Oh, he trusts me," said Xanthia. "The man has the instincts of an alley cat. He knows who his enemies are."

"And yet he does not suspect you," Kemble pointed out. "A spy beneath his own roof — even in his own — well, never mind that. But if he is so bloody clever, why does he trust you, the very woman Max sent to spy upon him?"

Xanthia felt the crush of guilt weighing her down. "Because I do not wish him ill, Mr. Kemble," she said. "I have believed — almost from the very first — that he was innocent of this crime."

"Oh, dear!" said Kemble softly. "Our little mission has been compromised."

She looked up at him wearily. "No, no, I went about this with an open mind," she said. "God knows Nash is no paragon of virtue. He might well sell a boatload of rifles to the Greeks — if such a thing occurred to him. But it simply has not."

Kemble seemed to be considering it. "Well, say nothing more for now," he replied, tucking the letters into his coat. "I shall take these over to Whitehall so their lads can have a look."

"Yes, the bloody things are in Russian, aren't they?"

"Indeed," said Kemble. "Letters from his cousin Vladislav. He is suffering the gout, and in a very ill humor."

"How do you know?"

"I daresay you've never had the gout, my dear, or you wouldn't ask."

"I mean — can you *read* them?"

"Oh, well enough," he answered, tossing his hand dismissively. "But there is no knowing what might be written between the lines. Perhaps *gout* is just a code word for *gunpowder* or *cannon* or some other sort of contraband. Spies have a thousand such tricks. Peel will hand those off to someone who will grasp all the subtleties."

He was heading toward the door when Xanthia seized his arm. "One more thing, Mr. Kemble," she said. "I wish to end this ruse about your working here. Kindly inform Lord de Vendenheim. I am in no danger — and I am certainly finished spying on Lord Nash."

"I shall tell him," Kemble agreed. "But he won't like it."

"Nonetheless, he must deal with it," said Xanthia, her conscience lightening. "I won't go back on my word of honor, Mr. Kemble, but from here out, my loyalties lie with Lord Nash. I am giving de Vendenheim the courtesy of a fair warning."

"You are very bold, Miss Neville," he said. "I hope you have carefully considered this matter."

"Oh, I have," she returned. "Will de Vendenheim give you any trouble?"

"He gives me nothing else," said Kemble.

"Fine, then. I shall send a note along with you and make it clear that this is my decision." She went to her desk and began writing. "And as to those letters, Mr. Kemble, you are welcome to take them, but I must have them back this afternoon."

Kemble looked at her incredulously. "This afternoon?" he echoed. "But we are talking about the Government here, Miss Neville. There will be forms. Procedures. Perhaps even a committee or two."

Xanthia glared at him. "Kemble, I must have them back," she insisted. "You must return them to Berkeley Square by midnight, at the latest. If you cannot — well, perhaps I shall feel duty-bound to tell Lord Nash where they are, and why."

Kemble lifted one eyebrow. "You meant to return them," he remarked. "How? When?"

"I do not know," she confessed. "But I *will* get in. I have to." But her voice broke rather tellingly on the last syllable.

Kemble grasped her other hand, and gave it a squeeze. "Oh, my poor, poor girl," he said. "Oh, my dear Miss Neville!"

"What?"

But Kemble was just shaking his head morosely. "You really are quite head over heels, aren't you?" he muttered. "Lord Nash is conveniently innocent. You are madly in love. And Max is going to blame this — all of this — on me!"

At two in the afternoon, Lord Nash still sat in his dressing gown, sipping at his morning coffee. It was, he thought, his third pot, but he was not perfectly sure. The first he'd managed to make himself. Of course, the day before, one of the servants had kindly ground the beans, set the pot on the hob, and laid the kindling beneath it. Even Nash was capable of lighting a fire.

The house seemed oddly empty today. Nash didn't know why. All the servants had returned promptly at noon, poker-faced and subservient, save for Gibbons. He was puttering about in the dressing room now, after making a great deal of fuss over all that had gone undone in his absence and the mess which had been left behind. The hibiscus petals Gibbons had ordered swept up at once, but curiosity still lay thick on the ground.

Well, let that curiosity run rampant. Nash had no intention of sharing even a hint of what he had experienced last night. He closed his eyes, cradled the warm coffee cup in his hands, and thought again of Xanthia lying naked across his bed, hibiscus petals in her hair. The entire evening seemed almost otherworldly to him now. A time out of place. A mood — a sense of serenity, really, which would likely never be recaptured.

Or would it? For a moment, Nash let himself consider it. Xanthia was not immune to his charms. In fact, she seemed to like him very well — and for himself, too, rather than for what he might give her. Unless one counted the sex, of course. Still, from the very first, Xanthia had brought with her a sort of quiet, which he found deeply comforting. But she was not, in the strictest sense of the word, a quiet woman. No, she was vibrant with life. Beautiful and confident. Gentle, but whip-smart, too, and —

Gibbons came trotting out of the dressing room with Nash's best evening clothes draped over his arm, whistling a merry tune — always a bad sign.

"What are you doing with those?" Nash asked suspiciously.

"Checking for moths," replied the valet testily. "We go to Brierwood next week, you will recall."

"Not in that rig."

"But there is to be a ball," sniffed Gibbons. "I had it from Mr. Hayden-Worth. Honestly, if I waited for you to tell me anything —"

"*Next* week," Nash interjected. "That, Gibbons, is the operative word."

"And if there are moths?" challenged the valet. "Have you any idea how long it would take to get a new suit of evening clothes made up?"

Nash shrugged. "I must have a dozen more in there somewhere," he said, picking up his coffee. "Just drag out a set of old ones."

"They mightn't fit," said Gibbons with another sniff. "None of us, I fear, are quite the men we once were."

Nash put his coffee down, and turned sharply in his chair. "What the devil is that supposed to mean?"

Gibbons smiled faintly. "You are almost five-and-thirty, sir," he said. "Things begin to shift — or spread — perhaps even *sag.*"

"I'll be damned," said Nash, leaping from his chair. He loosened the dressing gown and jerked it off.

"Really, my lord!" Gibbons rolled his eyes.

"The tape measure!" Nash growled, stripping off his shirt and hurling it to the floor.

"Get me the goddamned tape measure!"

Gibbons sighed, went into the dressing room, and returned with the tape, curled like a little snake in the palm of his hand.

Nash loosened the fall of his trousers, and held up his arms. "All right," he said. "Measure it."

"Sir, this really is not nec—"

"No, by God, I said *measure* it."

Gibbons wrinkled his nose and wrapped the heavy ribbon around Nash's waist.

"Ah-ha!" said Nash. "Thirty-two inches, is it not?"

"Tsk, tsk," said Gibbons.

"What?" Nash demanded.

"They do say a man's eyesight is the second thing to go," said Gibbons mournfully. "This tape plainly says thirty-three."

Nash gasped in horror. "You must be lying." He squinted down. Yes, Gibbons was lying. The tape very plainly said *thirty-four.*

"Oh, God!" said Nash.

"Not to worry, sir," said Gibbons placatingly. "Before your sucking gasp of horror, it was an even three-and-thirty."

And that was the beginning of Nash's new reality.

He spent the next two days wrestling with it — whilst already mired in the collective quagmire of all his other nascent emotions. Two days of soul-searching; two days to ponder the fact that his life was changing inexorably. For a man steeped in indulgence and hardened in habit, it was a bit much to take. But there was no escaping the truth. He was no longer young, but approaching middle age. His temples bore one or two strands of gray, and trousers which he'd worn for years were now an inch too snug. And in being forced to look back on his lost youth, he was beginning to wonder what, if anything, he had accomplished.

On top of all that, he was very much afraid that, for the first time in his life, he was in love. And he did not care. Or rather — he cared rather too much, and he had not a clue what to do about it. Indeed, of late his nights had been disturbed by tantalizing visions of Xanthia. Not the torrid sorts of nighttime visions he was accustomed to experiencing — though there had certainly been a few of those. No, the more tantalizing visions of Xanthia had been those of the most mundane — and more troubling — sort. Xanthia poking through his sideboard and looking very much at home. Xanthia in his dressing gown. Xanthia feeding him slices of cucumber from her fork.

So. There it was. He had had the unfortunate luck to fall in love with perhaps the one woman in all of London who would not have him. His title and his money meant nothing to her, of that he was utterly certain. Nonetheless, there were a great many things they both shared. A less-than-happy childhood. That constant sense of being different, of being an outsider. And, he believed, a sincere affection for one another. Surely those things were something on which one might build?

On the third day following his passionate tryst with Xanthia, Nash realized he would shortly be expected at Brierwood. God how he hated to leave without seeing her again. He had been half-hoping for another of her smuggled missives, even as he acknowledged how dangerous they were. Perhaps she had come to realize it?

"By the way, my lord," said Gibbons, who was just finishing off Nash's neckcloth, "there's been another letter from Swann."

Nash scowled. "I think it is high time we had something besides a letter from him."

Gibbons acted as if he had not spoken. "Most unfortunate news," he continued, giving the cravat one last fluff. "He fell off the roof of his mother's cottage."

Nash lowered his chin. "He fell?" he echoed incredulously. "Good God, what is a man of affairs doing on a roof — *anyone's* roof?"

Gibbons smiled tightly. "You will recall he is trying to let the cottage, my lord, but the roof was leaking prodigiously," he said. "He assures me that the break is not bad, but —"

"Break? What break?"

"The break in his shoulder," the valet clarified. "Well, the clavicle, perhaps? I believe that is a little less dire? In any case, he cannot be jostled in a horse or a carriage for a week or so."

"I am not fond of this long-distance relationship we seem to be having with Mr. Swann," Nash complained. "I need him *here.*"

"I am sure, my lord, that you do," said Gibbons. "But the stagecoach is a rough, miserable way to travel. Those contraptions could jolt one's intact bones out of place."

"I know! I know!" Nash grumbled. "I am dashed sorry he's hurt. But I have the most frightful pile of *things* heaped up on my desk. I have begun to forget, quite honestly, what's to be done with half of it."

Gibbons smiled solicitously. "Yes, you have had other things on your mind, haven't you?" he murmured. "Might I suggest we travel with Mr. Hayden-Worth to Brierwood? We won't be *too* snug, I think — and then you may send your well-sprung traveling coach to fetch Mr. Swann home in comfort."

"Oh, very well," said Nash. "Poor devil! Where is his letter?"

"On your escritoire, my lord."

Nash gave himself one last look in the mirror, then went to the little desk. "I shall tell him to expect the carriage on Saturday," he said. "Will that be too soon, do you —"

Gibbons approached. "My lord?" he murmured. "Is something amiss?"

Nash turned from the escritoire. "Gibbons, there were a couple of letters tucked in the front of this drawer," he said. "From my cousin Vladislav. Have you any idea what went with them?"

Gibbons shook his head. "Not a clue, sir."

Nash frowned. "See? This is what it comes to when Swann is away."

"Were they important, my lord?"

Nash shrugged. "Not really," he admitted. "But he's old and in the gout — and I do owe him a long letter soon."

"And his letters were to remind you?" said Gibbons. "Never fear, sir. I shan't let you forget."

"Thank you, Gibbons," he said earnestly. "I would really appreciate that."

A sound by the door caused them both to turn around. Vernon, the footman, stood on the threshold. "My lord, there is a caller downstairs," he said. "A young man by the name of Wescot."

"Wescot? *Wescot!* Oh, hell!" Nash jerked out his watch. "Vernon, I'm to meet my stepbrother at White's within the hour. What the devil does the chap want? Did he say?"

"No, my lord." Vernon shifted his weight uneasily. "But he looks . . . unwell."

"Unwell?"

"As if . . . well, as if he's been crying, my lord."

"Crying?" The last thing Nash wished to do was spend another moment with one of the infamous wailing Wescots. He rolled his eyes heavenward. "Do you know, Vernon — if this is God's way of telling me to quit gambling, it just might work," he said.

"He wants only ten minutes of your time, sir," the footman replied. "He really does look . . . unwell."

"Yes, *unwell*," said Nash dryly. "I have grasped that. Fine, Vernon. Put him in the library, and send for tea — and perhaps something a little more fortifying, just in case."

Nash followed Vernon downstairs. A moment later, Matthew Wescot was shown into the library. His country-scrubbed cheeks had succumbed to what looked like the pallor of death, and he had not recently shaved. Yes, just out of the sponging house, it would appear.

Nash offered his hand, but his greeting was cool. If the man were here to quarrel about the conveyance of his mill to his child, he would soon rue it.

"I've come to thank you, Lord Nash," said Wescot the moment their hands dropped.

"Do sit down," offered the marquess. "For what, pray, have you come to thank me?"

"For your kindness to Anna." Wescot settled onto the sofa's edge, looking as if he might spring up again at any moment. "Anna, my wife. She called on you late last week."

Nash was still standing. "I recall it," he said. "And you needn't have come. I shall keep my pledge to your wife."

Wescot looked up, and managed to collect himself. "No, you need not," he said softly. "That is why I've come today, you see."

"No, I do not see," said Nash stiffly. "If you mean to ask me to return the mill to you, I am afraid I simply cannot countenance —"

"No!" cried Mr. Wescot sharply. "God no! Your offer was more generous than I deserved. But . . . but I am afraid there shan't be a child after all."

"There shan't be a child?" said Nash.

"Anna fell ill," whispered Mr. Wescot. "It is entirely my fault, of course. Had I not gambled away everything we possessed, she would have felt no need to slip out into the rain and the fog the moment they hauled me off to the sponging house."

Dear God. Nash recalled how she had shivered in her damp cloak on his doorstep. He had been vaguely worried about the girl — worried enough to send her home in a cab. He wished now he'd found her a warm brick, or plied her with brandy.

At that very moment, Vernon came in with the tea tray, on which he'd prudently placed a decanter of that very spirit. Wescot looked as if he needed a dram. But Nash was still thinking about his wife. "So she . . . she lost the babe?" he said. "Is that what you are saying?"

"Yes, to a fever. It strained her poor body beyond tolerance, or so the midwife said." Wescot drew a handkerchief from his pocket and honked into it. "But I thank you, Nash, for hiring her a cab and having the good sense to send her to Harold's. I would likely have lost Anna, too, had you not done so."

"Lost her?" Nash felt oddly numb. "She

must have been frightfully ill."

Wescot nodded. "At death's door these last two days," he said. "They did not believe she would live until the wee hours of this morning. Then the fever broke, thank God. But we . . . we have not told her about the child."

"I am so very sorry," he murmured. "The babe — it was almost due, was it not?"

"Yes, a beautiful boy," said Wescot sadly. "We named him Harold, after Anna's cousin. We prayed that he might survive, but his odds were —" Here, Wescot broke down into wracking sobs.

Nash sat down and sloshed one of the teacups full of brandy. "You'd best have a sip of this, old chap," he said. "You must buck up. Crying won't help your wife."

Wescot nodded, caught his breath, and drank. "You are right, of course," he said. "But I was about to say 'his odds were not good.' "

"Well, they weren't, I daresay."

"But do you not see the horrible irony in that word, Lord Nash?" he asked plaintively. "*Odds?* I swear, if I never hear it again, I will be thankful. I have learnt I have neither the stomach nor the fortune for gaming."

Nash slid back into his chair. "Well, it is hardly the sort of life I would recommend," he said. Then he realized on a start that he actually *meant* it. "It is a life built on the weaknesses of other men," he continued. "Your weaknesses have hurt you badly, Wescot, and put your wife in a most precarious position. Now you must be strong when she cannot."

Wescot gave a watery smile. "You are not a man who minces words, are you?"

"What good would that do you?" asked Nash honestly. "You are in a devil of a mess."

"No, my lord, I am not." Abruptly, Wescot stood, and Nash followed suit. "I am the most fortunate man on earth, for I still have my wife," he earnestly continued. "I cry for her, Lord Nash, not for myself. But there will be more children, eventually. When she is ready to hear that, I shall tell her so."

"Very wise," murmured Nash. "And for all her frail appearance, your wife does not lack for fortitude or sense. In the future, I think you would do well to heed her advice."

Wescot offered his hand. "Thank you, Lord Nash," he said. "I shall. And now if you will excuse me, I'd best return to Anna's bedside."

They started toward the door. Wescot did indeed seem eager to be gone. "What happens now?" asked Nash. "Do you return to

Yorkshire when your wife is well enough?"

Wescot looked sheepish. "No, I dare not go back and suffer my father's wrath," he said. "He feared I would do something foolish with the mill — and I am ashamed to have proven him right."

Nash furrowed his brow. "Then where do you go from here?"

"Back to Spitalfields." Wescot smiled faintly. "Harold has very kindly offered to take me into the greengrocer's business — and I am deeply grateful for it."

The greengrocer's business? Good God! Nash pinched at the bridge of his nose for a long minute, Wescot looking at him oddly. Nash let go of his nose. "Wait one moment," he said.

He went to the desk, suddenly grateful for Swann's protracted absence. Knowing he might well regret it, he shuffled madly through the heap of papers until, halfway down, he unearthed Wescot's note. He snatched it and returned to the door. "Here," he said, handing it to the young man.

Wescot looked down incredulously. "No," he said firmly. "No, I do *not* want this."

"I hope that you do not," said Nash. "It would be a true sign of repentance."

With a stubborn set of his jaw, Wescot

stuffed it into Nash's coat pocket.

Nash pulled it out again. "Take it," he said more calmly. "Take it for your wife. Don't be a prideful fool twice, Wescot. Do you want her to live out her life as a grocer's wife when you know damned good and well she deserves something better?"

Wescot hung his head.

"*Take* it," said Nash again. "Take it for Anna. But if you bugger it up again, Wescot, I will cheerfully hunt you down and beat you within an inch of your life — if that makes you feel any better."

"Well . . . it does, rather." Wescot glanced at the paper, then took it from Nash's outstretched hand. "Thank you, sir. Anna thanks you. I — I won't bugger it up again. I promise."

Nash watched him go with a terrible sinking sensation in his heart. That poor, poor girl. So frail and lovely — and so full of hope when she had left him. Dear God, how fatal one little mistake — one small error in judgment — could be to one's happiness. And how very short life could be. He grieved for Anna Wescot even as he grieved for himself and all of his wasted days.

But he need waste no more — or at the very least, he might do something worthwhile with what was left of them. He knew, of course, what that something should be. It came to him with the clarity of a bucket of cold water tossed over one's head. He wanted to marry Xanthia Neville — or at the very least, *try* to marry her.

Good God. This was madness.

He had better think about this. He sat down on the sofa and poured a second teacup of brandy. It was not *quite* as insipid as he recalled. Judiciously, he eyed the decanter. There might be enough left to put him out of his misery. And perhaps when he awoke, this strange urge would have gone away.

No. No, it would not have. Because it was not an urge. It was a certainty which had been edging up on him slowly and steadily for some days now. The bottom of a bottle would not obscure it. Besides, what did he have to worry about, save for personal humiliation? Xanthia Neville would not have him, and his mind had already run through all the reasons. But the most telling reason of all was that Xanthia had already refused what little he had to offer her.

What, then, would you rather do with your life, Miss Neville? he had once asked her. *Retire to the country and raise a brood of children, perhaps?*

No, she had answered. *No, Lord Nash, I am*

already doing what I please with my life.

And she was enjoying that life. He could see it in the way her eyes sparkled when she spoke of her business and her work.

But her eyes sparkled when she was with him, too. And she had admitted that she adored him. She trembled with pleasure when he made love to her. And, yes, she liked him. So it probably wasn't a matter of losing her altogether. It was not quite the horror which poor Wescot had faced. No, he could keep Xanthia, he thought — keep her in his bed, at least. Until someone's suspicion caught fire, and she was forced to choose.

Was that enough? If he bided his time, would he tire of her? Nash stared at the brandy and shook his head. So there was but one option left to him — and it was a slender reed at that. Xanthia was a business-woman, and she understood the art of the deal as well as any businessman he knew. Therefore, he must offer her something *better.* Something which she could manage and make as successful as Neville Shipping.

Brierwood. It was one of the finest estates in England — and potentially the most profitable. Thousands and thousands of acres of fertile farmland and rolling timber. Half a dozen villages. Two miles of channel frontage. A chalk mine. A coal mine. Grain mills. A quarry. A fortune at his fingertips, had he ever bothered to tap it. Instead, he had chosen to let it limp along under the guardianship of an aged estate agent, whilst easing his conscience by reassuring himself that someday the whole mess would pass on to a distant cousin — someone who would give a shite for it. Instead, Brierwood could be Xanthia's. To manage and to build, and ultimately, to leave to her children.

Or . . . she *could* just keep her old job.

Did he give a damn what society thought of his wife? Well, no. She could trot off to Wapping until those spiteful fishwives down at Almack's bolted the bloody doors in his face — he'd never been there anyway, and despite his long-ago wager with Xanthia, he wasn't going.

Still, Brierwood was one hell of an ace for a chap to stick up his sleeve. It would take some time, however, and some delicate maneuvering to convince her. In fact, it would be best to begin simply by waving the temptation beneath her nose.

Nash pushed the brandy away and headed for the stairs. "Gibbons!" he bellowed up the stairwell. "Gibbons, fetch my boots, and my best riding coat!"

Gibbons met him at the door, a coat hanging from his fingertip.

"Not the brown," he barked. "That's the drabbest rag I own. Fetch the dark blue — oh, and a fresh shirt."

Gibbons trotted dutifully back to the dressing room again. The man had a surprising knack for knowing when to keep his mouth shut. After the coat, there were the boots to be decided on. And then Nash decided that his cravat was just a tad too lifeless after all. But eventually, he was dressed, his best horse was brought round from the mews, and Lord Nash was off in pursuit of his future.

A few minutes later, he found himself sequestered in Lord Rothewell's study, feeling foolish and more than a little frustrated. Xanthia was not at home. How had he imagined otherwise? She was not like the other women of his acquaintance, who rose at noon and did little thereafter. Xanthia had a business to run. But Lord Rothewell was in, his servant reported, and would be happy to receive him.

Nash questioned the word *happy,* however, upon seeing the gentleman himself. Rothewell entered with his usual determined stride, but his eyes were shot with blood, and his deeply tanned face would have been politely described as haggard.

"Afternoon, Nash," said the baron, going to the sideboard. "Will you have a drink?"

"No, I thank you, it is too early for me," he said. "I've been up but an hour or two."

"Ah, and I have not yet been to bed," remarked the baron, returning to his desk with a snifter of brandy. "Sit down, Nash. I don't imagine this is a social call?"

Nash looked at him curiously. "What other sort of call would it be?"

Rothewell hesitated, then smiled faintly. "One never knows," he murmured vaguely. "I rather assumed — but never mind. What brings you?"

"Frankly, I came to call on both you and your sister," he confessed. "I forgot she would not likely be at home."

Rothewell set his brandy down. "No, my dear fellow, you must rise at cockcrow for that."

Nash felt suddenly at a loss for words. Never had anything so seemingly small mattered so much — and he was loath to ask anything at all of Lord Rothewell. And yet, he must. "I am having a house party at the end of the week." His voice was surprisingly calm, faintly bored. "The party is at my estate in south Hampshire. I know it is a tad late, but I wondered if . . . well, if you and your sister mightn't care to join us?"

Rothewell's expression was unreadable. "We barely know one another, Lord Nash."

"Let me be frank, Rothewell," he said. "I wish your sister to come — I do know her well enough, I think, to ask such a thing. But I think she ought not come alone. It would be unseemly, particularly given my . . . my reputation, if you will."

Rothewell had begun to toy with various objects on his desk. "I thank you, Nash, for making my sister's good name your foremost concern," he said quietly. "Let me remind you that sometime past, you asked permission to court her. I discouraged it. She concurred. Have you some reason to hope that her opinion of you might have changed?"

"No, but on those brief occasions when we've met, I have enjoyed her company," said Nash. "And I think it would do her good to get out of London for a day or two. We are having party for my stepmother to celebrate her birthday. And I have two young sisters whom I should like Miss Neville to meet."

"This sounds a serious business," murmured the baron.

"No, pure pleasure, I do assure you," said Nash, feigning obtusity. "There is to be a dinner party, some dancing, and . . . and a picnic, I believe. Most of the guests shan't arrive until Saturday. But I should account it a personal favor if you and your sister might come down a day or two earlier — Thursday, perhaps?"

Rothewell laid aside the pen he had been toying with and lifted a pair of piercing eyes to Nash's. "Thank you, Lord Nash," he said softly. "I shall endeavor to ascertain my sister's wishes in this regard. But in fairness to you, perhaps I should make *my* position clear?"

"By all means."

"Xanthia is the most precious thing on earth to me," said Rothewell quietly. "I cannot know your true purpose in issuing this invitation, Nash. But if you toy with my sister's affections — if you cause her heart to be broken, or even the little nail on her pinkie finger to be broken — I will gut you like a hog at harvest."

Nash did not frighten easily, but he felt a slight chill settle over him.

Rothewell smiled. "So, with that in mind, Nash, do you wish to rescind your invitation?"

"Not in the least."

"Indeed," murmured Lord Rothewell. He took another drink of his brandy. "Then we have only to determine Lord Sharpe's plans.

As you know, Xanthia is chaperoning Lady Louisa."

Nash kept his gaze firm and steady. "I think your sister deserves a social life of her own, Rothewell," he said. "Perhaps you ought to see to that?"

Some dark emotion sketched over Rothewell's face, then relented. "Yes, perhaps I should," he said quietly. "In any case, my sister will return home sometime after five, I daresay. I shall send round our answer at once."

Nash rose. He thanked Rothewell with perhaps somewhat less enthusiasm than he had greeted the man and took his leave.

Following his guest's departure, Lord Rothewell and his boon companion, the brandy glass, paced the floor of the study for a time. After some thirty minutes had passed, he went to his desk and, with broad, decisive strokes, penned a few sentences on a sheet of his best letter paper. Then he went to the bellpull and summoned Trammel.

"I wish my coach made ready for a journey to Suffolk," he said.

"Yes, my lord," said the servant. "Will you take the coupé or the traveling coach?"

"The coupé but I do not go with it," he answered. "I shall have need of the big coach myself on Thursday."

"Very well, my lord," said the servant. "But where is the coupé to go?"

"To my aunt's house," he answered. "I have written Lady Bledsoe's address on this letter. I wish the coachman to deliver it to her in person. He is to await my aunt whilst she packs, then deliver her ladyship to her daughter's house in Grosvenor Street."

"To — to Lady Sharpe's, my lord?"

"Yes," said Rothewell in some satisfaction. "To Lady Sharpe's."

"But . . . but what if she won't cooperate, my lord?" asked Trammel.

"Oh, I think she will," he murmured, taking up his brandy again. "Yes, I think that this time, for once, Aunt Olivia will do the right thing — instead of the selfish thing."

Chapter Twelve:
A Rendezvous
in Hampshire

Xanthia leaned her head against the glass of her brother's finely appointed traveling coach and watched the neatly whitewashed houses of Old Basing go flying past. Unfortunately, the jostling motion of the carriage proved too much. Xanthia sat up again and tried to focus on the world beyond. It was difficult, for she was burning with impatience — and with curiosity, too.

Three days had passed between the morning she had left Nash's bed, and the afternoon he had arrived unexpectedly in Berkeley Square. Three days of utter agony. Three days of being unable to focus on her work, or anything else which mattered. Oh, she had gone through the motions, accompanying Louisa to a ball, a tea, and two musicales. Nonetheless, she could not have said with whom she had conversed, or what she had worn. Even her days in Wapping had been a blur. Everything, including her next breath, seemed to hang by a silken thread, awaiting Nash's next move — if there was to be one.

Well, move he had. And now she was en route to his home — and not in the dead of night, whilst hidden behind a veil, but as an invited guest. *To his stepmother's birthday party.* It seemed the sort of affair to which one would invite only one's closest and most significant friends. Did Nash hold her in such regard? Certainly he barely knew her brother. Kieran had insisted, however, that they go — which, the more she thought on it, seemed very odd indeed. He had made all the arrangements. He had written *something* to Aunt Olivia, though he wouldn't say what, precisely. And today they would arrive at Brierwood.

Already they had been five hours on the road, but it felt as if they were no closer to Nash. Xanthia was on tenterhooks — and yet filled with a sort of dread, too. Would Nash seem the same person when they were in the company of other people? What would his stepmother be like? Or his sisters? Would they like her? Did it matter? Good heavens, would people say they were *courting?*

It was all too much. Xanthia leaned against the window again, looking for something which might distract her. In the distance, she could see an ancient church, its squat gray tower stark against a near cloudless sky. Well-dressed men were streaming from the wide-arched doorway, and beyond them, by the churchyard, two gentlemen held open the lych-gate. They looked mournfully down the green slope at the pallbearers who were carrying the bier high on their shoulders. A funeral, then. Kieran's coachman had already slowed in deference to the dead.

"You look sad, Zee." Her brother was paging absently through one of the magazines he had brought along. "I hope I have not made a mistake in insisting on this trip?"

She smiled faintly. "No, there was a funeral," she said, gesturing at the window. "That's why we slowed."

"Ah." Kieran lowered his head to better see, but the churchyard was vanishing in the distance. "Nevertheless, you have been squirming like an impatient child this last hour or better," he remarked. "It makes me think of the old days, when Luke would dress us up and drag us into Bridgetown for Sunday services — trying, I suppose, to be a parent."

Xanthia sighed. "It really does feel as if we have been traveling for weeks," she complained. "Why must England be such a vast place? And why must it always be so cold when one travels?"

Kieran turned his gaze from the window and laughed. "Zee, England is a very small country," he answered. "You are used to the distances and temperatures of Barbados. And perhaps you are just a little anxious, too?"

Xanthia drew her cashmere shawl a little tighter and turned again to the scenery, this time the fertile, rolling fields of Hampshire. "What did you say, Kieran, to Aunt Olivia in that letter?" she asked. "Why won't you tell me?"

This time, he answered. "I simply told her it was high time she came down to London and did her duty by Louisa," his eyes suddenly dark and hard. "And by Pamela, too. She is carrying the woman's grandchild, for God's sake. A week in town shan't kill her."

"And she really is coming?" said Xanthia quietly. "We have not abandoned poor Louisa, have we?"

"She really is coming," Kieran reassured her, tugging out his watch and glancing at it. "Actually, she is probably there by now. It is not so terribly far to Aunt Olivia's."

In the confines of the carriage, Xanthia tried to stretch. "I still think," she said on a yawn, "that you blackmailed her."

Kieran hesitated oddly. "Blackmailed her?" he echoed. "With what, pray?"

Xanthia collapsed against the banquette and regarded him across the carriage. "I've no notion," she finally said. "But I know Aunt Olivia cares for none but herself. To bring her to London in the midst of the season . . . oh, yes, I think you had some sort of trick up your sleeve, brother dear."

Kieran's mouth merely quirked with humor. He returned his gaze to his magazine. Xanthia wadded up the carriage blanket she'd been wearing over her knees, stuffed it against the window, and rested her cheek on it. She drifted off to the rocking of the carriage and slipped into a hazy dream about Nash, who was wearing the black cloak and horns he'd worn at Lady Cartselle's masque and leading her through some sort of dark, twisting passageway.

When she stirred to awareness sometime later, the carriage was lurching left to make a turn between a pair of imposing stone gateposts. The massive monoliths were crowned with glittering falcons which were clutching golden orbs in their claws.

Kieran stared up through the carriage window as their huge coach swung through the gate. "I wonder," he said dryly, "if Nash has to climb up there and polish those silly fandangles himself?"

She looked up at her brother, and blinked. "We . . . we are there?"

Kieran nodded. "We are there," he said. "And soon you may see Lord Nash in the flesh, my dear, and fly at *him* with all your burning curiosity."

Alas, it was not to be.

"I am *frightfully* sorry to say that Nash has been delayed," said Lady Nash in a cheerful, chirpy voice. She was escorting Xanthia and Kieran up the sweeping stone staircase, and into a massive entrance hall laid with marble and dripping with gilt. "Tony did not know until the very *last moment,* you see, that Jeffers had even *died.*"

Kieran's brow furrowed. "And Mr. Jeffers was who, again, ma'am?"

Lady Nash smiled and clasped her hands in an almost saintly gesture. "Their childhood tutor," she chirped again. "A *lovely* and most learned man. But he retired to Basingstoke, then he died. I have noticed that happens quite a lot."

"I beg your pardon," said Kieran. "What happens?"

"Retainers retire — then they *die.*" Lady Nash seemed to take it as a personal affront. "I think the physicians should look into it.

It is such a frightfully odd coincidence — and then one must deal with *the funeral,* mustn't one? It is such a *dreadful* inconvenience, but Tony and Stefan — Nash, I mean — well, they could hardly pass *right by* the service, could they, when it was to be on their way here? Of course they could not."

"Indeed not, ma'am," said Kieran, though it hardly seemed necessary. Thus far, Lady Nash had answered all her own questions — and quite thoroughly, too.

Xanthia could already see their hostess might not wear well with Kieran. She was the sort of overly cheerful, pleasantly dull woman who twittered, and emphasized every other word as if it might be her last — and her most important. But it would be neither. Five minutes into their visit, Xanthia was confident Lady Nash would go on yammering from beyond the grave. The woman had not flagged since the moment she'd greeted them in the carriage drive.

"Now!" said her ladyship brightly. "You really *must* be worn to a thread. Why do I not show you to your rooms? And then the girls would *so much* like to have tea with you, Miss Neville — and with you, too, Lord Rothewell."

Footmen were moving efficiently about

the hall now, and sweeping up the double staircase with various bits of baggage, despite the fact that they had been given no instruction at all. Xanthia watched her dressing case vanish into the nether regions of Brierwood, and wondered if she would ever see it again. But one pile of luggage, a trunk and two portmanteaus in perfectly matched brown leather, remained untouched.

"I see that someone has arrived before us," Kieran remarked. "Do please ask the servants to see to their things first. We are in no hurry."

A frown sketched across Lady Nash's face. "Oh, those are Jenny's," she said lightly. "They came down hours ago. I mean, she is *such* a dear — but so dreadfully impatient and full of energy. I daresay she went down to the stables to see to her carriage. She *does* like things arranged just *so,* and the servants never do things quite perfectly, do they?"

Since Lady Nash had paused for breath, Xanthia turned around. "I beg your pardon, ma'am. Who is Jenny?"

Again, the angelic handclasp. "My *dear* daughter-in-law," she piped. "She is the most beautiful thing imaginable! Have you not met her? Oh, no, of course you have not. She has been either here or in France for much of the season. Jenny finds Tony's politics dreadfully dull, and she so *adores* Paris. She is *such* a fashion plate, and cuts *such* a dash when she goes to Town! Are you a lover of fine fashion, Miss Neville? Indeed, I can see you are. You really *must* ask Jenny all the best places to shop."

Even as Lady Nash escorted Kieran into his room, which shared a finely appointed sitting room with Xanthia's bedchamber, the prattle continued. Waistlines, it seemed, were going up — according to the knowledgeable Jenny. Sleeves, however, were getting fuller by the minute, and hats, Lady Nash warned, were shrinking to no more than befeathered teacups. Did Miss Neville like very small hats? No, of course she did not. Her hair was too long, was it not?

Nodding and smiling when necessary, Xanthia moved about the elegant suite of rooms, peeping out the windows and admiring the fine furnishings as Lady Nash kept asking and answering her own questions until at last, all the luggage was tucked away, and the servants were beginning, again unbidden, to carry hot water into their rooms. Suddenly, Lady Nash stopped dead in the middle of a recitation about how many new reticules Jenny had bought on her last Continental excursion.

"Oh, oh!" she chirped, looking about as if she'd lost one of her shoes. "What *have* they done with your maid?"

Xanthia felt her face grow warm. "I do not have a maid," she confessed. "I usually just snatch one of our housemaids. Should I have brought one?"

Lady Nash's eyes widened incredulously. "Oh, heavens no! We must have ten or twenty of them!"

"Ten or twenty?" But as Xanthia considered the house's size, and spotlessly clean interior, she did not doubt it.

Lady Nash smiled. "I shall ask Mrs. Garth to send up a few, and you may choose one you like," she said. "They are all named Polly — and they all have *frightfully* rough hands, so pray do *not* let them touch your stockings."

"Oh, please just send anyone," Xanthia protested. "Or no one at all. Truly, it does not matter."

"Very well then," she said. "We shall take tea in the Chinese salon, to the left of the hall. Will you join us there at your convenience?"

"Thank you, yes," said Xanthia.

She wondered if Lady Nash's smile was going to crack, but at last, the lady showed herself out and bid Xanthia to bathe and dress at her leisure. Her brother's door sprang open the moment Lady Nash shut hers.

"Lord, but I need a drink," he said, coming to stand in the middle of the opulent sitting room. "Is there any brandy in that sideboard?"

Xanthia waved him toward it. "You must find it for yourself, Kieran," she said, collapsing into the nearest chair. "Lady Nash has quite worn me out."

"My God, what a rattle!" he remarked, picking over the sideboard. "But harmless, I should imagine — and on the verge of perishing from curiosity. I suppose one must admire her for not simply demanding the scandalous details outright."

Xanthia looked at him oddly. "What scandalous details?"

Kieran glanced over his shoulder and grinned. "She is speculating about your relationship with her stepson," he answered. "I'd wager a pony you're the first female he's ever invited here. Perhaps she finds another Lady Nash a daunting prospect."

Xanthia felt her pulse leap. "Kieran, do be serious."

But her brother was warming to the topic. "No, think of it, Zee," he teased. "Why, I daresay the woman is quiet as a mouse under ordinary circumstances. You have likely terrified her."

"She has no cause for terror, or anything remotely like it," said Xanthia irritably. She toed off her shoes, and sank deeper into the armchair. She wondered if her brother had at last gone mad. Or could he be right? Dear heaven. "Will everyone be speculating about my relationship with Nash?" she muttered.

"Is there one?" her brother shot back.

Xanthia looked away. "I do not think I have to answer that," she said quietly.

Kieran looked at her a little grimly. "No, I daresay you don't — at least, *not yet.*" He had apparently forgotten his wish for brandy and was looking out one of the vast windows. "My God, I've never seen such a house as this," he said, his gaze drifting over the view. "I count six fountains in the front gardens alone! What is that place, Zee, in India? The fancy white mausoleum?"

"The Taj Mahal?"

"Aye, that one." Kieran turned and let his eyes drift over the frescoed ceiling. "It must look a bit like this, don't you imagine?"

Xanthia laughed. "Yes, but with more minarets — and fewer cherubs," she said, gazing up. "Remind me, brother dear, to give up my pudding when we get home. I should hate to begin to resemble that plump, pink fellow wearing nothing but a white banner across his belly."

Kieran lowered his gaze to hers. "What nonsense, Zee," he said. "You are rail thin, and always have been."

Xanthia dropped her chin. "But I shall be thirty in a few months' time, Kieran," she said quietly. "And I begin to feel as if life has —" She stopped, and shook her head.

Kieran stepped nearer. "It's Nash, isn't it, Zee? You may as well admit it."

Xanthia swallowed hard. "I . . . yes, I guess it is," she murmured. "Kieran, I — I might be in too deep this time."

His face was worried. "Well, I'm hardly qualified to give advice, my dear," he said. "But I do know this — if you find someone you love, you must seize hold of that love with both hands. Fight for it, Zee, if you must."

Xanthia looked at him, and smiled faintly. Then she bounced out of her chair. "Come on, old thing. Let's get this over with, shall we? I shall be ready to go down in fifteen minutes."

"I can think of little worse than tea in a roomful of prattling females," Kieran said, tacitly agreeing to drop the subject. "But coming here was my idea, was it not? And so I must bear my punishment with grace, I daresay."

Unfortunately, the arrival of a Polly — whose name was actually Rose — delayed rather than expedited Xanthia's departure. Rose was a pleasant girl with hands no rougher than Xanthia's own, and a great help unpacking Xanthia's bags but inexperienced with ladies' hair. Xanthia had to wait until the girl was gone before redoing it herself. By the time she arrived in the Chinese salon, with a bright smile plastered on her face and wearing her best blue day dress, she found that Kieran had already found a way to avoid his prattling females. She could see him through the long French windows strolling about in the gardens as one of Brierwood's retainers pointed instructively at first one plant, then another.

Lady Nash met her at the threshold. "Your brother professed *such* a fondness for roses," she twittered. "I could see that he was keen to go outside and have a closer look."

"Yes, Kieran loves nothing better than a rose garden," Xanthia lied. "How kind you are to indulge his eccentricities."

Together, they strolled deeper into the room. Two young ladies awaited by a low, elegantly carved table, which held a silver tea service of epic proportions. They made very pretty curtsies when Xanthia was introduced.

Lady Phaedra Northampton was thin and dark, and wore a pair of gold spectacles on her nose. She appeared to be in her early twenties, but perhaps it was just her serious demeanor. Phaedra's sister, Lady Phoebe, was perhaps fifteen or sixteen, with a vivaciousness which belied her age.

"It is a pleasure to meet you both, I am sure," said Xanthia.

They exchanged pleasantries about the trip down from London for a time, but that topic was soon dispensed with. Lady Nash was clearly more interested in the festivities to come. She began at once to rattle on about the guests who would be expected, what day they would arrive, and what gossip they might be expected to bring from Town. Then she began to describe her last half dozen birthday dinners; who had attended, and what they had worn. In the midst of it all, she began serving tea, saying that she did not expect Kieran to leave his beloved roses anytime soon.

"So we may as well go ahead, do you not think?" She did not pause for breath as she tipped the impossibly large pot. "I find that men do not really *like* tea all that well. What do you think, Miss Neville? My late husband — Stefan's father, of course — was fond of saying that tea was for ladies and that men only pre—"

"Goodness, isn't the weather lovely today?" interjected Lady Phaedra. "Do you think it shall rain tomorrow, Miss Neville?"

Xanthia's head jerked up. "Why, I daresay it might."

"Jenny says it will," chimed Lady Phoebe. "She says the roads will be nothing but mud by tomorrow afternoon. That is why she must leave for Southampton today."

"Well, at the very least, she might come down and say hello to Miss Neville before she goes," said Phaedra.

"Yes, I am very sorry not to have met your sister-in-law," said Xanthia. "I gather she is delightful."

Phoebe laughed. "Mamma thinks everyone is delightful so long as they will listen to her talk."

Lady Nash pounced at the opportunity to speak. "Jenny *is* delightful, you little minx," she said. "And she will be here *very* shortly. She promised me." Lady Nash then began to describe how her son had met his wife, how long they had courted, and every minute detail of her wedding dress.

She was calculating aloud the inches of

Alençon lace on the gown's hem when Phaedra interrupted again. "I think the weather will be fair tomorrow, Miss Neville," she said. "If it does, would you care to go riding?"

"I should love to," said Xanthia. "What about you, Phoebe? Do you ride?"

The girl's lower lip came out. "Not so well as Phae," she said. "Everyone likes to point that out."

Phaedra drew herself up an inch. "Complimenting me is not the same, Phoebe, as insulting you," she said. "May I not be allowed to do at least one thing well?"

"You do everything perfectly," retorted her sister. "And everyone loves to say so."

Lady Nash frowned. "This is a tea for adults, Phoebe, so if you cannot behave as one, you must go back up to the schoolroom." It was the first sensible thing she had said. "Miss Neville cannot possibly wish to hear you quarrel."

Phoebe fell back into her chair. "I wasn't quarreling," she said. "But I shan't say a thing if that's what you wish, Mamma."

"I wish nothing of the sort," she began.

But at that very instant, the butler threw open the salon's doors. A beautiful young woman with brilliant red hair strode into the room. She wore a carriage dress striped in shades of deep green and carried a dark green cloak over her arm and a pair of matching gloves in her right hand.

"That's Jenny," whispered Lady Phoebe.

The butler followed as if to take the cloak, but she shooed him away. "Thank you, Fedders, no," she said. "I'll be but a moment." Then she turned, and beamed a brilliant smile upon Lady Nash. "Mamma-in-law!"

"Jenny, dear, do join us."

The woman came at once to kiss Lady Nash's cheek. "And hello!" she said breathlessly. "This must be Miss Neville. How pleased I am to meet you."

Swiftly, Lady Nash made the introductions.

"I met your husband, Mr. Hayden-Worth, some weeks past," said Xanthia. "He seems a brilliant man."

Jenny's eyes appeared to glaze over. "Oh, to be sure," she murmured. "Quite brilliant." She took the seat next to Phoebe but remained on the very edge of the chair.

"Here is your tea, Jenny." Lady Nash offered the cup at her daughter-in-law. "I have already put your extra sugar in."

"Oh, thank you," said Jenny vaguely.

Xanthia set her own cup down. "Lady Nash was just telling us about your wedding dress," she said leadingly. "You are newly wed, I collect?"

"What?" Mrs. Hayden-Worth looked up from the plate of biscuits she was picking over. "Oh, Lord no. We've been married an age."

"Five years in July," said Lady Nash. Then her face fell slightly. "Jenny is leaving for France this afternoon. A prior commitment."

Mrs. Hayden-Worth looked sheepish. "A prior commitment which I forgot," she explained, selecting a biscuit from the platter. "Something I simply cannot miss. Isn't it perfectly dreadful? Mamma-in-law must never forgive me."

Xanthia hid her surprise. "Will you be back in time for the party?"

"I shall try very hard," she said, glancing down the tea table at Lady Nash. But even Xanthia could see she had no intention of doing so — indeed, it would hardly be possible unless she sprouted wings and flew.

Lady Nash cleared her throat abruptly. "Jenny has a great many friends abroad," she said. "It is such a quick trip to France from here, you know. And no, I shan't fuss, Jenny. I have had the pleasure of your company for some weeks now."

"*Thank* you, Mamma-in-law," said Jenny fervently. "You are always so very understanding."

Across the table, Xanthia saw Phaedra roll her eyes.

They made casual conversation over tea and biscuits for the better part of half an hour. But each time Lady Nash went off on a tear, Lady Phaedra would make some innocuous but sharp remark about the weather. Her mother would instantly fall silent. It did not take long for Xanthia to comprehend precisely who kept Brierwood organized — and it wasn't Lady Nash.

For his part, Kieran strode in just long enough to make a civil bow to Mrs. Hayden-Worth, then begged the ladies' indulgence. "Xanthia, I am studying the most fascinating *gallica* rose out by the terrace," he said in a voice most unlike his own. "Do have a look later. It is a — a — well, dash it, I forget the name. But it's a beauty."

"*La belle sultane,*" murmured Lady Phaedra, lifting her gaze to Kieran's. "The head gardener's latest conquest. But I prefer the *rosa damascena bifera,* myself. Which is your favorite of the damasks, my lord?"

Kieran faltered. "The — the damasks?" he said. "I am by no means an expert on damasks, but I prefer the — ah, the red one, I suppose." Here, he paused to glance out at the garden. "I'm afraid I forgot its name, too."

Lady Phaedra elevated a pair of dark, finely etched eyebrows. "The *celsiana,* perhaps?"

"Yes, by Jove!" Kieran agreed. "The *celsiana.*"

"Well!" said Mrs. Hayden-Worth. "This has all been perfectly fascinating. But I daresay I ought to be going."

"Oh, Jenny! So soon?" Lady Nash looked crushed.

Kieran seized the opportunity to vanish again. Jenny was already tugging on her gloves. "Fedders, has the carriage been brought round?"

"Yes, ma'am," said the butler. "Your things have been loaded."

Jenny brightened and bent to kiss Lady Nash again. "Have a lovely party, Mamma-in-law," she said. "If I miss it, I shall never forgive myself."

"Nor shall I," said Lady Nash, only half in jest.

"Why must you rush away this minute, Jenny?" said Lady Phaedra flatly. "You cannot get a ferry 'til morning, you know."

Jenny laughed. "I must think of my coachman, Phaedra," she said. "He is not as young as he once was. And the rain is coming. There might be ruts. I really think I ought to go."

"You had best wait for Nash," said Lady Phoebe, poking out her lip. "Mamma says it is his house, and we must show due deference. I cannot think it very deferential for you to leave before he even arrives home — not to mention Tony."

Lady Nash smiled nervously. "Hush, Phoebe," she said. "Nash will be sorry to have missed Jenny, and that is all."

"He will not notice I am gone," Jenny assured her.

"Perhaps not," said Lady Nash. "Now, have you a hot brick for your feet, Jenny?"

"Mamma-in-law, it is *May*," said Jenny, bending to kiss her again. "Now I am off. Miss Neville, it was a pleasure, I am sure."

They watched Mrs. Hayden-Worth cross the room with neat, quick steps. "How lovely she is," said Xanthia, when Jenny had vanished. "And her voice — she is American, is she not?"

"Yes, indeed," said her ladyship. "Did Nash not mention it?"

"The subject never came up."

Lady Nash laughed. "No, Nash would not bother," she said, almost to herself. "Jenny's father is a wealthy industrialist. He brought her to London to marry a title."

Phoebe leaned forward conspiratorially. "Yes, and she had a monstrous dowry," said the girl. "But then she met Tony, didn't she, Mamma?"

"What can I say?" Lady Nash lifted her shoulders. "My son *is* a politician, Miss Neville. He could charm the birds from the trees if he set his mind to it."

"I am sure he could," said Xanthia. "What sort of business is Mrs. Hayden-Worth's father in?"

"Oh, I cannot recall." Lady Nash made a vague gesture with her hand. "Metals, perhaps? Steel or iron or smelts or some such thing."

"Smelts are fish, Mamma," said Phaedra.

"Perhaps he *smelts* iron," Phoebe suggested. "One can do that, I think — whatever it means."

Phaedra shrugged. "Well, in any case, he has factories," she said. "Pots of them."

"Yes, in Connecticut," said Lady Nash, undeterred. "Or is it Massachusetts?"

The girls looked at one another and shrugged. Clearly the mysterious industrialist was not a topic of much interest at Brierwood. "So she will go from Southampton to where?" asked Xanthia. "Calais?"

"I am not quite sure," said Lady Nash vaguely. "She has friends everywhere."

"I see." Xanthia reached for another biscuit, but remembered the pink cherub on her ceiling. It was odd, really. She had never before given much thought to keeping her figure.

Lady Nash was still rattling on about Mrs. Hayden-Worth's friends. "Of course, I told Jenny that it was all very well to have *friends*," she was saying. "But some of them, I fear, are a little racy. And they do spend an *awful* lot of money on clothes, and on *frightfully* lavish entertainments."

"Oh, I am sure the well eventually runs dry for everyone," remarked Lady Phaedra. "Even for rich American industrialists."

"Not for Jenny's papa," said her sister. "He spoils her shamelessly."

Lady Nash scolded her daughters for gossiping, and returned to the topic of her dinner party. Lady Phaedra was required to invoke the weather-warning on but four or five more occasions, and eventually, tea was concluded.

"Oh, dear!" said Lady Nash as they rose. "Nash and Tony still have not come, have they?"

"Yes, Mamma, they slipped in amidst your recitation of the dinner menus for the next five days," said Lady Phaedra dryly. "You simply did not notice."

"Oh, you wicked girl!" Lady Nash frowned disapprovingly. "They did no such thing — oh! The dinner menu!"

"What now?" said Lady Phaedra.

"I forgot to tell Cook we were to have the asparagus, *not the sprouts!*" Lady Nash had clasped a hand to her forehead theatrically. "Nash does quite *loathe* sprouts. He really will *never* forgive me."

"Oh, Lord, it will be out on the street for us!" said Phoebe. "Phae, get your gypsy dress and your tambourine. We shall have to go down to the village and sing for our supper."

Phaedra set a hand on her mother's shoulder. "Just go downstairs, Mamma, and tell Cook to put the sprouts back until Saturday," she said patiently. "Sprouts will keep nicely. At your birthday dinner, we shall have so much to choose from, Nash will never notice."

Lady Nash was nodding intently. "Yes, quite so, quite so," she said. "My dear Miss Neville, will you excuse me? Phaedra will show you back to your room. I will go down to the kitchens."

They parted company near the grand staircase, Lady Phaedra at Xanthia's side.

"Well, that was interesting," said Xanthia as they started up the steps together.

Lady Phaedra laughed. "It always is," she said. "Mamma is a dear, but she never stops talking."

"I find her most gracious," said Xanthia. "But I do have one burning question, Lady Phaedra."

Lady Phaedra shot her a quizzical look. "Yes?"

"Just what color is the *celsiana* rose?"

The young lady grinned. "Oh, that!" she said. "Your brother's impressive horticultural abilities aside, I fear the *damascena celsiana* is always pale pink."

Xanthia laughed and looped her arm through Lady Phaedra's. "My dear, that is so cruel," she answered. "I think you must share your brother's black humor."

"Well, you know what they say," answered Phaedra equivocally. "A sharp wit is a dangerous weapon."

By the time they reached Xanthia's suite, she and Phaedra were laughing like old friends. Phaedra went directly to the door which opened onto Xanthia's bedchamber, and threw it open. "Ugh!" she said, recoiling in disgust. "That smell must be driving you mad!"

Xanthia followed her inside, and sniffed. The musky scent, which had been barely discernible upon Xanthia's arrival, was indeed powerful now. The late-day sun was streaming through the wide bank of windows, warming the air. Phaedra sneezed violently and headed straight for the windows.

"I am not terribly bothered by the scent," Xanthia reassured her.

Phaedra, apparently, did not agree. She was already throwing up the sashes. "Ugh!" she said again, straining at one of the windows. "I cannot bear it."

Xanthia went to help her. "What is it?"

"Nutmeg mace," she answered as the sash gave, and went rumbling up. "And some sort of musk, I think."

"It certainly is unusual," Xanthia remarked.

Phaedra was looking about the room as if she suspected vermin. She headed straight to the heavy mahogany wardrobe, threw open both doors, and pushed Xanthia's gowns aside. "Pardon my familiarity, Miss Neville, but you will thank me for this."

"By all means," murmured Xanthia, looking on.

Her nimble fingers went sorting through the wardrobe's contents. "Ah-ha!" Phaedra finally said, turning around. A round latticed ball on a pink ribbon dangled from the tip of her forefinger.

"What is it?" asked Xanthia. "Some sort of pomander?"

"One of Jenny's," said Phaedra in a put-upon voice. "She gets the scent in Paris. 'Tis bad enough she wafts it all over the house, but I wish she would not leave these lying about after she's gone. I think it is disgusting." As if for emphasis, she sneezed again.

"Oh, dear," said Xanthia. "I hope I did not take Mrs. Hayden-Worth's room?"

Phaedra hesitated. "No, she and Tony have a large bedchamber attached to his private study in the east wing," she said. "But Jenny often takes this one. She says she likes to see the front gardens."

"Oh, dear," said Xanthia again. "I should be happy to move elsewhere."

Phaedra's expression darkened. "Well, it's not your problem, I daresay, if she doesn't wish to sleep with her husband."

Xanthia scarcely knew what to say. "I am sure, Lady Phaedra, that it is not my business, either," she managed.

But the girl behaved as if Xanthia had not spoken. "Besides, Jenny will be away for a week, at least," she went on. "She finds Mamma's friends dull. And as to Nash — well, let us just say that he and Jenny are both possessed of strong personalities. I am not surprised she found an excuse to go away."

Phaedra's intimations precisely matched Xanthia's impression of Mrs. Hayden-Worth, but she said nothing. She decided it was prudent to change the subject. "Well, so long as we have the wardrobe open, come have a look, Lady Phaedra, at my favorite gown," she said. "You must tell me if you think it will do for Saturday's dinner party."

Phaedra brightened at once. "Oh, fabulous! No one ever asks my opinion about clothes."

Suddenly, however, the clatter of hooves and the jingle of a harness rang out across the front gardens. Phaedra's face broke into a huge smile, and she darted toward the windows. "Nash!" she cried, leaning halfway out. "Nash is here! And Tony, too! Hurry, Miss Neville. Let's go down."

Xanthia felt a moment of panic and went at once to the dressing table. As usual, her heavy hair was slipping from its arrangement, and she was a little pink from the overheated room.

"Come on, you look lovely," said Phaedra, grabbing her by the arm. "Nash would never have invited you if he did not think so."

Xanthia drew back, and cut a chiding

glance at the girl. "Phaedra, don't make more of this than —"

"I am making of it what it is," said Phaedra flatly.

"I beg your pardon?" said Xanthia.

Phaedra looked at her as if she feared Xanthia were slightly simple-minded. "Miss Neville, you are the only unattached female my brother has ever invited to Brierwood," she said. "And Nash — well, what can one say? He is known to be quite the connoisseur."

"Oh," said Xanthia quietly. "Oh, Lady Phaedra, I fear you have much mistaken the situation. We are good friends, no more."

Phaedra smiled with false brilliance. "Yes, and I am Queen of the Nile," she answered. "Now, come on. Do you mean to go down and greet your good friend — or not?"

CHAPTER THIRTEEN: TEMPTATION IN THE GARDEN OF EARTHLY DELIGHTS

In the end, Xanthia did not ride with Lady Phaedra the following day. Kieran did, accompanied by the jovial Mr. Hayden-Worth and Lady Phoebe, who planned a trip into the village to view the local church, and to permit Mr. Hayden-Worth to post an urgent letter. The latter declared himself devastated that Xanthia would not accompany them, and if he missed his wife, one could not discern it.

For her part, Xanthia found, somewhat to her surprise, that she rather liked Nash's stepbrother, though she recognized him for what he was — charming and handsome, but a politician to his very core. Nonetheless, he had kind eyes, and he utterly doted on his mother, which Xanthia believed spoke well of a man. But Mr. Hayden-Worth's charm aside, Xanthia's company had been claimed by Nash for the afternoon, who offered her instead a tour of Brierwood's magnificent gardens.

It was admittedly clever of him, for in the gardens they remained ostensibly under the watchful eye of his mother — and yet they were very much alone, for the gardens were inexhaustible, and Lady Nash's attention span was not. Their footsteps were quiet on the flagstone path that led around to the back of the house.

The front gardens were quite formal with many fountains, and a variety of hedges cut in complex geometric patterns, all of which were better viewed from the upper floors of the house. But in the rear of Brierwood, the gardens were gloriously English, with rambling paths of flagstone and pea gravel, and walls of stone cleverly interspersed with stretches of wrought-iron arches which allowed one a tantalizing peek from one garden into the next. Behind the wrought-iron arch would appear a fountain, a rose-covered pergola, or perhaps a clever piece of topiary.

Her arm linked in his, Xanthia ducked just as Nash smoothly lifted a lush, green limb from their path. "How verdant they seem," she said, admiring a long row of shrubs. "They are lilacs, are they not?"

"My dear, I have no notion," he said, drawing her a little closer and settling his opposite hand over hers where it lay upon his arm. "I can scarce tell an English oak from an English rose — save for that blush I occasionally see in your cheeks."

"So this garden tour was a sham?" Xanthia teased. "A mere ruse to lure me from your stepmother's side?"

"Pray do not look to Edwina to guard your virtue, my dear," said Nash dryly. "Can you only imagine what it will be like when Phae and Phoebe come out? I shall have to hire Bow Street Runners to keep watch."

"So we are quite alone in the gardens?" said Xanthia in a low, suggestive voice.

"I daresay," he responded. "The gardeners always respectfully disappear whenever I come out — which is perhaps once a year. Not such a dreadful imposition, do you think?"

Xanthia looked up to study his face. "It is so beautiful here," she answered. "And Brierwood is quite the most magnificent house I have ever seen. Do you find it intolerably dull?"

Nash looked down the garden path pensively. "Perhaps it is growing on me, Zee. I have begun to feel . . . differently about it, somehow. But come — let's not talk of such serious matters." He paused to stroke the backs of his fingers across her cheek. "I should rather we conspire as to how I might slip into your bed later tonight — preferably without being caught by your brother."

Xanthia laughed. "I think it will be a straightforward matter. There is quite a large sitting room between his bedchamber and mine, and my door onto the corridor has a most unreliable-looking lock." She looked up at him again. "On the other hand, I could come to you."

Nash smiled down at her, and appeared to be mulling it over. She could sense that something else was weighing on his mind, too. Last night during dinner, and the coffee and whist which had followed, he had remained exceedingly hospitable to all yet somehow removed from the crowd. He had the look of a man who did not quite fit in — and the quiet withdrawal of one who had something serious on his mind. Even Kieran had remarked upon it.

Dear heaven, she hoped Nash was not thinking about the missing letters! Xanthia had not seen Mr. Kemble since dismissing him in Wapping. Her heated threats aside, she would likely never get the letters back. She felt the needling sense of guilt return. A part of her wanted to confess, but she had given her word to Lord de Vendenheim. At least the correspondence she'd stolen had appeared benign — even Mr. Kemble had admitted as much. Perhaps by now de Vendenheim, too, was convinced. Perhaps he had given up on Nash and was in hot pursuit of some other hapless Englishman. The thought eased her conscience a bit.

Arm in arm she and Nash strolled through a pair of the stone gateposts which divided the shrub garden from an orchard which lay just beyond. Nash halted abruptly on the garden path and drew her to him, his heavy black hair falling forward to shadow his forehead. His exotic black eyes moved over her face as if searching for something unspoken.

"Kiss me, Zee," he rasped.

For an instant, Xanthia hesitated, but then his lips touched hers, so delicate and yet so hungry, she sucked in her breath. With it came the delicious, dizzying scent of him, and she was lost. Gently, Nash set her back to the cool stone gatepost and opened his mouth over hers. Unable to resist, Xanthia lifted her face to his and kissed him back deeply.

As always, he smelled of enticing citrus, and the heady fragrance of fresh linen and fine tobacco. But beneath it all was his own male heat, a scent too well remembered. The enticing combination conspired to throw her back to another time, another place — that dark, dangerous evening when she had first offered her lips to him on Sharpe's veranda. Then as now, Nash's tongue plundered her mouth and weakened her knees. Xanthia sagged against the stone post. The fear of being seen was melting away, draining with it her resolve. She drew him inside, entwining her tongue with his in a delicious dance of temptation — and of promise.

Yes, *this* was what she had come for. To others, she might deny the depth of her attraction — but her body would not be denied. She came away from the gatepost and leaned into him, allowing him to deepen the kiss as her hands slid down his back. The soft wool of his lapels brushed the silk of her gown, and her cashmere shawl went slithering unheeded onto the orchard grass. Already he seemed to know her body as he knew his own. Xanthia felt his hand on her buttock, warm and heavy as it circled. And when he lifted her against the unmistakable ridge of his erection and groaned, the sound seemed to come from the very pit of his soul.

Tonight, she thought blindly. Tonight he would make love to her again. He must — or she would die from the aching. And the ache was no longer simple lust. Indeed, it had long ago ceased to be, had she but allowed herself to realize it. Now she ached to please him. To share herself in every possible way with this man she had come to adore against her will. At that thought, a sudden surge of tenderness almost overwhelmed her.

He slanted his lips over hers again, raking her skin with the faint stubble of his beard, and she shivered. She drew back and stared into his eyes as she clung to him. "Yes, tonight," she whispered. "I will come to you as soon as I may."

Nash gave a muted smile and smoothed the fabric of her skirt back over her hip. "And what if we are discovered, my dear?" he murmured. "We might have a hard decision to make."

Xanthia dropped her gaze. He was asking, no doubt, if she would force him to do the honorable thing. It was something he feared, and she had known that from the first. Was it not the very reason he had come to call on Kieran on that long-ago afternoon?

"We shan't be caught," she answered. "But if we are, the decision will be ours, as you say. No one can force us to —"

He cut her off with another kiss, but swift

and short. "Come," he said, tucking her hand around his arm. "There is a pretty pond just beyond the orchard, and a little folly sits at its edge. I think we may dare to venture so far beyond the bounds of propriety."

Xanthia laughed and went with him willingly. "I cannot believe we are worrying so about appeasing your stepmother."

"We are not appeasing her," he said solemnly. "We are preserving your good name."

"But I venture regularly into places no lady would ever go, often in company no lady would ever keep."

Nash frowned faintly. "Yes, but that is not the same as being alone in *my* company," he pointed out. "What you do in Wapping . . . well, one might almost say it is out of sight, out of mind when it comes to the *ton.* But having an *affaire* with a man like me is another thing altogether."

Xanthia went up the steps of the folly and settled onto the semicircular bench. "So I am simply to give you up?" she asked, looking him straight in the eye. "Is that what you are suggesting?"

To her surprise, Nash looked away. "No," he said quietly. "Not . . . exactly."

"What, then?" she demanded.

Nash said nothing for a time. "I hardly

know," he finally confessed. "I have been thinking of you quite a lot, my dear. Thinking of how we fell into this treacherous business in the first place."

"Stefan!" she said chidingly. Xanthia slipped an arm around his waist and set her cheek against his shoulder. "It was desire at first sight. Sometimes, I think, it just happens like that. And I have been thinking of you, too — thinking of you at times when I really ought not."

He did not reply but instead glanced at the orchard behind. Then, as if reassured they were indeed alone, he set one arm around Xanthia's shoulders. It was a wonderfully comforting moment. The folly and its environs were charming, too. For a long time they simply sat thus, listening to the twitter of the birds and observing the tranquil, glistening surface of the pond. She felt a rightness in his embrace, a oneness with Nash she had never expected with any man. And there was a joy — a joy which she feared might be fleeting.

After a time, she drew a deep, uncertain breath. "There was one question, Stefan, which you have never asked me," she said. "I thought you would, after our little escapade at Lady Cartselle's."

"And what is that, my dear?" he murmured, dipping his head to look down at her.

For a long moment, she said nothing. "About my virginity," she finally answered. "About . . . why I wasn't one."

Did he stiffen slightly, or was it her imagination? "A virgin?" he asked, his voice perfectly normal. "Well, on that score, Zee, I fear I have a little confession to make."

She looked up at him strangely. "Of what sort?"

"Prepare yourself, my dear." He bent his head, and set his lips very close to her ear. "I was not a virgin, either."

She erupted in laughter and sat up again. "Yes, I had heard the rumors," she answered. "Now, Nash, will you please be serious?"

"I am being entirely serious," he said. "What business is it of mine if you have taken lovers before me? I have had more than I can count. But — very well, yes — I have wondered. I am a man, and we are weak, curious creatures. Nonetheless, I think I've managed to figure it out."

Xanthia crooked one eyebrow. "Did you indeed?"

He smiled lazily, and leaned forward to lightly kiss her nose. "I decided that you once fancied yourself in love with that angry young man in your office — Mr. Lloyd, was it?" he said quietly. "The fellow is quite handsome, and he looks at you with . . . well, with that look."

She laughed and pressed her fingertips to her chest. "What *look?*"

Nash shrugged, and dropped his gaze. "A possessive look," he said. "A heated lover's look. Do not tell me, Zee, that you have not noticed it."

Xanthia sighed. "I suppose so," she admitted. "It . . . it is hard to explain."

"And you do not need to."

She set one hand against his cheek. "But I think perhaps I should like to do so," she said honestly. "Or at the very least, Nash, I should like you to understand what our lives were like when we lived in the West Indies."

He hesitated a moment. "Then I should like to listen."

Xanthia chose her words carefully. "Barbados is an insular society," she said. "A small island with very few privileged whites. When Gareth came to the island as a boy, and began to work for Luke, we were thrown together. A sort of friendship sprang up between us. One might say we almost grew up together on the island. Neither of us had very much in the way of supervision."

"I think I understand," said Nash. "How

old were you?"

Xanthia lifted one shoulder. "Fourteen, perhaps?" she answered. "In those days, I did all Luke's filing, made the tea, swept the floors — anything to be with Luke, whom I worshipped."

"I felt the very same about Petar," Nash confessed.

She smiled a little sadly. "Luke found Gareth down at the docks, looking rather lost," she said. "He was just a few months older than I. We took him on as an errand boy, and then as a clerk, copying contracts and such."

"Where was his family?"

"I don't know," she confessed. "He never really said, but I know his parents were dead. So he was just an orphan, like us. For years we were . . . well, best friends, I suppose? But we grew up and began to live separate lives. Unfortunately, one evening, when we were working late, a terrible storm came up — almost a hurricane, really. I had sent the staff home, and Kieran was inland, at one of the mills. Gareth and I were trapped in the shipping offices alone."

"My dear girl." Nash took her hand in his, and squeezed it hard. "You must have been terrified. How old were you?"

"Oh, I was a woman grown — almost

twenty, I think." Her voice was low, and fraught with memories. "But we both were terrified. Barbados rarely got such storms. The sea was wild; even the careenage was storm-tossed. We were caught in a whirlwind of debris; shingles and torn sails and palm fronds flew at the windows. Then something metal — part of a windlass, I think — shattered a window, missing my skull by an inch."

Nash winced. "My dear, you could have been killed."

She nodded. "We knew it, too," she agreed. "But we pulled some furniture against the leeward wall, and hid behind it. And then . . . well, we began to cling to one another. In looking back, I can honestly say we thought we might die."

"You were fortunate to have survived."

"There were a few who did not," she answered grimly. "But what I did with Gareth that day — it seems so foolish now. And it was not just once, Nash. It went on for months afterward."

"Perhaps it was a little foolish, my dear," Nash murmured, tucking an errant strand of hair behind her ear. "But you were fond of him, and such things happen. Nonetheless, it was wrong of Lloyd to continue to take advantage of a lady's affections."

Swiftly, she looked away. "He did not take advantage," Xanthia answered. "I — I think perhaps *I* did. He wished very desperately to marry me. Indeed, at first he simply assumed that we would wed — and when I resisted, he attempted to persuade me. But when I kept refusing him, Gareth ended it. He went to Kieran and demanded my hand. He believed that . . . that *because* he had taken my virginity, I was his to possess. But I thought such logic medieval."

Nash turned her face back into his with his fingertip. "Zee, it does not matter now," he said. "And Barbados, I imagine, is very different from England."

"In a thousand little ways," she agreed. "Certainly, we had no Almack's patronesses to govern our social hierarchy. And on Barbados, there is a sense of timelessness, which is hard to explain. Virtually every day seems hypnotically the same — beautiful, of course — but after a while, one can scarcely see the world beyond, or even into the future. So often, there is only the here and now."

Nash was quiet for a moment. "I can only imagine what life on such a small island would be like," he acknowledged. "But at the risk of repeating myself, Zee, you must know that this is a rather dangerous *affaire* we are having. This is not the West Indies. What you are doing here — with any man, let alone one of my reputation — would ruin your name beyond repair, were it to become known. There would be no hope of your marrying and little hope of keeping your place in society. You understand that, do you not?"

"It will not become known," she insisted.

"I hope your confidence is rewarded," he answered coolly. "You have never wished, I take it, to marry?"

"No husband would allow me to lead the life I do," she said quietly. "You know that, Nash. I would be but a possession. And I would likely lose control of Neville's. It would become my husband's property, just as I would."

"You have the misfortune to be a woman before your time," he admitted. "Perhaps someday your sort of life will not be so unusual. But is that your only protest against marriage? Your work? The loss of authority? Does it matter so very much?"

"Of course it matters!" she snapped. "Neville's is the thing which defines me, Nash. It is all I have known, the whole of my adult life — and a good part of my girlhood, too. And it is why I did not marry Gareth, even though I . . . yes, I loved him, in my own way."

Nash sat silently for a moment. "I see," he finally answered. "I believe, my dear, that your Mr. Lloyd has my deepest sympathies."

"Has he?" asked Xanthia archly.

Without answering, Nash looked up and narrowed his eyes against the sun. "Well, I daresay we'd best go in now," he said. "The others will be returning for luncheon shortly, don't you imagine?"

"Yes, I suppose."

The conversation had come to a strange and sudden end. But Xanthia had lived with her brother long enough to know that one got nowhere in questioning a man when he was in a strained, temperamental mood. Nash drew her up from the bench, placed her hand upon his arm again, and together they began their sedate promenade back to the house.

They arrived to find that the riding party had indeed returned, and had brought with them Lord and Lady Henslow, whose carriage they had met in the village. Lady Henslow greeted Xanthia with overt curiosity and declared herself charmed to meet Kieran. She then returned to her sister's side, where she remained almost dotingly. She good-naturedly allowed Lady Nash to dominate the conversation, pausing to do no more than pat her sister's hand. It was becoming ever clearer that Lady Nash was accustomed to being cosseted by her family.

After a pleasant meal of cold chicken and roast beef, the group dispersed, with Lady Nash insisting the new arrivals must have a nap. Lady Phaedra accompanied Xanthia upstairs.

"Shall you have a rest now?" asked Phaedra, when they reached Xanthia's door. "If not, perhaps you would like to see the old ruins? It is a lovely walk."

Xanthia smiled and squeezed the girl's hand. "I fear I cannot," she said, feeling the press of duty. "I am so sorry. I have some letters to write which will take me most of the afternoon."

"Heavens, that sounds like a lot of work," said Phaedra.

"Work, yes," said Xanthia. "Exactly. Might we see the ruins another time?"

Phaedra smiled. "Yes, of course."

Xanthia went in, found her satchelful of papers, and went to the rosewood secretary, which sat between the windows in the sitting room. There were several matters which she had assured Gareth she would see to during this trip, and she meant to keep her promise, no matter how tempting it might be to do otherwise. Moreover, work would help to keep her mind off Nash and stop her from fretting over the unusual mood he had taken on — a mood which had only hardened throughout luncheon, until he had seemed as cool and as distant as Xanthia's brother.

With that thought, she let the drop-front of the secretary down and began praying she would find an inkwell inside, for she had forgotten her lap desk altogether. To her surprise, the desktop was frightfully untidy, as if it had been shut it up in some haste. Mrs. Hayden-Worth, no doubt. Xanthia picked up a crumpled piece of notepaper and sniffed it. It still held a hint of her strange scent of mace and musk. Perhaps in their rush to clean the room, the servants had failed to open the desk. In any case, the notes appeared very dull, consisting mostly of chicken-scratched lists of things to do, or to purchase, and duns from various shopkeepers.

Impatiently, Xanthia began to stack the jumbled papers neatly into one corner. Beneath the mess she found a well-worn prayer book embossed with the gilt initials *J. E. C.* With an inward shrug, Xanthia picked it up by its spine, meaning to lay it aside, but she caught it awkwardly, and another half dozen bits and pieces of equally unimportant-looking papers slid out.

"Bloody hell," said Xanthia under her breath.

She began to stuff the bits back into the prayer book as best she might, but one of them, a piece of folded ivory foolscap caught her eye. The paper was thick, and looked to have cost a small fortune. Xanthia flipped it over. It was addressed to Mrs. Hayden-Worth at Brierwood, and had obviously come from America. Inordinately curious, Xanthia flicked it open with her thumb, and let her eyes skim over the words, which were as dull as the shopping lists had been:

26 March
Dearest Daughter:
I am in receipt of your letter dated last month, and trust that you are well. How glad I am to hear that you will be in Cherbourg on the twentieth of May. I trust you will have fair weather. There will be two thousand pounds awaiting you there. Pray do not spend it all at once, and write to me immediately upon your return from France.

With all my love,
Your indulgent Papa
P.S. I am sending the seed pearls you

requested via Captain Tobias Bruner on the *Pride of Fairhaven.* Please count and sew them carefully, to see that none have been lost in transit. I am sure they will look lovely on you.

It seemed an odd letter, for reasons Xanthia could not quite put her finger on. Jenny's father was a man of few words. He scarcely enquired after his daughter's health and gave her no news from home. But clearly it was just as Phaedra had implied. Jenny's father indulged her dreadfully — and perhaps without the knowledge of her husband. She could see, too, why Jenny might have been in a hurry to go to France. Two thousand pounds of Papa's pin money would make for a very fine shopping spree.

A little ashamed, Xanthia tucked the note back into the prayer book. She did not care for Mrs. Hayden-Worth, it was true. But that was no excuse. She ought not read another person's correspondence. She shoved the untidy pile as far away as possible and began to lay out her things.

It was there that Kieran found her some hours later. "Aren't you going to change for dinner, Zee?" he asked as he came through the door.

Xanthia looked up in some amazement,

and laid her pen aside. Beyond the windows, the sun was slanting straight into the windows. "Oh," she murmured.

Kieran strode over to the secretary and pulled out her chair. "Up with you, old thing," he ordered. "This may have been my idea — but I don't dare go down to that dinner table alone."

CHAPTER FOURTEEN: AN ADVENTUROUS ASSIGNATION AT BRIERWOOD

In the gloom of a near-moonless night, Xanthia stealthily wound her way through the passageways of Brierwood, stepping tentatively as she went. Her slippers peeped from the hem of her silk wrapper as she mounted the first flight of stairs. Excitement, and the deliciousness of anticipation, drove her forward, impelled her toward Nash's arms.

Already, her body shivered with eagerness. She thought of his kiss this afternoon — so skillful, so rich with sensual promise. No, this one thing she would not be denied.

What if we are discovered, my dear? he had asked. *We might have a hard decision to make.*

She had insisted they would not be caught. But in hindsight, he had not seemed especially concerned. Sometimes she found herself wondering if he almost . . . but no. It was not possible. It would not work. They were both too set in their ways for her to have hope. Nash was a philanderer, and she — well, she was just enjoying the opportunity his philandering provided. In that respect — actually, in *every* respect — Nash was the perfect lover for her.

But they must not be discovered. Xanthia set every foot with the utmost care. From time to time, a seam of light would appear beneath a door, but no one stirred. On the last landing, a squeaking floorboard gave her a fright. She froze, and heard nothing. A few more steps, and she reached the door which opened onto his bedchamber.

She knocked lightly, and as if he had been waiting by the door, it opened. He wore only a dressing gown, this one of raw black silk, edged in gold, and his hair was again drawn back, this time with a black silk ribbon. But she had little time to drink him in, for within an instant, he had pulled her into his arms and was burying his head in her hair.

"You came," he murmured. "You fool."

"I am a fool for you," she admitted.

He set her a little away and stared down into her eyes. For an instant, it took away her breath. It was too much; she glanced away. A massive, almost medieval-looking bed sat in the center of the room, the wood black with age, the canopy full and arching. It was hung with dark blue silk, and the matching silk coverlet was already turned back, the sheets almost seductively rumpled. A low fire burned in the grate, the room's only light, and a carafe of port sat on the night table, a glass beside it.

"What a magnificent beast of a bed," she murmured. "I hope you mean to put it to good use?"

He chuckled and threaded his fingers lightly through her hair. "Lord, I was half afraid that between this morning and dinner, you might come to your senses," he said. "Where's Rothewell?"

She shook her head. "In bed — I hope. But I cannot be sure. He often cannot sleep."

Nash's exotic black eyes roamed over her face. "How long can we go on like this, Zee?" he whispered.

Once again, she was not perfectly sure what he was asking. "As long as we wish, Stefan," she said. "Until . . . until we tire of one another, I daresay."

Something flared in his eyes — a powerful but inscrutable emotion — and he bent over her and gathered her gently to him. "What if we do not?" he murmured. "What if it . . . it just gets worse?"

She tried to laugh. "My dear, you go through women like other men wear out stockings," she said, gently urging him away. "And I am just a woman, like any other."

"Don't push me away, Zee, when I am being perfectly serious," he said. "And you are not just any woman. You are *my* woman. At least for tonight — yes?"

She nodded, but said no more. He held her gaze for what seemed infinity, then slowly he lowered his lips to hers again. His mouth melted over hers, coaxing her desire and drawing the most exquisite feeling from the depths of her womb. The pleasure twisted sweetly through her, all the way up, until she was shuddering against the wall of his chest as his warm, familiar scent surrounded her.

Somehow, she pulled her mouth away. "Make love to me, Stefan," she whispered feverishly. "I have thought of nothing save your touch. To see you, yet be unable to touch you — oh, it has driven me half-mad, I think."

He drew her to the edge of the bed. Xanthia sat and looked up at him expectantly. His hands went to the tie of his dressing gown. "Tell me, Xanthia, how to please you tonight," he murmured, his eyes never leaving hers.

She trembled again, visibly this time. She looked away as the silk slithered down his body. "Possess me," she rasped. "Take me, Stefan. I want to feel as if you own my very soul. I . . . I sometimes wonder if you don't."

Something wild and primal flared in his eyes as he knelt before her, naked. Slowly, he unfastened her wrapper, tossed the tie onto the bed, then pushed the fabric off her shoulders. She wore a simple nightgown, the thinnest she possessed, and beneath it, her areolas were obvious. His gaze warming appreciably, he took one dusky peak between his lips and sucked hard, drawing it fully into his mouth. She gasped at the intensity, but his other hand slid over her belly, the palm open and warm. He stroked up her ribs, all the way up, until he caressed the weight of her opposite breast.

Xanthia speared her fingers into the softness of his hair and let her head fall back with a soft groan. *This* was what she had come here for. *This* was what he gave her, the thing she could no longer do without. He was her addiction. Her only wicked pleasure. She opened her mouth to tell him so, but no sound came out. She was lost, lost in the sweet, sensual onslaught.

Nash's mouth left her nipple and skimmed up her throat. His lips caressed the curve of her neck, the turn of her jaw, and then he kissed her again, lingeringly. "Take this off," he rasped, pulling at her nightdress.

He rose from his knees, and she stood. He drew the nightgown up and tossed it carelessly aside, his gaze running boldly down her length, heating as it went. "By God, Zee, you are a beauty," he whispered. "I want you, body and soul. I want you here to do my bidding."

She lifted her arms to circle his neck. "Perhaps I am," she murmured. She drew him down and kissed him, hot and open-mouthed. "Bid me," she challenged when their lips parted. "Hold nothing back, Stefan. I am no simpering virgin."

He pushed her down onto the bed, which gave to their weight with a soft squeak. The rumpled sheets were cool beneath her heated flesh. Nash crawled almost predatorially up the length of the mattress until he straddled her hips. Already, his erection was firm and jutting. Xanthia took the heated weight of him between her palms and drew them slowly down his length.

Nash's head went back, his face a mask of exquisite agony. Over and over she stroked him. Tormented him. Until he began to shake ever so slightly, the tendons of his neck straining. His eyes opened then, and his hands captured hers. "Enough, wench," he growled, pushing them high above her head. "You are here to do *my* bidding, are you not?"

Lightly, she laughed. "But I love to torture you."

With an almost disdainful grunt, he reached for something just beyond her shoulder. She felt rather than saw the cool silk draw taut around her wrist. Something like panic caused her to jerk, but he drew the silk tight with another sound of satisfaction. Her panic turned to something else.

"Stefan?" she whispered uncertainly.

"If there's any torture to be done tonight, my love," he rasped, "the doing of it will be *mine*."

He had her other wrist now, bound tight to the first. Experimentally, she tugged on them, but the silken tie held fast. Still holding them high above her head, he bent down, nuzzling at her breast, then drawing it lovingly back inside his mouth. Xanthia moaned, her body arching involuntarily. In response, Nash drew the silk tie tighter still, as if to show her who was in command.

When she began to writhe uncontrollably beneath him, however, Nash rose to a kneeling position and looked down at her naked body, a wicked light in his eyes. "Sit up, love," he softly commanded. "Let's have you on your lovely knees, *hmm?*"

Willingly, she did so. To her shock, he rose higher onto his knees, stretching their arms well above her head. She could easily have slipped the knot, but inexplicably, she did not. Instead, she looked up to see he was looping the silk tie around the highest slat in the wooden canopy. She felt enthralled. Oddly aroused.

"Stefan?" she said again.

He pulled the knot fast and drew her arms taut. Xanthia's breath ratcheted up a notch. She felt stretched out. Fully exposed. Again, she tested the knot with a little jerk. It gave but slightly, and yet it was not uncomfortable. Still, she was trapped on her knees. Naked. In the middle of Nash's massive bed.

Nash slipped one finger into the thatch of curls between her thighs. "Now you are truly in my power, my dear," he murmured, indolently drawing the finger through her curls, up her belly, over her navel, and all the way up between her breasts.

"Yes," she said weakly, watching his hand. "I do seem to be your prisoner."

He leaned into her, and opened his mouth over hers for a kiss which was invasive and possessing. "Do you wish to be released from your prison, sweet?" he rasped, when his mouth left hers.

"No," she said swiftly. "Not . . . not yet."

He laughed deep in his chest. "You find this intriguing?"

Xanthia felt her face heat. "I . . . I do not know."

He let his lips play down her neck. "You are a deeply sensual woman, Zee," he murmured. "You are curious, I think. I saw it in your eyes once before."

"Yes . . . perhaps," she admitted.

"There is nothing wrong with erotic play," he said reassuringly. "Not if both partners wish it. And there is certainly nothing wrong with your curiosity."

Xanthia's breath was coming rapidly. "And do you wish . . . to play?"

"I wish only to please you," he answered. "The simplest act of lovemaking would please me, so long as you are my partner."

"W-Would it?"

"I think you know it would." His teeth grazed her throat. "But I think, my dear, that you need a strong man in your bed," he whispered seductively. "I think that you want to be — shall we say, subjugated just a bit?"

"Yes." The word escaped on a sigh before she could snatch it back.

He bent his head and lightly licked the hard, pink bud of her nipple. "Do you know why, Zee, you want that?" he murmured.

"N-No." But she *did* want it, and his words fired her blood like fine cognac.

He slipped one finger into her curls again, deeper this time. "It is because strong women need strong men," he whispered, easing his finger back and forth in the silken heat between her legs. "You yearn for a man who can control you, who knows what you crave — and can give it to you."

"Is that what you mean to do?" Her voice came out soft and thready. "Give me . . . what I crave?"

"If you will let me," he answered honestly. "Will you?"

Xanthia looked up at the knotted silk. "Yes," she whispered, closing her eyes. "Anything."

He pinched lightly at her nipple. "Say please, my love."

"Please." She breathed the word into the gloom.

"Do you trust me?"

"Yes."

"Good." She felt his teeth nibble at her other breast, and her eyes flew open. "But what . . . what are you going to do? Are you — are you going to . . . to do anything wicked?"

"Wicked?" he murmured. "Oh, I hope so."

"No, I mean . . . I mean like the things you told me about," she whispered. "Are you going to . . . to punish me?"

His hands slid round to lift and spread her buttocks. "Oh, that depends, my dear," he murmured. "Have you been a naughty girl?"

Xanthia closed her eyes and nodded. "I think very naughty thoughts," she confessed breathlessly. "Ever since I met you, Stefan, I . . . I keep imagining wicked things. Wanting things. Things no lady ought to want."

Suddenly, she felt the sting of his hand across her backside. "Oh!" she cried, jumping

But Nash's hand was already massaging her buttock, easing away the burn. "There, perhaps that will remind you to be good," he murmured, rubbing her with both hands now. "Will it, my love?"

They stood on their knees, bodies pressed together, with his cock twitching impatiently against her inner thigh. A strange thrill had run through her at the instant his palm struck her flesh. She felt all quivery inside. Anticipatory. Curious. She licked her lips uncertainly. "I think . . . I think perhaps I have been more naughty than you realize."

He pressed the heat of his body to hers, his hands skimming restlessly down her back. "Have you now, my sweet?" he murmured. "Perhaps I ought to untie you, and just bend you over the pillows for a proper paddling?"

"No," she said swiftly.

"No — ?" The word was rich with curiosity.

"I like this," she whispered. "I like you standing over me. But I have been just a *little* bad. Like tonight. At dinner."

He gave her a curious half smile. "At dinner?"

Xanthia closed her eyes again. "I kept watching you and . . . and remembering that first night," she confessed, her voice dreamy. "How we met. How we kissed. I kept thinking of your hand between my — well, of your hand . . . pleasuring me in the darkness — whilst all the others danced, never knowing what we were doing together. And I kept remembering how . . . how powerful your cock felt when it brushed my body. How hard it felt beneath your trousers."

"Oh, that was very naughty indeed," he admitted. "I think the best way to punish you is to torment you until you beg."

"Oh," she whispered, trembling against him. "Oh, *God*."

He was kissing her now, light, gentle kisses all along her cheek, and circling the swell of her buttock with a gentle, certain touch. She lifted her face from his shoulder, and this time, she looked him directly in the eyes.

"I like this," she said again. "Your being . . . the one in control."

Something in his gaze softened, and he bent his head to kiss her gently. "Oh, my love," he whispered. "You must get so very tired sometimes. Tired of being strong and in command. Tired of having no one with whom to be . . . just yourself."

"You understand," she whispered dreamily.

"Yes," he murmured. "I do." Then his hands came up to cradle her face as he slanted his lips over hers in a kiss of exquisite tenderness. It was a caress of sensual promise, and of something else, too. Gratitude, perhaps? But it was no less erotic for it. The kiss deepened, became something more. A bond. A promise. She felt her body melt and join to his. A rich sensual heat swirled about them, and it was just *them.* The two of them, sharing a oneness no one could understand.

They came apart gasping, holding one another's gaze as if wondering what they had wrought. At least *she* was wondering. It was the most bizarre thing imaginable: to be tied in such a way that one could not move; to be totally at the mercy of another — and to want it. He sat back on his heels and let his gaze trail over her nakedness again.

Do you trust me? he had whispered.

And that was the essence of it, was it not? As lovers, did they have trust? She looked at him, taking in the powerful, bulging thighs, and the broad shoulders, which were limned with light from the flickering hearth. At the thick, straight, too-long hair and harsh black brows. At the almost intimidating size of his erection. *A strong man.* Oh, yes. He was certainly that.

Nash reached past her and picked up his glass of port. Still watching her, he drank with relish, then banded one arm about her waist and kissed her deeply. Xanthia was amazed when her mouth flooded with the rich taste of wine. The sweet, heavy liquid swirled sensuously in her mouth as his tongue thrust deep. She swallowed, and it was a heady, purely erotic experience.

He drew back, his eyes burning with intensity. "Good God, you are the most sensual creature I have ever known," he rasped. To her shock, he lifted the glass and let just a little of the port drip down the valley between her breasts. Her nipples puckered into impossibly tight buds as the port ran lower, down her belly, and farther still, teasing at her skin as it ran.

At the very last instant, Nash bent his head, thrust his tongue into her curls, and licked. Xanthia shivered at the sudden intrusion, and he made a soft sound of reassurance. Again, he stroked, sliding deeper. And then the wet warmth of his tongue trailed up her belly. Delved into her navel. Stroked along her breastbone, lapping up every trace of the rich, red wine.

Trapped on her knees, her arms tied high, Xanthia could do nothing but tremble with the pleasure of it. Nash brushed his lips along her jaw. "Do you wish me to stop, my love?"

"Nooo," she whispered. "Don't stop. Please. Go . . . back."

He chuckled deep in his chest. "Go back where, love?"

Xanthia swallowed hard. "Back . . . down. *Please.*"

He stroked two fingers deep into her folds, just grazing her clitoris. "Back . . . *here?*"

Eyes closed, she nodded.

"Tell me where," he murmured. "Be a good girl, and tell me just what you want."

"Taste me," she whispered, her words barely audible. "Use your tongue — and — and your fingers. Touch me. Oh, please, Stefan. *Touch* me. You know how to do it. How I want it."

For a moment, he hesitated, tormenting her instead with his hand. He watched her face — she knew it, though she did not open her eyes. The sound of her desire was wet and erotic. The scent of raw lust was everywhere. Xanthia wondered how he maintained such restraint when she ached with the need to explode.

And then he bent lower, the soft, curling hair of his chest teasing at her thigh. When his tongue slid deep, she cried out, her eyes flying open. Xanthia could not move. The rope held her fast to his hot, ravening mouth. She was gasping. His finger slipped into her wet sheath, and on a sudden instinct, her every muscle seemed to contract. Nash played his tongue delicately, working her to the point of madness, until she was gasping, then fighting to suppress a cry of release. The waves of pleasure washed over her, making her jerk at the silken rope, which drew her body taut.

"Oh, let me down," she whimpered as the heat of his body pressed against her, surrounded her. He was kissing her again —

her throat, her breasts, her collarbones. It was not enough. "Oh, Stefan. *Please.* Let me down. I want it — *ah!*"

The thrust was hard. Gloriously hard. Deep and sudden. He had lifted her with one arm about her waist and impaled her on the hot length of his cock. He lifted her again, with a masculine grunt of satisfaction, and let her body slide down his own as he pushed himself deep inside her. He was so unyieldingly large, and she so slender, he held her weight easily and caught her nipple in his mouth as she descended. For a long, impossible moment, he held her there, bound by his arms and by the silk tie knotted about the canopy, a prisoner to his lust.

"Again," she whimpered. "Stefan, again."

Nash let his hands slide down her back, all the way down, until he cupped her buttocks in his palms. Then he obliged her, lifting her just a few perfect inches as he spread her wide to take his thrust. *"Ah — !"* she cried. "Oh, God. So perfect."

"Perfect," he echoed. "Yes, love. You are perfect."

Xanthia let her head fall back. Felt him suckle her again. Felt him lift and drive deep again. And again. Their bodies grew damp as they slid and thrust. It was such a sensuously decadent sound, the sound of their flesh moving over one another. The sound of exquisite, perfect pleasure.

Their motions grew feverish. Urgent. Xanthia ached for him. A sob tore through her, deep and tremulous. A coal sheered off in the hearth, sending sparks into the air. She could hear his name, softly chanted in the gloom. Her voice. Her need. Again he lifted her. Opened her. Took her deeply. Over and over, until Xanthia was sobbing in earnest. Sobbing into his mouth, crying out his name. The waves of shuddering passion rolled over her. Against her length, his body shook with such primal strength the bed and canopy trembled with the force of it.

Xanthia returned to the present, still shaking. Nash's head was tucked into the turn of her neck, and there was a warm wetness on her shoulder. She turned her head and kissed him, but for a time, he did not respond. When at last he lifted his face from her neck she saw his eyes were glistening.

"I am lost, Zee," he whispered. "Oh, God. I am in so deep. I . . ."

"What?" She held his gaze intently. "Tell me. *Trust* me."

"I love you." He barely spoke the words. "The awful, gut-wrenching, head-over-heels kind of love — may God help us both."

She did not look away. "You are not the only one," she finally said. "You are not the only one in this bed who is . . . well, just a little frightened, I daresay."

He reached high and deftly freed the knotted silk. Xanthia's arms fell, and the silk slithered off her wrists. Wordlessly, he bore her down into the feathery softness of the bed. He set his lips to the warm turn of her neck and drew in her scent. It was as if they had mutually agreed not to speak of it; as if whatever it was that had sprung up between them was as yet too nascent. Too tender.

"Are you warm enough now, my love?" he murmured.

"Yes." She breathed the word on a sign of exquisite pleasure. "Wonderfully so."

He smiled softly. "You once said to me — it was the very night we met, in fact — that you hadn't been warm in an age," he said. "I thought — yes, in that very moment — how much I should like to make it my life's mission to change that."

My life's mission . . .

Xanthia went very still beneath him. But Nash had resumed nuzzling her neck. He did not seem to be as deeply serious as he had been a few moments earlier. She relaxed and let her hands caress the taut, muscular swells of his buttocks.

"You have accomplished your mission, sir," she said lightly. "Now kindly do not move. I shall go to sleep now, in utter warmth and comfort, and I shall try very hard not to snore."

"Dear me," he said. "Do you snore?"

She giggled. "Not usually," she admitted. "But you are squishing me — albeit in a perfectly delicious way."

He rolled to one side, and trailed his fingertip down her cheek. "Do you like it here, Zee?" he asked. "Do you like Hampshire? Brierwood?"

"It is a beautiful place," she said, wondering at the question. "And the estate itself — well, is there another so fine in all of England? I have not seen it."

He twirled a strand of her hair around his finger. "I wish it were just the two of us here, Zee," he whispered. "We have so much to learn about one another. I dislike having all these people around us."

"They are your guests and your family, and they are all lovely," she said. "And as to the servants, I fear this house is too large for you to send them all on holiday."

"Then there is but one solution." He looked up at her mischievously. "We must run away."

She laughed. "Where, pray, would we go?"

"To the Isles of Scilly," he said.

"That sounds lovely," she said. "But . . . no, too near. They might find us there."

"Morocco, perhaps?" he proposed. "Or Crete?"

"Ooh, Crete," she agreed. "Now all we need is a ship. Why do I never have one to hand when I need it?"

"Ah, but you are not the only one with a fleet at your command, my love," he said.

She looked at him in mild surprise. "Am I not?"

"My yacht is at anchor in Southampton," he suggested, throwing out his arm as if to direct her down a path. "My lady, the *Dangerous Wager* awaits your pleasure."

Xanthia laughed so loudly she was compelled to slap a hand over her mouth. "The *Dangerous Wager*?"

"That's how I won her," said Nash. "Some fool in Brooks's made such a wager one night and did not heed his friends' advice."

"And you won her from him?"

"Yes, and changed her name in honor of his folly," said Nash. "The *Mary Jane* just didn't have the right cachet."

"No, indeed," she said. "I must call on you, my dear, when next we christen a ship."

"Ah, some small way in which I can further Neville's business interests," he said, smiling. "Alas, I fear it is the only skill I have. You will not need to worry, my love, that I will ever meddle in your work."

"Oh, I think you have other skills which I can put to better use," she murmured.

"Have I?" he asked. "I wonder what they are?"

He chuckled again, then drew her to him. Instinctively, she turned, and nestled her back to his chest. His arm came around, firm and strong, and his hand settled warmly on her belly. Xanthia had never known such comfort — or such joy. In her drowsy, satiated state, she wondered vaguely at some of his words. He spoke with such hope and such certainty — almost as if he knew something she did not. Certainly he did not sound like some casual philanderer who meant to break her heart and move on. But Xanthia was so physically sated by his lovemaking, she could barely think coherently.

She gave in to the sweet lethargy and relaxed in his embrace. In short order, Nash's breathing shifted to the slow, rhythmic exhalations of deepening sleep. Xanthia lay still, drifting. This had been a wonderful, almost magical evening. She was not at all certain of where this strange liaison was going — but wherever it was, she was beginning to believe it was meant to be. She was beginning to believe that together, she and Nash might just be able to overcome any obstacle. Besides, what choice had she now? She, too, was head over heels. And Nash, she knew, would be worth it.

CHAPTER FIFTEEN:
TERRIBLE TROUBLE
IN HAMPSHIRE

By midday on Saturday, all of Lady Nash's extended family had arrived at Brierwood. Xanthia could already see that the affair would be much larger than she had anticipated. Lady Henslow's grandchildren alone were numerous enough to field a cricket team of sorts — which they did, with the good-humored assistance of Mr. Hayden-Worth. Shortly after noon, he herded a group of them out onto one of the few patches of lawn in Brierwood's front gardens and began to set up the wickets.

Caught up in the spontaneity, Lady Nash ordered a white tent and a pair of tables to be set up along the edge of the impromptu cricket ground, for the day had turned gloriously bright. Ladies began to drift from the house in light summer frocks, and carrying lace-trimmed parasols, as servants moved sedately through the sculpted gardens bearing wide silver trays of lemonade. Xanthia wandered along the edges, feeling neither a part of the festivities nor precisely an outsider, either.

Xanthia knew many of the guests vaguely, having met them at Lady Henslow's picnic. All were friendly enough. But after a brief introduction to Xanthia, their surreptitious glances and the inevitable whispers always followed. Clearly, speculation was running rampant as to precisely why she had been invited. Xanthia did not know whether to curse Kieran or kiss him for having had the audacity to agree to this visit.

At that very moment, Lady Henslow's eldest grandson, a long-legged young man named Frederick swung the bat with a most impressive crack. Xanthia looked up to see a streak of red go flying through the air toward one of the more distant fountains. The crowd sent up a loud cheer as Frederick and his second batsman went streaking up and down the field — not once, but twice. A moment later, the ball came in, shattering the wicket as the young men passed, but it was too late. The damage was done.

"Oh, bravo!" cried Xanthia appreciatively.

"An impressive lad, is he not?" said a quiet voice at her elbow.

She looked up to see Nash, still in his

boots and breeches, standing at her side. He looked imposingly large today in a snug brown riding coat and glossy black boots, which seemed to have molded to his calves — and a fine sight they were, too.

She felt a faint blush settle over her face. "Good afternoon," she said, smiling as he offered his arm. "I have missed you."

"And I you, my love." He patted her hand gently.

"I hear you have been paying tenant calls today," she said lightly. "Did any of them recognize you?"

Nash laughed ruefully. "Barely, I should think." But he looked oddly somber.

"How did you find them?" she asked more seriously. "The crops have made a good beginning, I hope?"

Nash lifted one shoulder. "The Oldfields lost their eldest last week," he said. "The most foolish thing — the boy fell from an apple tree and fractured his skull — and they are simply devastated. They have only daughters now. Oldfield is worried sick about the family's future."

Xanthia lifted one eyebrow. "Can a daughter not take over the farm eventually?"

"I cannot see how," he admitted. "The sheer physical strength required — well, I don't know, Zee. It is not for me to decide."

"But the Oldfields fear you *might* decide it, I daresay," Xanthia continued. They were strolling away from the billowing white tent and along the edge of the cricket field now. "You could choose not to renew the lease, and look for a more long-term tenant when the time comes."

"I would not do that," he answered. "Oldfield is a good tenant, and Brierwood is profitable enough without my stepping up on the backs of my own farmers."

"Then perhaps you should tell him so," Xanthia suggested. "At Neville's, we sometimes pay a premium in order to retain a more experienced captain for a certain voyage. In the end, it is for the best, even though the man may sit idle a few weeks more than he otherwise might. Perhaps Mr. Oldfield should begin looking about for a fine, strong husband for one of those daughters? Perhaps he would do precisely that had he some guarantee of retaining his lease."

Nash laughed, and covered her hand with his most protectively. "You are always planning and strategizing, aren't you, my dear?" His mood seemed considerably lightened. "And as usual, you are not wrong. I will speak to my estate agent, and we will see what can be arranged for Oldfield."

"I think it will be to your advantage," she

said. "A farm is like any other business. One must always think long-term."

He drew her closer, and tightened his grip on her hand. "Do you know, Xanthia, how much I like having you here?" he asked quietly. "I value your thoughts and ideas. Your enthusiasm is almost contagious."

Another crack of the bat rang out, and a second cheer went up from the field. Xanthia barely heard it. As if by mutual agreement, she and Nash had slowed to a halt. She had turned on the graveled path to face him and to study the harsh, lean planes of his face. He lowered his thick black eyelashes, and something in her heart leapt. Her stomach twisted with an ache which was not sexual desire, but something deeper and more fearsome. It was a yearning — a wish to spend every day of her life like this. With *this* man. Simply hanging on his arm and discussing the events of the day together.

She set one hand against his chest, an intimate and instinctive gesture. But she dropped it at once, remembering where they were. Nash's dark eyes snapped opened, and his gaze drifted over her, searching her face. *What was he asking of her?* she wondered again. Where was this going? There was something . . . an unasked question. A hesitation. *Something.* Or perhaps it was but wishful thinking on her part. Xanthia blushed and turned away.

Just then, the sound of a carriage reached her ears. She looked past Nash's shoulder to see a solid black barouche drawn by four glossy black horses come hurling down the carriage drive. There was a flash of recognition, and then . . . uncertainty. With a slightly unsteady hand, she pointed. "Stefan, who is that?"

Nash glanced over his shoulder, and smiled. "Just another of Edwina's friends, I daresay."

But it was not a friend of Lady Nash's. Xanthia somehow sensed it. A little numbly, she turned and watched the carriage draw up before the massive double staircase. Two footmen went down the steps to meet them. With a cheerful wave, Lady Nash hastened from the white tent and started across the gardens. They were expecting guests. Luggage. Conviviality.

But these were not guests. Xanthia suddenly remembered where she had seen the carriage. She closed her eyes on a wave of nausea. Nash's hands come out to steady her shoulders.

"My dear, are you all right?"

She set the back of her hand to her forehead. "Yes, I — I think . . . it is just the sun."

"How thoughtless of me," he murmured, his grip tightening. He escorted her to a nearby bench. "I wished to have you all to myself for a moment," he said, fanning her with his hat. "When you are feeling better, I shall return you to Edwina's tent."

She nodded, but within moments, she heard footsteps crunching in the gravel. It was one of Brierwood's footmen. "I beg your pardon, my lord," he said. "There are two gentlemen just down from London who urgently wish to speak with you."

Nash's expression darkened. "I have guests."

"Yes, sir," the footman acknowledged. "But they say it is an emergency, my lord. They have come from Whitehall in some haste."

"Good Lord, *Whitehall?*" Nash shook his head. "You've misunderstood. It's my step-brother they want."

The footman shook his head. "No, my lord," he answered. "They were very clear. Shall . . . shall I ask them to leave, sir?"

Nash looked down at Xanthia, who was still fighting the urge to retch. She let her hand slide from his arm. "You had better go," she said quietly.

"Walk with me back to the house." His face was lined with worry.

Xanthia drew away. "No, I — I am feeling better now," she murmured. "I had best find my brother. People are staring. Please go."

Nash nodded curtly and moved away.

Xanthia watched him stride across the gardens, tears pressing against her eyes, hot and desperate. Her every instinct screamed at her to *go*. To follow him. To protest his innocence — if indeed it was an accusation which had brought de Vendenheim so far from London.

But of course it was an accusation. And once Nash heard it — once he fully grasped all that had gone on — the very last person whose support or consolation he would wish for would be hers. Her only hope was that he would *not* fully grasp it — that he would never know just what had gone on or who had been involved — but it was a faint hope indeed. Xanthia set her hand on her diaphragm in an attempt to quell the nausea and set off in search of Kieran.

Nash escorted his unexpected guests into the Chinese salon, the room nearest the great hall, and bade them be seated. He glanced at the cards which the gentlemen had presented. "I hope you will understand, Lord de Vendenheim-Sélestat, that I have a houseful of guests," said the marquess without sitting down.

"Just de Vendenheim will do," said his guest.

The man was both leaner and taller, even, than Nash himself, which was most unusual. His eyes were heavy and hooded, and his olive skin was certainly not that of an Englishman.

The man's piercing black gaze caught Nash's. "Italian," he said. "And Alsatian."

"I beg your pardon?"

"You are speculating as to my origin," said the man calmly. "No, I am not English."

"I daresay that's no one's business save yours," Nash returned.

"Nonetheless, sometimes it is easier simply to dispense with the curiosity," said de Vendenheim.

"You must suit yourself." Nash smiled faintly, then returned his gaze to the cards. "And . . . Mr. Kemble, is it? Do we know one another, sir?"

"Perhaps we've met," said the man vaguely.

"Ah." Nash laid the cards aside and sat down. "Well, I cannot imagine what the Government wants with me. After all, I take so little interest in it. In any case, how may I help?"

The man called de Vendenheim looked suddenly ill at ease. He cleared his throat roughly. "The Home Office has been making certain enquiries, Lord Nash, regarding some irregularities within the diplomatic community," he began. "We would like to ask you certain questions in relation to those irregularities."

"I do not know anyone to speak of within the diplomatic corps," said Nash calmly.

There was a flicker of satisfaction in de Vendenheim's eyes. "Oh, but we think you do," he responded. "The Comte de Montignac, an attaché to the French embassy, has been in receipt of a large sum of money — *your* money, to put it plainly."

Lord Nash went perfectly still. Alarm surged, but somehow he managed to suppress it. The memory of that tawdry night in Belgravia came back to him — and the threat which had followed some weeks later at Lady Cartselle's masque. But it had been the Comtesse de Montignac's threat, not her husband's. And why would the Home Office give a damn about what was little more than a case of subtle blackmail?

"Lord Nash?" said de Vendenheim.

The marquess cleared his throat. "Whatever lies the Comtesse de Montignac may have told you are simply that," he said quietly. "Lies."

"But you gave her money to pass on to her husband, did you not?" said Mr. Kemble certainly. "A large sum of money. We should simply like to know why."

Nash glowered at the man, wishing to the devil he could place him. "It is none of your damned business, sir," he said stiffly. "I do not owe you any explanation, and indeed, I shan't give you one. And no matter how one looks at it, it is hardly the business of the Home Office."

De Vendenheim's frown deepened. "Diplomats are prohibited from accepting bribes from citizens of the country to which they are assigned."

At that, Nash threw back his head and laughed. "Prohibited by whom, de Vendenheim?" he asked, incredulous. "By their home country? Surely you are not so naive. In any case, the Home Office should concern itself with English law — none of which I have broken. As to French law, why, the entire government of France would collapse were bribery and blackmail to cease."

He could see de Vendenheim's frustration growing. "You do not seem to take this matter with the gravity it warrants, Lord Nash," he snapped. "I can assure you, England still considers treason a hanging offense."

"Treason?" said Nash very quietly. "By God, that is a dangerous word to bandy about, sir. You must hold your life cheap indeed if you dare come into my home and fling it at me."

De Vendenheim did not look especially concerned. "I won't give you satisfaction, Nash, if that's what you are after," he said with a dismissive gesture. "I am no gentleman, and I do not feel compelled to behave as stupidly as some of them do."

Nash started from behind the desk. "Actually, I would feel pretty well satisfied to simply throttle you here and —"

"Please, Lord Nash!" Mr. Kemble held up a staying hand. "Might I suggest we all pause a moment to collect ourselves? My friend here has let his concern get the better of his tongue."

"Yes, and his sense, too," said Nash, "— if he has any."

"But certain facts do remain, my lord," Mr. Kemble calmly continued. "And some of them are, on their face, treasonous. French and English couriers have been secretly coming and going from the vicinity of this house for over eight months now, and —"

"What, you people have set *spies* on me?" Nash roared. "You have been *watching* my house? What else, I wonder, have you been up to?"

For an instant, Kemble faltered. "Only what was thought necessary, my lord," he finally said. "You see, a few weeks past, one of the couriers was murdered at the White Lion Inn, just five miles south. He carried, as most of them likely did, some very interesting information well hidden upon his person, much of it in code."

A grave unease was creeping over Nash, but he fought it down. "But you said from the *vicinity* of this house," he repeated. "Not *from* this house."

"We have no witness who can put any of them within the walls of this house, no," Kemble admitted.

"Then I think this conversation is finished, gentlemen."

Mr. Kemble glanced at de Vendenheim with an *I-told-you-so* expression.

De Vendenheim returned his steady gaze to Nash. "It took some time to decode the cache of papers found on the dead man," he said. "But when we did, we found a list of weapons to be smuggled, and a map to this specific house, with this address written on it. I do not think we will need a witness,

Lord Nash."

"*Weapons* to be smuggled?" Nash felt the blood literally drain from his face. "Good Lord. Weapons from where? And to whom?"

"We are not at liberty to say," said de Vendenheim.

Nash jerked to his feet. "By God, this is a serious charge you have hurled at me," he said. "I think honor compels you to explain it."

For an instant, de Vendenheim considered it. "Very well," he finally said. "American rifles. Carbines, to be precise. And they are believed to be going to the Greek revolutionaries via France. Does that sound in any way familiar?"

"Carbines?" *Dear God . . .*

Nash could not get his breath. He paced toward the window, praying for clarity. For control. He had to think; to focus on what it all might mean. He knew he could not let de Vendenheim see him rattled. He set one hand on his hip and stared out into the brilliance of spring, at the innocence and gaiety holding forth on his lawns. How carefree everyone looked. And how very harsh the world could be. *Smuggled rifles!* He had been given a hard scrape from which to drag the family this time — if any of this were true . . .

"Lord Nash, these weapons are in transit even as we speak," de Vendenheim continued from across the room. "I am warning you — our government will not allow them to reach Greece. We need to know where that ship is this very moment, so that the Royal Navy may board it. Lives are at stake here."

The marquess whirled around. "And you think *I* know where the damned thing is?"

"Someone in this house does," said de Vendenheim quietly. "And we know, Lord Nash, that you have connections in Russia. We know your family has a history of antipathy toward the Turks."

"My family has a history of being *murdered* by the Turks, you fool," spit Nash. "As do the Greeks. As do the Albanians. Tell me, de Vendenheim, have you interviewed every bloody foreigner in this country? Because that is what it may well take to get the answer you seek."

De Vendenheim looked as if he might spring from his chair at any moment. Mr. Kemble must have sensed it, for he rose, went to his companion, and set a hand on his shoulder as if to restrain him. "Lord Nash, the map bore the address of this house," he said quietly. "There is no escaping that fact. Now, perhaps if you would simply work with us to —"

"Who are you?" Nash suddenly snapped.

"I beg your pardon?"

"Just who the hell are you?" Nash stalked toward him. "By God, I *know* I have seen you somewhere — and very recently, too."

Mr. Kemble let his hand fall and made no answer.

Nash felt his vision begin to darken, as if he might faint. Or commit murder. "In Wapping!" he muttered. "Yes, you were in Wapping, were you not? At Neville Shipping. I saw you there."

Mr. Kemble smiled faintly. "I suppose it was too much to hope that you would not remember," he said quietly. "Most people would not have, you know. They never see the servants who are there, simply toiling in the background."

A *servant?* This man was no servant.

"What were you doing there?" he rasped, already fearing the answer. "*What?* Tell me, by God!"

Again the visitors exchanged telling glances. De Vendenheim spoke first. "You must not blame Lord Rothewell or his sister," he said quietly.

Nash tried to absorb the words, tried to find another meaning for them. He could not. His ire was turning into a strange sense of foreboding and to something worse. A sickening fear. Just then, a firm knock sounded on the door. Nash strode across the room and jerked open the door. In one sweep, his eyes took in the brace of pale footmen beyond, and Tony on the threshold. Across the great hall stood Xanthia and Rothewell. Rothewell looked grave. Xanthia was whispering something in his ear, her face bloodless, her expression urgent.

Xanthia. His eyes caught hers, beseeching. *Begging.* She looked away.

Nash's knees felt suddenly as if they might buckle. A stake had just been driven into his heart. It was as if unconquerable waves of grief and anger were crashing down on him, as if his ship were sinking, splintering to jetsam beneath his very feet, leaving him to grasp at the wreckage as he wondered whom to save — and whom to let drown.

Good God. Xanthia. It was not possible. It was *not.*

Tony stepped into the room. Nash drew in a ragged breath and somehow forced his attention to his stepbrother, who still wore his cricket whites. "Stefan, you look ill," asked Tony very quietly. "Mamma said there was angry shouting. Is everything all right?"

Nash seized Tony by the arm. "You will excuse me," he said to de Vendenheim over his shoulder. "I wish a moment of privacy with my brother."

Nash propelled Tony away from Rothewell and down the opposite corridor in haste. He had to force himself to walk, to think. His hands were shaking now. He wanted to run back to Xanthia, and demand the truth. But the truth would kill him. Indeed, it already had.

"Where are we going?" Tony's voice was edged with alarm. "Who the devil are those fellows?"

"They are your worst nightmare, Tony," Nash gritted, pushing open the library door. "And we must decide just what's to be done about it — and we must decide now."

With the door closed, Nash dragged both hands through his hair. But it was not Tony's decision to make, was it? It was his life which lay in tatters, for Tony's might yet be saved. Nash wanted to sob. To let his fists fly at someone — Tony, Kemble, de Vendenheim, anyone — anyone but *her* — and hurt them badly. He had been spied upon. The man named Kemble had not been at Neville Shipping by accident. And Xanthia had not been in his bed by accident. The inescapable horror of it was pressing down upon him.

"What did I do, Nash?" asked Tony quietly. "And what can I do to help?"

"Tony," said Nash grimly, "if you had done what I have been asking you to do these last five years — to take hold of your wife, and keep her in check — you would need do nothing now."

Tony's face paled until it matched his cricket whites. "Dear God," he rasped. "What has Jenny done this time?"

"I think I can guess," Nash growled. "But I cannot yet prove it. Look, Tony, we have no time. I wish you to go upstairs and collect your things. We must go. *Now*."

"Go?" he said incredulously. "But what about Mamma's party?"

"I am sorry," said Nash curtly. "This is your political career we are talking about, Tony. I think I know what your choice will be. Now go find Gibbons and tell him he's to put up my kit — and my cashbox. I want them downstairs in five minutes. I am going to the stables to have your carriage made ready and brought round."

He had Tony's full attention now. "In two minutes," he agreed. "But where, Nash, do we go?"

"To France," said Nash tightly. "We are following Jenny to Cherbourg. My yacht lies at anchor in Southampton. If we hurry, Tony, we can be there by dusk."

Her stomach still churning with nausea, Xanthia watched Nash practically drag Mr. Hayden-Worth down the passageway in the direction of the library. She had been unable to miss the hurtful accusation in his eyes. Dear God. *He knew.* It was over.

Unthinkingly, she left her brother's side and stalked into the Chinese salon. "How could you?" she hissed at de Vendenheim. "How could you do this to me?"

"To *you*, Miss Neville?"

"Yes, and to Lord Nash, for God's sake!" she answered. "How dare you violate the sanctity of a man's home — and under such circumstances? He has a houseful of guests — important guests. What are these people to think?"

"It is most regrettable, Miss Neville," said de Vendenheim calmly. "But we received some urgent information. A load of American rifles is thought to be en route to Cherbourg — but we do not know precisely when, or under whose flag the ship will be sailing."

"And your interrogation simply could not wait?" she demanded.

"It could not," said the vicomte quietly.

"This ship must be stopped. Matters in Greece grow more perilous by the day. And I think, Miss Neville, that for your own sake, you should not be in this room."

She felt Kieran take hold of her arm. "He is right," Kieran warned. "If you remain, my dear, Nash will know you were a part of this."

Xanthia whirled on him. "He already knows!" she cried. "Because he has brought Mr. Kemble!" She thrust a finger at de Vendenheim. "He *saw* him, Kieran — *weeks* ago. It was at a distance, but yes, but he saw the man in my office. Nash already knows the truth, and it is *his* fault."

"Miss Neville, how was Max to know we would find you here at Brierwood?" said Kemble soothingly. "Seeing both you and I here — yes, Lord Nash will likely put it all together. I daresay he has already done so. I am so very sorry."

Xanthia wanted to weep with despair. "And you are so certain he is guilty!" she cried. "Yet you two have looked no further than the nose upon your face."

"Xanthia, calm yourself," her brother commanded. "Still, I think she is right, you know," he said aside to de Vendenheim. "I have been asking a few questions of my own about this business. And Nash knows nothing. I am quite certain of it."

"Regrettably, my lord, the facts rather speak for themselves," said de Vendenheim.

Xanthia almost lunged at him. "There are other people who live here!" she interjected. "Mr. Hayden-Worth, for example? What of him? Have you thoroughly investigated his background?"

"We have not."

"No, because he is wholly English — *and* a politician," she said derisively. The tears were flowing now. "You suspect Lord Nash because of his foreign blood. And that is just *vile,* Lord de Vendenheim. It is bigotry, plain and simple."

The vicomte's mouth turned into a sneer. "I assure you, Miss Neville, that no one is more acutely aware of the difficulties foreigners face in this country than I," he answered. "My suspicion of Lord Nash is based on fact. He *does* have regional ties to Eastern Europe. His family is *known* to hate the Turks. He *has* funneled at least one large sum of money to the French diplomats who are serving as liaison to the Greeks. And Brierwood is *his* home, no matter who may live here."

Later, Xanthia was never sure just what it was that drove her. Instinct, perhaps? She jerked from Kieran's grasp. "Stay here —

all three of you," she commanded, dragging a hand beneath her eyes. "There is something I wish to show you."

Propelled by her anger, Xanthia flew up the stairs. She passed Mr. Hayden-Worth coming back down with two servants on his heels. She was so ashamed, she felt compelled to look away. And so she did not see the portmanteaus, which the servants carried, or the stark, bloodless expression on Mr. Hayden-Worth's face.

Nash strode back through the west wing of Brierwood, his mind in turmoil. He had left the grooms in a panic, but by God he would have his carriage within moments — of that, he was sure. Of all else, he was less certain. But he pressed on, striding up the hill like an automaton, in part because he was afraid to slow down. Afraid to think. Afraid of the awful knowledge which was bearing down upon him.

But there was no escaping it. The bittersweet vignettes kept reappearing in his mind. Xanthia, chatting so casually about the turmoil in Greece. Teasing him about customs and taxation. Subtly suggesting that there were ways around such things. He had wondered at it, even then. Her words had seemed so disparate from her nature. But apparently, the woman was well schooled in deception. And it explained why she had followed him onto the terrace that very first night at Sharpe's.

Yes, she had been very clever indeed. She had played hard to get like one of Drury Lane's best. He recalled how he had seen her bent over the desk in his library, looking for the letter paper which had lain in plain view in the top drawer. Then there was the matter of Vladislav's missing correspondence. She had probably taken it. But why? Was there no end to the woman's audacity? How had he not seen it? Had he not chanced to see Mr. Kemble today — had something in the man's face not driven him to distraction — good God. What a fool he had been about to make of himself.

His life — the life he had never really known he wanted — was over. He was a little ashamed to feel the hot press of tears behind his eyes. His hands curled into tight fists as he willed them to recede. And slowly, the grief began to boil down to a righteous fury, a simpler, safer emotion.

Nash strode into the great hall to find his stepbrother waiting. Tony still wore his whites, but Gibbons and Tony's valet were ready with portmanteaus in hand, and fresh suits of clothing over their arms. Both servants looked unflappable.

"I apologize for the haste," said Nash to the three of them. "The carriage will be coming round shortly. We should make the coast by nightfall."

Just then, de Vendenheim stepped from the shadows of the salon, his footsteps ominous on the marble floor. "I hope, Lord Nash, that you do not mean to leave the country," he said *sotto voce.*

"That is precisely what I mean to do," Nash answered. "Have you sufficient evidence on which to hold me?"

De Vendenheim hesitated. "Not quite."

"Then stand aside, sir," Tony ordered, injecting himself into the conversation. "I scarcely know who you are, but I daresay you do know who *I* am."

"Yes, Mr. Hayden-Worth." De Vendenheim sounded inordinately weary. "I am all too aware."

"Then impede us at your peril," Tony snapped. "And kindly remember that I am not without influence in Whitehall."

"Yes, that's another thing I'm well aware of," said the vicomte dryly. He returned his attention to Nash. "My lord, I must ask again that you remain in England, on your honor as a gentleman."

"But my dear fellow, like you, I am

scarcely a gentleman," said Nash. "Indeed, I am scarcely an Englishman."

De Vendenheim frowned. "Lord Nash, I really think —"

"And I think you have a lot of gall, invading the sanctity of my home," Nash coolly interjected. "I am going to France, gentlemen — specifically, to Cherbourg — where I shall have the French police do what you people seem incapable of. And when I return, if I am feeling charitable, perhaps I will even bring you your foreign spy, de Vendenheim."

De Vendenheim's lips thinned with irritation, and he stepped away. It was only then that Nash noticed Xanthia's brother hovering in the depths of the salon.

"Lord Rothewell," he said curtly, "you and your sister will be so good as to leave my house — tonight if at all possible. Tomorrow morning at the latest. Do I make myself plain?"

Lord Rothewell stood impassively in the shadows, his face as veiled as his character. "You are making a grave mistake, Nash."

"No, thank God, I am not," Nash returned, his voice dangerously soft. "But it was a near-run thing."

Just then, the clatter of a carriage sounded beyond the front door, which still stood open. Cutting one last look of contempt toward de Vendenheim, Lord Nash went down the stairs, Mr. Hayden-Worth and the servants on his heels. In an instant, the coachman snapped his whip, and they were off.

"Maledizione!" spit de Vendenheim, pounding his fist on the doorframe.

"Well!" said Kemble with false brightness. "That could hardly have gone worse."

Lord Rothewell and de Vendenheim glowered at him. Kemble was saved, however, by Xanthia. The carriage had not quite vanished by the time she came back down the stairs. She ran to the open door, and set one hand against the doorjamb, watching forlornly as the trail of dust vanished.

When both carriage and dust had disappeared, she slowly turned around. "He has gone to France, has he not?"

Mr. Kemble looked at her strangely. "Yes. How did you know?"

Xanthia dropped her chin, and blinked back what was left of her tears. "Come with me into the salon," she said. "I want to prove to you Lord Nash's innocence."

Mr. Kemble set a hand over hers. "Miss Neville, you are distraught," he murmured. "There is no need to do this now."

Xanthia jerked away from him. "But I

must do it now, don't you see?" she cried. "Listen to me, Mr. Kemble — do you remember how you once told me about how conversational things written in letters might have special meanings?"

Kemble followed her into the salon. "Yes, but both parties must know which words mean what," he said. "It is the simplest sort of code there is — and more or less impossible to break."

Rothewell slid a hand beneath her elbow. "Nash has asked us to leave, Zee," he said softly. "Perhaps we had best do so now?"

"No." Xanthia sat down in a chair by the front windows and extracted the letter from Mrs. Hayden-Worth's prayer book. She handed it to Kemble. "I wish Mr. Kemble to read this first."

"What is it?" asked de Vendenheim, craning over Kemble's shoulder.

Xanthia bit her lip. "It is a letter to Mrs. Hayden-Worth from her father," she answered. "She is American. Did you know that?"

De Vendenheim and Kemble exchanged worried looks.

"No, I thought not," she retorted. "Her father is a wealthy American industrialist. He lives in Connecticut, I believe. That is rather near Boston — precisely where your ordnance is being smuggled from, is it not?"

"Yes," de Vendenheim admitted.

Kemble's eyes were swiftly running over the words. "The letter is oddly brief," he said, handing it back to Xanthia. "But other than that, what am I to see?"

Xanthia held the letter in one hand, and the prayer book in the other. "Do you not think the tone of the letter is strangely stiff?" she asked. "And the mention of a specific date — how was Mrs. Hayden-Worth to know that she was to be in Cherbourg on that particular day, so many months beforehand?"

"I cannot say."

"It must have been a very important appointment," said Xanthia. "And yet, when I first arrived here, she claimed to have forgotten she needed to be in France altogether. She flew out of here two days past in a very distracted state — almost on the eve of her mother-in-law's house party."

"What is your point?" asked de Vendenheim.

"How long does it take the post to go back and forth to America?" asked Xanthia. "This appointment was important enough that Mrs. Hayden-Worth wrote to father and remarked upon it. And important enough that he wrote back, repeating it. And then *she forgot it?*"

"Or perhaps not," said Kemble in a low undertone. "You are suggesting that perhaps this letter was in fact the first time Mrs. Hayden-Worth had seen that date? That the letter might actually be a form of instruction?"

"Collusion or instruction — either is possible, I suppose." Xanthia sighed. "Or neither. I am probably just clutching at straws."

"Probably," said de Vendenheim. But he was leaning over Xanthia's shoulder now, and there was a little edge of hope in his voice.

Xanthia handed him the letter. "Are you a married man, Lord de Vendenheim?" she suddenly asked.

The vicomte's dark eyebrows lifted. "Yes, happily so."

Her eyes ran over his obviously expensive clothing. "I daresay your wife is very lovely, and dresses elegantly," said Xanthia. "Does she ever wear seed pearls? The little ones which are sometimes stitched onto one's gowns?"

De Vendenheim nodded. "Catherine often wears them on her evening dresses."

"And where does she get them?"

De Vendenheim looked at her oddly.

"They come that way from the dressmaker," he said. "But wait — I see your point. Catherine keeps a little boxful on hand, for repairs and such. She sews them on herself. But I haven't a clue where she gets them."

"In Oxford Street, I daresay," said Xanthia. "They are unaccountably common, and not frightfully expensive."

"So why would she write to her father and ask for them?" murmured Mr. Kemble. "Any woman would know that seed pearls can be had almost as easily in London."

Xanthia lifted her gaze to Kemble's. "When I met Mrs. Hayden-Worth, she seemed preoccupied," she mused.

"And she has gone to Cherbourg," murmured Kieran. "What an odd coincidence."

De Vendenheim's olive skin had slowly turned a strangely ashen shade. "There is no such thing as coincidence," he said grimly. Without another word, he tucked the letter into the pocket of his coat.

"Cherbourg," muttered Mr. Kemble. "It is a reasonable location for American merchant ships to refit on this side of the Atlantic, is it not?"

"Not the most likely," said Xanthia. "But reasonable, yes."

Kem lifted his gaze to Max's. "Perhaps we

have the wrong brother, old chap," he suggested. "Perhaps we should look more closely at Mr. Hayden-Worth's loyalties. It would not be the first time an M.P. had his hand in someone else's pocket."

"Or perhaps he is as ignorant of all this as his stepbrother," interjected Rothewell.

Suddenly, the salon doors flew open, and Lady Nash rushed in, Phaedra on her heels. "Oh! Oh! What has happened?" she cried, clutching her hands together. "Where has Nash gone in such a rush? Where is my Tony?"

Xanthia went to her at once, and took one of her hands. "Do not worry, Lady Nash," she said, her voice surprisingly calm. "They have had to go to France. A minor emergency — but all will be well, I do assure you."

"An emergency?" Lady Nash pressed one hand to her cheek. "Oh, dear! What has happened?"

Xanthia was scrambling for a good lie when Mr. Kemble approached. "Mrs. Hayden-Worth has been taken ill," he said.

"Ill?" shrieked Lady Nash.

Kemble seized the other hand, and began to pat it. "She *was* ill," he corrected. "But she is better now. Just a little *mal de mer.* Still, Mr. Hayden-Worth was worried."

"As well he should be!" cried her lady-ship.

"And you *know* how he does dote on her," said Mr. Kemble.

"Yes. Yes. He does indeed!" said her lady-ship. "Tony is a devoted husband."

"Oh, what a pack of nonsense!" said Phae-dra, looking at Kemble suspiciously.

"We all of us show our fondness in our own unique way," said Mr. Kemble a little snidely. "Mr. Hayden-Worth is worried sick."

Phaedra drew back. "Who *are* you?" she demanded. "And what are you doing in our house?"

Lord de Vendenheim stepped forward. "We are with the Home Office." Smoothly, the vicomte made the introductions. "We work for Mr. Peel."

"Oh!" said Lady Nash. "Mr. Peel is very important, is he not? And Tony is very well thought of in the Government. I daresay they must have sent you?"

Kemble was still patting her hand. "Lord Wellington himself insisted, ma'am," he answered. "He wished Mr. Hayden-Worth to hear the news at once."

"Oh?" Phaedra set her hands on her hips. "And just how did Lord Wellington catch wind of this dire tragedy?"

Xanthia caught Phaedra's gaze and lifted her finger to her lips.

Phaedra's brow furrowed in confusion, but Mr. Kemble seized the moment. "The Prime Minister heard of it through his *important secret channels*," he said knowingly. "He had a spy, I daresay, on the very same ferry. And even though Mrs. Hayden-Worth is feeling much better, he knew her husband would not rest until he was by her side and reassured of his wife's good health."

Phaedra crossed her arms over her chest. "And Nash had to go along to help, did he?"

Kemble smiled down at Phaedra as if she were a prodigy. "Yes, of course," he said. "Mr. Hayden-Worth was in no shape to travel alone."

"Just because Jenny cast up her accounts on a ferryboat?" Phaedra clarified.

"Quite so."

"Yes, it all makes perfect sense now." Lady Nash was dabbing at her eyes with a lace handkerchief. "And Nash is always so very thoughtful. Poor, poor Jenny! I daresay she will wish now she had stayed for my birthday party!"

"Yes," murmured Lord de Vendenheim dryly. "I daresay she soon shall."

Xanthia crossed the room to Phaedra's side. "I rushed upstairs to get this," she said, handing Phaedra the prayer book. "I thought it might comfort her, but they drove off before I could return. It is Jenny's, is it not?"

Phaedra took it. "Yes, where did you find it?"

"Inside the sitting room secretary," said Xanthia. Lightly, she touched the gilt initials. "This must have been Jenny's before she married."

"Oh, yes, she brought it from America," said the girl. "See? J-E-C. Jennifer Elizabeth Carlow."

Mr. Kemble's head jerked up, and his gaze snapped to Xanthia's. "Carlow?"

Phaedra looked at him disdainfully. "Yes? What of it?"

De Vendenheim stepped nearer. "Her father is a wealthy American industrialist," he murmured, as if to himself. "How remarkable. I do not suppose . . ."

"Yes?" said Phaedra impatiently.

De Vendenheim lifted his eyes to Phaedra's. "That would not be the Carlow of Carlow Arms Manufacturing, would it? The rifle works in Connecticut?"

"Why, just so!" cried Lady Nash. "Rifles! I have had the most frightful time recalling it. In any case, Mr. Carlow is such a dear — and he just *adores* Jenny."

Mr. Kemble and Lord de Vendenheim exchanged dark glances and started at once toward the door.

Phaedra's confusion suddenly cleared. "Oh, dear," she murmured to Xanthia. "Jenny's bollixed something up again, hasn't she?"

"We must hope not," said Xanthia quietly. "And if she has, we must trust that Lord Nash can set it to rights."

Phaedra strolled to the window, peering out as the two gentlemen in black piled back into their carriage. "Well, I don't know how Nash will manage it," she muttered, "but I somehow get the feeling that dear old Jenny is going to be saying a few prayers — with or without this book."

Chapter Sixteen: The Denouement in Paris

Summer spread up the Seine Valley like a damp blanket, layering the land with a thick, unseasonable warmth. In Paris, the streets were stifling but tolerable. Inside *l'hospice de la Salpêtrière,* however, the stillness and stench were almost overpowering. Lord Nash stood beside one of the narrow windows which overlooked the deceptively verdant lawns, pinched the bridge of his nose, and did his best to shut out the groans and screams which resonated through the ancient building.

He scarcely heard the sound of the door, which opened behind him — but he heard his name, a distant, bloodcurdling cry, over and over, like that of a wounded animal. It echoed down the hall, then was mercifully muted again by the thud of the closing door. The hand which touched his was cool.

Nash looked down at the slender wrist which extended from the sleeve of a starched white alb. He turned slowly from the window. *"Bonjour, mon Père."*

Father Michel studied his face. "My son, how are you?" he murmured. "Tired, I think?"

Nash bowed his head. *"Je vais bien,* Father," he said. "But yes, tired. The comtesse, I can see, still knows my name."

The priest smiled wanly. *"Oui,* she will do so for some time yet." He made the sign of the cross. "But she is now — how do you say it? Caught with the arms?"

"Bound?"

"Oui, bound — so as to do herself no harm. But her temper will soon cool."

Nash felt a moment of grief. "Pray for her, Father."

"I do, my son," he said gravely. "And for the other woman, your American sister."

"Merci, mon Père."

The priest gave another faint smile. "Come, my lord, and walk with me back to the chapel," he said. "I believe there is much on your mind."

Father Michel clasped his hands behind his back and set a sedate pace down the seemingly endless corridor. If the occasional moaning and screaming gave him pause, one could not discern it. Perhaps he had been so long at *la Salpêtrière,* he was inured

505

to the horror. Or perhaps God had simply given him the grace to bear it.

"*Le commissaire de police* has released your sister, I hear," said the priest conversationally.

"Yes, Father," said Nash. "She has been given into my custody — with certain understandings."

The priest looked surprised. "Then your family is most fortunate, Lord Nash," he said. "France has shown you mercy."

"Yes," said Nash dryly. "For a price."

Father Michel cut a swift, assessing glance at Nash. "Ah! *Je comprends.*"

Nash carefully considered his next words. "Father, the comtesse . . . do you really think she is insane? From what I have seen, she still has her wits about her."

The priest puffed out his cheeks thoughtfully. "Some would say that to use her name and position to violate the laws — not to mention the economic interests — of her homeland was in itself insane," he answered. "But is she insane from her disease? No, not yet, I do not think."

"And yet the doctors have confined her."

The priest smiled hugely. *"Oui,"* he said. "For a price."

"Ah!" said Nash. "Her husband's doing?"

"Far better she should be here than

506

prison," said the priest, as they started down the stairs. "Here, our rats are smaller."

Nash was not perfectly sure he believed that. In the past fortnight, he had seen more of *la Salpêtrière*'s infamous vermin than he cared to count.

They reached the bottom of the stairs, and Father Michel pushed through the door into sunshine, and to air which smelled marginally better. Here, the crisscrossing paths teemed with people — the doctors in their black frock coats, the plainly clad clerks scurrying from building to building, and the white-aprons maids who trotted to and fro with buckets the contents of which Nash had rather not know.

He paused on the path. "Thank you for agreeing to look after the comtesse, Father," he said. "In my absence, may I . . . reimburse your expenses?"

It was an offer of a bribe, and they both knew it. But the priest merely smiled beatifically. "I take on such obligations often, my son, and only for the glory of God," he said. "He will recompense me. You do not need to."

Nash narrowed his eyes against the sun. "How long will it be, *mon Père?*"

The priest shrugged, lifting his black cassock on his narrow shoulders. "Syphilis is an unpredictable malady, my son," he said. "But it is as good an excuse as any to keep her from the prison cell, *non?*"

"I daresay," answered Nash quietly.

The priest patted him soothingly on the arm. "But if I had to guess, my lord, I think *la comtesse* will not know her own name by Christmastime. The thinness of the body. The whiteness of the skin. The beginnings of *la démence* — the brain madness. No, my son, the end is not far for her."

"Will she feel pain?"

"No, my son," he said. "Only the pain of purgatory. I will ensure that the doctors see to it. De Montignac has paid them well for the proper medicines."

"Her husband — he does not seem overly distressed."

Again, the shrug, and a Gallic lifting of the hands. "A convenient solution for *le comte,* is it not?" he said. "But a mortal danger to his soul. I think you know the sin of which I speak?"

Nash nodded. "Yes, Father."

His expression solemn, the priest leaned very near. "De Montignac is a depraved man, my lord," he murmured. "His unholy desires are a weakness of the flesh, which is like a poison. In the future, you must keep your brother far from him."

Nash's mouth pulled into a scowl. "Ah, the comtesse has been carrying tales, I see," he said. "Tales she was well paid to keep secret."

"*Oui, oui,* there were some *lettres d'amour,* I understand," murmured the priest sympathetically. "A very dangerous business for a politician to engage in, my lord. And in England, the penalty for such unnatural acts between men is still death, is it not?"

"Whatever his feelings for de Montignac, my stepbrother should never have written them down," said Nash grimly.

"And you, a good brother, have very deep pockets, I am sure," said the priest. "Do not worry. There will be no more talk, for I have given her absolution. But in any case, *la comtesse* has syphilis, so she says many things which may not be true, *n'est-ce pas?* And here, well, whom would she tell?"

Nash closed his eyes, and tried to bite his tongue — but if one could not trust a priest, who else was left to him? "The comtesse asked to be generously compensated for her risk," he said quietly. "She claimed that her husband would be insane with anger once he realized she had stolen his love letters, but that she wished to help me protect Tony. It was blackmail, of course — but of the

509

politest sort."

"Eh bien!" muttered Father Michel. "We French are known for our *politesse.* All the same, one hand usually knows what the other is doing. I doubt *le comte* was innocent."

"I fear you are right." Nash shoved his hands into his pockets and stared at the graveled path. "Some weeks past, she hinted that de Montignac may have more letters. We shall see, I daresay, if he has the audacity to play the blackmail card himself — and this time to my brother's face."

"Your brother has ended this . . . this forbidden liaison, *j'espère?*"

"He swears it," said Nash. "And if he has not, this time I shall leave him to deal with the aftermath."

"A fool must learn from experience," said the priest sadly. "Only a wise man can be told. I hope, my son, that your brother repents and turns from these sins of the flesh. The salvation of his soul will depend upon it."

Nash said nothing, for he was in no position to throw stones at Tony. He had committed too many mortal sins himself. Besides, it was de Montignac whom Nash objected to — beyond that, Tony's choices were his own. "Thank you, *mon Père,* for looking after the comtesse," he said. "I must leave you now. I am to sail for England in the morning."

The priest reached up and clasped Lord Nash's shoulder. "Then *bon voyage et bonne chance,* my son," he said. "I will look after *la comtesse* as best I can, until the end of her time comes."

"Merci, mon Père."

Father Michel smiled, and tightened his grip. "And for you, my son, it is time to go home," he said reassuringly. "It is time to get on with your life."

It was a wet, blustery day when the *Dangerous Wager* sailed with the tide into the Pool of London, en route to the more exclusive portals of Westminster. Despite the nasty drizzle, Nash stood topside, hatless, with the wind in his hair, looking starboard as Wapping and all of its bittersweet memories went sailing past. He had been less than a month in Paris straightening out the mess Jenny had left them, but already it seemed a lifetime.

The pain, however, had not dulled. The aching sense of loss was the very same; keener, perhaps, in this moment, when he could almost make out the very window which looked out from Xanthia Neville's office. For an instant, he imagined that he saw her, saw her standing at the window, staring out into the rain with her fingertips lightly touching the glass. In his mind, it was a girlish, wistful gesture — as if she were hoping for something.

But Nash was not hoping for anything. Not any longer. He had but one duty left to carry out, then it would be back to life as usual for him. He told himself he looked forward to it. Again, he turned and looked at the window. No. There was no one there. And there never had been.

He had set Tony ashore at Southampton, with orders to go back to Brierwood until he could determine how matters stood in Town. If there had been any news, any hint of gossip or any blackening of Jenny's name, Nash had thus far heard nothing of it. The letters from Edwina and Phaedra had been filled with questions but no news. But would they have heard anything, isolated in the country as they were?

He thought that they would have. Lady Henslow was well connected. Had she chanced to hear her favorite nephew's name aspersed in any way, she would likely have gone haring off to Brierwood on her next breath. Yes, Tony was probably unscathed. But Nash had learned one thing for himself from this tawdry little mess — it was time to stop playing the big brother to a man who had probably never wanted one in the first place. God knew his own childhood grief had been little assuaged by it. And now Tony's secret — the secret which had never really been a secret to Nash — was out, and the two of them had got past what little embarrassment there had been.

He had believed, Nash supposed, that by being a good brother to Tony he could expunge some of the guilt for having survived his own. But Petar was still just as dead. Nash had not honored his memory. Perhaps he had even hampered Tony by giving him a crutch to lean on. It was odd how clearly he saw it all now.

Yes, it was time to let Anthony Hayden-Worth, dashing bon vivant and up-and-coming M.P., sink or swim of his own accord. And Tony, he got the impression, would not object. Perhaps, left to his own devices, Tony would even be capable of making some hard choices — choices which would be needed in order to preserve his political career. But that would be up to Tony. Having a disgraced, sexually ambiguous stepbrother was no impediment to Nash's sort of life. And as to Phaedra and Phoebe, Nash could dower them well enough to overcome most any social obstacle.

And that was just what he would do, Nash decided. It was as good a use as any for his ill-gotten gains. Better by far than bailing Tony out of trouble. Nash bowed his head against the spitting rain, and tried to feel joy at his homecoming. But it was hard. Yes, very hard indeed.

Xanthia barely heard the creak of the door which opened behind her. She leaned into her office window and watched the tide come in, heedless of all else. She felt a strong, warm hand touch her arm.

"Come away from the window, Zee." Gareth Lloyd's body seemed to radiate heat. "You cannot keep standing in the draft. You'll get cold. You know you will."

"No," she said faintly, lifting her hand to touch the glass. "I've become used to it, I think — the cold of England, I mean. I think my blood has finally thickened. Or thinned. Which is it?"

Gently, he set an arm about her shoulder as if to turn her. "I'm not sure," he admitted. "But I am quite certain you'll get sick standing here."

"Wait, Gareth," she murmured, pointing through the glass. "Look — do you see that sloop just there? Coming up the near side of the Pool?"

Gareth leaned into the glass. "What, that forty-footer with the bowsprit?" he answered. "Yes. Why?"

"Can you make out her name?" asked Xanthia hopefully.

Gareth squinted into the rain, watching as the nameboard came into view. Slowly, he shook his head. "Sorry, no. Not through this drizzle."

The disappointment was oddly crushing. But why? It was just a pleasure boat like a dozen others which had passed by today. "Nor can I," she said wistfully. "But for an instant, I thought perhaps . . ."

This time Gareth did turn her from the window. "You thought perhaps what, my dear?"

Her smile was wan as she looked up at him. "Oh, nothing."

"You are cold, Xanthia," he said with mild approbation in his voice. "I shall have Mr. Bakely bring up tea."

"Tea would be nice," she murmured, sitting down. "Thank you." Xanthia began to shuffle through the papers on her desk. "Did you meet with Captain Rangle?" she asked absently. "I need his voyage expenditure sheets. His purser is late again."

Gareth left the door and returned to Xanthia's desk to pluck the documents from amongst the untidy mess. "You saw Rangle here yesterday, Zee," he said worriedly. "You exchanged pleasantries. He gave you this list himself. Do you not remember?"

Xanthia set her palm to her forehead. "Yes, yes, of course I remember!" she insisted. "Really, Gareth, there is no need to be sharp."

Gareth pulled his chair to her desk. "Xanthia, I was not remotely sharp," he said, straddling the chair backward. He crossed his arms over the back, and looked at her assessingly. "I mean this in the kindest way, Zee, but what the devil is going on?" he said more gently. "You've not been yourself of late, and it is getting worse, not better. Yesterday you snapped at poor old Bakely."

"Yes, and I apologized," she said defensively.

"So you did." His tone was soothing. "Zee, we are friends, if nothing else, are we not? I am not worried about Neville's. I am worried about *you.* Look — why do you not take a holiday? They say Brighton is lovely. Make Kieran take you. I can see to all this for a fortnight, truly."

Damn it. Why did Gareth have to be so kind? Xanthia set her forehead on the heels

516

of her hands, but she could not stop from heaving a deep, shuddering sigh.

"Oh, Zee!" Gareth whispered, leaning nearer.

Xanthia closed her eyes and willed it not to happen. But it was too late. "Damn you, Gareth," she choked. "Just . . . *don't*."

"Oh, Zee," he said again, more gently still. "Oh, I am so sorry. Please, my dear, *please* don't cry."

"I'm n-not crying," she whimpered. But the tears were running down her face, hot and acrid now. "J-Just d-don't be so nice, Gareth. Just *st-stop*."

Gareth stood, drew a handkerchief from his coat pocket, and spun his chair around. "Look, sit up straight, then," he ordered with mock severity. After a moment, she did so. He blotted the tears from her eyes and let his gaze drift over her. He tried to look stern, which made it all the worse. "It's that Nash chap, isn't it, Zee. The fellow who came here a few weeks past."

"N-no," she said, snatching the handkerchief, and blowing her nose furiously. "It is *not* him. I — I won't let it be! I just won't!"

A little dejectedly, Gareth sat back down. "Ah, Xanthia!" he murmured, propping one elbow on the corner of her desk. "Oh, my dear girl. Did no one ever tell you?"

She blotted her eyes again. "No," she sniffed. "Tell me what?"

Gareth looked at her sadly. "We do not get to choose," he said quietly. "No, we none of us do, my dear. Not even you." He took her hand, and squeezed it hard. "I am sorry, Zee. I truly, truly am."

Lord Nash's welcome in Park Lane was warm — almost as warm as the bathwater which Vernon so cheerfully hauled up the stairs. Swann stuck his head inside the door to say that he had cleaned the piles of paperwork from Nash's desk and that he appreciated Nash's patience and understanding. *Monsieur René* sent up a tray with a slab of bloody beefsteak and a pile of escaloped potatoes a chap could have wallowed in. Agnes set a vase of fresh flowers on his escritoire, and remade his bed with fresh linen. And Gibbons was in alt — having all of twelve coats to choose from instead of just the two they had been stuck with — and he began laying out an ensemble suitable for an afternoon call at Whitehall.

Everything, in short, was back to normal in Park Lane. It should have been enough. For a man who loved nothing so well as the comfort of his own home and a life of uncomplicated leisure, this was bliss. So why did he feel . . . nothing. Or something painfully close to it?

But there was no point in pondering it, was there? What was done was done, and now, there were greater things than himself — and his own misery — which required attention.

In short order, Nash was dressed and ready for the meeting he had been dreading since setting sail from France. "There, sir," said Gibbons as he patted the folds of Nash's neckcloth. "From the look of you now, no one would guess you'd spent weeks with those uncivilized Frogs."

Nash glanced down at the valet. "You have been quite civil yourself these last few weeks, Gibbons," he said. "Feeling sorry for me, were you?"

"Yes, but it won't last," said Gibbons. "Do not accustom yourself to it."

Nash grinned and set off on foot for Whitehall. Yes, everything was settling down. In that regard, at least, he was glad to feel life returning to normal. In other ways, however . . . Ah, well. He could drink himself into a stupor when this vile business with de Vendenheim was done.

He was fortunate enough to find the gentleman in his office — and in a state which could only be described as extreme civility, or restrained fury. Nash couldn't tell, and he didn't much give a damn. He had tried to let go of his anger these last few weeks, and for the most part, he had done so. Jenny's nefarious scheme had cast blame upon him unfairly — but had he been in de Vendenheim's shoes, Nash supposed he might have drawn a similar conclusion.

He relayed the story of the Comtesse de Montignac's smuggling operation, and Jenny's complicity in it, with words which were succinct and unembellished. "I have brought with me the statements from *le commissaire de police,* should you doubt my veracity," he finished, placing the man's card on de Vendenheim's desk. "But I imagine your contacts at our embassy in Paris have kept you fully abreast."

De Vendenheim, who had been pacing back and forth before the windows, made a dismissive gesture with his hand. "Yes, yes, the embassy took care of everything," he murmured, almost to himself. "But two women, gunrunning and smuggling! What is the world coming to?"

Nash smiled faintly. "You must have known very few women in your day, de Vendenheim," he answered. "They can be as cool, competent, and patently cruel as any man when they wish to be."

"And the Comtesse de Montignac — she will not live?" De Vendenheim asked the question almost hopefully.

Nash shook his head. "There is no chance," he said. "Her disease is advanced, and *l'hospice de la Salpêtrière* is notoriously infectious. If syphilis doesn't get her, cholera likely will."

Some of the tension seemed to drain out of de Vendenheim. "I don't wish her dead, but thank God the French are our allies," he said. "And that they were willing to arrest her."

Nash gave a muted smile. "The French are the allies of the French," he said. "The ship was sitting loaded in their harbor — hard evidence to ignore. Besides, it always comes down to money, does it not?"

The vicomte gave a bark of bitter laughter. "Oh, to be sure," he said. "But to what, specifically, do you refer?"

Nash relaxed in de Vendenheim's very comfortable armchair. "The French have lucrative trade deals with the Turks," he said. "And French investors are knee deep in Turkish state bonds. None of it will be worth a sou if Russia overruns the Turks."

De Vendenheim looked at him appraisingly. "You are remarkably well informed."

"From time to time, it pays to be a citizen of the world," said Nash. "And to understand that there is a little more to it than just England. But I somehow suspect I am telling you little you did not know."

"No, you are not," he admitted. "And alas, I must now bring up a far more delicate matter — that of your stepbrother's involvement."

"There was none," said Nash swiftly. "Anthony knew nothing. Didn't your contacts at the embassy make that plain?"

"They did . . . but I was not sure I believed it."

"You may believe it," said Nash. "Whatever my stepbrother's shortcomings, Tony is a fervent patriot. As to his wife — well, *that* I should rather forget."

De Vendenheim looked at him skeptically. "How could he not know what she was doing?" the vicomte gently challenged. "She was a wealthy heiress, and he was her husband. What was hers was his."

"The estate supports Tony with a generous allowance," Nash replied. "And Jenny supplemented her expenses with whatever she could wheedle from her father — or so we believed. Have you any idea, de Vendenheim, what it costs to be a member of the Commons? I speak not of just the palms which must be greased, but the life one must maintain. The campaigns. The carriages. The clothing. Tony had little left — apparently not enough to appease his wife."

De Vendenheim coughed discreetly. "Yes, I have learnt a little more of her American connections," he said. "Carlow Arms is quite an operation. I am sorry to say that we will, of course, have to prosecute her."

Nash made a dismissive gesture with his hand. "That I cannot allow," he said coolly. "Much as I might like to see the old girl hang, de Vendenheim, my stepbrother's career would be ruined if this business is not hushed up."

"I fear, Lord Nash, that you shall have little say in the matter," said the vicomte. "Mrs. Hayden-Worth will be detained and interrogated by agents of the British government upon her reentry. I am sorry."

Nash smiled faintly. "You may save your sympathy, de Vendenheim," he replied. "I sent Jenny back to Boston with her father's carbines. She will not be returning. *Ever.* And do not even think of extradition."

De Vendenheim looked grave. "It was not your place to interfere, Lord Nash," he said. "Moreover, our government can apply a great deal of pressure when it chooses to do so."

Nash laughed. "Have you any notion, de Vendenheim, just how dependent the American government is on their arms manufacturers?" he asked. "Carlow's rifle-works is a part of America's military might. Had the woman assassinated old Prinny himself, you would not get her back on British soil in this lifetime — nor the next, I daresay."

A sour smile twisted de Vendenheim's face. "Checkmate, Lord Nash," he murmured. "That was brilliantly done. I will, of course, discreetly pursue extradition and arrest, but you are likely right. Your stepbrother will attempt to divorce her, I collect?"

"He cannot," said Nash. "Again, his career would suffer. My stepmother is putting it about that Jenny has returned to her father's sickbed. It seems Mr. Carlow has recently discovered that his heart is slowly — *very* slowly — failing. I expect it will be quite a prolonged illness. I gather Jenny will be happy to be back in her homeland, and I don't think Tony will really notice she is gone."

Nash finished the meeting by presenting the few papers which *le commissaire de police* had bade him provide the English authorities. And at last the tawdry business was settled, with de Vendenheim giving Nash a stern lecture about his interference in government affairs. Nash, however, got the last word — he thought.

"But I am a peer of the realm, de Vendenheim," he said. "If I wish to interfere in the affairs of government, I have only to turn up in the House and exercise my right to do so. In effect, as frightening as it sounds, I *am* the Government."

Indignation flared in de Vendenheim's eyes again. "And why do you not do precisely that, my lord?" he returned. "If you don't care for how we do things, you have a right to participate in your government — notice I said *your* government, for it is yours, much as you might disdain it. You are an English peer, like it or not. You are stuck with the job. Just do it."

"Dear me, you sound bitter," murmured the marquess.

"I bloody well am bitter," de Vendenheim agreed. "I can do none of those things, Nash. My government — indeed, my very land — was burnt to ashes before my eyes. My elaborate title isn't worth a shovelful of horse shite, and by God, yes, I resent it when I see you English lords pissing your lives away. But the French nobility was busy eating cake and letting their country crumble, a fate which the English have avoided — *thus far.*"

"Well," said Nash coolly. "I shall keep that in mind if gambling, carousing, and womanizing ever begin to bore me — which I doubt."

De Vendenheim's temper had not much cooled. "Yes, and that's another thing," he began. Then he checked himself and practically bit his tongue.

"Yes?" said Nash. "Don't stop now, old fellow. You are on such a tear."

De Vendenheim was pacing again. "It is about Miss Neville," he began. "It is none of my business, of course —"

"No," Nash interjected. "It is not."

"— but I involved the poor woman, as I'm sure you gathered."

"Yes, I gathered," said Nash grimly. "Had I not, the guilty look on her face — and her brother's — would have been quite a clue."

"Yes, and I feel a grave obligation about that now."

"Do you?" asked Nash bitterly. "To do what?"

"To . . . to set to rights anything that is wrong," said the vicomte vaguely. "To correct any misimpressions you may have regarding her involvement in this sordid mess."

Nash rose from his chair. "Oh, I think I have quite a clear grasp of her involvement," he said. "But I am a gentleman — or at the very least, I mean to behave like one." He paused to snatch his hat from the vicomte's desk. "I give you good afternoon, de Vendenheim. Convey my warmest regards to the Home Secretary."

His hand was on the doorknob when de Vendenheim spoke again. "She believed in you, Nash," he said quietly. "When no one else did, Miss Neville believed in you. And she fought for you. Even after your asinine behavior toward her brother at Brierwood, she fought, and she believed, until she thoroughly convinced the rest of us."

"I do not care to hear this, de Vendenheim," said Nash calmly. "Nor do I even credit it. But you are kind, I daresay, in trying to paint the woman in a favorable light."

"Oh, I would not trouble myself," said the vicomte. "My nature is not all that generous. So just tell me this, Nash, and I will drop the matter — why did I not follow you to France? Surely you do not believe I was afraid to do so?"

"No, you seem remarkably stubborn and heedless," said the marquess.

He smiled faintly. "Worse has been said of me, I daresay," de Vendenheim answered.

"But I did not go to France because Miss Neville convinced me of your innocence."

"I am amazed anyone could succeed in that."

"She is quite the negotiator when she wants something," said the vicomte. "It was Miss Neville who found the evidence implicating Mrs. Hayden-Worth, though she had been telling us for weeks that you would never involve yourself in such a scheme. So I decided to cool my heels and let our embassy in Paris monitor events as they unfolded. The rest, of course, you know. But it is unfair to blame Miss Neville or her brother. We approached them because of the nature of their business, and they were simply trying to behave as any patriot might — whilst protecting their company's financial interests, too, of course."

"It was cleverly done, I'll grant you," said Nash. "I wondered why Sharpe had invited me to that ball. But to have the woman follow me onto the terrace — well, I am shocked I fell for it. But daresay we all of us have our moments of naivete."

De Vendenheim's brow had furrowed. "I think there must be some mistake," he said. "I did not approach Lord Rothewell until some days after Sharpe's ball. In any case, Miss Neville is an amazing and determined young woman."

"Indeed," murmured Nash coolly. "Perfectly amazing. Well, good day, de Vendenheim. Better luck catching your criminal next time, eh?"

De Vendenheim watched him through his heavy dark eyes for a moment. *"Non ci credo!"* he muttered, throwing up his hands in obvious disgust. He flipped open a folder which lay in the center of his desk, extracted a sheaf of well-creased letter paper, crossed the room, and thrust it at Nash. "I don't know why the devil I let Kemble talk me into this sort of nonsense."

Nash glanced at the paper. It was a letter — more of a note, really — but written on the letterhead of Neville Shipping. Swiftly, he read it. Then he looked at the date. "I see," he said, handing the paper back. "So Miss Neville was overcome by guilt and sent your cohort packing. But what does that change, really?"

Again, de Vendenheim lifted his hands in the air. "Nothing?" he suggested. "Everything? *Dio mio,* Nash, you figure it out. I am just here to do a job for Peel."

"Oh, and you have done it," said Nash a little bitterly. "Accept the thanks of a grateful nation and move on to your next inquisition."

De Vendenheim's long, serious face fell. "I am sorry," he said after a moment had passed. "This has been hell for you and your family. And none of it was your fault."

Nash's lips thinned. "Apology accepted."

"Yes, well, don't be too quick about it." De Vendenheim looked suddenly uncomfortable again. "Before you go, there is one last thing."

"Am I ever to leave here, de Vendenheim?" asked Nash dryly. "You seem just full of surprises."

De Vendenheim strode back to his desk. "Well, you may like this one a good deal less than my defense of Miss Neville."

Nash had slowly turned from the door. De Vendenheim extracted a small key from his waistcoat pocket and opened the top drawer. He withdrew a sheaf of folded papers which were tied together with a red ribbon. He passed them across the desk with an acutely uncomfortable expression.

Lord Nash took the bundle. "What are these?"

"To be honest, I do not know," he said. "My associate Mr. Kemble found them."

"Kemble?" said Nash. "Where?"

"After we heard of her arrest, Mr. Peel asked us to make a discreet search of the comtesse's home in Belgravia," said the vicomte. "We found nothing about the smuggling; she was wise enough to handle everything from her home in Cherbourg. But Mr. Kemble found those. They were locked in a desk in the library."

De Montignac's library? Bloody hell. Nash sorted awkwardly through the pile, his apprehension growing. Letters — perhaps four or five — and all of them addressed to de Montignac in Tony's hand. "Dear God," he murmured, almost to himself.

"I have not read them," said de Vendenheim swiftly. "And I think, perhaps you ought not, either? Mr. Kemble assured me that the letters had nothing to do with smuggling, but were . . . well, of a personal nature."

"He read them?" asked Nash a little weakly. "*All* of them?"

"He had to give each at least a cursory glance, yes, or he would not have been doing his job," said de Vendenheim a little defensively. "He read them, he took them away, and he ordered me to lock them in my desk until such time as one of you might retrieve them. I have left several messages for your stepbrother, but he has not come. Frankly, I don't want the bloody things here, locked or otherwise."

"Tony has been with me," said Nash dully.

"I left him at Southampton."

"Then you may reassure Mr. Hayden-Worth that Kemble is the soul of discretion."

"Well, we shall see, shan't we?" murmured Nash, tucking the letters into his coat pocket.

"*You* may have to see," said de Vendenheim. "I already know. Whatever personal information is contained within those letters, one would have to pry it out of Kemble under torture."

"That honest, is he?"

"No," said de Vendenheim slowly. "He isn't honest in the least. He just lives by his own rules — honor among thieves and all that rot, I collect."

"Indeed? I like him better already." Nash paused and stared down at the pile. "Do you imagine that he got them all?" he asked a little hopefully.

"I am certain of it," said de Vendenheim. "Kemble is very thorough. He rolled up the carpets, pried up the floorboards, and took the mirrors off the walls. There is nothing left in that house which one of us has not seen."

Nash felt a sagging sense of relief. *At last.* He had them all.

"Do you know, Nash, we are an awfully

lot alike, you and I," remarked de Vendenheim out of nowhere.

"Indeed?" Nash lifted his gaze from the letters. "How so?"

De Vendenheim flashed an acerbic smile. "Oh, I suspect we both often feel like outsiders here," he answered. "We will never really be English, you and I, despite my position in the Government, despite your lofty title or your father's name. And society will always account us different."

"The latter little troubles me," said Nash.

De Vendenheim's smile faded. "We are alike in another way, too," he continued. "We are arrogant, and entirely too certain of our opinions. I hope you will think long and hard, Lord Nash, before you close any doors which cannot be reopened. I very nearly did that once, a few years past. And now I thank God every day that I did not do so. My life . . . it would have been ruined, I now realize."

Nash did not know how to reply to that. After a few parting words, he bowed his way out of de Vendenheim's office, feeling far more charitable toward the man, and walked slowly toward Mayfair, his mind a whirling chaos.

Tony was safe. Jenny would never dare show her face in England again. Both those realizations were a relief to Nash. But it was not enough. The questions about Xanthia still tormented him.

He hoped he had hidden the depth of his despair from de Vendenheim. What Xanthia had done had hurt him, and more deeply than he wished anyone to know. But the letter de Vendenheim had shown him was a bit of a balm to his wounds, he supposed. Perhaps she had begun their *affaire* for all the wrong reasons, but it seemed she had come to believe in him. That was something, wasn't it?

Actually, it was quite a lot. Her letter to de Vendenheim had been cold and concise. She was washing her hands of the matter and ordering Mr. Kemble off her property. Nash tried to think it through. Had she meant it? She must have done; there was no other reason to say it.

Nash remembered something else de Vendenheim had said — something which, in the midst of Nash's hurt and anger, had not properly registered. The Home Office agents had approached Xanthia — and Rothewell — but only *after* Sharpe's ball. A few days after, de Vendenheim had said. The passionate kiss which they had shared, then, had not been a setup at all. Perhaps the sudden desire which had flared between them had been as real as he had once believed.

The thought inexplicably comforted Nash. But why? Xanthia had still led him a merry dance and betrayed him in the end. Hadn't she? Nash shook his head to himself and almost stepped out in front of a brewer's dray making the turn from Cockspur Street. The cart flew past, missing him but a few inches, the beefy, red-faced driver shaking his fist at Nash.

He stepped back onto the pavement and drew a deep breath. Good Lord. Had he survived a broken heart, a run-in with French police, and a fortnight in and out of Paris's most notorious insane asylum simply to die beneath the wheels of a beer cart? The thought struck him as oddly hilarious. And the old adage was true. Life could be so bloody short.

Yes, life was short — and briefly, his had been sweet. Would it ever be so again? Would he ever feel the stirring of hope in his heart? Or the fleeting sense that there existed a perfect joy which was his for the taking? Would he ever dare to love again?

That might be difficult, when he had never stopped. No, despite his anger, he loved Xanthia still. But their joy had not been perfect. It had been flawed, just as life itself was flawed. Did he need perfection? Was *that* what he had loved? A perfect dream? A fantasy? Or was it just Xanthia, with all her human frailties and conflicted emotions?

She believed in you.

De Vendenheim had been emphatic. And really, what had she known about him at the first? Just two things: That he was the sort of man who would take shockingly intimate liberties with women whom he barely knew. And that he was arrogant enough to think he was being trapped into marriage because of it.

Yes, even then he had been leaping to conclusions about her character, whilst she had seemed to reserve judgment. The worst he had ever seen was mild irritation in her eyes — offset by her wry, quizzical smile. Yes, that day in her brother's study, she had been all but laughing at his presumptuousness. She had teased him. But she had never truly upbraided him as he deserved.

Perhaps if *she* had judged *his* character on that one mistake — that angry, arrogant assumption which he had so quickly leapt to — then they would not now be in this mess. He would never have kissed her again. Never have made love to her. Never have decided that he wished to marry her.

Whatever her suspicions had been, whatever nonsense de Vendenheim had told her, in the end, he thought, she had been *his.* She had truly longed to be with him, he was almost certain. And he was not a man ordinarily given to flights of fancy, or to false hope. It was a part of what made him such a bloody good cardplayer. He could sense the essence of what people were, of what they were thinking.

What was Xanthia thinking now? he wondered. She was regretting all of it, he feared. She would take away precious little joy, perhaps not even a sliver of sweet memory, from all that they had shared together, given how things now stood between them. And suddenly, Nash found that heartbreaking.

Just then, somewhere above his head, a little bell jangled as if to recall him to the present. On his right, a white-aproned shopkeeper popped out of a tobacconist's to sweep the front step, cutting a suspicious glance at Nash as he did so. It was only then that Nash realized that he was still standing at the foot of Cockspur Street. People were beginning to stream past him, en route to supper, or to a nearby coffee shop as their workday drew to a close. The tobacconist gave his broom a good whack against the step to shake out the loose dirt, went inside, and flipped over his CLOSED sign, then through the glass, shot Nash one last suspicious glower.

It was time to go home. Time to decide what must be done and what sacrifice his pride was willing to make. But suddenly, it seemed as if there was very little sacrifice involved. He went home, feeling a little hopeful but inordinately weary and emotionally drained.

Gibbons greeted him downstairs with a decanter of *okhotnichya* and a chilled glass.

With a rueful smile, Nash refused it. "What day is today, Gibbons?" he asked, collapsing into a chair.

"It is Tuesday, my lord," said the valet.

Nash scrubbed at his day's growth of beard thoughtfully. "Which means tomorrow is Wednesday," he murmured.

"Yes, that's generally how it works," said Gibbons.

Nash did not even note the sarcasm. "Where is Swann?"

"In the library, my lord," said Gibbons. "Shall I fetch him?"

"Yes, and send for my gig to be brought round," he said. "Tell Swann we are going for a little drive into the City."

"To the City, sir?" But Gibbons was halfway to the door. "At this hour?"

"Yes, to see my solicitors." Nash's rueful smile returned. "I don't think they'll shut the door whilst my foot is in it, do you?"

"Given what you pay them, I doubt it," the valet agreed. "Shall I tell Swann why?"

"Yes, I have a new challenge for him," said Nash musingly. "I need some important papers drawn up by tomorrow evening."

"Indeed, sir?" said Gibbons. "Swann will need to know which files to take. What sort of papers do you require?"

"If I knew that, Gibbons, I would not need Swann, now, would I?" said Nash. "Now go on, you noisy old hen, and fetch the man in here. As you say, the day grows late."

The valet sniffed affectedly. "Well, really, sir! I am only trying to help."

"Oh, I doubt it," said Nash evenly. "You are looking for gossip to trade over dinner tonight, more likely. But if you wish to help, brush and press my best suit of evening clothes for tomorrow."

"Tomorrow, sir?"

"Yes, and I wish them to be perfect."

The valet looked surprised. "You have a formal engagement, my lord?"

"No, Gibbons, I'm going wear them down to Mother Lucy's whorehouse," he returned. "Yes, I have a formal engagement. In point of fact, old chap, I am going down to Almack's."

The valet recoiled with horror. "To . . . to

Almack's, my lord?"

"Yes," said Nash with mild satisfaction. "And with any luck at all, you'll *really* have something to gossip about when I get back."

CHAPTER SEVENTEEN:
A WALTZ
IN ST. JAMES

Xanthia was waiting by the front windows and wearing her favorite ball gown, a rather frothy creation in ice blue satin, when Lord Sharpe's carriage drew up in Berkeley Square. Knowing full well Lady Louisa's tendency toward tardiness, Xanthia had anticipated her late arrival. She hastened down the front steps just as Sharpe's footman opened the carriage door. But when she climbed up into the carriage, it was to find both forward seats occupied.

"Oh!" she said in some surprise. "Aunt Olivia."

Her aunt glared imperiously through her lorgnette. "Sit down, girl," she said. "What is that on your bosom? Cake icing and whipped cream?"

"Grandmamma, it is ruching and lace," Lady Louisa complained. "I think she looks very fetching."

Xanthia ignored both of them. The pair

541

had been squabbling for the last month, and each day Xanthia assumed, would be her aunt's last. Spending the latter half of the season in London had done nothing for Olivia's haughty disposition. Still, her continued presence had got Xanthia off the hook, socially speaking, on several occasions.

"I thought you had planned to return to Suffolk today, Aunt," she said, carefully arranging her skirts.

Aunt Olivia sniffed disdainfully, making her diamond earbobs jiggle. "What, and leave a job half-done?" she answered. "This chit needs a husband, and the season is nearly over."

It was on the tip of Xanthia's tongue to tell the old woman to suit herself, then clamber back out of the carriage. Xanthia would have much preferred to stay home and lick her wounds in private. But she hesitated a moment too long. The steps went up, the door thumped shut, and they set off toward St. James with a jerk and a jingle of harnesses.

"Well, what a treat this is," Xanthia managed, settling her spine against the velvet banquette. "Almack's, with my favorite cousin and my only aunt."

The drive down to St. James was but a

short one, thank heaven, since Olivia and Louisa continued to peck at one another for the duration. Inside the ballroom, the air was already growing stuffy, and if there had been any ice at all in the orgeat, it had long ago melted, leaving the dreadful concoction more insipid than ever.

Aunt Olivia had her lorgnette up again and was surveying the room. *"Where is he?"* she muttered to herself, thumping her walking stick on the ballroom floor. "Show yourself, you fainthearted fool."

"To whom are you speaking, Aunt?" asked Xanthia. Louisa was fanning herself furiously.

"Cartselle's boy," grunted Aunt Olivia from behind the glass. "The chit wants him — and so she shall have him. Before the season is out, too, I vow. And *then* I shall go home."

"And how do you plan to do it?" asked Xanthia.

"I shall employ the green-eyed monster," said Aunt Olivia, dropping her lorgnette. "Ah, he is just there, Louisa, by the windows! Come along now. I wish you to dance with every gentleman in attendance whilst I go exchange gossip with Lady Cartselle."

Xanthia hung back, half-afraid of what her aunt might do. But most likely, she would achieve her objective. For all her absence from Town, Lady Bledsoe was still a grand dragon of the *ton,* and few had the strength to stand in her way. Xanthia gave an inward shrug and looked about for something with which to amuse herself — well, perhaps *amuse* was not the right word. What she needed was something which would keep her from bursting into tears at an inopportune moment — a habit she seemed to have developed of late.

Just then, across the crowded ballroom, she spied some neighbors from Berkeley Square who had a daughter Louisa's age. They looked as weary as Xanthia felt. Perhaps it was time to commiserate? Xanthia set her orgeat on the tray of a passing footman and hastened off in their direction.

Lord Nash presented himself at Almack's at precisely a quarter to eleven, fashionably late, yet just early enough to avoid incurring the wrath of the persnickety patronesses. He made his way into the ballroom as languidly as possible whilst pretending he did not notice the stares and whispers which came his way.

He nodded in acknowledgment to the few gentlemen he knew. Then, taking up a place opposite the orchestra, he looked about the room. It took but a moment to catch sight of Lord Sharpe's chit. She was dancing a quadrille with a fresh-faced lad who possessed a startling shock of red hair. Her smile was almost falsely bright as they bobbed and weaved their way through the delicate steps of the dance.

Xanthia was here, then. Nash was sure of it, though he saw her nowhere. Already he felt her presence in the room. He was suddenly very grateful that Swann had kept up the subscription to this frivolous little affair. Nash had expected to have to bludgeon his way in — if one could bludgeon past Almack's steely-eyed gorgons. But good old Swann, ever determined to keep up appearances, had once again laid smooth his path.

And so he was here — and feeling more than a little nervous, though he would have admitted it to no one this side of the afterlife. His unease aside, however, Nash had given quite a lot of thought to what he was about to do. If only he could find Xanthia, perhaps the nervousness would pass, and his visceral certainty would return.

Suddenly, he noticed an elderly woman leaning on a gold-knobbed walking stick near the windows. His heart sank. It was Lady Bledsoe, he was unutterably certain, though he had met her but two or three times in his youth. And if she was here, it probably meant Xanthia was not . . .

No. Xanthia was here. His every nerve was vibrating with the certainty of it. On impulse, he set a determined course for Lady Bledsoe. The old battle-ax caught sight of him and lifted a bejeweled lorgnette to her eyes.

"Lord Nash is it?" she said, peering haughtily at him. "Or do my eyes deceive?"

"How do you do, ma'am?" Nash bowed stiffly. "I trust I find you well?"

The old lady sniffed, and lowered the glass. "Well enough, I daresay," she replied. "You know Lady Cartselle, do you not?"

He leaned forward to see her ladyship standing on Lady Bledsoe's opposite side. "Indeed, I attended her delightful masque a few weeks past."

"Did you?" said Lady Bledsoe archly.

"How do you do, Lord Nash?" twittered Lady Cartselle.

"What a shock to see you here," said Lady Bledsoe, when her companion had turned away again. "Tell me, how is that silly mother of yours, my boy?"

"I believe you mean my stepmother, ma'am?"

"Yes, whatever," said Lady Bledsoe. "Still as scatty as ever, is she?"

"Edwina does have her own sort of charm," said Nash. "But I am excessively fond of her."

Lady Bledsoe harrumphed. "I daresay," she answered.

Nash was saved from a further reply by Sharpe's chit, who returned to her aunt's side on the arm of her red-haired partner, breathless.

"Ah, there you are, my pet!" said Lady Bledsoe a little loudly. "Make your curtsy, Louisa, to Lady Cartselle and Lord Nash."

Lady Louisa did so. The red-haired lad accepted his dismissal with grace.

"Now who is your next partner, my pet?" asked Lady Bledsoe, snatching her granddaughter's card. "Oh, excellent! The Marquess of Langtrell! What a lovely man!" Then, aside to Lady Cartselle, she said, "Lady Louisa has been engaged for every dance this season, you know. She has taken very well indeed. One can hardly walk through Sharpe's drawing room without tripping over another vase of flowers, or some puppy awaiting an audience."

"Indeed?" said Lady Cartselle. "What an inconvenience that must be."

Lady Bledsoe smiled. "So I should think, but her papa is thrilled."

Lady Cartselle turned a vague smile upon

the chit. "How lovely you look tonight, my dear," she said. "I do hope you saved a dance for Peter?"

The girl's eyes widened. "Oh, I fear I did not," she said almost rotely. "Ought I have done?"

Her grandmother patted her hand. "There, there, dear child," she said. "The early bird gets the worm, does he not?"

The chit wrinkled her nose. "Eww, Grandmamma!"

Lady Cartselle opened her mouth as if to protest the oversight; but just then, true to her grandmother's prediction, the girl's next partner swooped in to claim her.

With a fleeting but satisfied smile, Lady Bledsoe returned her narrow gaze to Nash. "And what of you, my boy?" she murmured. "The rumor mill has it that you have been petticoat-chasing in earnest — and a lady of quality this time. I should have a care, if I were you."

"How kind of you to give advice," said Nash dryly. "I have so little experience with petticoats."

The old woman cackled. "I said *in earnest,*" she reminded. "And yes, you have too much experience to suit me. Tread cautiously, Nash. Sometimes the only thing which truly tempts us is the thing which we cannot have."

"My, you are practically oozing sage advice, ma'am," he murmured, his eyes running over the crowd. "But I think you need not worry yourself on my behalf."

"Oh, I shan't," she reassured him. "But poor Edwina — now, there's the rub! Lady Henslow has frequently mentioned how often her sister frets herself into a state over you — not to mention that glad-handing stepbrother of yours."

Nash breathed a small sigh of relief. It seemed Lady Bledsoe had caught wind of a rumor but no name to go with it. Thank God Edwina's relatives had kept their mouths shut about the debacle at Brierwood. No one but immediate family knew Xanthia had been there — he hoped.

Nash plucked a glass of something dubious from the tray of a passing footman and carefully considered his next words. "I think Edwina may soon cease her fretting, ma'am," he murmured over the rim of the glass. "Indeed, I shall do my best to ensure it."

"Shall you?" The old lady looked at him suspiciously. "I rather doubt that, my boy. And now that I think on it, what is a man of your ilk doing in Almack's anyway?"

Nash hesitated but an instant. "I have

decided to look about for a wife, Lady Bledsoe," he coolly answered. "Is this not the proper venue for such an endeavor?"

"Do not be ridiculous." She rapped his knuckles with her lorgnette, almost causing him to drop his glass. "You are not the marrying type."

Nash turned to look at her pointedly. "A man can reform, can he not?" he murmured. "Tell me, Lady Bledsoe — who amongst this fair gathering would you recommend?"

"None of them!" she responded. "If you must marry, Nash, for God's sake, chose someone of experience if you can find her. A widow. Or a woman of common sense. I vow, you would scare a debutante to death."

"Then introduce me to your niece, Miss Neville," Nash suggested. "Is she here?"

Lady Bledsoe's visage stiffened. "Xanthia?" she answered. "Surely you jest?"

Nash shrugged. "Is she not an uncommonly sensible woman?"

Lady Bledsoe looked at him askance. "Well, yes, but . . ."

Nash smiled. "Surely, ma'am, you worry unnecessarily," he said. "A sensible woman could hardly be lured in by a man of my reputation."

The old woman laughed. "No, not that

one, I'll vow," she said. "You are quite right. She won't give you the time of day — though perhaps she ought, given how long *she's* been on the shelf."

"A small wager on it, then, ma'am?" Nash suggested. "Twenty pounds, perhaps? Just to make your victory ever more sweet?"

Lady Bledsoe considered it. "Very well, you upstart," she said. "Twenty pounds says the girl won't so much as dance with you."

Lord Nash extended his hand. "You are on, ma'am."

Lady Bledsoe put her nose in the air, lifted her lorgnette, and went clomping across the ballroom at a healthy clip despite her stick. In a distant corner, tucked behind some withering palms, Xanthia was parting company with a smiling, middle-aged couple. Upon seeing her aunt's approach with Nash in tow, she stiffened, color flooding her face.

Swiftly, Lady Bledsoe made the introductions.

"I — yes, thank you, Aunt," Xanthia stammered. "But I already have the pleasure of Lord Nash's acquaintance."

"Have you indeed?" said her aunt, looking back and forth between them. "So you already know he is thought a scoundrel, eh?"

"No." Xanthia's head jerked up. "I mean — well, I did not say that. Not precisely."

"Then I don't suppose, Miss Neville, that you would care to dance with me?" Nash interjected.

Her eyes widened. "I think not, sir."

"Well, my boy, there you have it." Lady Bledsoe smiled. "A woman of sense and discernment. You may send the twenty pounds round to Grosvenor Street at your convenience."

"Ah, such is the life of a gamester!" Nash murmured. "You win some, you lose some."

Xanthia looked as if she meant to edge away. "I can't think what the two of you are talking about."

Gently, Nash took hold of her arm. "Miss Neville will make good my wager, Lady Bledsoe," he said. "She owes me twenty pounds on a previous bet."

Xanthia jerked from his grasp, her elegant eyebrows sharply arching. "I think you must be mad."

Nash looked at her in all seriousness. "Do you not remember, Miss Neville, that afternoon I came to court you in Berkeley Square?"

"To — to *court* me?"

"To court *her?*" chimed Lady Bledsoe.

Nash ignored Lady Bledsoe and held Xanthia's gaze as steadily as he could. "Well, to ask your brother's permission to do so," he corrected. "I think, you see, that I was already half in love with you. But in any case, you bet me twenty pounds that — now, how did you put it? Ah, yes! — That you would 'lay odds' Almack's wouldn't let a man of my 'ilk' in the front door."

"Yes, I did," she coolly admitted. "Fine, then. I shall pay it. Now kindly take him away, Aunt."

"No, I don't think I shall," said Lady Bledsoe. "This is vastly entertaining."

Nash slipped a hand discreetly into his coat pocket, then took both Xanthia's hands in his. "I shall leave, then, since you wish it," he said quietly, continuing to hold her gaze. "I am sorry, Miss Neville — deeply sorry — for all the confusion which has gone on between us."

Xanthia's eyes were wary. "Yes, my lord," she murmured. "As am I."

Nash dropped her hands. "Then I bid you a good evening." He turned and bowed. "Lady Bledsoe, your servant."

"Good Lord, girl," he heard Lady Bledsoe say after him. "Have you brought that black-hearted devil to heel?"

Five minutes after Nash's departure, Xanthia excused herself and went straight to the ladies' retiring room. It was empty, thank God. She drew open her reticule, and pulled out the note which Nash had slipped into her palm. Her heart in her throat, she read it.

If I dare hope, please come to me tonight.
I will await you in the garden at Berkeley Square.

Xanthia's knees began to shake. She felt almost blindly for a chair and fell into it. Just then Louisa came in. "There you are, Cousin Xanthia," she murmured. "Are you perfectly all right?"

Xanthia lifted her gaze to meet her young cousin's. "No, actually, I'm . . . I'm not."

Louisa nodded knowingly. "I have said to Mamma three times this week that you seemed not yourself lately," she replied. "Have you the headache?"

Xanthia set her fingertips to her temple. "Yes, a headache," she agreed. "I believe, Louisa, that I shall hire a cab and go back to Berkeley Square. Will you mind awfully?"

"Indeed I shall." Louisa knelt, and clasped her hands. "I will send round for our carriage. They may return for Grandmamma and me afterward."

Xanthia smiled weakly. "Thank you, my

dear. I would be most grateful."

In Berkeley Square, the house was dark. Kieran, she knew, was out for the evening. The carriage set her down at the front door. She ordered the footman not to ring the bell and waved them away, much to his consternation.

"No, please," she said insistently. "I have the headache, and I wish to take the air. I shall just circle round the square before going in."

Finally, the footman tugged his forelock and climbed back up to his post. Xanthia watched them rattle round the square and back down toward St. James, then she rummaged in her reticule for her ring of keys, of which there were but three — one to the house, one to Neville's, and the last, which she never used, into the square's garden.

Her hands shook as she crossed the street and fitted it into the lock. What had he meant by such a note? Did *she* dare hope? What did it matter? She had done nothing lately *but* hope. And of course he would not be here yet. He would have expected her much later. She prayed to God that he would come. Indeed, she would simply wait until he did.

Or perhaps not. The gate would not open. "Oh, drat!" she said, pounding on the wrought iron with her open hand.

"Here, allow me," said a deep voice from the gloom.

She dropped her keys, and looked up to see Nash on the other side.

With a resolute jerk, he pulled open the gate, and stepped back.

"Stefan," she asked inanely. "How did you get in?"

In the gaslight, she could see his faint smile. "I am almost embarrassed to say," he answered. "I forgot that one needs a key to get into these places, so in an act of sheer desperation, I climbed over the wrought iron."

"Good God." She rushed in to lay a hand upon his arm. "Are you all right?"

"I survived, yes, but my breeches did not," he replied. "I fear I must now walk with my hat rather strategically placed over my hindquarters lest I give offense."

Xanthia dropped her arms. "I have already seen your hindquarters."

His eyes held hers in the gloom. "Yes, I recall it," he said. "Vividly."

For a long moment, there was nothing but the whisper of leaves on the wind and the distant rattle of traffic in the streets below. Xanthia drank him in — the exotic eyes, the hard, harsh bones of his face, and the hair which fell forward to shadow his brow. He was so beautiful, even more so than she had remembered.

"I owe you a deep apology, Stefan," she whispered. "Whatever . . . whatever your note meant — and I pray you will tell me soon — but whatever else I might say tonight, I will never have words to sufficiently apologize for what has happened."

Nash picked up her keys from the grass, and closed the gate. "Let us go toward the center of the garden," he suggested. "There are some benches there."

She allowed him to lead her deeper into the greenery and sat down. He joined her on the bench and took one of her hands into his. "Why, Xanthia?" he asked. "Will you just tell me . . . why? And then . . . well, we may never speak of it again, if that is your wish."

She squeezed his hand, and looked away. "I think, Stefan, that it was just a foolish notion," she quietly confessed. "I was . . . so *intrigued* by you. To me — at first — de Vendenheim's request was just . . . just an excuse to try to spend time with you, I suppose. An excuse to pursue my little fantasy, and to tell myself it was — oh, God! — all for a good cause! That I was protecting Neville's interests. Is that not inane?"

He bowed his head and said nothing.

"I am so sorry," she said again. "I — I wanted you. From the very first, I wanted you. I . . . I should have simply said so. I never believed you guilty, Stefan. Well, not after the first time we . . . well, never mind that. I am sorry. Just so very sorry. And yet I would not give up the memories of what we shared, Stefan — no, not for anything on this earth. Can you possibly understand that?"

"I am glad, Xanthia, that you have good memories," he finally answered. "It was my sister-in-law who did it, you know. And there were others, of course. But given the evidence, I suppose I cannot blame de Vendenheim for laying the suspicion at my door."

"Mr. Kemble called some days past to tell us in confidence what had happened," said Xanthia. "I am sorry that scandal has touched your family. I hope you have managed to hush it up?"

Again, the faint smile. "I daresay," he answered. "I am not sure I really care all that much anymore."

Xanthia leaned forward on the bench, far enough to set her cheek against his. "Then what do you care about, Stefan?" she whispered. "I know I do not deserve it, but please, *please,* say that it is me."

He turned his head, and set his lips near her ear. "It is you, Zee," he answered. "It has always been you. I love you with my every fiber. I cannot seem to stop."

She let one hand slide up his chest. "I pray you never will stop," she said with a catch in her voice. "For I love you. I love you more than is wise, I know. But there is no use fighting it. There — it is said. I cannot live, I do not believe, without you in my life. Please, Stefan, please say that we can begin again? That we can pick up where we left off?"

"What, with a torrid, illicit *affaire?*" he murmured. "No, my love. That is where I draw the line."

Her hand still pressed against the warm wall of his chest, Xanthia drew back. "What . . . sort of line?"

"A very dark, very thick one," he answered firmly. "Xanthia, I won't go back to that. I cannot. My love, I am very much afraid that . . . well, that you must marry me."

"I . . . I beg your pardon?"

He tried to smile. "I have grown a little tired of being used for my good looks and my — well, whatever other talents I possess," he murmured. "Yes, Zee, I am holding out for marriage."

"For . . . marriage?"

He set his head to one side and studied her, his eyes anxious. "That, I fear, is your only option," he said quietly. "What will it be, my girl? Am I worth it? Will you do it?"

The answer exploded from her lips. "Yes!" Her arms were around his neck and her lips pressed to his face almost before the word was out. "Yes, yes, oh, yes, Stefan! A thousand times, yes."

He laughed, then set her away a little, his eyes roaming over her face. His expression was still grave. "Are you sure, my love?" he asked quietly. "We have not even talked about Neville's. We must, you know."

She dropped her gaze. "Yes, I know," she answered. "I love you, Stefan. I — I will do what I must to have you. And I know it is unreasonable — perhaps even scandalous — for me to continue on as I have, but I cannot give it up. Please. Not entirely. Help me find a way. Please?"

He was already shaking his head. "Well, I will admit that I had hoped to persuade you to run Brierwood for me instead, but I will —"

"*Brierwood?*" she interjected.

He looked at her warily. "Yes, had you not guessed?" he asked. "That was why I invited you down, you know. I had hoped . . . but no, it won't do. I see it quite clearly now. You are a Neville through and through, and that business is yours."

"Well, it will be yours if you marry me," she murmured.

He shook his head. "I do not want it," he said. He released her right hand and withdrew a fold of papers from his coat pocket. Solemnly, he handed them to her.

She looked at him blankly. "What are these?"

"Legal papers," he said. "Papers which waive my right to your property upon our marriage."

Amazed, she unfolded them. "Can . . . can one do such a thing?"

"My solicitors are not perfectly sure," he admitted. "Certainly it is rare, but there are ways, perhaps. I think you must discuss this with your brother; perhaps even take the papers to your own solicitors. They may redraft them, if they please. If you will just marry me, Zee, I shall sign anything you put in front of me — and I would be disappointed, I think, if you wished to give up the running of your business."

Xanthia stared at the papers in her lap. Even had there been enough light, she could not have read them for the tears welling in her eyes. "And you will do it, then?" she asked. "You would marry me . . . and let me go on as I am?"

He set a strong arm about her shoulders, and his familiar scent of smoke and citrus and warm, strong male surrounded her, comforting her as it always did. "I fell in love with you, Zee, just as you are, did I not?" he asked. "Why should I wish to change anything?"

She laughed, but it was more of a snuffle. "But it will be thought scandalous," she warned. "And what of the children? You wish to have children, do you not? I do — *desperately* so."

"Oh, I am accustomed to being thought scandalous," he countered. "I think I will take a perverse pleasure in continuing to do so. As to children, Zee, yes. I wish to have as many as you and God can be persuaded to bestow upon us. But we can hire servants to —"

"No," she interjected. "Servants will *not* raise my children."

He brushed his lips across her forehead. "Servants raise most all children, Zee," he said gently. "No one will think the worse of you for that."

"My brothers raised me," she countered. "They ran businesses and plantations and, for a part of it, they were little more than children themselves. But they managed to do it."

"And so shall we, then," he answered. "Together, Zee, we will think of something."

She dashed at her eyes with the back of her hand. "All right then," she said. "You resign yourself to a life with a woman who is thought *outré,* and to a houseful of children who will be haphazardly brought up. Do I have that right?"

"Absolutely, Miss Neville." Nash leaned forward and kissed her nose. "I wouldn't have it any other way."

Xanthia lifted her chin, and caught his lips with hers. For a moment, silence fell across the little park. When at last they parted, she looked at him and said, "When, Stefan? Soon, I hope."

His eyes crinkled with humor. "What are you doing tomorrow, my dear?"

Her eyes widened with delight. "You cannot mean it?"

"I have the special license in my pocket," he confirmed. "Tomorrow, or next week. But please, no later than August, I beg you! And then, my lady, the *Dangerous Wager* awaits."

"Does it indeed?" she whispered. "Where do we go?"

"On a wedding trip, if you have time?" It

was a question, not a command. "I think we shall sail round Italy, then up the Adriatic to Montenegro."

Xanthia kissed him again. "I shall make time," she promised breathlessly. "Oh, for *you,* Stefan, I shall always, always make time."

Epilogue:
Safe Harbor
by the Thames

"No, not green silk." Lady Phaedra Northampton's voice was sharp. "It just won't do, I tell you."

"But I have a vision." Mr. Kemble was making an expansive gesture about the dark, grimy room, and all but ignoring her presence. "This chamber simply *must* coordinate with Lady Nash's office opposite."

"This isn't a chamber, Mr. Kemble," said Lady Phaedra. "It is a nightmare. A hell-hole. A *hovel*."

"But I have a vision," he repeated, both arms stretched heavenward. "I see light! I see watered silk! I see *swathes* of brilliant color!"

"And I see a lunatic on the loose."

With a sigh of mild exasperation, Xanthia lumbered from behind her desk, one hand on her belly, the other set at the small of her back, which was aching like the very devil. "My dear Phaedra," she said, crossing the passageway into the newly emptied storage room. "Must the two of you quarrel? Can we not settle this by compromise?"

"Zee, everything in life is not a business negotiation," complained Lady Phaedra, both hands on her hips. "Mr. Kemble is interested in no one's opinion but his own. He wants *green* silk hung on the walls."

Kemble was still strolling to and fro over the worn floorboards, his eyes sweeping through the room. "And coordinating draperies in butter cream," he added, drawing his hands down a window in a long, dramatic gestures. "Yes, *toile de Jouy,* I think — printed with little cows? Or dancing ponies?"

Lady Phaedra looked as if she might pull her own hair out. "But the room, Mr. Kemble, is to be a nursery," she returned. "Have you any notion what a toddling babe will do to walls hung with green silk?"

Mr. Kemble stopped abruptly.

"And cream-colored *toile?*" Phaedra pressed.

Mr. Kemble's face fell.

"Children will chew and spit and wipe their nasty little hands all over the fabric," Phaedra continued. "And then they will draw pictures on the walls with chalk and paint, and with anything else they can get their hands on. Think *strawberry preserve, Mr. Kemble.*"

Mr. Kemble drew himself up haughtily. "Then someone must simply explain that it won't do," he said. "We have a vast deal of work to do if we are to turn this filthy hole into an elegant nursery in three months' time. There is no point in permitting some *enfant terrible* to ruin it, is there?"

Lady Phaedra shook her head. "Mr. Kemble, were you never a child?"

The gentleman set one finger to his cheek, as if pondering it. "Actually . . . no."

As if vindicated, Phaedra turned to her sister-in-law. "Do you see, Xanthia, what I am up against?"

Xanthia put her hand back on her belly, and stared at them pointedly. "My dears, I have not slept in a week," she said. "I am dyspeptic. I have three merchantmen overdue in port, and a hold of lemons rotting in the Pool because half the stevedores are down with the grippe. Just paint the blasted room yellow, throw some sort of floorcloth over those boards, and hang some plain chintz curtains. Beyond that, the two of you have *carte blanche.*"

"Well!" said Kemble and Phaedra as one.

"I guess we have our marching orders,"

Phaedra added. "But really, Zee, a *floor-cloth?*"

Kemble shook his head. "You will never be confused with the Duchess of Devonshire, Lady Nash," he said ruefully. "*That* is for certain."

Xanthia felt a smile curve her mouth. "No, I never shall," she agreed, waddling back to her desk. "A circumstance for which Her Grace cannot but be grateful."

Just then, heavy footsteps sounded in the stairway below. Xanthia turned to see her husband appear at the top of the steps, his broad shoulders filling the doorway. He was dressed in an elegant black riding coat, and wore tall black boots which shone like glass. In one hand, he carried his riding gloves, and in the other, a small stack of papers. His face broke into a smile when he saw her.

"My dear girl, you look ravishing!" he said, approaching her desk. "I adore that rosy glow in your cheeks."

Xanthia smiled as he laid down his gloves and letters. "That glow is exasperation, I fear," she said, catching his hands in hers. "What a lovely surprise, Stefan. How are you?"

"Well enough, I daresay — for a man who is a little short of sleep." Nash bent to kiss the tip of her nose. "You left early this morning, my dear. I missed you."

"You enjoyed last night's dinner meeting with Tony and his political cronies, I hope?"

"Actually, I did," Nash admitted, grinning. "It is a little shocking, really. I cannot say it is a cause to which I would willingly give my life, as Tony has — but I believe there is important government work to be done. And de Vendenheim was right, you know, about doing one's part."

"Was he?"

Nash nodded. "It all seems so very clear to me now."

"Does it?" She looked at him curiously. "Why?"

"Because, Zee, we are to have a child," he quietly confessed. "And it changes everything. Everything a man values. Everything he is willing to sacrifice for."

Xanthia gave his hand a swift, hard squeeze. "I am so proud of you, Stefan," she said fervently. "No matter what you do — or don't do. You know that, I hope?"

"I do know it," he said. "And it is just one of the reasons, Zee, why I love you so. But here, I've brought you this morning's post from Park Lane. I thought you might find it of interest."

"Shall I?" Xanthia drew back, and looked

at the pile. "Have we something exciting there?"

Nash shuffled through the letters with his index finger. "There is a letter from Gareth," he said, deftly sliding it from the pile.

"Ah!" said Xanthia. "Wonderful. What does he say?"

Nash winked. "I am not yet in the habit of opening your mail, my love," he answered. "You must read it for yourself. But do not hold your breath, Zee. I rather doubt anything has changed."

Xanthia was quiet for a long moment. "He is never coming back, is he?" she finally said.

Nash shook his head. "No, my love, he is not," he answered. "He cannot — and it would be selfish of us to wish otherwise."

Xanthia turned, and went to the window. "I wish only for his happiness, Stefan," she said. "But I do miss him dreadfully. I shan't pretend I don't."

She felt Nash's warmth behind her and leaned back against him as his arms came about her waist. "You need never pretend with me, Zee," he murmured into the softness of her hair. "Besides, I miss him dreadfully, too."

"Do you?"

"Well, I miss my wife," said Nash with chagrin. "Since she is doing two jobs now, instead of just the one."

Xanthia laughed. "Mr. Mitchell starts next week," she assured him. "And whilst he comes dear indeed, he is exceptionally skilled. Give me a fortnight to bring him up to snuff, then I shall be all yours for a while."

Laughter rumbled low in Nash's chest. "Yes, that is what you said about the last fellow," he said. "How long did he stay?"

Xanthia sighed. "Three months, perhaps?"

"Yes, perhaps," her husband conceded. "Now, my dear, I must tell you that there was something else in that pile of post — something which I *did* open."

Xanthia turned in his arms, her eyes alight. "What?"

"Do you remember, Zee, that little villa on the Adriatic which you yearned for during our wedding trip?" he reminded her. "You will never believe it — the owner is willing to sell it after all."

"No!" Xanthia grabbed his forearms. "Stefan, my God! Are you jesting?"

Nash bent his head, and kissed her brow. "I've this instant come from the bank, my dear," he confirmed. "Everything has been arranged. And perhaps by summer — provided your Mr. Mitchell has stuck it out — we can take the child for a long visit?"

"Oh, Stefan!" Xanthia found herself blinking back tears. "What wonderful, wonderful news!"

A warm, satisfied smile spread slowly across his face. "I will be very happy, I think, to have a home in Montenegro again," he remarked. "And happier still to share it with you."

Just then, the rumble of conversation in the storage room rose to another crescendo. Nash crooked one of his slashing black eyebrows. "Dare I ask how the nursery goes on?"

Xanthia winced. "I fear both our decorators are possessed of an artistic temperament," she confessed. "I think we are going to end up with green watered silk, and some sort of fancy French draperies with dancing cows."

"Ah," he said. "And is that your wish?"

"No, but I know when I am beaten," she admitted.

Nash threw back his head and laughed. "Then George Kemble is a better man than I," he admitted. "I find you quite indomitable. But honestly, Zee, you must admit he's done wonders with this room. And the new melon-colored paint and green Turkish carpet downstairs look remarkably fine — and have you noticed the clerks seem so much more cheerful? Old Bakely was singing 'God Save the King' when I came in just now."

Xanthia gave a sharp laugh and let her head fall against her husband's shoulder. She did not care, really, about the décor of her new nursery. She cared only for the child who would soon occupy it — and for the man who had made it all possible, the man who thought no less of her for wanting the best of both worlds and was determined to give it to her. And as her arms slid round his waist, and the wool of his coat grew warm against her cheek, Xanthia's heart swelled with an almost breath-stealing joy.

"Oh, I love you, Stefan," she said softly. "Do you know that, my darling? Do you have any idea of the depth of my devotion?"

He set his lips to the top of her head. "As deep as the Seven Seas, I think," he murmured. "As deep as my love for you — and just as never-ending. You are my safe harbor, Zee. And I am so glad to have found you at last."

He held her quietly for a time, just standing there by the window as the clouds above the Thames scuttled past, and the wintry sunlight shifted across the window's stained and ancient glass. And amidst the peace and the joy which surrounded them, nothing else held sway, not the squabbling nearby, nor the door downstairs which kept slamming, nor even the teeming commerce on the riverfront below.

He kissed her again, then whispered, "Look, my love." He turned her in his arms to face the window again. "Is that not the *Mae Rose* coming up past Wapping Old Stairs?"

Xanthia's face broke into a smile. "Oh, thank God in heaven!" she said, pressing one hand to her chest. "She's in! Six weeks late, but in and safe."

"Who is at her helm?"

"Captain Stretton," she answered.

Nash squeezed her shoulder reassuringly. "Then let us go down and greet him, Zee," he said. "Let us go down together, and welcome the *Mae Rose* safely home, too."

Xanthia looked up at the man she loved, then took his hand in hers. And together, they went down the narrow steps and out into the mottled sunshine of a perfect afternoon. Together, they walked toward their future.